TIERNEY JAMES

DANCE
OF THE
DEVIL'S TRILL

Publishing Coordinator – Sharon Kizziah-Holmes
Cover Design – Jaycee DeLorenzo

PRESS

Owasso, OK

ISBN 978-1-965460-33-7 (Paperback)
ISBN 978-1-965460-34-4 (eBook)

Apparently they were going to let her live, but what kind of life would she have without her music...

On some subconscious level, Catharina realized there were five or six men. They wore ski masks and black hoodies. Twisting to be released only managed to tighten the man's grip. When she opened her mouth to scream, a hand covered her face, before shoving her into a wall.

"Is that her?" The ghetto accent sounded deep and ominous as the first man yanked her to wobbly feet. As she staggered, he pulled a picture from his pocket, eyed it, then her. His open mouth, embedded with one gold tooth in the middle of his crooked smile, sent a chilling warning that forced her to wobble toward the stairs.

Somewhere she heard doors opening from above. Other tenants would hear the commotion. Just as she tried to call out a warning, one of the men grabbed her hair, throwing her to the floor. When she crab crawled backward, he stomped on her fingers so hard no amount of prevention could stop her from screaming. Another man jerked her up, took his gun, and held it to her shoulder. The smell of gunpowder, and the realization that she'd never play the violin again, overpowered the deafening noise that pounded her eardrums when he pulled the trigger.

Looking down, she saw that black streaks covered her coat. In shock, she could only look up into the dark eyes of one of the men as he pointed the gun at her kneecap. "No more dancing for you."

"Just do it," ordered the first man who had started the invasion. "We got a lot to do here." He turned around to look at his followers. "Where's Ty?"

The others stopped to let their eyes adjust to the dark. Several shrugs followed as a shadow hurled over the second floor bannister, followed by a loud thump hitting the floor. "What the hell was that?"

The leader ran to the large dark object on the floor and jumped back then spun around with his gun drawn. "It's Ty. He's dead."

KUDOS for *Dance of the Devil's Trill*

In *Dance of the Devil's Trill* by Tierney James, Catharina "Cat" Spokane has her hands full running a small coffee shop in Union Station Hotel in St. Louis and taking care of her ex-marine brother with PTSD. Still fighting the war in the Middle East in his head, her brother Zane is slipping away from her, and Cat is desperate to save him. Then Zane starts hanging out with a strange creature of the night they call The Watcher. Although Zane seems to get better after being with The Watcher, Cat is concerned over what the consequences of the healing might be. Is The Watcher endangering Zane by convincing him that he can protect the homeless and other defenseless souls preyed upon by the gangs, drug lords, and greedy criminal elements of St. Louis? She wants her brother to get well, but she also wants him to live long enough to enjoy his freedom from the demons that haunt him. Even though she tells her brother that The Watcher is dangerous and Zane should stay away from him, she can't help being drawn to this strange man herself. James weaves a chilling but romantic tale of greed corruption, courage, sacrifice, and unconditional love. A must read for all paranormal romance fans. ~ *Taylor Jones, Reviewer*

Dance of the Devil's Trill by Tierney James is a paranormal romance/thriller with some unusual twists. The story begins in 1740 when the devil tempts a musician, promising to give him a masterpiece composition in return for his soul. The archangel Rocco arrives and fights for the musician's soul. He wins, but the musician remembers and claims the masterpiece even though the devil doesn't get his soul. And apparently, that's a no-no. As punishment for this faux pas, Rocco is sent to Earth as an avenging angel, to protect the helpless against those who would prey on them. He is promised that, eventually, he will find a woman who is able to love him both as an angel and a man. If she is willing to sacrifice everything for him, he will be forgiven and allowed to walk upon the Earth as a mortal man. Some two and a half centuries later, he meets Catharina James. Cat seems an unlikely prospect for this willing sacrifice, as she is struggling to overcome an abusive childhood, run a fledgling coffee shop in a luxury hotel, and take care of her ex-marine older brothers who is not only homeless but suffers from a severe case of PTSD. Rocco scares Cat, both because of her feelings for him, and because she fears the price he might exact for healing her troubled brother. Dance of the Devil's Trill casts a spotlight on the sad fate of so many of our returning veterans who, haunted by the horrors of war and unable to meld back into society, end up on the streets. It's also a thrilling love story about a young woman who deserves a break and an old soul who has more than paid for a lack in judgment—a heartwarming story you'll want to read again and again. Well done, Tierney. ~ *Regan Murphy, Reviewer*

DEDICATION

To
Jeremiah Essmyer

Hebrew 12:2

Do not neglect to show hospitality to strangers,
for thereby some have entertained angels unawares.

ACKNOWLEDGEMENTS

I would like to thank all the staff of Union Station, St. Louis for making me feel welcome while I did my research on this project. You are the most helpful and supportive people a writer could wish for in creating a story. I think you were my angels for a short time. Blessings to you all.

Prologue

1740:

The French astronomer rubbed his chin, looking doubtful at the young Tartini. The story, although bordering on insane, forced Jerome to stand and look out the window toward the heavens. Soon darkness would fall. Shadows grew long against the candlelight. In 1740 young men still believed in the devil and very little science.

With a sigh, the astronomer returned to his table of heavenly charts. "Tell me again, Tartini. Tell me the dream."

Tartini looked at his violin in awe before placing it with utmost care on the wobbly table. "I went to bed late that night. My thoughts of creating music left me drained and empty. There was nothing left in me." The young violinist pulled out a chair and sat down clumsily as if he'd been drinking. "I wanted to quit."

"But you are a fine musician. Even Vivaldi thinks this is true. What changed your mind?"

Tartini ran his fingers through his hair before meeting the eyes of his friend Jerome. "The devil."

"The devil?" Jerome smirked skeptically as he shook his head. "Did he knock at your door? Drop by for dinner? Or maybe he was passing by when—"

"No! You're not listening to me."

Jerome nodded, composing a solemn face.

"I fell asleep. I awoke to him bumping against the foot of

my bed."

"And what did he look like? Is it true he has horns?"

"He was both hideous and beautiful."

Jerome leaned back in his chair to eye the young violinist. "What did he want?"

"My soul, of course. He said he would serve my every need and desire if I but gave him my soul." Tartini shook his head then looked up at the ceiling as if searching for clarity. "My music had faded. I needed help."

"So you said 'yes.'" Even though he was a man of science, even as an astronomer, Jerome knew that wasn't a good idea.

"No. He picked up my violin and began to play with such virtuosity, I became too enchanted to speak. My soul became enraptured with his music, even as he danced around the room like a lunatic. Then the song slowed, as all sonatas do at some point and I fell into a deep sleep. The next morning when I awoke my violin stood propped in the corner."

"And why have you come to me? I know nothing of music or of dreams."

Tartini stood then lifted his precious violin. "I want you to listen. If I never write another note, *The Devil's Trill*, will be my finest work."

As darkness fell, a cold breeze swept in through the open window and flickered the candles that separated the men from powerful forces even science couldn't explain. With each passing moment, Jerome experienced a power never before known to him. Soon tears streamed from his eyes as Tartini's shadow twirled on the walls made for maps instead of ghostly aberrations.

Exhausted, Tartini finished the sonata and smiled at his friend. "The look in your eyes tells me you believe."

"I believe you have created something very powerful."

A smile spread across the young violinist's face. "More than you can imagine." Tartini glanced over his shoulder as if another watched over him. "If it had not been for an angel, my soul would be lost."

Chapter 1

Present day:

Hiding in the deep shadows of night, his body became invisible. Even when he ventured out among those who bore the scars of homelessness and mental incapacity, no one really noticed him. The cloak of darkness covered the truth of what kind of creature roamed the streets each night between the hours of twilight and dawn. Sometimes he rested, but rarely did sleep take advantage of such moments.

There remained work to be done, even on wintry nights when snow blanketed back alleys, someone always appeared that needed to be taken care of in the most permanent of ways. The helpless, misguided, and haunted warriors residing in makeshift houses of cardboard or slept on park benches, knew he was there watching, protecting, and sometimes delivering justice to whoever dared harm them. Both fear and reverence kept his existence secret until the night Catharina brought them *The Devil's Trill*.

♫ ♬ ♫

"Forgive me, Father, for I have sinned." The raspy voice confessed to the priest kneeling next to the creature.

"Only the Heavenly Father can absolve you of sin such as this. You burden me once again with carrying this secret." The priest kept his eyes on the cross above the flickering candles. Time meant nothing to the creature of the night. Sometimes, he appeared in the hours before dawn and other times not for weeks. "I continue to pray for you."

"That is all I ask."

The priest could feel the boring gaze of the creature turn upon him. "I dreamed of a girl."

"A man of God must still possess desires from time to time." It was the first time the priest detected a hint of amusement in the creature's voice.

"It was not desire. She comes for you." Even though the priest dared not look at the creature, he felt the sudden burst of heat radiate from the black hooded garment covering his tall body. He knew without looking that the creature's chest glowed with a dull pulsating beat which could frighten the faint of heart.

"I know of no such person, priest." A hint of concern resonated in his words. "All these years, no one came forth."

"Be careful my son. In all your evil, never forget there is good left in the world. May God bless and keep you tonight and the nights that follow." The priest stood with knees that popped before turning to his visitor, only to find him gone. With a sigh the priest bowed his head and walked away.

♫♬♫

"Any progress with moving forward in purchasing the Essmalory Building?" The mayor stood at the window looking out over the city of St. Louis, admiring the lights sprinkled across the landscape. The silhouette he created with his back to the darkened room put the others on edge.

"The tenants all own their apartments, Mayor LaPlante. Their board came back yesterday. It was unanimous among all the tenants. No one was willing to sell. The title of the building is in all of their names."

"Did you up the price?" The mayor turned his body slightly to look at his advisors sitting in chairs across the room where sconces pushed dappled light up the walls. The people appeared almost mannequin-like. "Well?"

"A Mr. Chevon owns the top and bottom floor of the building so he has the greatest influence. He plans to put a few shops in on the first floor where access can be gained from the street." The voice, deep and rich, hinted at education. "The top floor he occupies. He doesn't care if he makes more money. His tenants love the place as much as he does." A notebook opened on the table. "Looks like he has plenty of money to sustain the place with repairs. The monthly fee everyone pays is way below other places in the city."

The mayor walked to his desk, rolling the black leather chair out to sit down. "Meaning?"

"In spite of being prime real estate, it's the cheapest place to live, drawing tenants that are not necessarily top notch professionals like lawyers, doctors, businessmen, and such."

"They must not be down on their luck if they own their own apartment." Mayor Kragan LaPlante eased down into his chair, and then leaned back, causing a sudden squeak.

"Correct. But not six-figure occupants either. Mostly service industry workers, a couple of teachers, Peabody Opera House employees, secretaries, and so on. Oh and there is one tenant who got the coffee house contract at Union Station."

"Find a weakness. I want that building torn down so we can move forward with our plans." His voice grew void of emotion. "What have you done to make the place less appealing?"

A woman cleared her throat then pushed her frosted blond hair behind her ears. "A few gangs took the incentive of stirring up trouble."

The mayor leaned forward revealing his narrow face. "How is that working?"

"Great until some psycho started showing up to protect people on the street." The third person, a man dressed in casual clothes stood and walked to retrieve a cup of coffee. Finding the pot empty he opened the top to double check. Puffing out his cheeks, he continued. "They're calling him The Watcher."

The woman took a long, slow breath. "He may be our best shot here, Mr. Mayor. The police think besides being homeless, he may be taking the law into his own hands."

The mayor's interest piqued. "How so?"

"One of the gang leaders swears some of his members have disappeared after sneaking into one of the homeless areas."

The mayor chuckled through clenched teeth. "Spooks. All of them. They're not smart enough to know the homeless are probably setting a trap for them. That or they're drugged out."

The black man with the law degree and expensive suit stood up. "Either way, we need that to work to our advantage." He nodded to the woman. "Morgan, you're the public relations guru around here. Tap in to the police department. Find out who they think this vigilante is. Let me know when the police won't be around the area of the Essmalory, perhaps when they're concentrating their patrols around the Scott Trade Center. The Blues play soon. Have one of the gangs step up their mischief."

"I like it." The mayor smiled. "Just get it done. Do not bring me anymore bad news." The three nodded and moved toward the door. "Morgan. Can I have a word with you?"

The men looked at each other knowingly before slipping out the door.

"Of course, Mr. Mayor." Morgan closed the door behind her partners before leaning against the lacquered finish, her palms spread out on each side of her body. Looking toward the dark shape at the desk, she smiled seductively. "What can I do for you now, Kragan?" She took a step forward. "As if I didn't know."

♫ ♫ ♫

Yawning, Catharina unlocked the glass doors to her coffee shop inside the Union Station Hotel. Every time her toes touched the 120 year old tile, she found herself sucking in a deep breath of awe. With restoration finally complete, the shop had opened several weeks earlier. Before the doors opened to the public, the job of supplying the quaint gathering place kept her running between tasks.

Fortunately, the hotel provided the table and chairs found in some forgotten storage area. The owner didn't want their millions of dollars in renovations to skimp on something as ordinary as a coffee shop. Assuming the decorating responsibilities, the owner installed a working electric train set that filled half of the shop—the hope being children might drag their parents inside to get a closer look just as they caught a whiff of her US— Union Station—brand of coffee.

Without knowing it, the hotel owners opened a door of possibilities for her to put a bid in for the job. Finances, despite saving for six years, left her on the verge of being homeless after signing a two year contract with Union Station.

Every day she arrived at 5:45 a.m. The bakery that supplied her pastries arrived at 6:00 a.m. and the first cup of coffee served at 6:30 to the Assistant General Manager, Jeremiah Welding.

"Good morning, Cat." No matter the time of day, he smiled and looked pleased with the world. He forked out two dollars then shoved two more in the tip jar against her protests. "Just the way I like it."

Catharina took his cup and refilled it then added vanilla creamer. "Mr. Welding. Please. No tip. I'd gladly give you your coffee. You've led many a new customer in here. These past two weeks have been very successful. Thank you for giving me this chance."

With a shrug he took the cup. "Call me Jeremiah. People like you. Have you had any luck in hiring anyone to help you?"

"I've interviewed a few girls. For now, I think I'll just do it myself."

He pointed to a croissant sprinkled with almonds. "Seven days a week?" He fished out more money. "You'll burn out. Won't be long and you'll need to extend the hours."

"Money is tight for a while. But I'll be okay." Something caught her eye outside the glass walls of the shop. "Looks like you need to put out a fire, Jeremiah."

He turned around to wave at a bellman who motioned for him to follow. "See you tomorrow, Cat."

Another twenty minutes and hotel guests would be trickling in for their caffeine to jump start their day. During this lag time, she poured herself a large black coffee, selected a bear claw only to set it aside to nibble throughout the day. She couldn't afford to eat lunch so the bear claw would have to do until dinner. Dinner would be delicious tonight at the homeless kitchen where she served each night. For her efforts, Father Xavier saved her a plate. They would eat together after serving the last wayward soul. But she couldn't allow herself to think about food now as three customers meandered in. One strolled over to look at the train display, the second stared at the pastries, and the third ordered a small coffee.

"Great coffee, Cat."

Cat smiled. "In town long? Where ya from? Business or pleasure? Try the muffins. Nice tie. Want that to go? Come back next time you stay at Union Station." These comments were made over and over each day until three in the afternoon when the coffee shop closed.

The hours ticked by with little time to consider that her feet hurt or that the afternoon light faded to evening. She believed each customer needed extra attention to keep them coming back.

♫ ♬ ♫

With the last morsel of bear claw popped into her mouth, she savored each crush of flavor as counters were disinfected, trash emptied, and coffee machines prepared for the next day. A glimmer of hope arose about an hour earlier that two bagels would make it home with her, but a hungry salesman decided to take them for his next day early departure. He tipped a dollar after she threw in a mini tub of cream cheese, in case they were stale by morning.

With lights off, except for the case with the model train, Catharina backed out of the shop then locked the glass doors with care. Fishing for her keys, she barreled into a tall man in a suit standing outside her shop.

Startled, she bounced back against the doors, making them rattle. "Oh. So sorry. I didn't see you. Did you want something inside the shop? I just closed."

She thought she might be stammering as the man's pale blue eyes narrowed in a suspicious way that made her shiver.

His black hair had several strands that fell across his

forehead and a five o'clock shadow that looked like it might be permanent on his hollow cheekbones. "Who are you?" The British accent came across as impatient.

"Catharina. I operate this coffee shop. If you'll only come back–"

"Jeremiah?" Touching an ear piece, he lifted a small microphone to a mouth that looked too perfect for a man. "Can you come to the coffee shop please?" The man clicked off and tilted his head at her.

"Is there a problem?" Catharina felt uneasy when the well-groomed stranger before her arched an eyebrow and stepped back as if he thought her toxic.

Lifting her hand to her left shoulder, she began to rub vigorously, feeling a heated pain throb against the tattoos that spilled down her arm. The man lowered his head slightly but never looked away. The over-six-foot frame intimidated someone of her average height.

Jeremiah hustled up through the business center located outside her shop and slid to a stop. His lopsided grin eased her discomfort. "What is it, Damien?"

Pointing to Catharina with one finger, the stranger turned his back on her. "Who is this?"

"That's right, you two haven't met. This is Catharina our new barista. Everyone calls her Cat."

The man turned to eye her from head to toe with a disapproving nod.

"Damien Cruz is the head honcho around here, or general manager," Jeremiah continued. The demeanor of this general manager was about as opposite of Jeremiah as one could get. "Don't let his evil eye scare you, Cat. He's really a nice guy." Jeremiah patted his boss on the back. "Damien has been on vacation."

"And this is who you hired to run the shop?" The manager spoke as if Catharina wasn't present. "Did you not mention there was a dress code?"

Catharina folded her arms across her chest and stood ridged. "Excuse me. I got the bid for this place. Jeremiah didn't hire me. I have a two-year contract. I'm working hard to add to the ambience of this monstrosity of an old railroad station. My question is—" She turned her glare on the assistant manager. "—why is someone with no personality in charge of management?"

Damien straightened, pulling his shoulders back, before his deep voice responded. "I will be by in the morning to inspect the premises. See that you're prepared." He stormed away toward the Grand Hall of Union Station.

"What was that?" Leaning against the glass doors in relief, Cat continued to rub her shoulder, feeling the pain subside.

A nervous laugh escaped Jeremiah. "I know he's a bit over the top, but trust me, he's the brains behind this place. He actually owns this monstrosity as you called it." Placing his hands on his hips, he looked after Damien as he stopped in the Grand Hall to speak to a guest. "I've learned so much from him." Jeremiah waved his hand, clearly trying to sound reassuring. "He fired thirty people his first day on the job. He even fired my mom."

"What? That's horrible. I'm so sorry." Trying to cover her shock, she forced out a sudden exhale of breath.

"Nah. She was going to retire anyway. They made a deal so he looked like the bad guy. Let me tell you everyone shaped up pretty fast." He leaned in with a smile. "They call him the hatchet."

Blinking back a sudden need to cry, Catharina gulped. "The hatchet? Dear Lord."

"Not to worry, Cat." Jeremiah stepped closer and fist bumped the arm that didn't hurt. "He's really a nice guy, but you didn't hear that from me."

Rubbing her hand down her funky mismatched clothes from the Goodwill Store, then up to the jagged haircut that sported two different colors, helped her realize for the first time, she would never be mistaken as one of the wealthy guests buying her coffee. "I didn't know there was a dress code."

"You're good. I kinda dig the Bohemian look." He started to walk away as he smoothed his tie. "Don't change a thing. We need a little diversity around here. You add color to what would normally be stuffy."

"Thanks, Jeremiah," she called after him. "Coffee is free tomorrow."

A guest stopped him at one of the computers, diverting his attention immediately. With a shrug, Catharina took a deep breath before heading out into the Grand Hall to go home.

♫ ♫ ♫

Standing in the shadows, the woman failed to notice the man in the limestone archway. He watched her shade her eyes as she looked up at the blue sky. The old bicycle she mounted wobbled before her feet pumped the pedals to speed up. A wire basket held the canvas bag she used as a purse. In seconds, she disappeared around the corner.

Knowing he could easily follow, the creature decided to wait. This time of year darkness came early, in spite of the warmth of late autumn. Tonight he would find her.

Chapter 2

The smell of garbage and body odor grew stronger in this part of the city, even though just a mile away stood one of the most beautiful hotels in St. Louis. Families, the wealthy and the influential, stayed in chic accommodations that these shabby street residents would never enjoy. Most days, they picked through trash or worked minimum-wage jobs to have enough to eat. The lucky ones had cars to sleep in and were able to drive to a job the Salvation Army found for them. In between jobs, the homeless who could use computers visited libraries to do internet searches for postings of jobs or to update their resumes. People would be surprised at the capabilities of the down and out.

There remained others, Cat knew, who were just too sick to find jobs. Some bore the demons of mental illness while former warriors continued to fight wars at the sound of loud noises. Her brother was one of those—a Marine home from Afghanistan and badly scarred by the horrors of foreign conflict. Living on the streets gave him peace—no time clock to pressure him to perform, and no boss to give him orders. She realized Zane might never be well.

"How's my baby sister?" Zane walked the last two blocks with her to The Kitchen that served several hundred people each night. "You look tired. Everything okay at the coffee shop?"

He still managed to walk and talk like a soldier. Sometimes it was difficult to remember that things weren't okay with him.

Catharina dismounted from the bike. "Worked hard today. Business was good. Met the big boss, too."

"And?"

She shrugged. "Arrogant maybe. Jeremiah says he's okay so it must be so."

Zane nodded as he took the bicycle from her hands and walked it between them. "Good. Good. Good." It was when he repeated things over and over that she became aware her hero brother who served his country was a walking time bomb.

"Did you work today?" She hoped so. Money was so tight for her.

Nodding, he smiled like a little boy. "Yep. Father Xavier had me rake leaves all day. Said I could come back tomorrow to help him out if I want. Paid me already. Maybe I'll buy you a present."

Catharina stopped and leaned across the bicycle, pulling him closer. With a kiss on his scratchy cheek, she added an awkward hug. "Use it for food, Zane. I don't need any presents. Come by tomorrow morning and I'll fix you up with some coffee and a donut."

"Can I bring my friend Gideon? He's the one who fixed my car last week. Remember?"

"The black guy with all the red tattoos?"

Zane nodded. She'd met Gideon a few days after the repair and was surprised he, too, lived on the mean streets of St. Louis. How he managed to keep his head shaved and face free of a beard amazed her. He stood over six foot six, making the new friend stand out among the other homeless friends Zane collected.

"Yes, I remember him. Bring him along, but make it really early or near to closing. Don't come in the front door. I'll tell the bellman to let you in through the luggage elevator."

"Sure. Sure. Sure."

"Remember, Zane. I can't lose this job. I've invested all our money or at least what's left of it. If I make a go of it, I may be able to branch out on my own in a few years. You could work for me and we can be a family again."

Catharina stroked his arm, knowing Zane would gain clarity. "I'd like that. I'll remember, Cat. You'll like Gideon. He's my new best friend."

"Okay. But don't give him any money and don't tell him when you have some. Promise?"

"Yes. Yes. Yes."

Just then a car passed them and backfired. Zane dropped the bike and grabbed her. Slamming her up against the brick wall of a building, Catharina felt the wind knocked out of her.

He yelled, "Incoming!" as he covered her body with his, forcing her head into his chest.

His entire body shook after a few minutes. She waited for the calm to be restored. Running her hand up and down the front of his camo jacket, she could feel her brother's rapid heartbeat return to normal.

With a sudden release of his grip on her body, Zane turned nonchalantly to pick up her bike. In an unconcerned voice, he said, "Come on. We'll be late for supper. Father Xavier will wonder where you've gotten to."

Taking a deep breath, she blinked at the harsh reality. "Sorry. I got distracted."

"It's okay. Now, come on."

♫♬♪

"Put on that apron, Cat," the priest ordered as he pointed to a hook near the stainless steel sink. "I was getting worried. A little shorthanded tonight."

"Isn't the parish from The Hill coming to help out?"

The Hill boasted a very active Italian community of Catholics that never missed an opportunity to serve.

"Yes, they're coming, but they need to leave early." Father Xavier carried the last metal tub of green beans to the steam table as she came along side tying her apron. "Maybe Zane will stick around and help clean up. Oh, and I brought your violin. The music store called to say it was ready. You need to keep your phone turned on, Cat. What if Zane needed you?"

"My minutes ran out. I'll buy more in a few weeks. You're a worry wart, Father." Catharina waved to a couple of familiar faces, both women pulling children by their hands. They smiled shyly as they pushed their little boys forward. "You look hungry." She began filling their plates, making sure the helpings were larger than they needed to be. After all, if it was too much their mothers would most likely gobble it down. "How was school today?"

It was something she always asked, knowing that an education was their only possibility of escape from poverty. The mothers filled her in on school and then the news they secured a job in housekeeping at the Sheraton a few blocks away.

The line stretched outside The Kitchen of Hope as darkness fell. In spite of several flickering light bulbs, a false layer of warmth pushed the cold at bay for a couple of hours. Only a few families walked through the door. They usually went to shelters, the Salvation Army Center or churches that took turns serving dinner throughout the city. Here, the crowd consisted of the hardcore homeless. Most were men, but a few older women staggered in each night, smelling of cheap wine and smoke.

Zane held out his Styrofoam plate for a scoop of fruit salad. "Sis, this is Gideon. Remember?"

Catharina met the black man's eyes with hers, causing him to look down nervously. A rush of sadness washed over her noticing his discomfort. "Yes. I remember. Nice to see you again, Gideon."

He extended his plate for her scoop of salad before sneaking a peep at her. "Zane says you'll give us coffee tomorrow." Catharina thought Gideon's voice too soft for a man who appeared rough around the edges and so muscular.

"That's right. My way of saying thanks for looking after my brother." This made him smile then elbow Zane good naturedly. "Can you guys help us clean up tonight?" she asked.

They promised to stick around until closing then moved to a table to enjoy the quiet noise of contentment. There wasn't much time to contemplate whether she possessed enough energy to keep serving or if her brother was adequately fed for the day. The hungry kept coming, some for a second and even a third helping. Most didn't make eye contact, but others grunted a thank you or offered a crooked smile with missing teeth.

"Get you a plate too, Cat. You're skin and bones." Father Xavier pulled the strings of her apron. "Go. I can handle the rest." He nodded to the crowd. "See they're leaning back in their chairs now. I'll say a few words and offer words of encouragement in a few minutes."

She filled a plate with the last cup of spaghetti, salad, green beans, and a piece of stale, crusty bread. The peach cobbler had disappeared an hour ago. Leaning against the cabinet, she remained standing to eat.

In spite of being in his sixties, the priest worked tirelessly for the people of his city. His thick mane of hair had grown white since their first meeting when she was only ten. Watching him walk among the men who embraced being ignored, she learned yet another lesson in humility. From time to time, he sat with a loner or patted a few veterans on the shoulder, thanking them for their service, then moved on to another table, another need.

This was why she loved him—not as a priest but as a father.

Tossing the plate, she gulped down a carton of chocolate milk and dumped it in the trash as well. Beginning the cleanup felt harder tonight, but it went quick enough. The room remained full of men, hesitant to go back into the night. It was always this way. She wanted to go home and sleep. Couldn't they leave, just this once?

"Finished sweeping, Cat. Gideon took out the trash. Looks like the good father is a bit tired too, tonight. Told me he hasn't been sleeping very well. Did he say anything to you?" Zane sounded concerned as Gideon joined him.

"Thanks, Gideon. I know Father Xavier appreciates the help." She eyed the priest again. "No. He never mentioned that to me."

Her brother slipped an arm around her shoulders. "Maybe he can work for you too when you get your own coffee shop outside the hotel."

She felt his body tense then straighten. "What is it, Zane? Are you all right?" Looking up at him, she followed his stare to the door. "Who are they?" But she already knew. They were gang members who preyed on homeless people for sport. "Don't do anything stupid, Zane. Please."

Dropping his arm from around her shoulder, he whispered

to Gideon. "Insurgents. Ready yourself, Gideon."

"No. Don't ready yourself, Gideon. Zane, you listen to me. They aren't insurgents—"

Zane rolled his shoulders back like an imposing gladiator. "Get the priest, Gideon. He's out there without a weapon."

Gideon laid a hand on Zane's chest and spoke in the most rational, calm voice. "His weapon is God. Be not afraid."

The gang of five men in their early twenties sauntered in wearing black tee shirts. Their jeans looked faded and worn, but it was their faces that bore the battle scars of inner city poverty. Every eye turned toward them in anticipation of trouble. Several bumped into frail old men, causing them to stagger or spill their coffee. One remained at the door with his arms folded across his chest.

"Welcome." It was Father Xavier. "I'm afraid all the food is gone. There may be some coffee left."

The leader eyed the priest, who stood a head taller, before stepping around him toward a table where one man still ate. Reaching down, he took the uneaten bread and sniffed it, only to drop it to the floor and crushed it with a stomp of his foot.

Catharina felt her brother's muscles flex. She needed to diffuse the situation before all hell broke loose. Zane wasn't the only post-traumatic stressed warrior in the room, all still capable of great harm if pushed.

"Hey!" she called.

A look of confusion crossed the gang leader's face as he turned his eyes toward her. She imagined how she must appear to him, a rag tag girl climbing up on the front table with a violin.

"Almost forgot the entertainment tonight," she continued with false cheer.

The priest hurried up to stand beside her brother. "Cat! Get down from there. What are you doing?"

The next instant, Catharina began playing her violin. A hush fell over the crowd as she twirled and bent backward to play some haunting melody. When she got too close to the edge, Zane lifted her to the floor as if she were a tiny ballerina. All the while, she played and danced around the room, mesmerizing the down-and-out with the richness of her talent.

At the conclusion of her performance, she stopped in front of the gang leader to bow her head. Without fear, she lifted her eyes, to confront the tormentor.

Without warning the thug began to clap, slowly at first then quicker as everyone joined in to offer her praise.

"You are welcome here, but don't come back if you mean us harm," Catharina warned.

A smirk played at the edge of his mouth as he eyed her scrawny body, and her green eyes with gold flecks, then the others in the room. He noticed, in that moment, several men stood who didn't look so down-and-out—like the big one who lifted her off the table or the big black man with the angry eyes. Then others stood, gaining confidence in the musician's words. He started to back out, and his gang followed.

And then they were gone. A loud jubilant roar of proud victory spread through the remaining dinner guests as Catharina looked at her brother, now calm as if nothing had happened.

"That was beautiful." Gideon bobbed his head and looked like he was trying to smile without revealing missing teeth. Zane began bragging about his little sister to several men. "He's proud of you," Gideon whispered.

"I'm proud of him too." She looked around the room. "Where's Father?"

Gideon looked around the room then jumped back behind her in fear. "There in the window."

Catharina turned her eyes toward the plate glass window at the front of The Kitchen to see the priest pleading with hand gestures to a man she'd never seen before. His clothes looked almost medieval in the street lamp that shined from above. A dark cloak covered his shoulders and kept his profile hidden. Together, both men turned to look inside and she realized they were staring at her. Even then, she couldn't determine his face with the hood pulled so far down over his forehead. Raising his right hand, he touched the glass. His skin appeared to glow just as a jolt of pain hit her shoulder where the tattoos spread down her arm. When he withdrew his hand, the pain stopped.

"Who is that with Father Xavier, Gideon?" She looked behind her and saw the black man moving behind the steam table with several others who watched the stranger outside. Whoever he was, they were afraid.

♫ ♫ ♫

"No. I forbid it, Rocco." The priest didn't dare touch him in this current state of turmoil. "She is not the one. It can't be."

"She is the one." Rocco's voice grew raspy and dark as he turned his pale eyes upon the girl inside. "I can feel it."

"Dear God. Please not my Catharina. She's all I have, Rocco. Find someone else. She and her brother are all the family I have. Don't take her from me. I'm begging you."

"Did you not say you dreamed of a girl that would come for me?"

"Not Catharina, Rocco. It wasn't her."

"I am tired, Father. I've waited hundreds of years for her to find me." When he withdrew his hand from the glass, the creature watched the girl continue to rub her shoulder where he knew she had bled for the tattoos that would free him. "It is God's will, not yours."

"I can't bear it," Father Xavier choked, looking inside at the men edging toward her to offer praise.

"She is beautiful in her own way. I want to know everything about her, priest. You will tell me."

"I won't!" Father Xavier insisted.

The creature jerked his head around, glaring his anger. "You come close to blasphemy. It is not for you to interfere. Even now—" He turned his attention toward the girl who tried to move forward to get a closer look. "—she seeks me out."

The heart he'd felt long dead and cold began to beat again. It was almost painful to know he was so close to being set free. But if he wasn't careful, all would be lost forever.

The priest covered his face with his hands to hold back the tears of loss he already felt. "Dear God in Heaven, protect my humble children from the monsters of the night."

A hand touched his arm. "Father? What's wrong?" It was Catharina. "Are you all right?"

The priest looked around him before grabbing her elbow to

lead her inside. "Yes. Just needed a moment to pray for every-one."

"Who was that man I saw you talking to?"

"Just another creature of the night, my dear."

"He frightened me." Catharina turned to face him. "Are you sure everything is all right?"

"Everything is in God's hands. Just like always."

Chapter 3

The full moon appeared to bounce on top of skyscrapers as narrow clouds moved across its brightness, hiding the glow for mere seconds. The wind picked up, channeling down Market Street. The remaining leaves that clung to trees released their hosts and swirled in the night as Catharina and her brother headed toward her efficiency apartment.

It was almost eleven as they neared the building—older than the others, but still possessing the charm the newer ones lacked. More and more people moved downtown, liking the community of businessmen, theater, restaurants, and sporting events close at hand. Now that the economy pendulum swung toward better times, the prices of these units increased daily.

"Stay with me tonight, Zane," Catharina begged. "I don't like you walking all the way back by yourself. My couch makes into a bed. Remember?"

He'd insisted she ride the bike as he ran alongside, saying he needed to keep in shape. "Your neighbors might not like seeing me come in their fancy smancy building." He stopped when she dismounted the bike about a half block away. Breathing deeply, he looked around them as if looking for problems. The area, normally well lit, now had a few missing street lights.

"Don't worry. I'll call the street department tomorrow to have them fix the lights. So what d'ya say? Stay with me. You can take a shower in the morning and head out if you like. By the way, where is your car?" It would be just like him to have loaned it to someone.

"Father's is in the shop. I told him to use mine as long as he needed."

"So you'll need a place to stay tonight. Please, Zane. I don't want to be alone."

The former Marine smiled at her as his fingers touched the violin case in the basket of her bicycle. They began walking again, enjoying the last of the autumn nights. Soon riding a bike and walking would be impossible with St. Louis winter weather.

"What ya got there in the basket?" A voice startled them coming out of the alley next to her apartment building. A man stepped out accompanied by three more that looked like they escaped a chain gang from some movie set.

"Get the hell out of our way," Zane growled as he pulled Catharina with his free hand around the front of the bike then behind him. "We don't want any trouble."

With her hand in the middle of her brother's back, she tried to nudge him forward without success. Backing down from a fight was not in his DNA. "Let's just go around them," she whispered, feeling the fear rise up inside her.

Just then one of the men grabbed the violin case, causing Catharina to gasp and reach for it. This amused the thugs as they jerked it back then lifted it into the air. One dark man tossed it to another, then another, until tears began flowing down her face at the prospect of the condition of her precious instrument.

"Please. Just leave us alone. We don't have any money."

One of the men, who looked to be in his thirties, eyed her. "Maybe I don't want money."

With that, Zane landed a punch in the man's eye, forcing him to fall to the ground. They began to brandish knives as their posturing changed from taunting to threatening. "Get him," the one on the ground yelled as he stumbled to his feet.

A scream escaped Catharina's throat as she watched two jump her brother. They were no match for his quickness and strength as he easily handled them. She thought the sound of a broken bone meant they might run, but the two left came at her, causing Zane to get distracted. Since Zane managed to remove both their knives, the injured one with a black eye landed a blow to her brother's kidney as he turned to help Catharina. A groan sent him staggering as she felt the grip of one of the attackers grab her around the waist and lift her feet off the ground. With a ferocious attempt at saving herself, she began kicking and scratching at the man's face. Her heart sank as another shadow emerged from the alley, almost in slow motion. The flickering street lamp caught the steel of two swords he withdrew from under his robe. In that fleeting moment, she realized it was the hooded man Father Xavier cornered outside The Kitchen of Hope.

The next instant, the stranger plunged his sword so deep into the man's back that the tip emerged through his chest. The attacker dropped her to the ground. The savior rushed up, looking down at her for mere seconds before he turned to her brother. Her first thought was that Zane would be next.

Zane staggered to his full height, apparently, shaking off the pain. "I need a weapon!"

In the blink of an eye, the rescuer tossed him a sword and, together, they began battling the vile muggers in some synchronized dance of death. When one of them pulled a revolver and pointed it at Zane, Catharina believed all was lost.

"No," she screamed between sobs.

The stranger stepped in front of Zane, just as the assailant pulled the trigger, taking the bullet full force.

Holding her breath, she managed to get to her feet. Knowing that the stranger saved her brother's life, she waited to see him fall from what must have been a fatal gunshot wound. The attacker also stared in horror—not at what he'd done, but that the man in the black hood did not fall. His two companions turned and ran, but he could only stumble backward, hypnotized by the man walking toward him. Without mercy, the stranger took the attacker's hand, turning it around so that the revolver pointed at his heart. Taking one step back, the stranger commanded, "Fire." The trigger pulled again and the attacker fell by his own hand.

Catharina stared in horror, trying to make sense of what just happened. Her brother lowered his sword like an exhausted Knight of the Round Table, unafraid and calmer than she'd seen him in a long time.

"Zane."

Keeping his eyes on his fighting partner, her brother ignored her call.

Looking back over his shoulder at Zane, the stranger appeared to be evaluating the situation. The distant sounds of traffic crowded in as did the sound of a police siren. Walking to the dropped violin case, the stranger picked it up before carrying it cautiously to Catharina. He stopped several inches from her before handing her the case.

Catharina stared up into strange pale eyes that both frightened and intrigued her. A feeling of joy entered her soul as she tried to see his face, lifting her hand to touch his skin. He knocked it away, then jerked her to his chest with his free hand, squeezing the breath from her lungs.

"Hey! Turn my sister loose!" Zane put a threatening hand on the stranger's shoulder, causing him to whirl around and place the tip of his sword at her brother's throat. Zane's eyes widened slightly then narrowed at the stranger.

The stranger took a step back and lifted his sword before his face in some odd salute. "You are a warrior, Zane Spokane. Do not give up the fight." The raspy voice sent shivers up Catharina's back.

Zane nodded before tossing him the second sword. "I won't. Thanks for all your help."

The stranger turned back to Catharina. "You. Play your violin again tomorrow night for The Kitchen."

"But I—"

"She'll play," Zane voiced as he came to stand next to her. "Promise."

Looking up at her brother, she let him pull her into his arms. The sirens grew closer. How would they explain all this? "Zane, you need to let me talk to the police when they get here. I'll explain about the dead men and how they attacked us."

"What dead men?" Her brother sounded so matter-of-fact, she couldn't help but look to where the two bodies lay on the street. In that split second, she realized the bodies disappeared before her eyes as did the hooded stranger. Stepping from the safety of Zane's arms, she let him pick up her bike as he nudged her toward the front door. "Who was that, Zane? Better yet, what was that?"

"The Watcher."

♪♫♪

Riding her bike to work in the rain the next morning was out of the question. The splurge on a bus ticket came as a result of over sleeping. It took a while to fall asleep with her brother deciding to remain the rest of the night.

"No interrogations, little sister. I'm staying because it's late and you're scared."

He didn't even bother opening up the bed in the couch—just curled up and fell asleep like a baby. In his mind, all was right with the world. In hers, all hell had broken loose.

Arriving fifteen minutes later than usual made preparing the coffee makers the day before worth the extra effort. The bakery arrived on her heels, even before she stripped off the wet parka. With squeaky shoes leaving a trail across the floor, she flipped the on buttons of the coffee then grabbed paper towels to remove the water she'd left on the floor.

Six-thirty came and went before she realized the assistant manager failed to come for his morning drink. After displaying all the pastries, she decided to secure an extra-large muffin for herself. Just as she sank her teeth into a warm banana nut muffin, she looked up to see Damien Cruz standing on the other side of the counter, staring at her. His hands were on both hips that forced his suit coat back from his pale yellow shirt making his skin a little darker and the areas under his eyes shaded.

With an arched eyebrow, he lowered his head slightly, giving the appearance of some sinister contemplation. "Do you always eat your inventory?"

The question came as he placed his hands on the top of the counter.

The muffin lost its satisfying taste as it turned to mush in her mouth. She tried to hurry and swallow. A slight tilt of his head gave him an impatient robot appearance.

"No. I mean—"

"Never mind, Ms. Spokane. I'll take a cup of your US coffee Jeremiah has been telling me about. He's become quite the cheerleader. Better make him one as well."

"Yes, sir." Turning away to fill the order, Catharina tried to relax. Her heart beat too fast and she was so nervous her hand trembled when she pulled the lever of the coffee machine. With the mirror behind her workstation, she realized Damien had leaned in to get a better look at her backside. Whirling around to confront him, she caught him off guard. "Looking for something, Mr. Cruz?"

The general manager showed no embarrassment or surprise as he straightened to his full height before smoothing his expensive suit coat. When their eyes locked, she felt something warm and frightening well up inside her.

"Actually, I think I've found everything I need."

A slight upturn at the corner of his mouth teased her with his hard sensuality. She surmised he used it on every woman he'd ever met. Catharina discovered, much to her distaste, it worked on her as well. Could one man be that handsome and obnoxious at the same time?

Glancing at his watch, Damien reached for the coffee she set on the counter.

"That will be six dollars," she said with as much indifference as she could muster.

"For coffee?"

"Eight, if you leave a tip. Jeremiah always leaves a tip."

Taking out several bills from his pocket he handed her a ten. "Keep the change. I'd hope we would have time to chat about what I expect of you and your little operation here." His walkie talkie crackled to life as he touched his ear fob. "But apparently there is a leak in the dining hall over the police chief's table. Besides—" He glanced toward the open glass doors. "—your first customers appear to be anxious for some of your coffee and muffins." He pointed to her face then dabbed at the corner of his mouth. "Better fix that, Ms. Spokane."

Grabbing a napkin to brush away the crumbs, she watched him stride out into the business center, stopping to greet several guests. He pointed to the inside of her shop and bobbed his head, as if confirming something important. The guests smiled and mouthed a "thank you" as they headed her way.

Without warning, he turned to look back at her. This time, his smile widened at her nervous confusion. Lifting the cups of coffee in a salute, Damien walked away into the Grand Hall.

Feeling a hot blush of irritation creep onto her face, she realized Damien Cruz succeeded in making her lose focus. There had been no men in her life for several years now and, even then, they were always a few dates from getting kicked to the curb. Taking care of her brother, a few night classes, and violin lessons didn't leave a lot of time for romance. Most of the men she'd known couldn't measure up to her warrior brother or the wise priest that helped raise her.

Catching a glimpse of herself in the mirror, she wondered what such a handsome man thought of her mismatched clothes. The chopped off black hair with blond tips fell thick and straight to the bottom of her neck. Thick eye liner and mascara accented her best feature—green eyes with flecks of gold. She always hoped it diverted people's eyes from the jagged scar down the left side of her face, reaching from under her bangs, down the edge of her face, to her chin. The dangly ear rings had been a gift from her brother, adding to the impression she'd fallen off a wagon while traveling with a band of gypsies.

♫ ♫ ♫

It was the end of a long day. Touching her scar with the palm of her hand, she poured yet another cup of coffee for a policeman who wandered in. When he started to pay, she refused, but he tipped her anyway.

"I heard a lot of sirens last night, Officer. I live over in the Essmalory apartment building. Anything I should be concerned about?" She made an effort to sound mystified.

Taking a sip of the brew, he shook his head. "Not sure. Someone called about a fight, some sword play. Probably some kids trying to play Luke Skywalker or something. They were gone by the time police arrived." Another sip. "Good coffee." He started toward the door. "Just the same, a young woman shouldn't be walking the streets after dark in that area. A few snatch and grabs and a couple of car thefts in the last month not far from there. Then there's the homeless. The problem seems to be growing. A lot of those people are desperate."

"Thanks. I'll be careful, Officer. I'd appreciate you sending business my way."

Thankfully, he'd been gone several minutes before Zane and Gideon arrived, looking timid and ill at ease in the fancy hotel atmosphere.

With a hug for Zane and a smile toward Gideon, Catharina led them to a table where they couldn't be seen so easily from outside the shop. Serving them a real mug of coffee with slices of pound cake, Catharina stood watching the two men. Her brother looked as he always did on the outside, calm, collected—normal. Apparently, the drama the night before left no lasting effects. If anything, Zane looked almost happy.

"What have you boys been doing today?"

Gideon shrugged first then pointed at Zane. "He took me to mass. Father Xavier took us into his home and fed us scrambled eggs and bacon."

"That was nice of him."

Scraping the last bite of pound cake off the plate with his fork, Zane chuckled. "Told him about our little adventure on the way home last night."

"Shh! Zane, don't ever mention that again."

Troubled eyes of confusion then looked up at her. "Okay. Okay. Okay."

She patted his wet head then his shoulder. "It's all good. Really. It's our secret, though, Zane."

Gideon nodded. "Secret," he echoed.

"What secret?" came the deep voice of Damien Cruz from behind her.

A quick turn-around took her off balance so she fell back against the table. A blush crept up her face as her hand tried to cover her scar along her face. Until today she hadn't paid much attention to it.

"My secret to a great cup of coffee, of course." The artificial smile forced its way onto lips she'd just covered in red lipstick.

Damien looked down his narrow nose at her, suspicion

registering in narrowed eyes. "And who do we have here?" His voice became cool and accusing as he stepped around Catharina. "If I didn't know better, I'd say these men were homeless, Ms. Spokane."

The two men remained still as church mice under Damien's penetrating gaze.

"Yes. Well, I invited them, Mr. Cruz. You see—" She extended her hand to her brother then hurried behind him to place her hands on his shoulders. "—this is my brother and his friend Gideon."

Zane's muscles tightened beneath her hands but he remained quiet. Gideon, on the other hand, appeared to be headed for a nervous breakdown. His hands shook as he stood then backed behind Catharina.

The manager reached across the table and extended his hand to Zane. "Then you'd be Sergeant Zane Spokane, former Marine. Served with Her Majesty's SAS in the Nimruz province myself."

Zane grabbed his hand like a life line. Damien's smile grew wide as he stole a quick glance at Catharina.

"Damn," Zane exclaimed. "You're a Brit. Those guys in Nimruz killed a lot of Taliban."

"That we did. We must swap war stories sometime soon."

"How did you know I had a brother?" Catharina sounded leery.

"I read your file today. You mentioned him, I believe." Damien's shifted his focus back to Zane. "Your sister is doing a terrific job for us. I know you must be very proud."

"Sure am. She's going to branch out one of these days."

"Zane!" Horrified, she allowed herself to look into the eyes of Damien Cruz who appeared more than amused. "That won't be for years, of course, Mr. Cruz."

"Hmm. I'm not sure about that. Your coffee is quite good." The callous look of contempt shifted to Gideon. "Giving away your fine brew for free to anyone who walks in off the street might very well prolong those plans."

Gideon started to pace. "I gotta go."

"This is Gideon, my brother's friend, Mr. Cruz. I invited

both of them here today. I hope you'll forgive me this one time. It wasn't their idea to come here."

Damien walked around to face Gideon, which stopped his pacing. "Gideon and I are old friends. Isn't that right?" Gideon began nodding without taking his eyes off the floor. "He likes to beg outside the front entrance which scares hotel guests," Damien continued.

Catharina frowned at the intimidation tactics being used on Gideon. "It won't happen again, Mr. Cruz. They came to walk me home, so I invited them in while I finish up."

Zane drained his cup and stood, before draping his arm around his sister's shoulders. "Not safe where she lives. Thugs tried to jump us last night."

Damien shrugged then nodded. "We'll talk tomorrow, Ms. Spokane. Allow a little time for me at the end of the day, please, before you leave." He turned his strange-colored eyes back on Zane and smiled. "No need to worry about her safety. I'll have the hotel car take her home or—" His gaze moved from Zane to her. "—wherever you need to go for the evening."

Chapter 4

like that general manager at the hotel," Zane confessed as they walked inside The Kitchen of Hope. "Those SAS guys were serious as a heart attack. Wonder why he ended up here."

Catharina moved behind the counter to don her apron, then offered a back pat to Father Xavier. "He seemed to like you too," she said with a little too much cynicism.

For the first time in a long time, Zane laughed. "I think it's because I have a pretty sister." He winked at her.

The sound of his laughter gave her hope things might be changing for the better. "Oh, Zane. I love you so much."

"What's not to love?" He faked the pose of a body builder, while holding out her violin case, and made her burst into laughter.

"Hearing my two favorite people kidding around brings me great joy." Father Xavier handed Zane an apron. "Need your help tonight, son. Do you mind?"

"Glad to, Father."

A few extra servers arrived from St. Louis University as part of a volunteer project, along with several from Father Xavier's church. No one had to work too long or hard for their dinner. For the first time in a long time, the priest got to sit down and eat with the men coming through the doors.

There were about twenty more people needing a hot meal tonight. Maybe it was because of the misty rain that blanketed the streets or the sudden drop in temperatures. Catharina was thankful they all had a place to go. Several older men stole glances at her for the first time. Their grizzly faces of hunger and poor health hid identities. The only unique thing about these people was that they lived in their own little world of torment and could survive harsh conditions. Some smelled of alcohol, cigarette smoke or body odor. It had taken Catharina a long time to ignore the smells of homelessness.

Determined to keep her brother clean, she made him bath every few days at her apartment. With each cleansing, he emerged with some magical kind of clarity that would last for hours. They would talk about old times, the future, world events, and even the weather. By morning, the haunted Zane would have returned, often quieter and staring into space where his ghosts lurked to digest his sanity.

"The men are wondering if you'll play that fiddle again to-night, Cat." It was Gideon. He stared down at his mismatched shoes. "I'd like it if you did."

Untying her apron, she smiled, pleased that it meant so much to them. Was this her gift to them now? Removing her ankle boots, she felt the coldness of the concrete floor seep up through the balls of her bare feet. It was then she noticed a hole in her black leggings and thought how perfect her imperfection was in such a place. She rattled her bangle bracelets to get everyone's attention, then stood with her legs spread apart.

"Tonight I need your help. Can you do that?" Some shook their heads while others just appeared confused and frightened. "Zane, remember that drum beat you used to do for me when I was learning to play?" Without her telling him what to do, he started tapping on a gallon size empty can of green beans. "Now you!" she commanded of her audience.

A slow rhythmic beat began to fill the room as all eyes focused on Catharina. With her violin, she began to play a haunting melody that soon had the men bobbing their heads to the beat of the music. When her melody sped up, she couldn't help but twist and turn, dancing to some forced magic she always felt when music filled her.

Spinning between the tables, bending and sometimes even hopping, Catharina lost herself in the performance. A joy filled her. A peace soothed the worries for her brother, carried like bundles of rocks in her heart.

Three songs later, she held up her violin in a victory stance, breathing so hard it was difficult to laugh. Their applause made her feel like she had just performed at Powell Hall.

Spinning around, she faced the plate-glass window that fronted The Kitchen. Standing alone, with his head bowed before her was The Watcher who commanded her to play from the night before. His waist length robe, damp from the night mist, opened at his waist, revealing leather clothing underneath. Tight pant legs, shoved in his thigh-high boots, left nothing to the imagination as to his strength and capabilities. Both hands were gloved and he also wore red bands around his wrists.

Stepping forward, he placed his hand against the glass then raised his head slightly.

Catharina took a step closer, raising her hand to touch the glass where his hand rested. Just as she started to make contact, Father Xavier stepped in front of her. "Stop!"

Startled out of her reverie, she looked up into the fearful eyes of the priest. "Why?"

He took her by the shoulders and turned her around to face her fans. They looked past her out the window at the man who rescued them the night before. "The homeless are afraid of him. Do not encourage his attentions."

When Catharina turned to look back out the window, the man had disappeared. The tattoos on her shoulder began to burn until she rubbed them with her free hand. "Who is he, Father?"

"Never mind that. Is that the man who helped you and Zane last night?"

"Yes. Without him—"

"I can only imagine." The priest took her elbow and maneuvered her to the front of The Kitchen where her brother began cleaning away the night's work. "He protects those who cannot protect themselves. These people think he's some kind of savior for them."

Digging in her heels, she forced him to stop. "But they look frightened of him. Why?"

"You saw firsthand what he is capable of, Cat. Doesn't that tell you why?"

It was the first time Catharina could ever remember the priest sounding irritated with her questions. "You know him."

"Yes." His voice became low and controlled and he made the sign of the cross. "He visits me for confession and for me to offer prayers to our Heavenly Father."

"Should I go to the police? He killed two men, father."

"*No*," he snapped. "No," he continued in a softer tone. "His work never harms an innocent."

"Work? He goes around like a vigilante, Father."

"All is not what it seems, dear Cat. Do not encourage him with kindness. He is not like us."

"How so? You act as if he's some kind of creature."

Father Xavier sighed. "Do as I say, child."

Her brother's gestures of heading to the alley to dump the trash forced her to acknowledge there must be more important things to fret over besides some lunatic trying to be a street superhero. Seeing him whirl his sword like some Knights Templar the night before struck a romantic notion of justice and being rescued from the burden of taking care of a brother. Zane, for a few minutes, had morphed into a strong warrior with purpose, defending *her*, instead of the other way around. Together, the two battled evil men who would do them harm. One thing she knew for sure, her brother didn't need to collect another new best friend who carried a sword and made dead bodies disappear.

Tucking her violin into its case, she closed it with the utmost care.

Gideon waved goodbye as did several other men who, except for the color of their skin, looked a great deal like Gideon; tall, shaven, bald, or at least well-groomed mops of hair. Only their clothes told of their destitute circumstances. Hunched shoulders hid their confident strides out the door. The smell of incense followed them. In that moment, she noticed Father Xavier staring after them, clutching the large crucifix around his neck with the grip of desperation. His lips moved in silent prayer.

Catharina started to tell the father about taking out the last bag of trash when she noticed an elderly couple seek out his confidence. Leading them to a table, he began consoling them on some matter of concern to them. Her heart filled with love once more, seeing how the priest ministered to the people of the street. He really was a man of God.

Tying the ends together of the trash bag, she carried it to the backdoor and saw it still ajar. She stepped outside, the red exit light creating an eerie glow on the puddles next to the overflowing trash bin. A scrawny cat leaped off the pile, forcing her to catch her breath in fear. In that instant, she wondered as she tossed the leaky bag of Styrofoam plates and melted Jell-0 cups, where Zane had wandered off to. Had he forgotten about taking her home?

Voices farther into the darkness drew her attention, recognizing one of them as her brother's. Hesitant at first, she worried he might be hallucinating again and might need her to snap him back to reality. She'd gotten good at soothing the savage beast within his troubled mind. Following the hushed voices, she saw him standing in front of someone in dark clothing. Was it a drug dealer? Maybe it was one of the gang members, who preyed on the helpless, and who thought he could get Zane to do his dirty work. Either of those options could mean danger if she approached too quickly. Most of those men carried guns.

"Zane?" she called in a soft voice so as not to alarm either man. "Zane. Time to go."

Her brother looked around whoever he was talking to and held up his large hand for her to be patient. Then both men clasped forearms in some strange bond of loyalty. Catharina felt her shoulder come to life with fire, forcing her to stumble backward. Both men approached with caution.

"You!" Catharina choked when she realized Zane was with the hooded stranger. Reaching up, he pulled his hood a little farther down over his forehead so that his face became bathed in darkness. "Who are you?" she demanded.

With his leather clad hand, he reached out and touched the left side of her face where her scar trailed down. The contact electrified her senses, compelling her to grab hold of his wrist. A fleeting question of why her brother allowed this beast to touch her evaporated as the sting of something wonderful entered her body. The beat of her heart quickened and all fear disintegrated, erasing any thought of escape.

"I am Rocco."

Her eyes shifted to Zane, who smiled like a little boy hitting his first homerun. She tried to step away, but moved closer as the hooded man pulled her so close she could feel the hilt of his sword press against her ribs.

"The music soothes my soul. Will you come again tomorrow night?"

Aware that this time it wasn't a command, but a request, Catharina breathed a "Yes."

A tenderness mixed with enormous strength surged through Catharina as he passed her to Zane. "God be with you, Catharina. Blessings upon your music that conquerors the darkness in us all."

In the time it took to glance at her brother then back at the man of shadows, Rocco disappeared. All reality crashed upon her, driving uncontrollable trembling to rack her body. She experienced chills and heat, fear and comfort.

Zane seemed to sense her confusion and wrapped his arms around her.

"It's okay, little sister. Promise." He kissed the top of her head as the backdoor swung open, revealing the form of Father Xavier. "Not a word of this, Cat," Zane whispered, a request that meant a lie to the father figure who taught her to overcome life's pitfalls with grace and hope. "Not a word."

"What are you guys doing out here? Time to go home. Cat, we'll drop you off then Zane can take me home."

Catharina walked into the light of the hall. "Sounds good. Just need to get my violin."

Father Xavier looked from her to Zane with a frown. "Everything all right?"

The Marine veteran patted the priest on the back before turning to lock the door. "Never better. Never better. Never better."

The fog that came into the eyes of the man he loved as a son, convinced the priest nothing was amiss.

♫ ♫ ♫

Another rainy morning meant Catharina needed to take the bus to work. This time the alarm clock woke her in plenty of time to get ready. Lace tights, a thigh-length black and white polka dot dress, with a red denim jacket she secured from The Goodwill Store, seemed almost festive on such a dreary day. Along with the jacket, she'd found some black designer boots for ten dollars with only a few scuff marks. Wondering what it must feel like to buy them new crossed her mind as she slipped on her bangle bracelets and hoop earrings.

Brushing her teeth then applying the ritual eye makeup, she kept track of the time. Fumbling through her one drawer of colorful accessories, Catharine found the sparkly headband and black leather belt to finish her Bohemian appearance. Smiling at the unconventional combination, she could only imagine Damien Cruz's reaction when he saw her today for their meeting.

Lifting the headband to her unruly hair, Catharina froze. Pushing the blonde tipped ends of her black hair away from the side of her face, she realized the scar had begun to fade.

Chapter 5

The coffee shop remained busy throughout the day. November rains drove people indoors instead of taking advantage of The Arch or St. Louis Zoo. Coughs, mixed with a few sneezes, echoed in the business center outside the shop, forcing a few loose-tie executives to wander inside for a cup of soup Catharina prepared the day before, knowing the weather meant extra money in her pockets. The pastries disappeared by ten, the cheese and crackers by eleven, so the only choice became vegetable soup, bottled water and coffee. She made a mental note to add a few salads.

Groups of two and three business men or women occupied the tables later in the day. Wednesdays didn't bring children with traveling parents. School cut down on that kind of coffee drinker. Busy parents didn't tip very well, anyway. A few architecture students from Drury University in Springfield spent hours combing the nooks and crannies of Union Station, but when it came time to eat or drink, they sat at one of her tables to nibble on a sack lunch instead of buying anything.

She'd been in the same situation many times. The truth was she still needed a sack lunch most days. In spite of the non-paying clientele, she figured her profit around two hundred dollars for the day. "God bless rainy days" became her mantra.

The phone behind the counter buzzed just before closing. With the adjusted lock in place, the obsessed gamer, sitting in what looked to be pajama bottoms and a Ram's tee shirt outside in the hall of computers, gave her a nod of understanding that the refills were over on his herbal tea. Untying her apron,

Catharina raced to catch the phone on the fifth ring, only to hear it click as she lifted it to her ear. Shifting her eyes to the clock, the time frame for cleaning would be tight today since she needed to meet with Damien Cruz at four. On a normal day she would have begun wiping down tables and chairs an hour earlier. Even as she started that process the phone buzzed again.

This time she caught it on the second irritating sound. "Yes." Running across to catch it left her a little breathless.

"Do you always ignore your calls, Ms. Spokane?" There was no mistaking the deep richness of Damien Cruz's voice.

"Always," she retorted a little more blah than she felt. His voice managed to send shivers up her spine for some odd reason. In spite of being on the phone, she could imagine him staring at her with an arched eyebrow over blue eyes that bore through her ability to think straight. "What is it?"

A warm, unsettling chuckle answered her flippant attitude. "Remind me to speak to you about your phone manners when you come at four. I hope you haven't forgotten our date."

"It's more of a command than a date." Catharina bit her bottom lip, wondering if she came across as suggesting further contact outside of work. "I mean, I'll be there. Well, unless you keep talking to me then I'll have to see you tomorrow. I have a lot of work to do. Goodbye."

Dropping the phone like a fourteen-year-old klutz must have sounded like she slammed the phone down. His opinion of her, already questionable with bringing in a couple of homeless guys, now might have her permanently on his bad side. Maybe if she apologized, explaining she dropped the phone, he wouldn't give her that better-to-eat-you-with-my-dear look.

Even as she finished her chores, his voice played around the recesses of her mind, toying with her common sense. The shape of his wide, perfect mouth, the eyes that looked like blue lasers of desire, cutting through her defenses, registered caution deep in her core. The day before, when he stood rigid and tall, she became aware there wasn't an inch of fat on him. His expensive suit fit him like a glove, hinting he had a tailor. The dark hair and olive skin gave him an east European appearance rather than British.

Even though Catharina saw him as handsome, his hollow cheekbones gave him a sinister edge that some women might see as too hard, too angular.

Being caught up in imagining Damien in various stages of undress resulted in her missing her four o'clock appointment with him. She tried to smooth down her hair then press her dress down lower toward her knees, afraid she'd be too inappropriate for the very sophisticated Damien Cruz's taste.

"Is Mr. Cruz still in?" she panted as she ran into his outer office where a male secretary typed a document. "I had a four o'clock."

"He'll be with you shortly." He never stopped typing or bothered to make eye contact until she remained standing at his desk. Then, with indifference, he pointed to a French settee covered in blue silk. "Sit."

For someone about her own age, the secretary apparently felt pretty confident in ordering her around.

Backing toward the settee, looking around the room with awe, she failed to realize how close the settee was until she bumped into it and flopped down like a beached whale. The secretary glanced her way, raising both eyebrows without ever stopping his tapping on the keyboard.

Blushing, Catharina lifted her hand and smiled. "It's all good." She thought he exhaled a "humph," but wasn't sure if maybe the furnace hadn't kicked on instead.

At 4:50, she continued to wait. The secretary started shutting down for the day, clearing the clutter of one coffee cup which bore the St. Louis Cardinals insignia and several already stacked documents next to the computer. Tennis shoes replaced his wingtips and an all-weather coat covered his suit.

Catharina stood, slipping her purse strap over her shoulder.

"Where do you think you're going?"

His look of confusion stopped Catharina in her tracks. "Home. You're leaving. I thought—"

"I'd wait if I were you."

It sounded like a warning as he disappeared out the door.

At 5:15, Catharina, huffed a disgruntled sigh and stormed toward the hall as she dug in her purse for bus money. If she hurried to the corner, she'd make it. Walking five blocks in the rain didn't sound like something she could handle tonight. It would be dark soon. Maybe she should just take a cab to The Kitchen, but that was ten dollars she could use elsewhere. Her glance of the clock over the door forced her to speed up to a run. As she plowed through the doors, Damien stepped in front of her, coming in from the hall.

"Ugh," she grunted then bounced back off his chest, only to be caught in his arms which pulled her in close.

"Are you all right, Ms. Spokane?" He continued to hold her as he looked down his narrow nose at her.

The timid push away from his embrace left her a little shaken. "Yes." Why could she not be as chatty with him as she was with her customers?

"You seem to be in a hurry. We have a meeting."

"We had a meeting at four."

His sinister smile toyed with any self-respect she had left for herself. In a few seconds, she worried there would be nothing left of her but a melted, steamy puddle on the floor.

He stepped around her. "You were late."

"I was here 4:10."

He moved toward his office door and tilted his dark head for her to follow. "That constitutes late in my book, Ms. Spokane. I'm a busy man. I had other things to attend to besides wondering if you'd show up." He glanced over his shoulder to verify she was behind him.

"Ditto," she snapped with her weight shifted to one hip and her arms crossed across her chest.

Surrendering to his silent command, she followed then stopped in the middle of his office, trying not to notice the impressive masculinity of it all.

Rolling a leather chair up close to his desk, Damien lifted his head, indicating he wanted her to sit. When she didn't, he insisted. "Please sit, Ms. Spokane. This won't take long."

She eased into the chair. It moved slightly, making her grab the arms. "If you're upset with me because of yesterday, it won't happen again. I take care of my brother and I needed to know he was okay. He's gone through some tough times."

Damien sat on the edge of his chocolate brown desk, looking down at her with reserve. He loosened the black tie and opened the top button on his pale blue shirt. Catharina couldn't help but stare at his throat and wondered, in that moment, if there was a woman in his life. No wedding band indicated there might be but wasn't it possible that a handsome creature like Damien Cruz possessed a whole harem of willing females?

"You're staring." He broke into her train of thought, causing her to blush. "I know all about your brother. I did a little digging after they left. You're to be commended."

"Oh. Thanks. I guess." Catharina wasn't sure where the conversation was headed. "Then why did you want to see me? Is everything all right?"

"Yes. Quite satisfactory. Your brew is delicious and your unorthodox way of dressing seemingly fascinates the guests. They think it's all part of the atmosphere."

It sounded like a back-handed compliment to her. "Then why am I here?"

"I wanted to let you know I've moved the weekly meeting of the mayor to your shop on Tuesday mornings. He comes and drinks coffee with city officials, citizens, anyone who wants to listen to his dribble." His contempt showed as he slipped his thumb under the tie to loosen it further. "Then on Wednesdays, I've moved the police chief and his detectives to the shop. They actually talk about work and change. The restaurant is too busy to just be serving coffee. Their coffee and donuts are always complimentary."

"Stop right here. I can't be—"

"The hotel will pick up the tab, as always. Keep track of the charges, add in whatever tip you think appropriate. It pays to have the police watching after you in this part of the city. We may be a luxury hotel, but crime is just a few blocks away. We take care of them and they take care of us. Simple as that."

"I don't know what to say, Mr. Cruz." Catharina felt mortified at wanting to scratch his eyes out a moment earlier. Grateful he interrupted her before she could spew insults about working hard and no way was she giving anything away for free unless she wanted to, would certainly have squelched the warm fuzzy feelings tapping at her common sense.

With a mischievous smile, he slid off the end of the desk. "Thank you is traditional."

Having the feeling they were finished, Catharina scooted to the edge of the chair. "Thank you, Mr. Cruz."

"That's another thing. Call me Damien. In spite of this place looking like royalty lives here, we're pretty informal. However—" The eyebrow arched again, sending shivers up her spine. "—I so enjoy how Mr. Cruz rolls off your tongue."

Aware that he'd emphasized the word "tongue" caused Catharina to push up out the chair, sending it rolling backward. "Please, call me Catharina or Cat."

His mouth widened. "Cat. Sounds like a creature of the night."

"Or Bengal tiger who can devour its mate."

This caused Damien to chuckle deep in his throat as if he were deciding on some kind of action to take. "I've noticed you keep looking at the clock. Do you have some place you need to be? A jealous boyfriend impatiently waiting at home for you?"

"I work at The Kitchen of Hope at six. I missed my bus. I'll have the guys downstairs hail me a cab." Slipping the strap of her bag onto her shoulder, she turned to leave.

"Nonsense. I promised your brother I'd make sure you'd arrive safe and sound. I didn't realize it would be The Kitchen." He dialed and requested a car. "I see. Then bring my car around please. I'll need it right away."

Catharina felt a wave of panic wash over her, knowing Damien intended to drive her to The Kitchen. "That won't be necessary, Mr. Cruz, I mean Damien." The whole "tongue" comment popped into her head. "A cab will be okay."

The phone disconnected as he walked over to retrieve his coat from a closet. "If you can work all day then serve the homeless, then I can certainly give their angel of mercy a ride on a cold rainy night." Even though she'd started for the door before him, he cut her off in time to swing it open. "Is there anywhere else you need to go?" The question sounded as if he already knew the answer.

The thought of him knowing where she lived unsettled her,

in spite of knowing the information was in her file, on his computer and Google Earth. Providing him with an up close and personal location of her life after working at Union Station all day did not sit well with her.

She caved. "I promised to play my violin tonight. It's at my apartment."

"No problem. We'll just make a quick stop. It's on the way." Shoving his hands in the pockets of his London Fog coat, he smiled over at her.

Catharina stopped, shooting him a skeptical look. "How do you know that?"

Taking her elbow, Damien ushered her down the grand staircase toward the street. "I've been stalking you," he said flippantly. When she jerked away to glare at him, a deep throaty laugh escaped into the chilly night air. "I know of no other Kitchen around here and your address, according to your contract, is just a few blocks from here. I'm not a rocket scientist, but some things are not that difficult to figure out. You're very suspicious, Cat."

"Oh," was all she managed to utter as the valet handed Damien his keys then opened the door for her to slip in his black Mercedes.

She tried to huddle into a small ball, squeezing her knees together then pulling her jacket together before staring straight out the windshield. Feeling his eyes on her, Catharina glanced over, confused. "What?"

Ignoring her impatient tone, Damien reached across her to grab the seatbelt then dragged it across her chest before fastening it. His hand remained on the buckle and his face inches from hers. "Don't want anything to happen to you on such a stormy night." A wolfish smile played at the corners of his mouth. Taking a few extra seconds to explore her face and hair, he turned away to pull out into traffic.

With as much calm as she could muster, Catharina offered directions to the apartment building, but didn't try making conversation. The tension between them reminded her of downed electrical wires dancing around the ground after a wind storm.

"You can pull over here." He obeyed then turned off the car

and opened the car door. "No. You don't need to come in. I'll only be a minute." His eyes narrowed in some kind of amusement as she escaped the car to enter her building.

In less than ten minutes, she was buckling herself back into the Mercedes, clutching her violin case like a baby. "Thanks for doing this."

She resisted calling him by his name. He offered a straight smile across closed lips that drove her heart beat into double time. In that instant, she wondered if it would be wrong to pray there would be no parking place and he'd be forced to drop her off without any further feeling of obligation.

"How fortunate." The car slowed and pulled into a spot in front of The Kitchen.

"Thanks so much, Mr. Cruz." Up went the left eyebrow. "I mean Damien. I appreciate it."

"My pleasure."

Fumbling with the door handle resulted in Damien's quick exit of the car, only to catch the door as she began to exit. Cocking his head to the side, his eyes shifted from her to the inside of The Kitchen. Closing the door, he fell in step with her.

"You don't need to walk me in. Thanks again."

"Are you trying to get rid of me, Cat?" He sounded amused as he opened the door to The Kitchen for her. "I'm feeling kind of hungry."

Stopping in the doorway, she looked up into blue eyes evaluating her discomfort. "You can't park your hundred thousand dollar car outside and waltz in here wearing a five hundred dollar suit and expect these people to feel comfortable. You look like you've come to see how the other half lives. You need to leave. Now." She stole a glance into the room, noticing everyone now looked her way. "Oh geeze."

Damien continued to push inside and shook off the rain from his coat. He nodded to onlookers without the slightest concern. "Relax," he whispered in her ear.

The feeling of his warm breath on her ear sent goose bumps up her arms. They stared with stubborn resolve into each other's eyes, failing to notice the approach of Father Xavier.

"Cat, who have you brought us tonight?" The priest smiled

and extended his hand to Damien. "You've been missing mass, Damien," he scolded, pulling him forward away from the door.

"You know him?" she said with bewilderment.

Walking away from her, the two men forgot her, lost in their own conversation. Laughter passed between them like long lost buddies.

Irritated at the surprise, Catharina grabbed her apron after securing her violin case. Extra volunteers arrived so that Father Xavier could minister to his hungry flock of forgotten souls. When he and Damien came through the serving line, they barely acknowledged her efforts. Only her brother spoke cheerfully, asking her how her day went. He offered to relieve her but she declined, afraid the priest would somehow insist she sit with their new guest.

"Hello, Gideon." She hadn't seen him arrive. "I've heard the meatloaf was made by the Baptist ladies from the church on Grand. Let me sneak you an extra piece." The tall black man didn't make eye contact. She thought they'd gotten beyond the awkward stage, but he kept looking over his shoulder at Damien. "Don't worry, Gideon. He won't be staying long."

She noticed several other men Gideon sat with each night huddled together looking in the same direction. Their obvious nervous behavior alarmed her that trouble might be brewing.

Removing her apron, she turned her responsibilities over to a volunteer then removed her shoes. She wiggled her toes, relieved to be free of their confinement. After lifting the violin from its cradle, Catharina walked around the steam table and waited. She bowed her head to say a pray for her gift to give peace to her homeless audience then raised the violin out shoulder height in one hand and the bow in the other hand the same way. A hush fell over the room as someone turned out all but one light in the middle of the room.

A slow beat of hands on tables brought her instrument to rest under her chin. The rapturous feeling of the music yet to come, began to fill her with euphoria. Everyone disappeared as the bow touched the strings.

Even the penetrating eyes of Damien Cruz failed to distract her from the gift God gave her. Maybe the creature of the night lurked in the shadows on a street nearby and listened to sooth his soul once more. She began to twirl with the rhythm of her song. Leaning backward so that her hair nearly touched the floor, she created a web of music and desire inspired by a man she'd only met a few days earlier.

Another song, then another and another, caused her dancing to swing between ballet and jazz. So lost in the music, that when she stepped up on the top of a table to finish followed by loud applause, Catharina looked down into the face of Damien Cruz. Raw pain filled his eyes as did what looked like emotion. He reached up for her hand to guide her down to a metal folding chair then lifted her off her feet to the floor. The touch of his hands on her waist sent shock waves through her body.

"The music soothes my soul, Cat." The words sounded like gratitude. Stepping back so others could approach and thank her, Damien continued to watch her with curiosity, never standing too far away or too close.

Chapter 6

The Watcher never showed in the plate glass window. She wondered if he might not be some place safe and dry. She played for him as much as the restlessness of Gideon's friends. Like other nights, those men were the last to leave. Something always looked different about them compared to the other homeless. They hovered like nervous guardians for Father Xavier. Sometimes Catharina imagined them to be angels waiting to fend off mutated gang members. *Maybe I should have been a writer instead of a musician*, she mused.

Damien made himself useful, helping to clean up and take out the trash. She worried The Watcher or whatever he was, waited in the alley. Would he flash his sword if he perceived Damien as a threat? When Damien didn't return right away, she went looking for him. To her surprise Gideon and his friends stood talking to Damien. There were no hunched, submissive shoulders, timid voices, or pacing. These men stood tall, unafraid of the man before them. He spoke with a quiet firm voice before taking out his wallet and handing them money. They nodded then backed away into the darkness.

When she tried to scamper back inside, she stumbled over a metal trashcan, making a loud racket that drew his sudden attention. In the flickering light of the exit sign, Catharina thought he was someone else. She turned to rush inside before feeling his hands on her shoulders. He forced her to turn around. In that instant, he drew her close enough that their noses touched.

The thought of him kissing her became a possibility when she realized he stared at her mouth. Powerless to stop what she shamelessly desired, her lips parted.

"Cat," called Father Xavier.

Damien stepped away and brushed past her. "Gotta go, Father."

"Good to see you again, son. Thanks for your help tonight and the donation. God bless you."

In almost a blink of an eye, Damien was gone.

♫ ♫ ♫

"Thanks for the ride." Catharina waved to Father Xavier as she entered her apartment building.

He pulled away from the curb only after she stood on the inside of the heavy security doors that locked each time they closed.

The Essmalory Building, built in the late 1930s, showed its age with chipped and yellow floor tiles. The mosaics of Athenian gods and goddesses decorated the lobby walls leaving the impression of gaudiness. Even the ceiling felt the artistic hand of the architect, grandeur with ornate designs, now in faded blues and reds. All the charm of a bygone era with its dark varnished baseboards and marble staircase reaching to the second floor, was one of the things that compelled her to sign a waiting list for an apartment.

After finishing her associate's degree at Forest Park Community College in business, she had received a notification about an available unit. With Father Xavier as a reference, her grades and two part time jobs at Busch Stadium and the Scott Trade Center, Catharina signed a one year lease agreement with a promise of a second. Three years later, residents were given the opportunity to buy their unit. Securing a loan proved to be a little difficult considering her age, yet it happened.

"God provided for you yet again, Cat. Be sure to thank Him each day," Father Xavier proclaimed.

The second story apartment meant Catharina didn't need to use the elevator which squeaked like a convention of hungry mice. Although the city inspection guaranteed residents of a safe ride to any of the ten floors, she opted to walk up each day.

The white marble felt cold through the thin soles of her shoes. Old and worn, they offered about the same support as ballet slippers. Now with her hand gliding on the wide railing of the staircase, she allowed herself to look up at the large windows at the top of the stairs. Lightning flashed followed by a low rumble of thunder. Reaching the landing, she inhaled deep and long, wondering if her brother slept in his car as he promised to do. Always something to worry about with him.

Juggling a violin case while fishing for her keys, Catharina kept her head down as she slipped the key in the lock. A clap of thunder hurried her steps inside before she toed the door shut then secured the deadbolt. A touch to the light switch revealed the power was out. She would be going to bed, anyway. Thankfully, the little apartment didn't need much heat for her to stay warm. Cutting back on such a luxury became routine over the years. Tonight, the five hundred square foot space felt colder than usual.

Only the bathroom allowed any amount of privacy. Brushing her teeth by a flashlight she kept in the vanity drawer, then washing her face before slipping into her cotton nightgown she kept on the back of the bathroom door, completed her nightly ritual. She hurried out to the room that served as kitchen, living room, and bedroom where a fake sheep skin rug offered warmth to her half frozen toes.

In that moment when she stopped next to her double bed, the sensation of not being alone filled her. Why hadn't she brought the flashlight with her? She reached out to grab the iron headboard just as lightning flashed in the double windows on the other side of the room. That's when she saw him sitting in the one comfortable chair she owned in front of the window. She made out the hood covering his head and his hands resting on his knees. Even though she couldn't see them, the touch of his pale eyes on her exposed neck and shoulder, where her gown slid off, ignited her tattoos.

Whether it was fear or perhaps courage, she released the headboard, stampeding to the front door with more swiftness than she thought possible.

She realized the deadbolt refused to budge beneath her

trembling fingers. Rattling the door did nothing to alleviate the problem.

Just as she banged her fist against the door and called for help, another clap of thunder muted her voice.

"Come here." The calm, raspy voice of The Watcher, or whoever he pretended to be, reached her from where she'd left him. "Come here," he repeated.

Catharina slid along the narrow foyer wall into the room, as if by doing so would conceal her existence. If only her cell phone worked. Maybe she needed a gun. Self-defense classes suddenly sounded like a good idea. But none of that mattered, because time had run out on those proactive things that single women did to protect themselves from situations like this.

He stood in slow motion, dropping his hands down to his sides. "Do not be afraid, Catharina." The lightning flickered several times. "I'm not here to hurt you. I do not have it in my power to hurt the innocent."

The swallow she forced down her throat sounded like thunder in her ears as she pushed off the wall. If she could get to the bathroom and lock herself in, then she'd be safe. In a burst of speed, she ran toward the bathroom door, only to find it locked. Whirling around, she pressed her body up against the door. Now she had trapped herself in an impossible situation.

"What is happening?" she mumbled.

With stealth-like movements, he walked across the room to stand before her. "You're trembling."

The city lights, still burning, shined through her windows, causing web patterns across the floor and walls. He reached over to the bed and pulled off a lacy shawl she used as decoration. As he stepped closer to her, a terrified moan escaped her throat. With the gentleness of a loving father, Rocco wrapped the garment around her shoulders before stepping back a safe distance.

"What do you want? I'm going to tell the police all about the other night and you." Her warning sounded less than convincing. "You need to leave."

"Soon." Reaching out, he rested his hand on the shoulder where her tattoos became visible as the shawl slipped down.

"Why do you have these?"

She shrugged, trying to push his hand away with little success. "Stop it. Don't touch me," she demanded.

Withdrawing his hand, he stood silent, drinking in the sight of her shadowy form. "You are good to those who have nothing. Why?"

Suddenly, she felt he really did mean her no harm. If he had, an attack would have already commenced. "Rocco," she whispered. "Rocco." The name sounded strong, almost warrior-like.

He extended his gloved hand toward her. Catharina looked at it only seconds before she entwined her fingers with his. A step closer did not make seeing his face any easier.

"What are you, Rocco?" Releasing his hand, she reached up and pushed back his hood. "I want to see you."

He nodded as the hood fell back on his neck. Closing his eyes, he bowed his head and waited to hear a frightened cry. When none came, he raised his chin to stare into the eyes of the one who could free him. "Are you frightened of my face?"

Catharina met his pale eyes with hers and shook her head. A darkness covered his face above his eyebrows, down across his narrow nose. Dark hair came over his ears and his wide mouth turned down in a frown. A four o'clock shadow felt prickly as she touched the sides of his face with her hands. She felt him pull away.

With a smile that felt timid, she whispered. "I won't hurt you, either."

His eyes opened then narrowed to slits in some kind of torment Catharina recognized from the other homeless men she'd met at The Kitchen. She'd seen him kill two men and had just promised to not harm him. The thought of her even trying probably would make her laugh in the morning—if she survived. A sad smile played at the corners of his mouth. "Of that, I am sure."

They still stood near one another, close enough to feel the breath of the other.

He reached out to touch her skin. Catharina stepped into his touch. She closed her eyes, feeling the painful burn drain from her shoulder, leaving a soothing emptiness. His touch remained cool, acting as a balm to her tortured body. A sigh of relief escaped her lips.

"How—" She wasn't sure of the question to ask because she couldn't wrap her head around the possibility that whoever this creature might be, he had removed the sudden flare of discomfort.

With a cringe, he withdrew his hand, turning away abruptly. He staggered only a step before Catharina wrapped her arms around him in fear that he would fall. Later, she would remember the firmness of his back, the toughness of his chest as her arms pulled him back against her. A tug backward forced him to sit on the edge of her bed. A moment's weakness left him vulnerable to Catharina's prying eyes. A glow radiated from inside his leather vest near his shoulder.

"Rocco?"

He became powerless against her fingers opening his vest, then his black shirt, peeling it open. His eyes met hers as she caught her breath. The tattoos that spread across his shoulder, then down the front of his chest, glowed like burning embers.

"Rocco," she cried in anguish, knowing the intense pain he must be experiencing.

Without thinking, she laid both her hands against his skin, feeling a surge of some unknown knowledge, power, and pain enter her palms then rush up her arms and chest.

For only a second, she tried to move away, but the creature spread his legs out so that he could pull her to him with such force that her ability to control the situation evaporated. The spread of his palms on her lower back felt like iron clasps, holding her in place. She dared to look down into his nearly opaque eyes and had the sensation of drowning in something beyond her power, which filled the longing from deep inside her. The need to resist vanished.

Closing her eyes, she looked upward feeling his hands stroke her spine in long, slow movements. When she dared to look down at his chest, the glow instantly disappeared as did the heat. Shifting her eyes to his face, she thought the darkness across his face had started to fade.

"Catharina, I have waited a very long time for you to free

me from this curse."

Rocco stood, causing her to stand against him like a lover. A wave of exhaustion descended over her so quickly that she felt her legs grow weak. "I can't stand—" She became aware that Rocco lifted her into his arms then laid her on the bed. "I'm afraid—"

The last words she heard as he sat down next to her were words from Psalms she used to say to herself when she lived in foster care. "Even though I walk through the valley of the shadow of death, I will fear no evil, for you are with me; your rod and your staff, they comfort me…"

Chapter 7

The alarm clock chimed like any other morning except that now, Catharina knew her safe life had shattered in the darkness of a storm. Darkness still fought against morning's light by layering clouds that promised to lift later as the sun burned off the fog and dampness of November. Even without looking, she knew it was already five by the sound of more traffic, along with a trash truck pulling into an alley across the street. A few pigeons began to pace along the window sill, in expectation of light.

Lying still, she took inventory of her body. Had he assaulted her when she became too weak to stand, to stay awake, or even care? With relief, she realized he had not violated her. What she did remember was hearing him recite scripture, comforting words meant to give her strength. The smell of incense remained as a faint memory of his presence. Sitting up in bed, she looked around the apartment.

"Rocco?" Pushing back the covers, she swung her legs over the side of the bed. "Rocco."

Nothing. Vanished into whatever dark corner of obscurity kept him safe. It left her wondering if it had all been a dream. The light over the sink was on as was the nightlight in the bathroom. The cold floor against her bare feet hustled her to the door, confused at how the deadbolt could be secure and Rocco gone.

It created more questions than answers. Nothing was out of place, not even the chair she believed was next to the bed where he sat until she fell into a deep sleep. The answer now became crystal clear. It was all a dream.

The habit of laying out part of her clothes for the next day made getting ready much faster, but there was nothing prepared today. With no electricity, she couldn't very well have chosen an outfit the night before, not that it mattered if it matched. The eclectic-Bohemian style she donned each day didn't really need a great deal of thought. A sigh brought her hand up to her throat as she pushed toward the bathroom in hurried steps.

Relief lightened her mood as she hurried to get ready. She caught the bus as it started to pull away from the curb. It was mostly empty and had been cleaned the night before so there were no strange smells, candy papers, or discarded coffee cups under the seats. The driver, large and black, looked like one of those posters in travel brochures, of beautiful Zulu men of South Africa. His face smiled, revealing yellow teeth but in good condition. The gray uniform looked as if it had been pressed professionally.

"Mornin', Miss Cat. Some storm last night." He pulled out into traffic then checked in his mirror to see if Catharina heard him. "You okay there? Storm keep you awake? My boys were up and down all night. Scared of the thunder."

"No. I'm fine. Just need my coffee, Harry. Thanks for asking."

"Hear anything about that ruckus last night up the street?"

The alarm bells went off somewhere inside her. "No. Went right to bed."

"Some guy with swords got into it with some gang members over stealing from those hobos down by Union Station."

"Hobos?"

"You know. The homeless guys that come around late at night. They were trying to find a place out of the rain. Terrible."

Catharina scooted to the edge of her seat as the bus turned on Market Street. "Was anyone hurt?"

The driver laughed. "Those drug-infested gang bangers got sliced up pretty bad. Won't be thinkin' they're so pretty now. Can you imagine? One guy takin' on five of those punks?" He shook his head. "Those homeless people can be a nuisance, but they don't deserve to be treated like scum. Heard one of those attacked was a veteran."

She grasped the metal bar on the back of the seat in front of her. "Veteran, you say?

"Yeah. He got hurt protecting some old woman and her dog. If that Watcher hadn't shown up—"

"Excuse me. Did you say Watcher?"

Harry pulled to the curb of Union Station. "Everybody is talkin' 'bout it. Some guy in a hood goes around protecting the homeless. It's driving the police crazy. They suspect him in a couple of missing persons."

Gathering up her things, she hurried down the steps. "Thanks, Harry."

She didn't wait to hear his farewell as her feet flew up the steps to the Grand Hall of Union Station. *My brother. Please don't let it be my brother who was hurt.* Without going to open up her shop, she ran out into the part of Union Station that had been converted into small boutiques. Her footsteps echoed as she ran down the length of the once bustling railroad station a hundred years earlier. In the distance, beyond the exit doors, flashing red and blue lights danced with strobes of bad news.

Pushing open the double doors, she ran toward the throng of police officers and first responders. The cold smacked her chest as her coat flew open. In her heart, she already knew it was her brother who had been injured.

"Zane. Zane," she yelled in hopeless desperation. Just as she neared, arms reached out and grabbed her around the waist.

Damien held her close. "Calm down. He's fine. Just a little banged up."

"I want to see him." She tried to look around Damien, but he managed to cut her line of sight off with his tall frame. "What happened?" she demanded. "I knew I should have made him come home with me. At least then I wouldn't have—" Startled, she cut her eyes up to Damien who watched her with concern.

Damien rubbed her arms as if trying to erase her unease. "Your brother checks on an old woman named Rose and her dog Jalopy. When he got there, some gang members were trying to take her dog, threatening her and stealing her stuff she'd collected during the day." He withdrew his hands and put them on his hips like she'd seen him do before. "Zane…"

Trembling hands covered her face. "Oh, Lord. Tell me he didn't kill someone."

"No. Rose was taken to the hospital a little while ago. Claims some guy in a hood came at them just in time. Just appeared. They pulled a gun on Zane, but 'The Watcher' as she calls him, cut off his hand with his sword."

Keeping her voice from quivering took all the strength she could muster. "That sounds crazy. What does Zane say?"

"Not much." He eyed Catharina. "I know he's an ex-Marine and served in Afghanistan, so he doesn't appear to be all that upset. What's your take on that?"

"I should talk to him." Rolling her shoulders back then swallowing took great effort as she tried to close her coat. Under the outdoor awning that stretched over what was once the railroad yard, the concrete remained mostly dry.

A paramedic bandaged a cut over Zane's eye. There was a patch on his ear and some scrapes on the side of his face. The paramedic talked in a low voice to him, nodding from time to time. She suspected the first responder was also a veteran and understood her brother more than most. The police stood close by, talking among themselves with an occasional glance his way. They were paid to be suspicious.

"Zane." It took great restraint in approaching him without bursting into tears and fussing that he needed to be more careful. "You're hurt."

His crooked smile nearly broke her heart. "Nah. Just a few bumps and bruises. I've had worse, little sister."

Damien came alongside and patted Zane's shoulder. "Will he need to go the hospital?"

Zane shook his head as he tried to adjust his camo jacket. "Not going to any hospital. Too expensive."

"Don't worry about that, Zane. You're on your sister's health insurance and I'm pretty sure it would be taken care of, anyway, with you being a veteran." Damien looked over at the surprised Catharina. "Right?"

She opened her mouth but nothing came out.

"I think he's okay." The paramedic stepped back and looked

pleased at his work. "You probably should take it easy today. Do you have some place to stay?"

"I'll call Father Xavier." The fussing started as Catharina touched his face then patted his knee. He sat on the back of the ambulance. "Where's your car, Zane? I'll drive you over."

He shrugged. "I think they stole it."

She covered her face with her hands again and shook her head. "This can't be happening."

"Zane, how about I drive you over? Or better yet you can stay at my place until your sister gets off work." Damien sounded more human-like with her brother than he did with her. He was polite—almost.

"Your place?" Zane slid out on steady feet. "All I need is a couple of hours of shut eye. Then maybe I'll look for my car."

Catharina cringed at the thought of her brother staying in someone else's home. He didn't always have the best hygiene and his clothes needed a good scrubbing. "I don't think so. But thanks, Mr. Cruz. Really. We appreciate it." She looped her arm through her brother's.

Zane grinned as he pinched her cheek. "Stop your fussing over me. I can make my own decisions. I'm not a cripple. My head is screwed on nice and tight." He knuckled the top of his head. Turning back to Damien, he smiled. "I think I'll take you up on that, you being a former SAS and all."

"Very good." Damien motioned for one of the police officers to join them. "Officer, if there isn't anything else, I'll be taking the gentleman with me to my apartment in the hotel. You know how to reach me." The officer nodded as his eyes slid to Catharina. "Oh, this is his sister. She owns and operates the Union Station coffee shop. Best coffee in town." Damien raised his chin in the air, making it easier to look down his nose at her. "Don't you have coffee to make, Cat?"

Damien's tone turned cool as he eyed her with a critical observation, making his eyebrow arch. She slipped her hand in Zane's as she forced herself to look away from the general manager's hypnotic glare. "I haven't charged my phone yet," she said. "You'll have to call me on the hotel phone if you need me." She dug in her shoulder bag to fish out a piece of paper and pencil. Scribbling across the old receipt, Catharina had to retrace a few numbers to make them legible. "Can you read it?" She handed it to her brother then put her finger on it for further clarification just as he snatched the paper up close to his chest.

"Cat, I know what to do. Stop treating me like I'm funny in the head," he barked at her for the first time since he'd returned from Afghanistan. "I'm going to rest a while, then I'll come to the coffee shop to check on you." The calm voice showed signs of the old Zane as he nodded to Damien then looked back at his sister. "Maybe we can talk about what happened last night."

A swallow stuck in her throat as she took a step away from her brother then looked with nervous anticipation at Damien. "Last night?"

"Yeah." Zane nodded in an all knowing way as he patted her cheek. "About our mutual friend."

It wasn't difficult to notice Damien shift his weight to one hip before dropping his hands to his side. Cutting her eyes between the two men standing next to each other, the realization dawned on her that they were very much alike. Although dressed for different worlds, the warrior in both men could not be ignored. Both stood with their legs slightly apart with their hands down and out slightly from their sides as if ready to do battle with unknown forces.

Baffled, Catharina looked at Damien, whose eyes bore into her with both contempt and interest. His bottom lip protruded in a pout that drew her interest in a carnal way. With his head dropped just inches so he could look at her with narrowed blue eyes, she experienced something familiar. A slight jerk of his shoulder drew his hand up as if he would touch her, but thought better of it. Stepping back behind Zane appeared to snap him out of whatever thoughts entered his head.

"We should go, Zane." His voice started out raspy as if needing to clear his throat but ended in a normal deep husky tone. "Both your sister and I have work to do." Stepping with purpose, Damien pushed past her as if she no longer mattered or existed.

Like an obedient puppy, Zane followed, leaving her standing in the old rail yard with a cold November wind teasing the flaps of her open raincoat. She looked back at the ambulance and police beginning to leave, extinguishing the flashing lights as they pulled away. Turning her eyes back to the two men who just left her side, she noticed how they walked in sync, as if marching off to war. The brother, haunted by battle, now walked erect like a proud Marine bent on making a difference. Damien, whoever he was, moved in the same determined fashion, creating a warm sensation inside her, that she knew needed to be squelched.

The bakery delivery man had come and gone by the time she reached the coffee shop. Jeremiah was carefully putting the delights away as she came inside. His smile greeted her, and she couldn't help but notice a little powdered sugar on the corner of his mouth.

"Jeremiah, how can I ever thank you?" She grabbed her apron as she flipped on the three coffee makers. "There was a problem—"

He held up his hand for her to stop. "Damien told me. That's why I'm here. No problem, Cat." He stepped around the counter to let her in. "I may have eaten one of your fluffy, English explosion things. Too tempting." Snatching a brown napkin, he wiped his mouth before fishing out a ten dollar bill.

"Stop right there. I'll not take your money. Come by in a bit and I'll have your coffee."

Straightening his yellow striped tie, he offered a mischievous smile. "I'm sending in someone I think can help you in here. Her name is Molly. Used to work for me in the restaurant but had to quit for school. Now her classes are all in the evening so she's looking for a few hours, plus some weekends. I already replaced her or I'd take her back. Interested?"

He waved to some hotel guests as he continued to talk to her and walk toward the doors. With such enthusiasm, how could she say no?

"Sure. Send her around. Maybe in the morning?"

Giving her a thumbs-up, he slid out into the hall like a teenager, causing the guests at the computers to chuckle. She wondered how Damien Cruz and his assistant could be so different. Talk about ying and yang

Chapter 8

Father Xavier." The surprise in Catharina's voice echoed in her empty coffee shop as she began to prepare to close. Coming around the counter, she stood on tiptoes to kiss his cheek. "What brings you out on such a cold day?"

Looking around the shop with pride, he couldn't withhold his smile. "The sun is out and the sky is blue as turquoise. Not so cold. It's nearly fifty degrees. I saw them putting up Christmas decorations all around town." Removing his coat and hat, he placed it with the utmost care on a nearby table and chair. "This is wonderful. Can I start the train?"

She laughed. "Men and their toys. Do you know how many men walk over here to start that crazy thing? They stand there with a funny grin on their face, just watching it go round and round."

With a flip of the switch, the train weaved its way through tunnels, towns, forests, and over bridges.

"Happy?"

The priest nodded before giving her a hug. "Tell me about your little business venture here, Cat."

"That shouldn't take long." In spite of the quick tour and routine she did each day, the priest seemed genuinely impressed at her accomplishments.

Taking a deep breath, he pulled out a chair to sit down. "Do you have any of that coffee left?"

"Maybe a cup. I'll get it. Pastries are all gone. Sorry."

"Watching my waistline, anyway." When she set the cup

down, he reached out to take her hand. "Sit with me a while. We need to talk."

She pulled out a chair and flopped down, feeling the ache in her feet and legs. "Okay. What about?"

"The good news is several other churches have stepped up to help us out at The Kitchen of Hope. You need come only on Wednesday and Thursday nights. The other times, I have plenty of help. You're wearing yourself out and I don't like it." His eyes drifted around the room. "All this takes a lot of energy and concentration."

"Will you continue to serve each night?"

"I believe several other pastors have stepped up for that as well. I'm not as young as I used to be." The smile he offered was sweet, followed by a wink. "So now maybe you can have a social life if you're not out with people of the night."

Catharina's mind snapped up a picture of Rocco. "I don't mind going, Father." She wasn't aware her eyes looked down at her hands folded in her lap.

"The man in the news—" He stopped talking as if gauging her reaction.

"Rocco." Lifting her head, she saw terror leap into the priest's eyes. "I need to know who he is. Don't tell me he's a homeless psychopath either. I watched how you talked to him and how afraid you were when I touched his hand through the window."

The priest began to stroke his crucifix with trembling fingers. "How do you know his name? I never told you that." His voice grew anxious as he leaned in toward her. "Has he sought you out?" When she didn't answer, he rolled his eyes upward and said a prayer of protection for her. "He is a dangerous—" The label he almost spewed stopped on his tongue as he licked his lips. "Now you listen to me, young lady. You are to stay away from him at all costs."

She reached out to take his face in her hands. "I love you, Father. But you can't protect me from everything. I need to know what I'm up against. Twice he has saved my brother. Twice," she insisted. "Tell me what he is. I know that he isn't a man—at least not like any man I've ever known. The homeless call him The Watcher."

Raising his hands, he placed them on hers. "That is what he is. A Watcher sent from God, the Almighty Himself."

"Do you know how crazy that sounds?" Withdrawing her hands, she leaned back in her chair and nodded for the priest to drink his coffee. "What is a Watcher, Father?"

"Rocco is the Archangel Zerachiel. It means 'God's command.' He leads souls to judgment, as evidenced by his work among those who would harm the hopeless and poor on the streets." He too, leaned back in his chair and sighed before sipping his cold coffee. "I read in the Book of Enoch that he is one of the seven archangels as well as an angel of healing."

Catharina touched her shoulder, remembering how he took the painful burn from her tattoos. For a second, his tortured face came into focus as she sensed his presence. "That sounds like a good thing, Father."

It was hard to know why her voice became a whisper, but when he responded, his voice also became low and guarded, as if he didn't want the holy powers to hear him.

"Rocco is also the presiding angel of the sun, prince of ministering angels. His job has always been to watch over mortals, especially children, particularly children of parents who have sinned. He tries to keep them from falling into sin as adults themselves. He is said to have dominion over the earth."

"This sounds preposterous. I'm a believer, Father Xavier, but this stuff you're talking about is all a little sci-fi-slash-paranormal." Standing, she walked away to continue the cleanup. It was a sign of dismissal. But he followed to stand at the counter as she continued to wipe things down. "So essentially, since he's The Watcher, it means Zane and I have nothing to fear." She cocked her head to give him a sideways glance. "Angels are a good thing, right?"

"Sometimes." Father Xavier rested his arms on the clean counter as Catharina continued to busy herself. "Remember, God kicked a bunch of those rascals out of Heaven when they thought they could be equal. They are the demons of Hell. Then there were the angels who came down and ended up mating with Earth women because of their beauty."

She twirled around and danced a little jig as she fluffed her hair. "Wow. You mean I might get an angel boyfriend? How cool would that be? He could pick me up for work every day and fly me over here so I didn't have to take the bus or ride my bike." She started laughing at the frown forming on the priest's face.

"Do not make light of this, Cat." His tone sounded insistent, but a grin played at one corner of his lined lips. "I'll talk to Zane about this. He's liable to be easily impressed with Rocco's strength and guardianship."

Tossing several soiled paper towels in the trash, she removed her apron. "It's not like I'm seeking the guy out. If he's really an angel, can't he do whatever he wants? I mean how could I stop him from just appearing?"

"Stop who from appearing?" came a deep familiar voice that sent shivers up Catharina's spine.

Damien strode in as he extended his hand to the priest.

Catharina watched the man as he turned his pale blue eyes to her. The quick visual sweep he made of her brought his gaze back to lock with her eyes, causing her to become rigid. This man seriously either had issues with her work or he was planning a way to get rid of her.

For a few minutes, the night before, she believed he might be interested in her in more than in a professional way. Now his imposing height of over six foot two managed to intimidate her.

"Kind of nosey aren't you, Damien?" She said his name as if taunting him. Keeping her voice steady became her big accomplishment for the day. "Where's Zane?"

"Left several hours ago. My assistant had the chef pack him some sandwiches."

Father Xavier pumped the manager's hand then pointed an accusing finger at her. "Mind your manners." He turned back to Damien. "You're a good man, Damien. I was just warning her about The Watcher. Were you aware he'd been prowling around here?"

"Yes, Father." His smile became thin as he shifted his eyes back to Catharina.

"The Watcher means well."

The priest was so matter-of-fact, it caused her to suck in her breath at hearing his words. Catharina spread her palms on the counter. "What? Are you implying that you talk to him on a regular basis? I thought it was just confession, Father Xavier." Watching the priest eye Damien carefully caused a rush of unease to engulf her. "When do you see him?" she continued as she came to stand near him.

"He seeks my counsel from time to time. That's my job. Nothing to be alarmed over." The priest patted Damien's arm. "Right, Damien?"

A darkness appeared to fill Damien's eyes as he looked back at the priest and nodded. "A priest should certainly feel a sense of protection from God when helping those who are disturbed." This time his smile widened. "I'm not too concerned about him coming back. The police are stationed around the back of the hotel since several restaurant owners have some concerns about their business being affected."

Father Xavier moved to get his coat. Damien grabbed it first and helped him into it with care.

"Thank you." Placing the hat on his head, the priest winked at Damien. "Thanks to your calls, I now have a full staff at The Kitchen of Hope. I don't know what you said to them but they were more than willing to step up and serve."

Damien offered a sinister grin. "Yes. Well, I can be very persuasive, I'm told."

"Put the fear of God in them, did you?"

The manager raised his chin a little too quickly, making him look down his narrow nose. "Something like that, Father. Either way, you now have plenty of help."

"It seems to me—" the priest said, nodding toward Catharina who stepped alongside him as he headed toward the door. He thumped Damien on the back. "—that two unattached people should have dinner since they're free Friday night."

Catharina cringed as she covered her face with hands that smelled of bleach. "Geeze Louise, Father."

A low chuckle started in Damien as he pushed open the door for the priest. "So besides being the confidant of The Watcher, you are a matchmaker."

"It pays to be diversified."

That eyebrow arched—the one Catharina had come to both despise and long to rub her fingers across. "Yes. I'm sure it does, Father."

Damien followed the priest out into the hall where the double row of computers for the business center stood. The door closed in slow motion as the two men took a few steps then stopped to face each other. Catharina watched as the priest took a step back and paled as the manager turned his back so she couldn't see his face. The priest began nodding then reached inside his coat to touch the crucifix she knew to be hanging around his neck. The empty business center brightened as the afternoon sun began pouring through the windows. Bands of what looked to almost be celestial light reached across the floor to where the two men stood, circling them. Father Xavier closed his eyes as he lifted his head upward. His lined lips moved in some prayer she could not hear. The hotel manager bowed his head and lifted his palms up and open next to his side, as if preparing to accept a blessing from God.

Standing transfixed, she stared at the scene, her heart beating faster. A warmth surged through her as she watched the priest and the man connect on some heavenly level that touched her deeply. Catharina wanted to rush out and participate. A twinge hit her tattooed shoulder as she watched Damien's back tighten and release beneath his suit coat. Then, just as quickly as the sun broke through the windows, it clouded over. The two men shook hands and parted.

Damien pivoted on his heels and stared at her, somehow knowing she witnessed some special connection between him and the priest. The skin under his eyes looked a little darker than before and he'd lowered his head in the way that gave him the appearance of being angry or…something else.

Swallowing seemed to be difficult as she hurried to snatch her coat and scarf. Pulling out her purse from a shelf under the counter, she lost her grip, spilling the contents on the floor. With her coat half on and off, she scooped the contents back inside before standing, only to see Damien come through the doors. He was at the counter by the time she tried to slip her arm in her sleeve. It disturbed her that he took her purse from her then assisted with the coat. She felt defenseless against a weakness she didn't know existed until a few days ago.

"Thank you." She took the purse then slung it over her shoulder in mock confidence. "Gotta lock up."

The smile he offered mocked her. His dark aura, combined with his good looks, managed to intimidate her into silence when he spoke. "May I take you to dinner tomorrow evening?"

Catharina was taken so off guard, she ran smack into the glass doors, bouncing back into his waiting arms. He pushed her at arm's length, even though he never removed his hands from her wrists. Considering how hot her face felt, she wondered if it burned as red with embarrassment.

"Thanks. No. You don't need to feel obligated because of Father Xavier's rude suggestion. He thinks I spend too much time with the homeless and my brother." A nervous laugh spilled out just about the same time she hiccupped, which drew a slight upturn of Damien's mouth. "The father wants me to have a family and make babies for him to baptize."

"Hmm," was his only response. His eyes narrowed as his gaze scanned her face and hair. "Interesting thought."

"Besides, that would be a little awkward don't you think since I work—"

"You do not work for me, Cat. This is your business. I operate the hotel, nothing more. I do not even hold your contract. The attorneys do that."

"Oh. Well, I donno—"

"I have box seats at the Fox Theater tomorrow evening. The violinist David Depraysie is performing. I thought you might like to have dinner then the theater."

She felt her heart leap. "The David Depraysie?"

"I'll pick you up at six."

Opening the glass doors, he allowed her to slide past him, but not without laying his hand lightly to the middle of her back, causing her to speed up. She turned to lock the door but was relieved of the key. "I didn't say I'd go, Damien."

Watching him lock up then outstretch his hand, Catharina slipped her fingers around the key only to have him clamp his hand over hers. Again the wicked smile followed by the sense of being captured. Startled she looked up at him, drowning in the eyes with the icy hot gaze.

"We both need a few hours away from the grind of everyday living." He allowed her to pull her hand free with the key tightly in her grasp. "I thought you'd enjoy hearing David play. I could even introduce you. He owes me a favor."

Catharina thought, from the way he slightly cocked his head, Damien might have been a vulture in another life. Was he trying to decide which part of her to devour first? "I can meet you there." She dropped the key in her purse before trying on her best look of condescension.

"Temptation is just too great, isn't it?" He walked alongside her as they entered the Grand Hall of the hotel. "I'll pick up you." The tone grew final as he nodded and disappeared toward the far end of the bar where the bellman motioned for him.

She didn't want to look back as she started down the stairs that would lead outside, but as he so aptly put it, 'temptation was just too great." Pausing on the top step, she looked over her shoulder just when he jerked his head around, as if knowing she looked for him. The bellman continued to speak, but Damien's eyes watched her as she disappeared, running down the stairs to safety.

Chapter 9

T he darkness surrounded him as the cooing of pigeons came to roost on the ledge of his safe place. The bare wood floors smelled of dampness and age, but smells which bothered others only managed to intensify his longing to experience the discomfort. Standing before the clock in the tower, he stared through holes at the city. The sounds of horns, sirens, and screeching brakes lifted from the street below, bringing him comfort in knowing he could walk freely soon, among the helpless who depended on him each night for protection. But like always, something was missing —the lack of human contact weighed heavier with each passing day.

Tired. Frustrated. Angry at the many who took life for granted or wanted life to grant them everything without earning that right. The children hurt him the most. They were the victims of abuse and neglect. He couldn't reach all of them in time. Even with the help of well-meaning public servants burdened with regulations and caseloads, it was not enough to save them. There were others like him, who moved about in the daylight, having forgotten their power because of sin. Now he must also watch after them until the time came for them to rise up and remember. Until that time, he'd expected to be alone, enslaved by his one indiscretion centuries ago with the violinist Tartini.

The concept of being alone forever no longer frightened him. With the acceptance of his duty, came the ferocity of his ability to seek justice for those who needed it the most. Then the sound of a violin and a dancing girl, so agile and genuine, prompted him to watch as she calmed the savage beasts of the streets and the emptiness of the forgotten. Only he could see the glow surrounding her as her music engulfed the room. For an instant, he was transfixed, feeling the rapture of every emotion he ever experienced. A tranquility filled him, as did a longing he thought vanquished centuries ago.

He must be careful. The price of freedom to someone like him meant possible death to a mortal like Catharina. Following the order of the universe created both winners and losers. The touch of her hands brought the burning desire to experience everything he'd lost. Patience was never one of his gifts. Seeking her out in her home nearly crossed the line. He could have risked everything.

♫ ♫ ♫

"I can't eat another bite." Catharina folded her napkin before laying it on the table next to her plate. She couldn't remember feeling so full in a long time. "I may not fit in that fancy seat tonight, Damien." She felt shy looking at him, but he didn't appear to notice.

Their waiter rolled a cart next to their table covered in rich desserts. Damien enjoyed watching her eat. "The bread pudding is the best I've ever eaten."

Laying her hand across her midriff, she rolled her eyes. "Sorry." She looked at the waiter. "It all looks wonderful, but I'll pass." When Damien laughed, she cut her eyes back to him. "Go ahead. Indulge yourself. I don't mind."

"Maybe we'll go for dessert afterward. Thank you, Ramone. Not tonight." The waiter nodded his acceptance before moving on to the next table. Damien turned back to her. "You look beautiful tonight, Cat."

Catharina liked this Damien Cruz. This man spoke in even-toned sentences, didn't arch his eyebrow in contemplation of wrong doing, or move like a stalking panther.

She looked at him as if seeing him with new eyes. "You sound surprised. Were you afraid I'd embarrass you?"

Damien leaned back farther in his chair, smiled, and unconsciously adjusted his tie. "I thought maybe I might continue to put my foot in my mouth. You don't appear to like me very much."

He couldn't help being surprised when she came to her apartment door. The black dress with the scoop neck wasn't expensive, but she looked elegant nonetheless. The funky black hair with blonde tips had been brushed smooth as silk. Simple pearl earrings added a layer of sophistication he hadn't expected. The gypsy look enticed him more than he thought possible.

She cupped her chin in the palm of her hand. "Maybe we got off to a bad start. Truce?"

"Truce." Damien stood then assisted Catharina.

Surrounded by the elegance and beauty of the Fox Theater, Catharina was driven to distraction. Paralyzed with awe, she stood patiently as Damien signed for their dinner, failing to notice the couple approaching them until they stopped next to her.

"I don't believe I've met Damien's latest." The blonde stood a head taller than her and smelled of heavy perfume. She extended a soft white hand the color of polished pearls, drooping her fingers as if the possibility existed Catharina should kiss the diamond studded finger.

"Oh." Catharina grabbed the hand and pumped it like a nervous lumberjack. "I'm Cat."

The smile of condescension, paired with an amused look of tolerance, forced Catharina to pull her hand back from the icy clasp of the stunning beauty before her.

"Morgan Knox. Public Relations for the mayor's office." Her brown eyes shifted to the man standing next to her. Damien continued with introductions. "Kragan, this is Catharina Spokane."

The mayor too, let his eyes slide down her body as if she were on the auction block. The icy gaze paired with the sinister smirk, caused a moment's hesitation as he extended his hand toward her. Before she could react, Kragan snatched her hand, almost playfully, and chuckled, as if he knew her self-confidence was about to tank.

"So you're the charming little vixen I've been hearing about who runs the new coffee shop at Union Station. No wonder

Damien has moved us to your place. I would be trying to gain a few favors myself if I were him." His eyes continued to smile in a narrowed way that appeared less than cordial.

Damien's frown deepened as he laid his leathery hand on Catharina's arm and guided her back from the mayor's touch. "I placed you there because of privacy and the coffee is the best in St. Louis, Mr. Mayor. If you'd rather me move you to the concourse outside the hotel, I can arrange that." Damien's hand made its way into hers, entwining his fingers with a firmness that offered a kind of security. "I thought the coffee shop would be a better fit for your so-called meetings with the public."

The mayor pulled back his shoulders, giving him a haughty stance. "Do I detect a tone of disapproval, Damien?"

"Not at all. I want only what is best for the city. People feel a little intimidated by the hotel's grandness. The coffee shop may be more inviting for citizens. It will also give you an air of being one of the working masses that run the city." Catharina looked up at Damien to see him smile like the devil she knew he could be. "Are you afraid you might actually have to visit with someone outside your office, Mr. Mayor?"

The mayor laughed good-naturedly as he waved to someone down the staircase. "Don't be ridiculous. I live to serve the city." He looked back at Catharina. "Maybe we can visit as well, Cat. Love the name by the way."

Morgan hooked her arm through the mayor's, offering a glare at Catharina. "You don't look like Damien's usual kind of date, Cat. How in the world did you snag him?" The feline smirk toyed at the corners of her mouth, letting Catharina know she'd just been insulted.

Catharina smiled her most brilliant smile. "Do I really need to explain that to someone like you?" She added a playful shrug, before looking up at Damien who appeared to be amused. "I'm sure you know what I mean." She nodded at the mayor then took a deep breath as she tilted her head at Morgan.

"The way you play the violin has me putty in your hands." Damien slipped an arm around her waist and smiled down into her eyes. He looked back at Morgan. "That's why we're here. David Depraysie is a friend of mind. He's playing *The Devil's*

Trill tonight and we're going to say 'hello' afterward." He squeezed Catharina closer to his side, forcing her to look up in to pale blue eyes that reminded her of someone else. The lights flickered, drawing his eyes upward as he dropped his hand back to her arm. "Nice running into you, Mr. Mayor. Enjoy your evening. Good to see you, Morgan."

As they took their seats, overlooking the audience below, Catharina was immediately handed a menu by another waiter. "You can't be serious. We just ate."

Taking the menu from her hand, Damien handed it back to the waiter. "Maybe later."

The lights began to dim as he turned his eyes toward the stage.

Catharina stole sideways glances at him, wondering why the old Damien had reappeared. Was it because of the mayor or the beautiful woman on his arm? Did he have feelings for such a cold-hearted person? When he saw Morgan with the most powerful man in the city, did he forget all about her, the coffee shop waitress with big ideas? As the curtain lifted on the stage, she felt disappointment rise within her. Maybe she was a distraction at best. Whatever the reason Damien invited her out tonight, it warranted a feeling of caution. Men like him traveled roads littered with broken and battered hearts.

It's a good thing I don't even like you, Damien Cruz. The thought gave her courage to patch the wall she'd begun to dismantle around herself. *What was I thinking? Truce? I should have said, "That which does not kill us, makes us strong."* Applause floated like a wave across the theater as she turned her focus on the performance, instead of the rising dread in the pit of her stomach.

♫ ♫ ♫

"Jealous?" The mayor took the menu from the waiter, entering his box as Morgan seated herself, careful not to wrinkle her amber-colored gown.

Without looking up at him, she began to smooth the shimmering folds of the fabric. "No. I can't help it if Damien is attracted to the underbelly of society." She rolled her eyes before patting the seat next to her. "Just surprised, is all."

Kragan lifted her hand to his lips. "He is a fool to have discarded you." The cold smile offered was meant as a slap with his remark. When she tried to pull free, his grip tightened, enough to make her flinch. "Tomorrow, I want you to find out everything about her. That name rings a bell. It would be just like Cruz to take an interest in my business for his own personal gain." He added a second kiss then sank his teeth lightly into her middle finger, causing Morgan to jerk her hand free.

"He didn't discard me, Kragan. We went our separate ways, is all." She leaned in enough to tease him with the brush of her body. "Besides, I'm with you now until you begin to bore me."

A puckered smile formed on his thin lips. "Be very careful with your insults, Morgan. I don't like threats and rejection even less." His eyes turned toward the stage as the curtain began to lift. "Try to enjoy the performance. *The Devil's Trill* is one of my favorites for some reason. I've never been able to explain the feeling it gives me."

A huff of discontent escaped her mouth as she turned her eyes to the stage. "Maybe we should make it your theme song for the next election."

The mayor answered with a wide smile and a nod as he began to applaud for the musician entering onto the stage

Chapter 10

Watching Catharina chat with the famous violinist after the concert helped Damien realize what a special young woman had wandered into his life. Her smile never faded as David, himself a shy person, seemed to open up, enjoying the questions enough to answer each one with a precise response.

In spite of being all dressed up in her finest, something quirky remained. Maybe it was the black hair with blonde tips, or the gold flecks in her green eyes, or the way she stood with a kind of nervous anticipation that tugged at his interest. He didn't want to evaluate it with too much intent.

"Thank you for sharing your friend, Damien." David rose from his stool and kissed Catharina on her cheek. The violinist winked at the man. "I don't think he has ever introduced me to a lady before, Catharina. You must be very special. We go back many years."

"Really?" She squeezed the hand he offered then beamed at Damien. "How long have you known each other?"

"Centuries." Damien quipped with a wave of his hand. "Or at least it feels like that."

The violinist bowed to his two fans. "Thank you, Damien, for bringing her. It gives me pleasure knowing you are not alone."

Catharina wanted to protest that Damien was indeed alone if it meant he thought she was a love interest. "Oh, Mr. Depraysie, we're not—"

"All is ready for you at the hotel, David," Damien quickly

interrupted.

Once they returned to the car, Damien offered a suggestion. "We can have dessert at the hotel if you like." He might as well have been talking about the weather.

Catharina, determined not to look at his handsome profile, kept her eyes forward. "It's getting late. I still have an early morning at the coffee shop. I should go home."

His silence drew her glance. Something tortured showed in his profile as shadows zipped across his face beneath each streetlamp they passed. The high cheekbones flexed until his face became a mask of cold indifference. As he turned onto her street, she realized he probably felt relief at being shed of her.

"You can let me out at the door. Parking is not always safe around here." The quicker this night ended the better, she reasoned. Ignoring her comments, he pulled into a parking lot across the street. A security guard took his ten dollar bill without hesitation.

The wind tunneled between the canyon walls of skyscrapers, forcing Catharina to pull her lightweight coat up around her neck as Damien took her arm and led her to the front door of the apartment building. She turned to shoo him away, but was met with a look of contempt.

"Open the door, Cat. A gentleman walks his date to the door at the end of the evening." If his British accent had not been so seductive, she would have told him to "get lost." But the richness and deepness of his voice tied up any resistance.

Her pace up the stairs left him walking behind her like a slow panther stalking his next meal. By the time she reached her door, her heart beat rapidly. Fumbling with her keys, made Damien relieve her of the ring of noisy chaos. How he knew which key belonged to the door momentarily puzzled her. When he pushed the door open, she realized she was trapped between the doorframe and his large body so that she couldn't slip inside and slam the door shut.

His serious expression became void of emotion as his eyes scanned her face. Wondering if he saw the remnants of her scar on the side of her face, she lifted her hand to touch it. A hard swallow caught in her throat, making her jerk her chin up. Why did he have to be so mysterious and handsome?

"Thanks for a very nice evening, Damien. I'm glad we had a chance to get to know each other. Everything was just lovely." She didn't realize her words sounded like the end of a promotional speech for cold soup.

A smile lifted the corner of his mouth; drawing her eyes and making her bite the lower lip. "Good night, Cat." He handed back the keys before putting some distance between them.

Catharina stood in the doorway as he headed down the staircase, hoping to hear him turn around instead of the closing of the exterior doors to the street. With the evening concluded, her thoughts now turned to The Watcher. Would he return tonight? Should she have told someone about the first visit? Should she have asked Damien inside to make sure all was safe? That probably would have sounded like a lame invitation to spend the night. She bolted the door after making sure she was alone then shoved a wooden chair beneath the doorknob for extra measure. Somehow she knew if Rocco wanted in, a wooden chair wouldn't stop him.

It was late. Sleep would elude her for a while so she postponed the nightly ritual and sat in a chair to stare out the window. Jumbled thoughts of Damien mixed with The Watcher and finally her brother. The woman named Morgan surfaced too, and she imagined her and Damien in the throes of passion, causing a twinge of envy. Catharina wondered about their history. Implying that now she and Damien might be more than friends wasn't the smartest thing she ever did. If Damien resented the implication, he didn't mention it later. Something about the woman rubbed her the wrong way. Was it that she somehow knew Damien in an intimate way or that Catharina wasn't much more than a cockroach beneath her expensive shoes?

When the phone rang at 3 a.m., Catharina realized she'd dozed off and pushed up out of the chair to locate the annoying ring. Just as she picked up the phone, it stopped ringing. The number wasn't one she recognized. Then it rang again.

"Hello." The words escaped in a yawn.

"Cat. I'm in trouble. Yep. I'm in trouble. Trouble, Cat." The undeniable voice of her brother sounded on the verge of tears.

"What's wrong? Where are you, Zane? Are you all right?"

"Going to hospital. Hospital. Hospital, Cat." He sniffed. "Big trouble."

"Which hospital, Zane? I can't help you if I don't know where you are."

"I donno. Donno, Cat. Donno."

"Is there someone there I can talk to?"

"Nope. All alone. All alone. They came at me from all sides."

"Who did, Zane?" Even as she spoke, she kicked off her heels then unzipped her dress.

"Taliban. Sneaky little hajis. I shot 'em." A haji could be an Iraqi or and Afghan. It was a nickname soldiers used for the locals. The word actually meant someone who had traveled to Mecca.

"You shot someone?" She tried to keep the panic out of her voice. The dress now crumbled to the floor as she ran to her dresser to remove a pair of jeans and a tee shirt. "Are the police there?"

"Affirmative. Patrol just arrived. Taking me into custody for my own protection. Big trouble."

"Are you injured, Zane?"

"Affirmative. Medics arriving. Need you, Cat. Big trouble."

The line clicked off, causing her to scream "No."

Dropping the phone on the chair, she pulled on her jeans. As she slipped her head through the neck of her tee shirt, Catharina saw him standing on the other side of her bed. With slow deliberation, she pushed her arms through their openings.

He stood rigid in his leather clothing with his legs slightly apart, hands out to his side, as if he prepared for battle against some demonic horde. The wool hood of his cloak hung down over his forehead, but she knew he stared straight at her.

Her words grew tight as if she might release a volley of insults. Breathing became deep and controlled. "How long have you been standing there?" Knowing he'd watched her undress made her angry.

"Long enough." Rocco spoke in the raspy tone she'd come to know, only this time his voice carried a hint of admiration. "I will take you to him."

"How did you know Zane was in trouble?"

Rocco started toward the door but she cut him off. It wasn't until then she became aware of his size and build. In spite of not being able to see his eyes, Catharina knew the depths of their emptiness. "Did you do this? Is Zane in trouble because of you?"

They stood less than a foot from each other. "No. I did not harm Zane. That would be impossible." His voice sounded so matter-of-fact that when he stepped closer, it didn't occur to Catharina to escape. "You know what I am."

"Yes. But I don't understand any of this."

She could feel his breath coming at her, the smell of incense and smoke clinging to his clothes.

His shoulder began to glow as hers began to burn so suddenly she bent over with pain. Catching her in his arms, she felt his hand shove through the low rounded neckline of her tee shirt. She tried unsuccessfully to push him away, but when his hand touched her tattoos, the ebb of fire eased from her skin. Staring in horror, she watched as the glow seeped into him, traveling up his arm then into his shoulder and chest.

His free hand now circled her back, drawing her against him. His cold lips touched her ear. "Be still. 'You shall not fear them, for it is the Lord your God who fights for you.' Deuteronomy 3:22." He withdrew his hand from inside her shirt, letting it come to rest around her shoulder in an embrace. "My presence brings your body to fire where you have buried the truth. Another time, you will tell me about the scars that are hidden by your body art."

The weight of truth Rocco spoke removed the last ounce of fear from her common sense, causing her to collapse against him, laying her head against his shoulder, wrapping her arms around his body. "Rocco." Her voice came out no more than a whisper. "I don't understand any of this."

He pushed her back at arm's length, holding tight to her upper arms. "Zane needs something you can no longer give him, Catharina." He walked over to the table where she'd dropped her coat. In seconds, he was helping her into it. Removing his own cloak, he fastened it around her. "The night turns cold. This will protect you. We must hurry."

If it hadn't been for the middle of the night, riding a motorcycle without a helmet or any idea what they were speeding toward, she would have thought the experience exhilarating. Her arms held tightly to his body. Several times she felt his hand touch hers. The gesture reassured her. Cold air pounded her face until she buried it in Rocco's back. He had tied the hood snugly beneath her chin so now his head was exposed to the frigid November weather. She wanted desperately to touch the black hair that tangled in the wind. The realization that she also wanted to smell it and run her fingers through the thickness caused a sense of shame to well up inside her, considering the predicament her brother might be in which could get him thrown in jail.

The thought never occurred to her he might be taking her some place to cause her harm. Something besides circumstances bonded her to whoever Rocco might be. Whatever she needed to do to save her brother from himself would be worth it. Would there be a price for Rocco's help?

Flashing lights caused the rumble of Rocco's motorcycle to slow as they approached with caution. Parking in an alley, he hurried to dismount then assisted Catharina to her unsteady feet. "If they see you in this cloak your life may be in danger. They search for me everywhere."

She nodded as her gloved hands pushed the hood off her head. Realizing Rocco stood a breath away, she let him release the bonds that he secured around her earlier. His hands stopped as the cloak opened, keeping his fingers on the lapels. "I cannot go with you." He slipped back into the cloak.

"What kind of trouble is he really in, Rocco?"

Rocco pulled her into his arms. His mouth came close to touching hers. "The worst kind. But I will protect him. Do not lose faith."

"What should I do? I'm afraid I'm losing him for good. His mind—"

"He is strong. Soon he will be free of his demons." Rocco began to back away into the alley.

"You." A uniformed officer approached with hurried foot-steps, causing her to whirl around, knowing guilt was etched on her face. "Why are you hanging around here?" he demanded.

A shiver of fear crept up her spine as she looked to the alley then back at the officer. Rocco and the motorcycle had vanished. "My brother. He called me." She stepped into the pool of light beneath the streetlamp. "Zane Spokane. Is he here?" The officer nodded then looked around to see where she'd come from and if there was anyone else. "I'm alone. I caught a ride with a friend who works late. He was just coming off work."

"A woman shouldn't be out here so late." He motioned with his head to follow. "Mr. Spokane is your brother?"

"Yes, sir. Is he hurt? He said he was in trouble."

They breached the circle of officers to reveal a dead man on the ground. Catharina caught her breath before gagging at the sight of so much blood. It was hard to tell if he was young or old, black or white because he had been slashed multiple times.

She felt the officer steer her away. "Sorry about that. Your brother is over here. He's been shot."

A cry escaped her throat as she rushed forward, seeing Zane being loaded into the back of an ambulance. "Zane!"

Rising up, he tried to wave two fingers at her. "Baby sister. I'm sorry. Sorry. Sorry."

She looked at the paramedic. "What happened?"

"Looks like a gunshot wound, ma'am. Doesn't look to be life threatening, but we need to get him to the hospital."

Catharina recognized the paramedic from a few days earlier. He had shown Zane kindness and understanding.

"Can my sister come too?" Zane seemed to snap out of it.

"We need to talk to your sister, Mr. Spokane. We'll see to it that she gets to the hospital." A detective came alongside her. "I promise to take good care of her." He extended his card to Catharina. It read Detective Jacobs.

As clear as she'd ever heard him speak, Zane looked at her with a seriousness and clarity that had been missing far too long. "Protect him, Cat." She stepped closer and tried to hug him but he held up his hand. "Do as I say. Protect The Watcher," he whispered.

When she bobbed her head, he relaxed and lay down, giving the paramedic a thumbs-up signal that he was ready to go.

The ambulance drove off moments later. Catharina pulled her coat tighter around her body. Silent tears cascaded down her cheeks.

"Protect The Watcher?" The detective stepped closer. His mouth looked like it had been stolen off the face of a marionette. Deep crevices around his lips, with sagging jaws, gave him a tired expression. "What do you know about The Watcher?"

With a shrug, she turned her face into the cold wind, wanting the sting to explain her tears. "Not much. My brother is a homeless veteran. They believe someone is watching over them." He looked skeptical. She shrugged. "I know. Crazy."

"Could your brother believe he is this Watcher? That fella over there on the ground is sliced up pretty bad. I'm thinking your brother took a swing at him with a knife we found on him."

"Zane doesn't have any weapons." Her insistence sounded confused. "He's a sweet, gentle giant. Besides, he's been shot."

"Granted. By the clothing of the deceased he's a gang member or drug dealer. Probably provoked your brother."

"I want to go to the hospital. He'll be calmer if I'm there."

The detective took out a small notebook. "Just a few more questions."

"Ms. Spokane is finished talking to you for now, detective." Both Catharina and the officer turned to see a tall man in a trench coat approach. It was Damien Cruz. "We'll wait for you at the hospital if you want to talk further. Ms. Spokane is her brother's guardian, and it would be advantageous for her to be at his side." Somehow a British accent sounded so much more authoritative.

"Mr. Cruz." The detective's surprise caused him to reinsert the notebook into his pocket. "Sure. Didn't realize you were friends."

Before the man could protest, Damien took Catharina's arm around his and began walking her out into the darkness toward his black Mercedes.

After seeing that she was safely inside the car, he slid in and gunned the car into an empty street. By the time they reached the emergency room of Barnes Hospital, Catharina shivered violently.

"H—how did you know Z—Zane was in t—trouble?" she managed to stutter as they walked into the ER.

"It appears we have a mutual friend."

Damien looked down into her terrified eyes and waited for realization to set in.

Chapter 11

e're prepping your brother for surgery." The doctor turned away, but stopped when Catharina stepped in front of him, feet parted to balance her weight and keep from toppling due to exhaustion.

"How serious is it, doctor?" She managed to keep her voice steady. After all, she was the responsible adult.

"Any surgery has the potential of being serious, Ms. Spokane. Your brother is fit, young, and the bullets didn't appear to damage anything important. There doesn't appear to be any internal injuries, but you really never know until he's opened up. Either way those bullets need to come out."

She felt Damien walk up beside her. "So he'll be okay?"

"I'm optimistic." The doctor tried to step around them but Damien held up his hand.

"Doctor, Ms. Spokane's brother is a veteran. He served three tours in Afghanistan. He's been through a lot." Damien's voice, although low and controlled, exuded a warning.

The doctor's eyes shifted back to Catharina, then he shook his head. "I'll be extra careful. I served in Iraq. I'll have someone contact the VA so you can get some help afterward." With a nod to Damien, he was allowed to pass through doors that whooshed open then closed in slow motion.

She stood there staring after the doctor, confused at what to do next. Every nerve in her body felt tense. Thoughts flip flopped through her brain of when they were children, lost and alone in the foster care system, finding Father Xavier in time to save them from the harsh treatments they'd learned to endure, and then their life now. When Damien touched her shoulder, she startled so violently, he pulled her into his arms.

"It's okay, Cat." His voice sounded soothing and familiar. The memory of smelling incense teased her nose again as she looked up into his pale eyes and windblown hair the color of ebony. Even though he looked down his narrow nose at her, he conveyed compassion rather than the harsh judgment that so often occurred between them. "Are you hungry?"

She started to laugh at such a thought, causing him to smile. "Still trying to feed the half-starved cat?"

"I seriously doubt you're used to eating three square meals a day. Let's get some breakfast. It's nearly five. The cafeteria is probably already serving." He took a step back and extended his hand toward the elevator. "My treat."

When Damien smiled at her then shoved his hands into the pockets of his open trench coat, Catharina felt her heart skip a beat. His timing had been impeccable when arriving at the scene of the crime. The darkness of the skin beneath his eyes made him look tired and sinister, but his beguiling smile sucked her into a warm desire she'd never felt before. Even the way he arched his eyebrow, in evaluation of her at times, sent shivers up her spine. The accent alone made her listen carefully to each word he spoke. Now, here he was, stepping in to be the knight in shining armor during her hour of need.

He lowered his head slightly, as if to evaluate and wait for her response. His stance with legs slightly apart, back rigid, and shoulders pulled back reminded her of someone else in her life. Rocco.

Were they connected somehow? What did Damien mean when he said "We have a mutual friend"?

He extended his hand toward her. "Don't be afraid. I'm here for you, Catharina.

Slipping her hand in his felt like the easiest thing she'd done in years.

♫ ♫ ♫

Mayor LaPlante shuffled through papers on his normally empty desk top. He'd learn to speed read in law school and manage his time like a four-star general in charge of ground operations for war. Learning to focus on tasks at hand helped shape him into the man he was today. That, and taking advantage of the disadvantaged and trusting souls who dared depend on his expertise when he worked in private practice. Accumulating wealth became an obsession and a god he bowed down to each and every day.

A tap at the door was followed by his secretary looking in. She waited for the mayor to look her way. "Mr. Crane is here to see you, sir. Do you have a minute? He's quite insistent."

"Did you block out the morning meetings and reschedule?"

"Yes, sir."

"Show him in."

An over-weight man with slicked back gray hair and a fuzzy mustache barreled through the doors in an agitated state. His black skin showed the creases and lines of a stressful job working for the city. The three piece suit failed to hide the cheap smell of cologne sprayed on too heavily earlier in the day. He was as wide as he was tall, causing him to look almost clown-like.

"What is it, Crane?" The mayor enjoyed ignoring the title of Chairman of the Board of Alderman. "Not enough legal work to keep you in the office?"

"With all I have to do for this alderman position, I'm lucky if I have time to take care of my practice and clients."

The mayor leaned back in his leather chair, rocking it until it squeaked. "If it weren't for me, you'd not have any clients at all, so stop whining. What do you want?"

"The other night I told Morgan to follow up on a few things. She never got back to me or returned my calls. What's going on?" He paced at first until he noticed the mayor looking sour. Squeezing his body into the armed upholstered chair forced him to unbutton his coat.

"Morgan answers to me. Not you. She has no relevant information for us at this time. But something has happened that might be of interest to you." Kragan shoved a file folder toward the alderman. "Morgan brought this to me an hour ago."

Opening the folder, the alderman read over the info sheet.

With a smile, he closed the folder and leaned back in his chair. "The coffee shop owner at Union Station does indeed live at the Essmalory."

"She's in over her head in debt and can barely make ends meet. Apparently, her brother is one of the homeless wandering around the streets at night. The police report that he's been involved in several suspicious altercations in recent weeks where gang members have been attacked or injured. Several have even gone missing." Kragan tapped his cheek with his index finger. "No big loss, but we're depending on them to get some nasty business done for us."

"Do the police think he's this Watcher everyone is talking about? I saw where KKOV plans to do a series on the homeless this week. It would be just like the media to make him out to be some kind of hero."

"If he's going around killing people, they won't. He may have slipped up last night."

Crane grabbed the arms of the chair, feeling the pinch of discomfort from not having enough space in his seat. "What happened?"

"This brother may have killed a man. According to the police report, the man may have been a drug dealer or—who knows?—one of our gang people. Anyway, the thug shot the brother. Somehow he managed to take him down. Cut him up pretty badly. Same as a few others who lived to tell about it. It wasn't the first time. He's in the hospital recovering from his wounds. The police say he's in and out of reality. The police don't think he's the culprit, but he did tell his sister to be sure and take care of The Watcher."

Crane began chewing the inside of his jaw. "And you plan to use this information how?"

"The coffee shop woman, Catharina Spokane, I met her last evening at the Fox Theater. She was with Damien Cruz."

Crane rolled his round eyes, blood shot from too much drinking the night before. "So what? He's a known womanizer. Probably slumming."

Kragan smiled as he leaned forward. "That, or he's after the Essmalory himself. Cruz is a shrewd businessman. Who knows how he's made his millions? Most people don't even know he owns that whole Union Station complex. He keeps that pretty close to the vest. If he's taken up with that little coffee rat, it's damn well because he's after something. I bet it's the building we want. He knows the value lies in its strategic location. That property is worth millions."

"What are you thinking, Kragan?"

"The brother just may get charged with murder if we play our cards right. I would bet Ms. Spokane would need to sell her apartment to afford legal fees." A chuckle escaped his thin lips. "Maybe you could even take the case at a reasonable price, provided I subsidize your efforts."

Crane nodded and let a belly laugh escape. "Anything else?"

"Yes." Kragan picked up another folder and thumbed through it before handing it over to Crane. "It seems that the Spokanes were once in the foster care system. They disappeared when they were quite young, yet the money never stopped being sent to a—"

"Father Xavier?" Crane looked at the name. "Isn't he the one who runs that Kitchen for the homeless?"

"The same." This time a wicked smile spread across Kragan's face that widened with each word. "I smell fraud, Crane. Wonder what the church would think if they knew the good father was stealing from little children in the foster care system? All that money with added interest could be a sizeable amount. His kitchen is also prime real estate. Just blocks from Busch Stadium, who knows what that is worth?"

Crane wiggled out of the chair then straightened his coat. "I bet you already know that information."

"Damn right, I do. And I intend to take it. The church doesn't need another scandal involving a priest." His voice had become a growl. "Now that we're up to speed, I've got work to do." Kragan started stacking the file folders spread across his desk as Crane moved toward the door. "Crane?"

He turned to look at the mayor.

"Don't ever barge into my office again and demand information." The alderman looked surprised. Kragan snorted. "I have other friends in low places that can replace you at a moment's notice. Understood?"

Crane's frown deepened as he nodded then rushed out the door.

The mayor reached over to turn on the CD player that would turn on the music he listened to each day for inspiration. *The Devil's Trill* began its beautiful melody, forcing him to close his eyes and breathe deeply. Some places he even began to hum until his vision of the future came into focus.

♫♫♫

Catharina laid her head down on the edge of her brother's bed, falling asleep an hour or so after he was brought into his room. Father Xavier sat on the opposite side, whispering a barrage of prayers to the Lord. The smell of an antiseptic room and the constant beep of machines attached to her brother lured her into a deep sleep. When she felt his fingers toy with her hair, she lifted her head and saw him smiling like the old Zane she knew before war and Afghanistan.

"Hey, baby sister. Why aren't you at work?" His voice sounded a little drugged and tired.

Father Xavier stood up and leaned over Zane, smoothing his hair with an arthritic hand. "My boy," he whispered with love.

Catharina stood and kissed his cheek. She asked the usual questions about how he felt, was he in pain, did he want water, could she get him something to eat. He smiled as his eyes went back and forth between the two people she knew he loved.

"I'm good, Cat. Stop your worrying."

Father Xavier moved to shut the door then came around to stand next to Catharina. "Zane, what happened last night?"

The former soldier shook his head as if to clear it. He squinted, apparently trying to retrieve a memory. "I drove my car someplace. I think it was near that children's hospital. That's right. Gideon needed a ride. He works there at the parking garage until one. Or is it two?"

"Then what happened, Zane?" Catharina stroked his arm like she used to do when they were allowed to visit each other when separated in foster care. "Did you pick him up?"

He nodded with a smile. "Yep. He bought me a cup of coffee and a biscuit." A pause followed as if he was trying to piece together the events that followed. "I was going to park somewhere to sleep. Gideon said The Watcher wanted us."

"The Watcher." Father Xavier sounded alarmed. "I knew it. I'm going to have to talk to him. This has got to stop."

"No. Father Xavier, he tries to help us. We met with others. He taught us how to protect ourselves then spoke of how we can make a difference."

Father Xavier shook his head in sorrow. "Zane, he is dangerous. You don't know what he is capable of."

"You mean because he is an angel?" The words sounded like something a child might say.

"Yes, Zane. Because he is an angel. He holds great power over the earth." Father looked at Catharina whose eyes had grown wide with fear. "Do you really want him around your sister, knowing he has killed?"

Zane took his sister's hand and squeezed before looking up at the priest. "It is out of our hands, Father Xavier. The time is close when he will be freed from his heavenly body to walk as a man."

"At what cost, Zane?" Father Xavier grew impatient. "Has he spoken of Catharina to you? Do you know he—"

"Stop it." Zane put his hands on the top of his head. "Do not talk bad about my friend."

"It's okay, Zane." She patted his hands as they slid back to his side. "He came to get me last night when you were hurt. Can you tell us what happened?"

"Gideon helped Rocco pass out supplies of toothpaste and brushes. There was even some soap. I got two bars," he announced with pride. "Then this guy showed up and started waving a gun. He knocked old George down and made him cut his head. George ran off, he was so scared. The others did too. Not me. I told him, 'get lost, creep.' He laughed at me. When he started waving the gun around it went off and shot me. Gideon pulled me away before he could pull the trigger again."

"What about Rocco?" Catharina held her breath.

"Diced him up good. But he said a prayer over him. I thought that was real generous, Father. Don't you?"

Father Xavier ran his hand over his face in frustration. "Cat, no one is going to believe this."

Zane looked troubled at the possibility. "Of course, they will, Father. It's the truth. You believe me don't you, Cat?"

"Yes. I believe you, Zane." She shot a concerned look at the priest. "So what happened to Gideon? He just left you there?"

Zane nodded and smiled. "Rocco ordered him to leave. Said his time had not yet come to fight the battles of the wicked."

"What does that mean?" Father Xavier snapped.

"Not sure. Sometimes Gideon isn't right in the head. Sometimes he's afraid of Rocco. Says he makes him do things."

The priest and Catharina stepped closer to one another.

"What kind of things?" she dared to ask.

"Bad things?" The priest asked with reluctance.

"Depends on how you look at it, I guess." Zane scooted down in his bed a little farther. "I'm going to sleep now." He began to mumble as his eyes closed, "'Though I walk through the valley of the shadow of death, I will fear no evil, for you are with me; your rod and your staff, they comfort me.'"

Chapter 12

Thanks, Jeremiah, for opening the coffee shop. Is the new girl in there now?" Catharina wondered if her lumbered footsteps across the Grand Hall made her look like one of the homeless that shuffled along on the streets and alleys of the city. Even before she turned to go down the business hall to enter her shop, she could see through the glass walls where a new person smiled and nodded to customers. "Is that Molly? The one you told me about?"

Jeremiah helped her out of her faux leather jacket, draping it across his arm as they walked. "I stayed with her for the first hour, but she's done this before. Basically, all I had to do was go over prices, taxes, and where you kept everything." His smile beamed. "She even said she'd work for free today until you approved of her work."

Catharina tried to fluff her wild hair so it didn't look as if she'd been sleeping with a cap tied to half of her head. She took a deep breath then let it go as they walked into the coffee shop. "That's all I need. Another angel." Her voice came out disgruntled.

"You can never have too many angels in your life, Cat."

"That's debatable, Jeremiah." She took the coat from him and offered a weak smile of thanks. "I appreciate everything you did."

"Well, the boss kind of insisted." He winked at her. "I think he has a soft spot for you."

"The boss wants business to run smoothly. But I will thank him as well. I appreciate everyone pitching in like they did this morning. I owe you."

Waving to Molly behind the counter, Jeremiah headed for the doors. "If you need to head out for your brother, just call." Then he was gone.

It didn't take long to feel as if Molly had indeed been sent by an angel. Tall and lithe as a willow reed, she moved about the shop as if she'd always been there. The dark brown hair caught the lights from overhead, creating shiny bands of sparkle. Catharina liked her right away. It was after lunch when customers dwindled long enough for the two to talk and get acquainted. Molly insisted on taking over for the rest of the day so Catharina could do paperwork at one of the tables. Four o'clock rolled around when she noticed the next rush of customers, driving her behind the counter to help her new hired assistant. By six o'clock, they'd become friends.

"I guess I can keep this place open longer now that you're here, Molly."

"Great. Guess that means I'm hired."

"Without a doubt." Taking off her apron, Catharina grabbed her purse. "Thanks for closing up. I need to head back to the hospital."

Molly nodded as she started making a cappuccino for one of the hotel guests.

Catharina walked to the corridor to take the elevator up to the fifth floor offices, in hopes of finding Damien. He had stayed with her until Zane came out of surgery, then passed her off to Father Xavier. His kindness didn't involve a lot of chit chat. They ate in silence and sat in the waiting room side by side, shoulder to shoulder. She felt herself dosing off once and woke to find her head cradled in the crook of his arm. Startled and embarrassed, Catharina jerked her head up. When she glanced at him, Damien smiled ever so slightly that made his eyes narrow so that she couldn't see the color. Withdrawing his arm, he sat straight and tall. He looked as if someone had posed him in that position. His hands rested on his thighs without so much as a twitch. Not until the surgeon came to talk to her did he show any sign of being a human, capable of emotion.

"Your brother will be good as new. Can he stay with you

while he recovers?"

Her voice choked with relief as she bobbed her head like a little girl. Damien's arm went around her, pulling her close to his side. "You'll remember about the VA, doctor?"

The doctor reassured both of them he would do it immediately.

Catharina lowered her head to hide the tears of relief trailing down her face, when Damien turned her to him. He cupped her chin in his hand and lifted until she looked up into his pale blue eyes. "You can do this, Cat." Placing his hands on each side of her face, he rubbed his thumbs at the tears. "I need to get to the hotel. Some of the staff came in to help at your coffee shop."

She gulped trying to say 'thank you,' but nothing came out.

Tears blurred her vision enough that when she saw a blackness swim across Damien's face, like a mask, she thought the lack of sleep had caught up with her. Blinking her eyes several times, cleared the fog. Her lips moved. "Thank you, Damien." It was not enough, but it was all she had to give, even as he pulled her closer and rested his forehead against her face.

"Stay as long as you need."

Releasing her, he strode away toward the elevators. She watched him until the doors opened. He stood for the longest time staring inside as if deep in thought. The doors started to close. At the last second he raised his hand to bounce them open again. Turning his head to look back at Catharina, he appeared tortured. There was a longing as if he waited for her to react to something.

She had the overpowering urge to run to him. For what? Comfort? Support? Love? A torrent of confusion swallowed any rational thought, paralyzing her with fear of making mistakes that would destroy what little self-respect and confidence she possessed. A man like Damien Cruz didn't make long-term commitments. Pivoting on her heels, she walked away. A wave of suspicion of his intentions washed over her. What could she possibly offer a man like that?

Now she hoped to thank him. Others had dropped by in the afternoon to check up on her and Zane's condition. Thanking them came easy. They offered a hug, promise of a prayer, to fill in for her if she needed it. Going to Damien felt different. The almost romantic evening at the Fox Theater ended up being awkward for her. Was it the woman who eyed him like forgotten dessert or that he could have kissed her goodnight and chose not to?

Stepping off the elevator, she walked out onto the balcony carpeted in a lush red design. The lights of the Grand Hall drew her to the edge. Looking over and down at the full expanse, she watched the grand lady come alive with people. When Mayor LaPlante came up the spiral staircase from the street, he stopped and looked around as if searching for someone. His steps held purpose as he moved toward the area beneath the covered baloney where she stood. Peeking over the edge, she could see Damien come out from the reception area. With his back to her, Catharina recognized the impatient stance. The mayor slowed his pace, stopping in front of the manager. They both appeared to look around them to make sure no one paid them any attention.

One of the things Catharina had learned about the Grand Hall when she first got the coffee house contract was that the acoustics were legendary. Whispers could circulate like beating drums at times. The two men, who now eyed each other with contempt, began to speak. She knew walking away would be the polite thing to do until she realized they were talking about her.

The mayor grinned as he removed his gloves, one finger at a time. "So you're buttering up the coffee shop girl to get what you want. That's despicable even for you, Damien."

"Stay out of my business, Kragan. You are so used to dealing in ulterior motives that it never occurs to you I might be turning over a new leaf."

This brought a sinister chuckle from the mayor. "I bet she is just mesmerized by all that British charm. Taking her to the dinner then the Fox, showing up to whisk her off to the hospital to be with her brother. Sounds pretty convenient to me. I think that drug dealer might be working for you."

Damien rolled his shoulders as if they were stiff. "That's your style."

"How did you even know about the shooting, Damien?" The mayor's grin started to fade as he questioned the man before him. "Seems to me you got there awfully fast."

"You know a great deal about my movements."

"Yes." Kragan spoke through gritted teeth. "After all, I am the mayor and the police work for me. They tell me that Mr. Spokane might be charged with murder. A knife was found with his prints on it." This caused Damien to jerk his chin up. "Don't act so surprised? So what is the plan? You swoop in and offer to buy Ms. Spokane's apartment so she'll have money to pay a lawyer for her brother's bail and defense? I know you've looked into buying that property as well as The Kitchen of Hope. My information tells me you've been running some trouble makers around the street she lives on to scare the tenants into selling. Shady business."

"Go to hell." Damien leaned in toward Kragan. "And I really mean that. Anything else?"

"Yes. When I find out who this Watcher character is, I'd bet my right arm he's working for you. Those unfortunate bums, wandering around the streets, think he's their protector. We both know he's just a psychotic killer with a hero complex. Tell me how you got him to participate in this plan of yours." Damien started to walk away until the mayor reached out and grabbed his arm. "Don't walk away from me. Whatever plans you have for that building needs to stop or—"

Damien tilted his head as he jerked free of the mayor's grasp. "Or what? You can't threaten me. I'm not afraid of your little puppet kingdom you run from city hall." He nodded to the bar. "One drink, then get out of my hotel." Damien disappeared back under the balcony toward the reception area.

Catharina jerked back to cover her mouth from gasping. If she had waited two seconds longer, she would have seen the mayor look up at the balcony and smile.

♫ ♫ ♫

Running to the clear glass elevator, she heard the gears turning to lift someone to either the guest rooms below or to the fifth floor she now longed to escape. She looked down into the elevator as the cables creaked with vibration. Damien stood at ease, staring down at the floor. His dark hair appeared combed and neat, unlike the night before when he stood with her in the dark at the crime scene. Turning, she ran to hide. The last thing she wanted was a confrontation about the possibility of him participating in the attack on her brother or leaving evidence that would implicate him.

A door, half the normal size, marked "maintenance only" was the first thing she found unlocked. Trying to pop it open didn't work so she jerked hard enough for her to fall backward on her butt. Hopping up, she slipped inside the darkness, drawing the door closed to where only a crack let in the light. In seconds, Damien walked by, then stopped abruptly, stiffening his entire body. He looked over his shoulder, turned, and came back to the cracked door. In slow motion, he reached for the doorknob. At the last second he pushed it closed, leaving Catharina in the dark. She heard the lock snap in place, throwing her into a state of panic.

When she thought enough time had passed that Damien had continued on his way, she began feeling around for a light switch or pull chain. Her fingers touched a plastic cover and she flipped it to the on position. It took a couple of seconds to come on. The wiring in such an old building needed to be upgraded. Since it wasn't cosmetic, she imagined the job wasn't high on the priority list.

Turning around, she found that there was another door. This one, flimsy with flaking paint, opened easier than the first. She stood there with her hands on each side of the doorframe, wondering if she should try to find another way out. The three narrow stairs were steep and hard to navigate as she took the first cautious step down. Once on solid footing again, she dug in her shoulder bag for the small flashlight her brother had given her. She sucked in her breath as the beam of light spilled a path before her.

Stained-glass windows of reds and blues, caught the moonlight and created ghostly patterns across the dusty plank flooring. The musty smell of abandonment and pigeon feces made her eyes water. The pitch of the roof created a narrow path but it appeared to be safe. At the far end she could see another room. This one had a ladder leading up. Since there was no alternative she adjusted her bag on her shoulder and placed the small flashlight in her mouth before starting to climb. She could feel the grime and rust stick to her hands as she reached the top and pulled herself up.

The realization she'd reached the very top of Union Station dawned on her as she saw the back of the clock that signified the tower. Its three-foot diameter provided enough light for her to click off her flashlight since the batteries were failing.

This area looked like a grand ballroom waiting to be restored. The rafters were beautiful and masculine. Her toes touched down lightly, expecting the creaky boards to give way with her weight. She was so mesmerized at the emptiness, she forgot her fear of being trapped. The cooing of pigeons roosting above and the faint sound of outside traffic gave her pause. Dampness of a former leaky roof still permeated the air. Her breath exhaled in translucent clouds of vapor.

The temptation to look through the clock brought her closer. Raising up on tip toes, Catharina looked down at Market Street. Several pieces of the white clock front had been chipped, allowing her to see out to the city. The cold air smacked her face, but it felt good after the climb up. Now her jacket didn't seem to be enough against the November air, hinting an early snowfall might be on the way. Since she didn't have a television, she had no idea of the forecast.

"I've got to get out of here." Her voice sounded like an echo. When she turned from the clock she saw it—a bed. Walking over to it, she thought maybe a homeless person had found a way in. If so, this could be a dangerous place for her.

She started to back away when the sound of something forced her to whirl around. A dark shadow in the recesses moved along the edge of the room, careful not to step out into the light of the watch tower. Something scurried across the floor, causing her to scream. A pigeon decided to fly around the rafters at her intrusion. The flap of its wings sounded almost like thunder.

"Whose there?" she asked as she fumbled with her

flashlight, only to drop it. Because the floor was uneven it rolled toward the shadow that had stopped moving.

Catharina knew she was in trouble. Why hadn't she just banged on the door of the maintenance closet to face Damien? Running from her fears always got her into trouble. Zane wasn't here now to protect her. What would happen to him if whoever lurked in the shadows killed her?

Run, Cat. Run, she told herself.

But even as her feet started forward, the shadow trailed back to cut off her escape.

Chapter 13

Mayor LaPlante sipped his whiskey at the bar as his eyes watched a hockey game on ESPN. The Blues were on the East Coast tonight so the game started earlier than usual. His eyes focused on the game but his thoughts were on Damien Cruz. He wasn't sure when he'd begun to dislike the man or even the reason, but the resentment ran deep inside him. Maybe it was the man's flippant disregard for the mayor's important position in the city. In spite of Damien's stand offish behavior, people seemed drawn to him. Kragan liked being the center of attention and had to work hard to make it happen. Even Morgan showed signs of being smitten the night at the Fox with the chance encounter. The spark of jealousy brought on by Damien's date, caused a rift between them she'd paid dearly for, at the end of the evening.

The lack of fear Damien had for him weakened Kragan's ability to threaten and intimidate. Money had a way of making you feel more powerful than you actually were. Kragan knew he just needed to find a weakness in the man who took great pride in ignoring him and withholding support on various issues in the city.

Kragan swirled his drink around in his glass as he looked around at the guests meandering through the Grand Hall. The recent crime spree must have the tourists and businessmen thinking twice about staying downtown. That could make him look bad. He needed to resolve this Essmalory Building issue so he could unleash the police on his hired trouble makers.

A smile touched the corner of his mouth when he

remembered touching a nerve in Damien at the mention of the building and Miss Coffee Shop. Playing that game might be fun. Kragan saw her on the balcony as soon as he'd walked in. Meeting Damien beneath it turned out to be perfect. Even he knew of the acoustics in the Grand Hall. She probably was upstairs giving him a good slap about now. He couldn't resist a chuckle drawing the attention of the bartender.

"Another one, Mr. Mayor?"

Kragan shoved his glass forward in acceptance as he turned in his seat to watch several ladies approach the bar. "See what they're having and put it on my tab."

♫♫♫

Just as Catharina rushed toward the door where the ladder led back down to freedom, she caught her toe on a loose board, sending her falling forward. A scream pierced the darkness as she propelled toward the opening. The flash of knowledge, knowing you could be plummeting to your death forced her to try and grab at the door facing without success. As she felt her body tilt toward disaster, hands caught the back of her jacket. The backward motion landed her against a hard body that smelled of incense. A tight grip held her in place so that she couldn't turn and face her rescuer. She tried squirming free only to have the arms tighten around her until she could hardly breathe.

"Why are you here?" The raspy voice at her ear did not hold the usual calm she'd come to expect from Rocco. The agitation frightened her to the point she wondered if he could hear her heart pounding. "You are here all alone," he growled. "No one knows where you are." The threat in his voice paralyzed Catharina with horror as he continued. "Snooping into places you know nothing about is very dangerous."

She felt one of his naked arms drop down to her waist and tug her in tighter while the other arm remained around her midriff. His legs were standing apart so that he braced against any attempt at escape. The touch of his nose at her ear then her hair made her try to step away, only to have him squeeze until she gasped for air. When he relaxed his hold, she took advantage of the moment and rammed her foot into his. Although he made no sound of feeling pain, Rocco dropped his arms and stepped back.

She turned slightly to elbow his chest, causing him to jump back. Then she grabbed hold of the ladder and started down. Like playing with a rag doll, Rocco reached down and grabbed hold of the front of her jacket. Lifting her back onto the floor, he shoved her away from the opening.

He took a step toward her, his arms out to his side. "You should not have come here."

Catharina realized his torso was naked. With the light of the city spilling through broken windows, she saw for the first time the beautiful ink of tattoos over his shoulders and arms. Backing away, she couldn't help but see that his eyes possessed an icy hot glow. The black shadow of a mask across his face widened as he took another step.

"I know. I'm sorry. It was an accident, Rocco. Just let me go. I won't tell anyone you're staying here. I promise." Keeping the quiver out of her voice was impossible.

Then he stormed forward, causing her to cry out as he snatched her arm, dragging her toward the bed, and she realized this was not going to end well. Swinging her fist at his head and chest did nothing to loosen his grip. Jerking her around to face him, he hesitated as tears flooded down her face.

"Rocco. Stop," she babbled as salty trails touched her lips. "Rocco. Please."

Without another thought, he shoved her down on the bed then stared down at her. His tattoos began to glow like fire as he staggered backward, then fell to the floor.

At the same time, Catharina felt her own skin catch fire and she cried out in pain. Her back arched as the pain spread through her body. Through her tears she watched Rocco rise to his knees and crawl toward her. Pulling himself up next to the bed, he laid his hand on her shoulder where the ink designs hid beneath her clothing. He began to speak in some Aramaic language then in English. His eyes looked upward and he struggled to speak. "'You shall not fear them, for it is the Lord your God who fights for you.' Deuteronomy 3:22."

As he rose up from touching her, his chest still glowed. Her breathing, still short and labored, began to even out as he collapsed on the bed next to her, pinning her down with his arm. Laying on his stomach, his face was inches from hers. Caution still choked her as she turned her eyes to stare into his.

He blinked slowly as if coming back to reality. "I only wanted to scare you. You should not be here." His raspy voice was barely a whisper. "I cannot hurt you, Catharina. You are the only one who can free me." He reached over to roll her onto her side before pulling her up against him. "I'm sorry you are frightened." Still she remained quiet, shivering under his warm touch. "I too am frightened. You hold a great deal of power for my future. I have waited a long time for you to find me. My patience wears thin. I fear now I have damaged your trust."

He touched her shoulder where he knew the tattoos hid beneath her clothing. She began to tremble as he peeled back her jacket, then unbuttoned her shirt. The touch of his hand against her skin made her eyes grow wide with terror. She tried to pull away, causing his hand to hover for a second above the ink.

"I only want to understand why you have done this to your body." He looked down at the intricate designs then rubbed his hand across it, causing a momentary glow to surface. "Tell me, Catharina." His hand withdrew from her shoulder to rest on the side of her face. A whisper escaped his lips, so near to hers. "Tell me so I can understand."

"I—I—" She swallowed, trying to sound brave, hoping it would be enough to make him let her go. "Please. I want to go to my brother. Let me go."

He took a deep breath and exhaled as if trying to be patient. Slipping his hand to her back, he stroked her as if memorizing each part of her spine. His fingers came back to push her hair behind her ears. For the first time, he offered a slow smile. The expression carried sadness. Catharina took a chance and laid her hand on his that rested on her ear.

"The dark spots in the design. Do you see them?"

He withdrew his hand as she pulled back her blouse enough for him to look closer. A shiver caused goose bumps to rise as he once again peered at them then ran his fingers over each design.

"Do you see them?" she repeated.

His eyes lost the cold glare and warmed at feeling her breath against his face. "Yes."

"Each dark spot is where my foster father burned me with a cigarette."

He jerked his hand back so fast it startled her so that she buried her head in the mattress and covered her head.

"No. No. Not you," he moaned as he sat up and pulled her up into his arms. "Why would someone do this to you? How long ago?"

"I was nine or ten." She started crying, remembering the abuse. "He made Zane watch. I wanted a cookie I'd brought home from a birthday party at school. Because I ate it before supper I got in trouble. Zane tried to protect me, but—"

Rocco began stroking her hair as his face rested against hers.

"Zane took me and we ran away. Lucky for us the social worker figured things out when she found us. It was our word against his. He was a respected man in the community. The social worker took us to Father Xavier, her priest." His arms cradled her as he rocked back and forth. "Father found us a home with an old couple in the church. It was so much better. But eventually they could no longer care for us and Father took us, hiding us most of the time with the help of others in the church."

"Father Xavier is a good man." The raspy voice sounded proud. "Who was this man who hurt you, Catharina?"

"I've tried to forget. The son was nearly as bad. He would steal and bully kids then blame Zane. Most of the time it was easier for Zane to admit he did it. My brother was afraid I would be the one who might pay the price." A sob escaped again, forcing Rocco to hold her against his shoulder.

"Who was this man?"

With a shrug, Catharina pushed back to look at her captor. "I don't know." She swung her legs over the side of the bed and stood. "Why did you drag me to the bed?" She stood again, losing some of fear she felt. Afraid to run. Afraid to stay. "You meant to…" She didn't want to think about the motive.

Rocco looked up at her, a sternness returning to his expression as he stood in slow motion. "I am tortured. Being with you was a way to feel human." He closed his eyes for a few seconds. "I regret that action. I dwell in two worlds. Each one with demands I find difficult to fulfill. Only you can free me."

"How? Let Father Xavier and me take you to get help."

He blinked then recoiled. "You do not believe what I claim to be."

"I don't know what to believe." The sound of a siren drew her eyes to an open window. She remembered the reason why she'd hidden in the first place. "Do you work for Damien Cruz?" The words were out of her mouth before she could stop them.

He moved passed her and picked up a shirt hanging on a hook she'd not noticed earlier. "I will take you out. I will show you a safe way and also an escape vent. If the time comes you are in trouble, you know where to find me."

"Does Damien know you are here? Does anyone?" Catharina dared walk up beside him and touch his arm as he slipped on his wool cloak. "Should I trust Damien?"

"Come, Catharina. I will take you to the street. There is work for me to do tonight."

He moved toward the end of the room where the ladder rested. When she did not immediately follow, he looked back over his shoulder at her slender frame, shivering in the darkness. Her hands were down at her side and from across the room, he could still see the terror in her eyes. In three strides, he reached her and lifted her off the floor with his arms wrapped around her. Their mouths connected in one searing moment, both emptying a longing into the other.

Rocco sat her down like a piece of delicate china before taking her hand and rubbing his thumb along the outside of her skin. "You must leave here. Now. God will strike me for what I have just done. I don't want you to see that."

He pulled her after him to lead the way to safety.

♫ ♫ ♫

The old man looked out his kitchen window into the yard where dark leaves rose and fell with each gust of wind. He cursed the trashcan rolling up against the house, knowing it to be the sound that startled him moments earlier. The evening news blared in the other room so he could hear it in the kitchen while he made himself a cup of warm milk. Maybe tonight he'd sleep better. Most nights, he didn't. It wasn't the mistakes he'd made giving him insomnia, but the lack of action he failed to take to cover them that haunted him. There was still plenty of money in his accounts to keep him comfortable. The doctor warned him to take it easy on the fatty foods and the smokes. Those warnings were ignored.

As long as he could walk to the recreation center each day to play cards with his buddies, life was good. Plenty of donuts and coffee there for breakfast then a nearby café for lunch. They swapped lies, bragged about the women in their lives and the shenanigans that lined their pockets with extra cash. He truly loved to reminisce about the old days. The wife died a decade ago and the hard-to-control son, spoiled and self-absorbed, left so long ago he could barely remember what he looked like.

None of the children he and his wife cared for in the foster care program bothered to reconnect. Ungrateful trash. The money was hardly worth taking them in until he discovered he could pocket most of it. His wife begged him to give her more. He refused. With a little physical persuasion, she'd come to see his point of view.

The lights flickered then went out completely. He looked out at his neighbor's house and realized their lights still burned bright. Rubbing his nose with the back of his hand, he smelled the sweet scent of tobacco. In moments, he'd lit a cigarette and moved toward the phone to call the power company. They had been trimming limbs all week away from power lines so something like this wouldn't happen.

Raising the phone to his ear, he discovered that too was dead. "Worthless," he mumbled out loud, giving some thought again to getting a cell phone. As he turned around to find a flashlight, a tall shadow moved away from the wall across from him.

"Who's there?" His voice sounded more irritated than frightened. "Get out of my house or I'll call the police."

The shadow took another step closer. This time the old man backed up against the stove.

"The phone is dead." The raspy voice grew deep and slow as the shadow began to move about the room. "Are you afraid?"

"Hell, no, I'm not afraid. Get out," the old man demanded. "Punk."

The shadow moved closer. With a flick of his wrist, the old man opened his lighter to cast an eerie glow onto the shadow's face. It frightened him to see the face of such a menacing creature who stood before him.

The old man tried to slide away. "What do you want?"

"I want to know why you tortured a little girl with a cigarette." The raspy voice grew angry as he cut off the man's retreat.

"I never did that." His voice revealed his fear of being discovered.

Rocco removed his sword in slow motion so that it made a metal sound against the silver trim on his belt. The man tried to escape, but with Rocco's long reach, he merely took hold of the man's arm and jerked him back, placing the tip of the sword under his chin. The man began to quiver.

"Why hurt little children, old man? They were entrusted to your care." Without lowering the sword, Rocco took the cigarette from the man's hand and blew gently on the end to make it glow. With the care of a surgeon, he placed it against the neck of the man until he screamed. "Why?"

"I tried to teach them respect. That's all. Ungrateful brats." The old man gathered up enough courage to slide out from under the tip of Rocco's sword. "Greedy, little trash bags. All of them. I did the best I could, considering what I had to work with." He started to rub the spot on his neck then his left arm as a pain flowed in his fingers and up to his shoulder. "Who are you? One of the worthless I tried to raise?"

Rocco drew closer, arching an eyebrow before pushing the sword through the man's clothing. A whimper escaped as the old man cowered in the corner.

"Remove your shirt. Now."

The even tone of his voice left no doubt his words were a command. The old man did so with awkwardness. Pulling the flannel shirt then the tee shirt over his head, he proceeded to drop them on the floor.

The Watcher laid the cold steel across the man's chest. "Tonight I stand for the children you abused. Tonight I right the wrongs you did to them."

"Money. I have lots of money. You can have all of it. Just let me go."

"I have no need of money. 'Wealth and riches are in His house, and His righteousness endures forever.' Psalm 112:3"

"I donno what you're talking about. Just let me give you some money and be on your way."

"'Riches do not profit in the day of wrath, but righteousness delivers from death.' I am angry. So unless you have an ounce of righteousness I come to deliver you into the hands of the death angels that stand like warriors at the pits of hell." He began to slice the man's chest with a slow downward motion that broke the skin enough to let his blood run freely."

The old man's whimper increased as he looked down at the second slice. "Please. I'm on blood thinners. I could bleed to death. What do you want?"

Rocco closed his pale eyes that now glowed with vengeance. "Revenge for a little girl and boy who trusted you."

As The Watcher stepped back and looked at his work the man grabbed his chest. "Help me."

Rocco withdrew and found the cigarette still burning on the counter. He rolled some paper towels down so that they touched the glowing end of the cigarette. Moving to the stove, he turned on the gas burner, not enough to light, but to let the gas escape. Walking back to the man now sitting on the floor staring up at him, he squatted down to look him in the eye.

"Please. Help me," the old man begged, clutching at his bloody chest.

"Soon," Rocco looked over at the paper towels burning then spreading to the curtains, "you will feel the flames of hell for eternity. This is but a taste." Rocco reached out and touched the man's mouth with his fingers that sealed his lips. "The little ones called for help many times without anyone hearing them. Now you will know for only a short time what they felt. May God have mercy on your worthless soul." He stood. "I have one more question. Where is your son?"

♪♫♪

Rocco walked down the middle of street until he heard the explosion. Stopping, he looked back at the orange glow lighting up the sky as he pondered the answer to the last question he ask the old man.

Chapter 14

The smell of antiseptic touched Catharina's nose as she entered Zane's room. Visiting hours had ended thirty minutes earlier. After tramping around in the rafters of Union Station, she was covered in dust. A hot shower and shampoo prevented her from getting to the hospital in time to talk to anyone in authority. She brought a small bag with a change of clothes, toothbrush, and makeup, planning on staying the night. With any luck, the doctor would make rounds in the morning before she needed to head to work. They could discuss her brother's progress and the possibility of him leaving.

A quiet noise of shuffling feet, the whoosh of doors opening and closing along the click of computer keyboards, drifted down the hall. A nurse stopped by to take Zane's vitals, causing him to awaken. His smile at seeing she'd returned, warmed her heart.

The shattered emotions of Rocco turning against her, although momentarily, filled her with anxiety. He wasn't human. She didn't know what he was, but it wasn't human. The strength in his hands alone told her as much. In spite of living in filth and roaming the streets, Rocco appeared clean. His body nearly glistened when she'd gazed upon his naked torso. The smell of incense that clung to him reminded her of mass on Easter Sunday. Even his clothes bore no signs of blood stains or spilled coffee like the other homeless she'd met. She turned her eyes back to Zane.

He reached for her hand. "Hi, little sister. How are you?"

Leaning in to kiss his cheek, she knew instantly he was the

old Zane. "Good. Thought I'd spend the night here. We can talk like we used to when Father Xavier let us sleep over at the rectory. Remember?"

He grinned. "I'd like that. I love you, Cat." Lifting her hand to his lips, he kissed her fingers then paused. "You've been with Rocco."

Pulling back her fingers to sniff, Catharina wondered how he could smell The Watcher after she'd scrubbed her body until it was nearly raw. "Yes." There wasn't even a hint of his odor. "How did you know?"

Ignoring her question, he asked, "Do you like my friend?" He eyed her as she pulled up a chair next to the bed. Then he started to smile again. "Or has he scared the pjesus out of you?"

"Yes. He does scare me, Zane. I don't think you should see him anymore. He's dangerous. If what you say is true—"

"If? You saw him that night near your apartment." His voice took on an irritated tone. "He protected us. Last night, he protected all of us from that druggy. He would've killed me if not for Rocco finishing the job." His eyes rolled to the ceiling and stared for a few seconds. "I know this is hard for you, Cat, but The Watcher is all the people of the street have to protect them. Every night, it's something. The police running us off or gang members trying to hurt the crippled and sick. At least with him walking around, those idiots think twice before they try and steal from the homeless."

Catharina realized Zane didn't include himself as one of the homeless.

"He helps me. Tells me I can get better. I feel like my old self when he's around. I've started believing in myself again."

She leaned forward to prop her chin in the palm of her hand. "I'm just afraid he'll get you in trouble, Zane. Those policemen are starting to think *you're* The Watcher."

Zane nodded then sighed as he once more took her hand. "I am very strong, Cat."

She smiled proudly. "I know that, Zane."

"No. I mean really strong. Hand me that metal pitcher on my tray."

She did as he asked. With little effort he crushed the handle in his hand.

Catharina jumped to her feet and covered her mouth then spoke with awe. "Zane! How did you do that?" She grabbed it from him to examine more closely.

"Rocco won't always be around to help the homeless. His time here is almost over." He turned his eyes on Catharina with an icy clam—something she'd seen in Rocco the first time they met.

"What is that supposed to mean? Is he leaving town?" The hairs were standing up on the back of her neck as she calmly turned on the television to watch the evening news.

"You know exactly what it means, Cat." His voice sounded like a proud father. Looking up at the screen, he smiled. "I think you should watch the news."

Turning up the sound, Catharina watched a reporter standing outside a burning house.

"I am at Kimber and Sanford where firefighters have extinguished a house fire. There was an explosion, drawing neighbors out before calling 911." She looked down at her notes then back at the camera. "The resident was an older man, a Mr. Glen Forrester who once owned the Soulard Plumbing Supply Warehouse. Many people were local patrons of the business until it was sold two years ago. Mr. Forrester had already succumbed to the smoke and fire by the time firefighters could get to him."

Catharina pointed the remote at the screen, hitting the mute button. Turning her eyes to Zane she let her words spill out in excitement. "That's him! That's the man who burned me and beat you, Zane."

The smile on his face was pure delight. She unmuted the sound to continue listening.

A wind blew the reporter's long hair across her narrow face as she continued to speak. "We're now getting a report that says the fire may have been started from a cigarette left near some kind of paper products. Also it appears the explosion could have occurred from the gas stove not being turned completely off. Neighbors say Mr. Forrester could be forgetful. Further investigation will continue during the light of day. Sicily Timbers reporting live from Kimber and Sanford."

Catharina turned off the television and stared at Zane. "I can't believe it," she whispered.

Zane nodded happily. "All good things come to those who wait." He chuckled. "I believe that is from the Gospel of Luke. Maybe chapter twelve." Slapping his hands together, he continued to smile. "Yep. Definitely chapter twelve."

"I don't understand. Since when do you know scripture? And why don't you seem surprised about this fire? Please tell me you didn't have anything to do with that?" The panic in her voice sobered Zane.

"I've been here all night. What could I have done?" Zane shrugged his shoulders then wrinkled his nose, as if he had a twinge of pain from the surgery. He reached for her arm and pulled her in closer to the edge of the bed. "I did nothing. Honest. Besides, you should be happy that monster got what was coming to him."

"Did you tell Rocco about him?" She was remembering the vengeance that replaced the calm in his strange pale eyes.

Zane tilted his head to eye her. With the calmest voice she'd heard him use since returning home from Afghanistan, a different kind of Zane emerged. "I think we both know you told him."

♫ ♫ ♫

Father Xavier kneeled at the altar, crossed himself, and then kissed his crucifix. A sound near the flickering candles forced his body to tense. He thought he'd locked up an hour ago. No one showed up for evening prayers in his Bible study group so he decided to turn in early.

"Hello? Anyone there?"

A moan from the shadows broke the silence.

The priest hesitated for only a second before moving toward a figure lying on the floor. The smell of smoke and seared flesh touched his nose as he bent down to touch the body.

"Father, forgive me for I have sinned."

The priest knew he spoke to God as he kneeled down. "Rocco, what have you done?"

The priest rolled him over and sucked in his breath as he saw

The Watcher glowing as if on fire. Father Xavier started praying as he pulled The Watcher into his arms, rocking him back and forth. Tears cascaded down his wrinkled face. "Heal your creature, dearest Lord in Heaven, and protect the innocent woman who makes him stray."

♫♫♫

Morgan Knox was ushered into the mayor's office the following afternoon. The red leather briefcase she carried matched her shoes. Dressed in a black suit, she looked not only stunning, but professional as she sauntered in, flaunting her own self-importance. Tossing her briefcase onto a cushioned chair, she took a moment to smooth her straight blonde hair then walked over to the cabinet where the mayor kept a decanter of bourbon.

The sound of ice hitting the bottom of her chubby glass was the first moment Kragan looked up to acknowledge her. Just as quickly, he looked back down at his paperwork before him.

"Have you seen the news?" She poured the bourbon over the ice before swirling it around like it were a fine wine instead of something that would burn all the way down her throat.

"No." He continued to work, making a point to not be baited into asking what she meant. "I have you for that."

Strutting across to his desk, she leaned over, propping her free hand on the mostly cleared surface. She understood that Kragan didn't like clutter in his personal or professional life. That's why they got along so well.

"Channel two is reporting that the police—"

He looked up, narrowing his eyes at her. "I don't pay you to get your information from the news media. If that's all you have, then please leave."

"Did anyone ever tell you you're a jerk?" Morgan snarled as she took a sip of her drink.

Keeping his attention to the work before him, Kragan snapped back. "Not if they hoped to continue working for me and, in your case, sleeping with me." He finally looked up. "Either way I'm sure I'd manage without you."

"Fine," she snapped then turned to sit down in a nearby

chair. Sitting the glass down with ease took restraint on her part when she wanted to hurl it at the mayor's head. Crossing her long legs, she took a nonchalant moment to smooth her skirt then rest her arms on the chair. "The Watcher apparently has struck again." Her breath slipped out in a bored sigh as she lifted her manicured nails up to inspect. "Guess we won't be pinning anything on that man shot down at Laclede's landing the other night."

Kragan laid down his pen. Other than his nostrils flaring, he showed no other emotions. "Why is that?"

"Really, Kragan, you need to watch the news. People were complaining last night that not only is there an increase in crime downtown, but now we have some kind of vigilante walking around, taking matters into his own hands. Several of your alderman said they'd be looking into it themselves with the help of police."

One corner of his mouth turned up in a smirk. "Again. You tell me the news." His voice grew taunt like a wire pulled too tight. "Who died? Anyone of consequence?"

Morgan tried not to fidget under his gaze as she picked up her drink and gulped it down. "Some old man. The preliminary coroner's report of the deceased ruled that a heart attack was the cause of death. However, there were slices across his bare chest, like the kind a sword would make. Some of the witnesses say they saw a hooded man walking down the middle of the street shortly after the explosion. He was carrying something long in his hand."

Kragan leaned back in his chair that swiveled. "Like a sword?"

"Who knows? Witnesses are terrible at remembering what they actually saw. By the time the news trucks showed up the guy was seven feet tall, dressed like something out of a video game. They're turning him into a romantic hero who protects the down trodden."

Kragan rubbed his chin in contemplation. "If he is such a hero, then why attack an old man?"

"Maybe it was a robbery gone bad. The guy used to own the Soulard Plumbing Warehouse. Probably had plenty of money after he sold it several years ago."

Kragan paled as he let his chair come back to a level position. "What was his name?"

"I think it was something like a glen or park. Nature kind of name."

Kragan's voice deepened. "Glen Forrester?" His eyes grew dark but his skin paled.

Morgan stood to refill her glass. "Something like that? Sound familiar? You were from Soulard right?"

"Yeah. I heard of him."

The voice, faint and unsure, drew Morgan's eyes back to him. "Are you all right?" She poured him a drink then walked around the back of his desk to sit it down.

Grabbing the drink, he downed it as if parched then handed her the glass to refill. "Another."

She took the glass and stepped away. "Kragan, what's wrong? Who was this man?"

"My father." He stared straight, as if looking in the past. "Find out the funeral arrangements. I want to be sure I attend. Let the media outlets know that their mayor cares about a citizen who dies by the hand of a madman. We need to show concern on this one." He took the new drink and swirled the liquid around to avoid looking at the shock on Morgan's face. "I'm done messing with this Watcher."

Kragan suspected The Watcher would be coming for him.

Chapter 15

eremiah, I haven't seen Damien in a few days."

As usual the assistant general manager came by first thing in the morning to get his cup of coffee.

Catharina struggled to act aloof. "Everything okay?"

He took the first sip and rolled his eyes. "Ahh. So good, Cat. Can I get one of those scones too? No time for breakfast this morning." She wrapped it in a napkin then a small brown bag. "Damien had to go out of town. He didn't sound so good. Sounded like he was sick or something. Not himself, that's for sure." He sat the cup of coffee down and reached in the bag. "I think I'll just eat this here." He pulled out the scone to take a big bite.

Wiping her hands on her apron, she tried to pull out more information. She didn't want to sound like she was too interested in the mysterious Damien Cruz. "Does he just up and leave like that? Sounds a little irresponsible."

"Pretty sure if you own the place you can do whatever you want." He took the last bite then licked his fingers before rubbing a napkin across his mouth. "You didn't hear me say that."

Pretending to lock her lips then throw the key over her shoulder, she whispered. "I kinda figured that one out all by myself." She took the bag with his trash to throw away. "I just never got to thank him for helping me and Zane the other night. He stayed with me until Zane came out of surgery."

Jeremiah cocked his head and winked. "Well, who knew the elusive Mr. Cruz had a soft spot. Better keep that under wraps. He's a catch for some lucky girl. Could be you."

"I'm not looking for 'a catch' as you call him. I'm too busy. Besides, he's a little too…" She started scrubbing the counter to try and find the right word. "He's too high and mighty."

Jeremiah chuckled. "Money will do that to you." He handed Catharina his cup for a refill then shoved a ten dollar bill in her tip jar when she wasn't looking. "Did you know that he donates to The Kitchen of Hope, several children's charities, and a scholarship for the children of fallen police officers?"

"No." She didn't mean to sound skeptical, but it was what it was. "Guess he lets everyone know how wonderful he is with that information."

"That's word of mouth. He never takes credit. I just happen to overhear the priest that comes around here sometimes to see you, mention it to Damien. The police who will be meeting in here this week told me ages ago what Damien did. And those kids, well he has a soft spot for them. Makes sure the Boys and Girls Club gets free tickets every Christmas for the Polar Express ride out back. Pays for it out of his own pocket then treats all of them to a fancy dinner and presents. Some of those kids are in the foster care program."

Catharina felt that tingling again creep up her spine then raise the hairs on her neck. "Okay. So he's a good guy. Doesn't mean I'm interested in Prince Charming."

Jeremiah grinned. "Maybe. But I think he's interested in you." His cell phone rang. Looking down at the caller ID, Jeremiah's eyes widened with amusement. "Speak of the devil." He clicked the answer button. "Hey, boss. How's it going?"

He was already headed out the door before Catharina could eavesdrop on the conversation.

The traffic in and out of her shop had been slow the last few days. She thought about making some coupons to get people to drop by until Jeremiah said the hotel just hadn't been able to book any big groups for a few weeks. At the rate she was going, her new assistant would need to find another job. Christmas was around the corner. The Polar Express was a popular family activity which generated revenue because of the popular children's book.

Crunching the numbers meant she could hold on a little

longer.

Her thoughts turned to Zane. At first he fussed about coming home with her, taking her bed so that she had to sleep on the old sofa she'd purchased at a resale shop on Cherokee Street. But in the end, he caved. Each night when she'd gotten home there was a hot meal on the table and the place was as clean as a Marine barracks.

"Should you be doing all of this?" She'd worried he would cause his wounds to bleed again.

Zane posed like a body builder with his arms in the air, demonstrating his muscles were good as new. There was no crazy talk of Rocco, repeating himself, looking out the window like he expected the Taliban to invade her building. She loved that they could play cards and talk about her new business. Being supportive had always been what Zane was good at. Him offering suggestions made her forget how he could turn on a dime and be the damaged warrior who'd returned from Afghanistan.

"Let's talk about Damien Cruz," he said one night as she did the dishes. If he cooked she cleaned up. "You interested in him?"

The glass she tried to soap slipped from her fingers into the suds, causing a splash on her blue shirt. "Don't be silly. I'm a little out of his league, Zane."

"He doesn't seem to know that. He took you on a date then came to be with you when I got shot. I won't be around forever. Knowing you have someone besides me is important."

Alarm bells went off inside her. Was he slipping back into the PTSD Zane? "I can take care of myself. Besides, I have you and Father Xavier." Sitting the last plate on a dish towel to dry, she wiped her hand on another with embroidery. "Damien has seen my one good dress. One date. One dress." She came to sit with him at the table where he shuffled a deck of cards. He rose up for a quick kiss on his cheek that made him smile. "I love you being here with me. Don't ever leave. Please."

A concerned look covered his face as he stopped shuffling his cards. "As the gospel of Mark teaches: 'For you always have the poor with you, and whenever you want, you can do good for them. But you will not always have me.'" Lifting his eyes to meet his sister's, he sensed he'd frightened her. "Let's play cards. Penny a point."

That conversation left her doubting Zane's mental recovery as his body healed.

Then her thoughts turned to Father Xavier. He hadn't been around to talk to her or even call her on the hotel line. Zane said he'd dropped by to visit him at her apartment, but her brother avoided talking about their conversations. She'd surely see him at The Kitchen when she went to play that night. Maybe her brother would like getting out for a while. The police found his car and gave her a courtesy call to go get it before it got stolen. Parked across the street from her apartment, it meant a few more dollars going out of her pocket but at least she could drive to work. She hoped it all worked out in the end.

♫♬♫

Father Xavier slipped the strap of the apron over his gray head before reaching for the spoon to stir the pot of chili on the stove. The aroma filled the room, causing him to take a deep breath. His helpers arrived early to start the dinner. They now busied with the task of creating peanut butter and jelly sandwiches. Peach and blackberry cobblers cooled on stainless steel counters next to paper plates and bowls donated by the St. Louis Cardinal organization. Once more the priest reminded himself there were a great many good people in the world.

Soon he would have to start begging for more money to run The Kitchen of Hope. Fundraising had never been his strength. Prayer. That's what he was into these days. Lots of it.

Between worrying about a place for the homeless to get at least one decent meal a day, Zane being shot, and Catharina's new business he spent a lot of time on his knees.

Then there was Rocco. He both feared and loved God's dark angel. The night he showed up at the church, simmering with God's wrath coursing through his veins, frightened the priest. Hiding him in the rectory was the only logical solution until Rocco could heal himself. The pain and suffering he appeared to endure was accepted without complaint. Together they prayed. Rocco failed to sleep or eat, only prayed for two days without ceasing, lips constantly moving, the hollow blue eyes rolled upward toward Heaven, sometimes begging for forgiveness, other times thanking God for the pain laid before him.

What had he done to be struck by God's whip of retribution?

Of course, Father Xavier knew of Rocco's activities on behalf of the homeless. There was honor in that. After all, that's what God intended for his angel to do for mankind—protect the innocent, the helpless, the sick, and the goodness of those who couldn't protect themselves. He remembered a conversation with him just that morning.

"Give my message to the Nephilim, Father."

The Nephilim were half human, half angel.

"I know of no such creatures on the Earth since the time of Genesis. You are ill. Rest."

"The Nephilim are everywhere and they depend on me to protect and guide them, Father. Without me, they may fall into sin again. You must speak to Gideon. Warn him to stand firm against those who would influence his loyalty."

Father Xavier paused over the chili pot, ladle suspended in air as he stared into space. He had patted Rocco down with a wet cloth to sooth his burning face.

But the priest had only exhaled a deep sigh and walked away. Nephilim? There were no Nephilim left. God destroyed them with the great flood. Hadn't He? A movement caught his eye, forcing him to turn around and see Gideon and several other friends of his standing in the doorway. All four of them were taller than Rocco's six-two frame. A fleeting thought of asking them to play on the church basketball team after Christmas made him smile and place the ladle on the counter.

"Gideon. Good to see you. Are you well?" Father Xavier walked to greet the men with outstretched hand. He motioned for them to come inside and sit. "Dinner will be ready soon. Coffee is ready. We have a few donations tonight. Have a look if you like. I think maybe there's some gloves and socks this time. Getting cold. An extra pair might come in handy."

Gideon nodded but stood perfectly still as his eyes shifted to the windows that revealed a darkening street. His friends looked clean tonight. But then again they usually were more ragged than dirty. He wasn't sure how they kept clean.

"Something wrong, Gideon?" Father Xavier sensed the giant of a man was nervous, but Gideon only shook his head, moved to a table, and sat down. The priest observed them all turn toward the windows as if waiting for something. "Are you waiting for Zane to arrive?"

"Zane?" Gideon looked interested. "Zane comes tonight?"

"I believe so. He called me this afternoon and said his sister would be bringing him."

The four men began to smile and nod. "She will play for us?"

Father Xavier chuckled. "I'm sure of it. Now get yourself some coffee and—"

"And what of The Watcher, Father?" Gideon's voice changed to deep and foreboding as he narrowed his eyes at the priest. "Has he recovered?"

Looking out the window in hopes of calming himself, the priest sat down next to Gideon. "Yes. He was much better when I left. Do you know what happened to him?"

All four men shook their heads in denial. "Only that God smote him." Gideon's voice lowered as he leaned in near the priest's face. "He will leave us soon."

"Leave? Where?" The priest didn't realize how alarmed his voice sounded. "Why?"

But the four men turned their eyes to two people coming through the door, arm in arm, smiling like kids on a scavenger hunt. One carried a violin case and laughed as the other waved to them. A chill reached up Father Xavier's spine as Gideon turned his eyes back to him. "'For I know the plans I have for you, declares the Lord, plans for welfare and not evil, to give you a future and a hope.' Have you read the book of Jeremiah lately, Father Xavier? Try chapter twenty nine, verse eleven. Do not be afraid. Tell Rocco we remain strong." His eyes went back to Zane and Catharina who approached. "We will follow him when the time comes or we are set free. In the meantime, we will fight at his side."

"Good Lord." Father Xavier shook his head. They were all half delusional, just like every other person on the street. What had Rocco been telling them? Had he convinced them they were part of the ancient group called Nephilim? Did they really believe they were the offspring of fallen angels that had sinned against God?

"Father Xavier." Catharina hugged the priest as he stood. "I've been missing you." She turned to the seated men and smiled. "Brought my violin just for you guys. Any requests?"

Someone from the steam table called for help so she waved, blew them kisses, and left.

It felt like the nights that Catharina served, more homeless arrived. Some were families living at shelters with children. There were the usual mental disorders, substance abusers, lost veterans and the array of down-on-their-luck men. Some would bounce back, others would not. Over a period of months some faces changed, others disappeared. Father Xavier loved them all. He just wanted them to be safe, fed, and warmed from winter's freezing temperatures.

There was so little to offer them, but they were so grateful for whatever they received. The music Catharina brought them continued to enthrall them. Their faces lost the pensive mistrust that haunted so many of them. A few said her gift to them was hope. He would laugh and say, since it was The Kitchen of Hope, it was a good thing.

After dinner, a hush fell over the room, now packed with the lost. Standing room only was a growing problem. No one now left on the nights Catharina came to play.

The room filled with the smells of chili, coffee, body odor, and soiled clothing. Steam frosted the windows from the combination of bodies and the heat put off by a gas stove and a noisy furnace. Little children drew pictures on the moisture-laden windows. Giant happy faces, tic-tac-toe boards, and even a palm tree decorated the glass even as it would drip to a blurred image.

It was time. Catharina knew they were waiting. Father Xavier nodded for her to go as he took her apron. She grabbed a paper towel to clear one of the windows to see into the street.

The streetlight revealed emptiness on the sidewalk until a man walked up and stood staring back at her. She noticed a black car parked near the door with a police officer standing guard.

His lanky frame covered in a warm coat, left him looking lonely as he shoved his hands into the pockets. The night breeze moved his hair that appeared to be peppered with gray. The hollow cheekbones on such a narrow face created a hardness to his smile that he now exhibited. She watched him stroll through the door and unbutton his coat. He looked uncomfortable as he looked around at so much pain and suffering.

She moved to his side. "Mr. Mayor? What are you doing here?"

"In spite of what the news may be saying, I care for all the people of this city. I have been hearing about good things this Kitchen does for the homeless. Thought it was time I found out more. Is that chili I smell?"

Catharina took him to a stool near the end of the steam table and introduced him to the priest. They exchanged pleasantries as she made him a bowl of the thick chili. One piece of blackberry cobbler remained, so she took it too, knowing she'd be giving her piece away.

The mayor took a small polite bite then set it down. "Thank you, Cat. I didn't realize you volunteered here as well as worked at Union Station."

The conversation between the mayor and Damien Cruz came rushing back. If it weren't for the mayor, she may not have been alerted to the possibility she was being romanced out of her apartment. She only smiled as the crowd grew impatient, tapping their feet, then the tops of tables in a rhythmic beat.

The mayor stole a glance outside at the officer looking inside then back at the room full of the unwanted and invisible. "What's going on?"

She smiled reaching for her violin. "I'll show you."

Just as soon as she lifted it up to her shoulder the silence became deafening. From the first stroke, she was lost in the music. Twirling to each note of her melody as it sped up and slowed, she created a magical world where nothing mattered but this one moment in time. A joy filled her. She felt Gideon and Zane lift her to the table so she could stroll down the center, swaying, hopping, and bending backward, then forward. Her black skirt swished over leopard tights, the black studded vest over a purple top. The bracelets and earrings seemed to keep time with the beat as she moved.

The only time she broke her train of thought was when she looked out the window for Rocco. She played harder. Where was he? The thought of his mouth against hers sent her into a frenzy of playing until she felt beads of perspiration form under her clothing. The crowd now clapped to her beat, driving her nearly mad with the desire to play song upon song until she finally knelt with exhaustion on the table next to the mayor.

Applause rocked the room as her brother came to lift her down. She collapsed in his waiting arms, where he offered her a kiss on the top of her head. Laying her hand on the places he'd been shot, Catharina realized they no longer bothered him.

Was that proof how strong he still was? Either way, she thanked God for his recovery.

Zane ruffled her jagged hair with the funny blonde tips. "Awesome, little sister."

The mayor stood, looking stunned. He opened his mouth to speak, but blinked in amazement instead. Turning his eyes to Zane, he was aware at how much bigger he was than Catharina.

"Kragan LaPlante. And you are?"

"Zane Spokane, sir." He forced out his hand and shook the mayor's hand. "Nice to meet you. Mayor, right?"

Kragan nodded then looked at Catharina, resting against her brother's chest, breathing like she'd run a marathon. "You are simply amazing. Your music should be at Powell Hall or the Peabody Opera House. Then there's your dancing." He shook his head and smiled. "I think I'm in love."

Zane laughed. "She gets that a lot around here." His smile faded as he eyed the mayor. "You look familiar. Have we met before?"

The mayor took his eyes off Catharina as he shifted his weight to one leg. Shaking his head, Kragan raised his chin. "No. I don't think so. Did you go to McClure High School or St. Louis University?" In St. Louis that usually was how you introduced yourself.

"Nah. I graduated from downtown then I went into the Marines." He stepped aside, so a helper could take out the trash, and noticed Gideon and his friends watching him.

Catharina took a deep breath and nodded, knowing her time with him was drawing to a close.

"Does your brother volunteer here too?" Kragan already knew everything there was to know about Zane Spokane.

"Yes." She didn't offer any more information.

"Damien Cruz never mentioned you were such an artist with the violin." He enjoyed seeing the guarded look come over her face. "Did you enjoy *The Devil's Trill* at the Fox?"

The talk of music suited Catharina more than talking about Damien Cruz. "One of my favorites." Why she felt so shy around a man like Kragan was understandable, since he was the most powerful man in the city. There was also something else she couldn't put her finger on—his voice, his walk? She wasn't certain.

"Well, we have that in common, Cat. It is also my favorite." The room had emptied out. "I know it's late, but would you like to get a cup of coffee?" He used the smile that usually won over reluctant ladies. "I mean unless you think Damien would mind." Lifting his eyebrows in an anticipation of a rejection did the trick.

"I'll get my coat. And just so you know, Damien and I are not an item."

Kragan helped her on with the faded blue coat. "I'm happy to hear that." His hand lingered a little too long on her shoulder as she faced him. "Very happy."

Chapter 16

he coffee shop turned out to be a diner on Laclede's Landing, down by the Mississippi River. On weekends, gamblers and club hoppers filled the lunch counter stools and booths decked out in a 1950s style. Catharina felt like she'd fallen into the Edward Hopper painting titled *Nighthawks*. The waitress and cook dressed the part, making her feel almost nostalgic for a past she'd never experienced.

"Thank you." Kragan nodded to the young waitress as she sat two pieces of apple pie before them then filled two chunky cups with coffee. "The pie is delicious here." He funncled a piece into his mouth after swirling it in the vanilla ice cream.

Catharina couldn't help but notice how the waitress glared at her from behind the lunch counter. She considered the possibility the mayor was a frequent customer and the waitress might be feeling a little protective. Taking a small bite, it dawned on her that she was sitting with the most powerful politician in St. Louis. The thought clouded the taste of the pie. She smiled to agree, but remained quiet.

Looking over the rim of his cup, Kragan took pleasure in making her feel uncomfortable. "Where did you learn to play the violin?"

This was a safe subject for her. "One of the parishioners of Father Xavier's church took me under her wing when she caught me listening to a Mendelssohn Concerto on PBS." She gave a nervous laugh. "I was an odd duck even then. Most little girls listened to whatever was in vogue at the time, but here I was drooling over the rock stars Mozart and Beethoven." She dared meet Kragan's eyes for a second before lifting her coffee to take a cooled sip. "Probably why I didn't have many friends."

"And the dancing?" He swallowed a second bite of pie.

"Again. Watching PBS. Rock videos. Street dancers." A shrug followed by a scrunched up nose, made her roll her eyes upward.

Kragan chuckled at her making fun of herself. "I think you're enchanting."

Startled, Catharina met his eyes. "You don't even know me." His praise was more than a little nerve wracking. She didn't like it.

"And if I may ask, how did you get the scar on the side of your face?" He cocked his head to examine it closer as she sat her cup down.

She touched the place on the side of her face. It had faded after Rocco touched her, but still remained somewhat visible. The unconscious reflex to pull her hair forward in hopes of hiding it occurred before she could stop herself. "An accident."

Kragan reached out and removed her hand, but continued to hold it. "What kind of accident?"

Catharina pulled her hand free as the memory of being slapped so hard she fell against a heater flashed in her mind. "Just an accident," she whispered, folding her hands in her lap.

The mayor eyed her with admiration. "Maybe that's why your music is so full of passion."

"I'm sorry. What?"

"Your past fuels your present. Those people tonight, for a short time, escaped into another world. A world of beauty and hope." Kragan forced his voice to be calm in spite of feeling a rising need to possess a woman from his past. If she knew who he really was, this moment would not have occurred. "I feel weak from listening and watching you tonight. Thank you."

Catharina couldn't resist smiling. "Thank you, Mr. Mayor."

His laugh caught her off guard. Something familiar surfaced. Good or bad, she wasn't sure, but the need to have a friend washed caution aside.

"You need to start calling me Kragan because I intend for us to become very good friends."

♫ ♫ ♫

Arriving a little earlier than usual at the coffee shop, Catharina fussed over preparing for the mayor's weekly meeting with citizens, followed by the chief of police. The order for pastries included extra sweet rolls and bear claws, hoping the temptation would be too great for anyone who meandered in to chat with Mayor LaPlante. A fire blazed in the fireplace, the smell of coffee permeated the air with soft sounds of Vivaldi playing on the overhead speakers exuded the feeling of warmth.

Lights turned on full brightness shattered the gloom from late November weather. Even so, Catharina lit a few fragrant candles to sit on tables nearest the double doors in hopes the scent of pumpkin would attach itself to a memory as customers entered for their morning caffeine.

The Assistant General Manager, Jeremiah, had come and gone in a hurry, saying the boss would be back today and he needed to make sure everything was as it should be. Nervous activity ran through the staff, much to Catharina's amusement. *You'd think it was the pope coming to visit with the way everyone's acting.* She made sure the bellman got his large cup of coffee. Usually, he enjoyed telling her about the latest ghost he'd seen prowling around Union Station but today he rushed in and out before they could converse.

"Mr. Cruz will expect everyone to be on their game as usual. Gotta go. Hugs!" And he was gone.

Her thoughts turned to Mayor Kragan LaPlante and the night before. Considering the late hour, they didn't linger at the diner. Relieved to be going, she grew concerned as the mayor's driver pulled up in front of her apartment building that he might want to come inside. The eerie quiet that sprang up between them—paired with him taking sidelong glances at her, void of expression—caused Catharina to dread the parting goodnight conversation.

"Beautiful old building," he commented as he walked her to the front doors. "I'll walk you to your apartment if you wish." Smiling down at her, he slipped his hands in his coat pocket.

She realized, now it had been forced. Was she boring him?

"No. Zane may be asleep and voices would just disturb him. He needs his rest. I see his car over there." She sliced her key card through the lock. "Thanks for the pie and coffee, Kragan. And thanks for stopping by The Kitchen tonight. It's nice to know people in power really care about the down-and-out. I've been there and it means everything." She could feel her face flush and wondered if he noticed.

"I will see you in the morning, Cat. I hear your coffee is the best in St. Louis."

The mayor waited until she was inside and on the staircase before returning to his car. Feeling his eyes on her, Catharina turned to lift her hand in farewell, noticing his eyes had grown narrow along with the smile that seconds earlier tricked her into thinking he might be one of the good guys. A chill surfaced as she ran up the stairs to the landing. Daring to look back again, she could see his car pulling away from the curb.

♫ ♬ ♫

Several people entered the coffee shop to stand with awkward expectations as they strolled around with their hands in their pockets, looking at the train set behind the glass enclosure. Not bothering to remove their scarves or gloves, they appeared to be waiting. With a glance to the clock, Catharina realized the mayor was fifteen minutes late. She reasoned such a busy man probably ran into problems at city hall.

The thought evaporated, seeing him stroll in as he removed his gray overcoat and blue scarf tossing it on one of the wing-back chairs near the fire. He shivered and rubbed his hands together as his gaze locked onto Catharina while she served a hotel customer. She offered him a smile and lifted an empty cup in greeting. He looked around to see if anyone waited for him. The two near the train set began to watch him with reserve.

"How do you like your coffee, Mr. Mayor?" She stretched out the title with a teasing smile.

"Black. Strong. Hot." He approached the counter and leaned over to watch her. "Looks like I might have some visitors. I was hoping no one would show." He rubbed his red ears, stinging from the cold.

Handing him a large coffee in a ceramic mug with a picture of Union Station on the side, she moved to the pastry display. "Why is that?"

He grinned. "I'm a little shy." This made Catharina laugh, causing an echo. She covered her mouth in embarrassment. "I guess that is rather ridiculous, isn't it?" he asked.

"The only thing that is ridiculous is you standing here when people clearly have come to discuss a problem." A movement nearby caused her to look up.

Damien Cruz loomed behind them, standing like he always did, omnipotent and judgmental. He had pushed back his suit coat with hands resting on his hips. The dark hair fell slightly down his forehead which made his eyes bluer than Catharina remembered. His cheekbones appeared to be a hollow as if he'd lost weight. The arched eyebrow showed his condescension as he looked down his nose at the mayor.

Kragan turned in slow motion and leaned back against the counter in a purposeful snub. "Good to see you, Damien. I understand you've been out of town. Missed a lovely performance—" His glanced back at Catharina for only a second before he grinned. "—by Cat last night at The Kitchen." He laid his hand over his heart. "I'm not sure I'll ever be the same."

Damien pushed up beside him. "That certainly would be an improvement, Kragan."

Concentration failed Catharina as a man walked into the shop, carrying a bouquet of roses so large she couldn't see his face. He sat them on the counter, careful not to tip them over. It was Jesse, the bellman who the mayor quickly tipped.

She felt her jaw drop open at the burst of red before her.

"For you, Miss Spokane." Kragan bowed then let his eyes caress her face. "Last night was a new beginning for me, Cat. I just wanted to say thank you." His smile lifted only one corner of his mouth, making it look more like a snarl.

With a nervous hand lifting to her throat, she felt her face grow heated. No one had ever sent her flowers. Shifting her eyes to Damien, she expected him to look surprised as well, but instead he looked like death warmed over, in a murderous kind of way. Anger brewed beneath his blue eyes that suddenly turned a glassy gray. His face grew a little darker beneath his eyes, reminding her of a Watcher named Rocco living in the hidden corners of Union Station.

"They're beautiful, Kragan. I don't know what to say." She fingered the flowers, forcing her eyes away from Damien. Even though the trust had shattered, seeing him appear again, helped her realize she'd missed him. He and Rocco were Ying and Yang, dark and light. Both were affecting the common sense she wore like a suit of armor.

The mayor leaned toward her, casting a fleeting glance at the two people waiting to speak to him. "Say you'll have dinner with me tonight."

"I—I don't know. I work until six and then—"

"We'll dine here at the station."

"I won't be dressed for dinner."

"There's a Caribbean Rib place in the station mall. Then I'll take you home." The words were followed by a coy expression that suggested he wouldn't be leaving this time. "I won't take 'no' for an answer."

"My brother—"

Kragan started to frown. "He's a big boy. I'm sure he wouldn't want you to miss out on an evening out."

Catharina wondered if he meant an evening out with the mayor. With Damien prowling closer each second, she worried angry words would begin and her coffee shop would take on the appearance of a soap opera.

"If I can, Kragan," she murmured.

He pulled himself up erect and turned to Damien, slapping him on the back as if he'd won a victory. "And that, Damien, is how you win the heart of a beautiful lady."

The two visitors finally got enough courage to approach. "Mr. Mayor?"

Kragan made a surprised expression with his eyes as if pleased to see someone before guiding them to a nearby table.

Moving with the grace of a stealthy panther, Damien stepped in closer to the counter to finger the roses. When he lifted his eyes to meet Catharina's, the realization she'd no longer felt the need to depend on him took him by surprise. Even her stance appeared stubborn and impatient, as she glared at him with animosity.

"I dropped by to make sure the mayor stopped in and hadn't blown me off because I no longer let him take up my tables in the restaurant." He looked over his shoulder at Kragan then back at Catharina. "I see now that may have been a mistake." He lifted one of the roses out of the silver vase and broke off the stem only to place it in his lapel. "How is Zane?"

"Better."

She turned to wipe a spill from the coffee spigot dripping on the counter. Having to stare into his luminesce blue eyes unsettled her ability to be angry at his betrayal. Knowing he had romanced her with dinner and music in hopes of securing her support to purchase the Essmalory Building grated against not only her pride, but her heart.

Just once I'd like to meet a man who likes me just the way I am. I should have known I wasn't good enough for the high and mighty Damien Cruz.

"I see that Mayor LaPlante has been smitten with your music. I gather he dropped in The Kitchen of Hope last night." His British accent seemed a little thicker and raspier, like he'd been smoking a pack of cigarettes a day. "Remember, he is a wolf in sheep's clothing, Cat."

Throwing down her rag, she rubbed her hands against an already soiled apron. Taking quick steps to the counter she leaned across to meet Damien's eyes. "I've spent my whole life knowing men like you." She nodded toward the mayor. "And him too, I imagine. I don't need you to remind me of that. After all, you're the one trying to romance me out of my home."

Damien straightened. "I am doing no such thing." He sounded insulted or wounded, she couldn't decide which. "We need to talk about this."

"I'm done talking to you. I appreciate what you've done for Zane and for me, but—" For some reason her bottom lip trembled. A flood of tears wanted to burst forth, but she sucked them back by raising up her chin. "I have to get back to work, Mr.

Cruz."

Refusing to use his first name appeared to be the ice water thrown in his face that forced him to turn on his heels and storm into the corridor without looking back.

Catharina wanted him to look back. Wanted him to be hurt. Why she even cared bothered that common sense factor again. Now he could figure out she knew about his plans to take over the Essmalory. What would he do with it? Tear it down and put up a glass and steel building with absolutely no character? Where would the people who lived there go? They wouldn't be able to afford living downtown. Neither would she for that matter.

People drifted in and out for the next few hours, visiting with the mayor. The police chief arrived and they decided to take lunch outside of Union Station. She was relieved to see them go. As Kragan left he held up six fingers, indicating when he expected her to meet him. She nodded but still wasn't sure about keeping the dinner date.

During a lull, she strolled to the wall of windows that looked out into the Grand Hall. She watched her brother top the stairs and stretch out his hand toward Damien. There was something familiar about the two of them standing there like combat buddies. Maybe it was because they had both been soldiers that easiness always appeared to exist between them. Zane had lost the hunched shoulders, standing tall in front of Damien. When both of them, without warning, turned their eyes to fall on her, Catharina knew she had been the topic of conversation.

Chapter 17

atharina's new assistant needed to study for an exam the following day so she was given the night off. The opportunity to wiggle out of a dinner date with the mayor didn't seem to set very well with him when he called at 5:30. The tightness in his voice revealed a new side to him Catharina already suspected.

"I'm not used to being stood up, Catharina."

Probably aren't used to working hard for a living either, she mused. "I'm really sorry. I don't have any other options." The truth being she just didn't feel like being social with a man so visible in the public's eye and was relieved to be free to go home, to soak her aching feet, sounded like Nirvana.

Customers continued to wander in until eight—some came for souvenir coffee mugs or tee shirts and others wanted to push the big red button to make the electric train speed around its artificial environment. Dimming the lights before she latched the double doors warned off any further distractions. By the time she finished cleaning up and preparing for the next day, the railroad clock struck nine.

The tips weren't that good today so she decided to walk home. It would be well lighted until she reached her block. The buses stopped coming an hour ago and cabs would be unavailable with the Blues playing tonight. Besides, she couldn't afford one with Zane's medical bills. She still wasn't sure how much the VA would cover.

The thought occurred to her that she might need a lawyer if he got into trouble again. She tried to call Zane to come get her, but it went to voice mail.

"'Then the angel of the lord went ahead and stood in a narrow place, where there was no way to turn either to the right or to the left.' Numbers 22."

Other than Zane's words being a little cryptic and crazy, his voice sounded strong. One minute she believed he was on the track to recovery then he spouted Bible verses.

By the time she'd reached her block, the cold wind had pierced her thin coat. The canyon of skyscrapers caused tunnels of November air to slam against her chest. Pausing to pull her hat down over her forehead then standing her collar on end did little to beat off the cold. She felt her nose start to run and tears sting her cheeks, she guessed would be the color of ripe cherries by the time she got home.

"What do we have here?" A scruffy looking man of undetermined age had run across the street with his hands in his coat pocket. Ignoring him, Catharina picked up the pace. She was close to the door of her building. "Got any change? I haven't eaten in a week."

That was the button to touch with her. What if it were Zane who was hungry or Gideon and his buddies? "Sure. Just a minute." She stopped to dig in her purse, failing to see the man look around her and nod. "Here. Will five dollars help?" Tip money. She extended her hand and noticed it trembled from the cold. Should she give him more? Even as she offered the money, she began to step toward the door, feeling uncomfortable with him snatching the money like a hungry alligator. "Night."

She took her key card out of her pocket, hesitating for only a second, hand suspended over the lock, when she saw other shadows lunge into the doorway. The first man grabbed her card but she held on, only to feel the backhand of his slap. Falling against the brick, she heard the safety lock click then push open.

On some subconscious level, Catharina realized there were five or six men. They wore ski masks and black hoodies. The one she'd given the money grabbed her by her collar to drag her inside. Twisting to be released only managed to tighten his grip. When she opened her mouth to scream, a hand covered her face, before shoving her into a wall. Falling to the floor, Catharina became aware of guns at their sides. One of the men took aim at the lights, quickly vanquishing any ability to see other than the street halos from outside.

"Is that her?" The ghetto accent sounded deep and ominous as the first man yanked her to wobbly feet. As she staggered, he pulled a picture from his pocket, eyed it, then her. His open mouth, embedded with one gold tooth in the middle of his crooked smile, sent a chilling warning that forced her to wobble toward the stairs.

Somewhere she heard doors opening from above. Other tenants would hear the commotion. Just as she tried to call out a warning, one of the men grabbed her hair, throwing her to the floor. When she crab crawled backward, he stomped on her fingers so hard no amount of prevention could stop her from screaming. Another man jerked her up, took his gun, and held it to her shoulder. The smell of gunpowder, and the realization that she'd never play the violin again, overpowered the deafening noise that pounded her eardrums when he pulled the trigger.

Looking down, she saw that black streaks covered her coat. In shock, she could only look up into the dark eyes of one of the men as he pointed the gun at her kneecap. "No more dancing for you."

"Just do it," ordered the first man who had started the invasion. "We got a lot to do here." He turned around to look at his followers. "Where's Ty?" The others stopped to let their eyes adjust to the dark. Several shrugs followed as a shadow hurled over the second floor bannister followed by a loud thump hitting the floor. "What the hell was that?"

The leader ran to the large dark object on the floor and jumped back then spun around with his gun drawn. "It's Ty. He's dead."

The ding of the elevator door drew their attention as Catharina's eyes focused on the slow motion of the wood doors opening. The light from inside revealed an ornate sword lying on the floor. They all moved as one as they approached the small opening to retrieve the three foot blade with ornate details tipped in the color of spilled blood.

"Damn. This thing is heavy." Reaching in to retrieve the weapon, the leader's voice came out louder than he intended. He looked back at the body on the floor. "What happened to Ty?"

A tall shadow emerged from behind Ty's body. The movement of his limbs appeared relaxed but prepared to do whatever it took to rid the lobby of these men. "I killed him." Hearing the raspy voice of Rocco gave Catharina hope that she'd survive. "Now I'm going to kill you." He withdrew another sword that caught the outside light momentarily, forcing the remaining men to stand back.

The thug with the sword put both hands on it after he shoved his gun into his coat pocket. "All right Obi-Wan, let's see what ya got." He swung the sword around like a kindergartener twirling a pipe twice his size, only to drop it. The clang of metal hitting the marble floor stopped him in his tracks. "Pretty hard to win against four with a sword, when we all got guns that will blow your fool head plum off."

For the first time, The Watcher lifted his chin and nodded behind them. "That's why I brought help." His hand stretched toward the sword as it flew into his grasp.

The masked men jumped around in panic like startled rattlesnakes. Rocco lifted his sword to the front of his face, speaking something in Latin. Catharina couldn't translate, but she knew the attackers were doomed.

She recognized Zane immediately, but not the garb of leather and wool he wore. He dressed like something from a video game. A hood covered his head with a little of his broad forehead showing beside the point that hung down nearly to his nose. Even in the darkness, she recognized the murderous rage brewing inside him. Another man stepped forward, then another.

They were dressed in similar fashion and were nearly seven feet tall. Gideon. He was Nephillian, she now knew. What that meant would need to be addressed later.

Several residents edged down the steps in hopes of helping her, but Rocco waved them back.

"And it begins." His voice sounded like the whir of many

blades as he spun around to slice off the hand of the first man who pulled a gun. They began to back toward the door until they turned to leave and found another hooded vigilante blocking their retreat. Crashing into each other they began shooting wildly. The bullets ricocheted time and time again off the blades held up to protect Catharina, who watched in horror, knowing blood would soon cover the floors of the Essmalory.

The bullets, miraculously bounced back to hit their owners. She heard the audible clicks of empty weapons as Rocco and his followers formed a wall to stand before them. "Never come back or God will never show mercy to your miserable souls when I send you to hell."

The door opened by the hand of one of Rocco's followers and the thugs spilled into the night like frightened bats surprised by an intrusion into their domain. Blood flowed in rivulets as they escaped. The severed hand of the first man remained on the floor. The door sentinel nodded to Rocco before turning his back to the door as if making sure the building remained secure.

For a moment the only sound in the lobby of the Essmalory was the sobs of pain coming from Catharina. She watched the men continue to stand like marble statues, staring out into the night. Not until Rocco spun around to look at her did the spell break. He shoved his sword under his cloak, as did the others. Both he and Zane rushed to her side. The others began to fade back into the darkness as sirens sounded in the distance.

"We don't have much time." Rocco lifted Catharina up into his arms as she glared at him through a haze of pain. Starting up the stairs, she watched Zane hurry past them, reassuring the few onlookers to return to their apartments. He sounded so normal and confident. They didn't need to be told twice as Rocco topped the stairs.

"Lay her down on the bed, Rocco." Zane's voice sounded concerned but not frantic.

Catharina became aware that her brother was cutting off her coat, the only coat she owned. For a second that became her major concern.

Zane sucked in his breath after he ripped open her blouse. She heard him say something about a hole in her shoulder.

Blood flowed down her chest as she lifted her hand that usually held her violin. Tears started again as she saw the broken bones, twisted with a macabre distortion.

Bending over her, Rocco smiled with such warmth and love, she wondered for a second if she hadn't died. A glow radiated from his body as he pushed back his hood. He brushed her hair out of her eyes. Lifting his hands out to his sides, palms up, he began to speak in a tongue that burned her ears. Slapping his hands together then rubbing them vigorously until they looked like flames of fire, Rocco closed his eyes and continued what Catharina imagined was a prayer.

"Have no fear, Catharina. The pain will soon disappear."

With his words, he laid his hands, that appeared to be full of flashing lights, upon her shoulder. The first touch forced her back to arch then relax as a spear of warmth penetrated her upper body then edged down into her torso and her arms. When the light hit her hands, Catharina lifted them to watch the crumbled bones straighten to their original shape. Pain evaporated as joy spread through her psyche.

Zane stood on the opposite side of the bed. He took the once wounded fingers in his and kissed them. His eyes went to Rocco and he nodded his thanks even as sirens drew near. Looking at the door, a flash of concern crossed his face.

"Not to worry." Rocco took out his sword, laying it across Catharina's body. In a split second the blood evaporated into the steel, causing the red hilt of the sword to glow for a few seconds before fading back to dullness.

A commotion started in the hall as footsteps could be heard, followed by running up the steps, followed by anxious voices.

"Rocco," Catharina whispered as she reached out to him. "You must go. You can't let them find you here."

Bending down inches from her face, Rocco smiled with the kindness of a patient father. "They will not find me. Rest. I will protect your brother. Never fear." He straightened, looking over at Zane. "It's time my friend."

♫♬♫

Two squad cars arrived with an ambulance close behind. The 911 call sounded like any other emergency call, frantic voices and all. It wasn't until they entered the lobby that it became obvious this crime scene bore the markings of The Watcher. Several detectives arrived with a crime scene crew not far behind.

"What a mess," Detective Jacobs uttered as he walked around the lobby. Several tenants stood to the side, answering questions for the police officers. Flashing red lights made strobes of light dance across the walls and floor. "What the hell happened here?"

An officer came up beside the detective only to nod toward the tenants. "Said looked like a half dozen hooded guys. But you never know. They were scared to death. Said another tenant, a woman, got roughed up."

Jacobs looked around to see if there was another body. "Where is she now?"

"Said a couple of guys in hoods carried her up the stairs. These two tried to come down and help but were waved off as the fight started. Wasn't sure if they were part of the mayhem. Said she looked pretty bad. Thought they saw blood."

The detective rubbed his tired eyes after removing his black glasses. Pinching the bridge of his nose, he closed his eyes to envision what must have happened. "Where is she now?"

"Second floor apartment." The officer looked down at his notes before telling him the number. "A Ms. Catharina Spokane."

"Spokane?" Jacobs shoved his glasses back into place and took the steps two at a time. "I'll need a couple of officers up here," he called back as he topped the stairs. Knocking on the door with his fist, the detective identified himself. "Detective Jacobs. Police. Open up."

The sound of locks unbolting and a security chain being released brought the impulse to rest his hand on his holstered weapon. With a sudden jerk, the door flew open, and a tall man stood in the doorway with an angry expression on his face.

"Mr. Cruz?" The shocked detective took a step back as the man before him arched his eyebrow in a show of contempt.

Chapter 18

etective Jacobs. Come in, please." Damien stood aside so the detective could enter but he refused to let anyone else by—holding up his hand to keep the others out. The door remained open.

The detective nodded as he slipped past Damien. He eyed the hotel manager with skepticism before turning his attention to the woman pushing herself up in the bed. Her brother sat beside her, stroking her hand.

"Are you all right, Ms. Spokane? The other tenants seem to think you were injured?" Jacobs turned back to the officer in the door and ordered him to get a paramedic. "You don't look so good."

With slurred speech, she touched her shoulder now covered in a white sweater. She looked at her crippled hand to find it healed. "I'm fine. I think they hit me."

"The police need to increase their presence on this street, detective," Damien growled through tightly clenched teeth.

"Damien?" It was Catharina, her voice small and confused. "What are you—"

Zane leaned in to kiss her forehead. "Remember he came over to play cards with me until you got home." Stroking the side of her head then patting her once-wounded shoulder gave him the appearance of a concerned big brother.

The detective watched Catharina's forehead pinch in bewilderment. "So you two were here when the ruckus started downstairs?" Jacobs took out his small tablet and pen from one of his deep pockets. "Did you go to assist your sister, Mr. Spokane?"

He shook his head then rolled his eyes up to the ceiling in a gesture meant to be to self-loathing. "No. I played the radio so loud I couldn't hear a thing." Resting his palm against Catharina's face, he offered a smile. "I'm so sorry, sis."

The paramedics pushed in and Zane rose to let them have a look. They checked her out and found only a bump on the back of her head. "I hit the wall when they shoved me." Her eyes went to Damien, standing stiff and sinister with his hands on his hips as if ready to inspect his troops.

"I'm sorry to ask you, Ms. Spokane, but can you give us a description of the men who attacked you?" Detective Jacobs watched her eyes narrow, as if in deep contemplation. "The other tenants said someone else showed up to fight them off. What can you tell me about that?" His pencil seemed suspended in the air, as if waiting for some revelation as to the events that had transpired.

Catharina rubbed her shoulder then looked at her hands, turning them palm up and down and wiggling her fingers. "Yes. I thought it was one of my neighbors who brought me up."

The detective eyed her as if observing Pinocchio telling a lie. He focused on her button nose, waiting for it to extend over the edge of the bed. "Could it have been The Watcher, Ms. Spokane? One of the tenants said they may have been wearing a hood." Shoving his hands into his coat pockets, the detective could feel his mouth begin to frown. "By the looks of the lobby, I'd say the intruders got the worse of it. We'll be running DNA to try and get a match. Could take a while so any information you have would be most appreciated."

Damien stepped forward to divert the detective's eyes. "I think tomorrow will be soon enough to interrogate, Ms. Spokane, Detective." He dismissed him by walking to the door and pushing it open wide enough to bang against the door frame.

"Just doing my job, Mr. Cruz. I want to get this all down while it's still fresh in her mind." The detective inhaled a deep breath and took stock of the room. There actually were cards on the table and a radio playing in the kitchen. "I'll only be a few more minutes."

"Absolutely not," Damien demanded with the edge of

contempt in his voice. "Ms. Spokane is a personal friend of the mayor. I'm sure if you call him, he'll agree this can wait."

Again the raised eyebrow that made the detective feel as if he'd been dismissed like a servant from Downtown Abbey.

The detective walked to the side of the bed as the paramedic closed up his bag and moved away. "I'm glad you're all right, Ms. Spokane. I'll be around tomorrow if that's okay." She nodded as her eyes went to Damien for what looked like approval. "We'll get to the bottom of this. In the meantime, we'll beef up patrols in the area."

"A little late for that, Detective Jacobs," Damien said, lifting his palm toward the door as he appeared to grit his teeth.

"Yes. Well, the department has its hands full these days." Jacobs moved toward the door and paused, looking Damien straight in the eye. "I don't guess you have anything to say about all of this, Mr. Cruz?"

Damien jerked his chin up to make a point of looking down his nose at the detective. "I do not."

"Good thing the Spokanes have you showing up in their hour of need."

"Good night, Detective Jacobs." Damien closed the door a little too quickly as the detective stepped over the threshold into the hall.

The police officer grimaced at the rudeness of the mighty Damien Cruz. The detective smirked as he looked around him then over the bannister.

"Think they know more than they're saying, detective?"

"Definitely."

"Should I call the mayor?"

"Not until I have more information. Seems to me that our coffee shop girl has friends in high places." He looked back at the closed door and wondered about the conversation that might be taking place inside Catharina's apartment. "I would bet money that brother of hers has a sword and a hooded cloak lying around some place. Better get a search warrant. Post an officer downstairs in case one of them decides to get rid of anything suspicious. I don't believe in the coincidence that Mr. Cruz and Zane Spokane are all that chummy. Talk about oil and water."

The detective looked around him one more time, in hopes of finding evidence to connect the dots. He didn't.

♫ ♫ ♫

Catharina paused just inside the double glass doors after flipping on the lights in her coffee shop. A quick glance at the clock said 5:30. She'd been awake since 4:00 when the sound of a door closing startled her into a wakefulness that shoved any thoughts of sleep away for good. Zane slept peacefully on the couch across the room. Someone else had been there. Who? The memory of someone sitting next to her in the winged-back chair, pulled close, as if to protect and defend, punctured any ability to make sense of the night before.

The only way to clear her head would be to work hard and maybe her joggled brain would start fitting together the mystery surrounding Damien Cruz and her brother's sudden friendship. She didn't like puzzles. They were impossible for her as a kid. One of her teachers referred her for testing, with the thought she might have some kind of learning disability. Having never owned any puzzles or been given much a chance to play, she'd become an observer to fit in.

"Let me help you set up for the day, Cat." Catharina jumped two steps away as Damien's voice came from behind her. She hadn't heard him come in. "I didn't mean to frighten you. I'm surprised to see you. I told Zane I'd take care of things if you wanted to stay home."

With a brisk escape behind the counter, she slipped on her apron and turned on three coffee machines. "Yes. He lectured me on the drive over how I should not overdue it."

When Damien didn't respond, she turned to see him watching her with such scrutiny, that the feeling of being naked in his eyes made her feel flushed. The dark shadows above his hallow cheekbones, gave the blue eyes a luminesce she'd seen in Rocco. Frightened at their penetration, but hypnotized by their beauty, she trembled. She grabbed hold of the granite countertop for support.

"Damien?" Saying the name was meant to sound

confrontational but ended up a whispered prayer. "I—I don't understand." She began to rub her forehead, aware that Damien had moved to join her behind the counter. Feeling his large hands slip behind her back, the fighting instinct took over and she jumped back. Her breath came in gasps. "No. Tell me right now what you are up to, Damien Cruz."

He eyed her very much like a hawk might examine a piece of freshly caught carrion. "Maybe you should first tell me what you're talking about. And why on earth would you walk home alone? I thought you were smarter than that. From now on I'll have a car waiting for you after you close."

She fired back with a growl. "I don't need your charity. Zane and I don't need you. So just stay out of our lives. You thought your feeble attempt at romancing me with dinner and music could get you in my good graces." She swallowed hard, then with an effort to look tough she folded her arms across her chest.

A narrow smile began to spread across his wide mouth that drew Catharina's eyes. "And why, pray tell, would I do that?" The eyebrow began to arch in anticipation of an exaggerated explanation.

"I know you want the Essmalory Building. None of us will sell so you thought I could be the first domino in the ultimate fall of resistance."

"You certainly give yourself credit for a great deal of influence over the residents of the Essmalory." His smile now grew thin and his eyes icy. "Did the mayor tell you that on your date last night? And why didn't he bring you home? He loves showing off his chauffeured sedan to babes in the woods, such as yourself."

She dropped her hands to her waist. "Not that it's any of your business, but I canceled. By the time I got out of here, the buses had stopped and all the cabs were at the Scottrade Center for a Blues game. Even you should know that." Something came over Damien as he appeared to pull back his shoulders and cock his head in surprise. "I tried to call Zane but he wasn't answering his phone." She stepped closer and spoke through her teeth. "I guess we both know why, don't we? You are somehow connected to this whole Watcher business." He remained quiet as she realized how close her body was to his. Looking up into his eyes, she saw that his gaze had softened.

Without warning, his hand took hers and he lifted it to his lips but stopped and examined her fingers as if looking for defects. The words '*Have no fear, Catharina,*' began to echo in her brain. Terrified at the thoughts rushing into her head, she stepped back, pulling her hand from his. She continued to stare at him in amazement.

"I think you should go." In spite of being unsure of the words coming out of her mouth, she managed to look toward the door in a motion of dismissal.

The pastry delivery man entered and carried his boxes to the counter then looked from Damien to Catharina. "Sign here."

Catharina complied with a quick signature to hurry him out and to his next delivery.

"I want to explain about the Essmalory, Cat." Damien cut her off as she tried to walk past him. "I'm not sure what you think you know, but it isn't nearly as bad as you imagine."

The nearness of his body for some reason forced Catharina to look at his shoulders and chest, wondering if they would glow like Rocco's. Was he one of The Watcher's followers? It would be just like a powerful man to look for something to intimidate others.

"I can imagine a lot of things, Damien."

"I have made an offer to buy the Essmalory."

A huffed breath of disapproval escaped her mouth as she pushed him aside with some effort. She began to wipe down the small tables so hard, Damien imagined the shine coming off with each swipe. "He came to me. Not the other way around."

She pretended to ignore the sound of his voice, which forced Damien to approach her with impatience. Covering her hand with his caused a sudden jolt to his shoulder making him jerk free of her touch.

Catharina felt it too. With a hand flat against the cool surface of the marble topped table, she raised her eyes to meet Damien's. "I. Don't. Believe. You." Something in his blue eyes revealed wounds, very much like she saw in her brother. "What are you trying to do to me?"

Even now, standing in his presence gave her an urge to cave to any request he suggested. Anything. Everything. Just to be with him. Hadn't she felt the same way with Rocco? Was she losing her mind?

The first customers wandered in, looking around in awe at the surroundings then to the menu board.

She brushed past him, but Damien reached out and caught her arm. "I have a proposition for you, Cat."

Jerking her arm free, she steeled her resolve to have mind over heart. "I just bet you do. I've got customers."

Greeting the hotel guests, she glanced over to see Damien storming out into the corridor then out into the Grand Hall.

♪♬♪

Kragan hurled his coffee cup across his office where it slammed into the wall. The sound of shattered ceramic brought his secretary to peek in, but she slinked back out as he leveled a dangerous glare her way. It was too early for a gin and tonic, but he poured one anyway. The voice of some detective still rattled around in his head after a brief phone call.

"Mr. Mayor, this is Detective Jacobs from Metro."

Kragan pinched the phone between his ear and shoulder as he reached for his cardinal mug with one hand and turned on the computer with the other. "Yes, Detective. How can I help you?"

"Are you acquainted with a Ms. Catharina Spokane?" The detective's voice sounded like he might be reading it off a list of some kind.

"Yes. She runs the coffee shop where I have my weekly meetings for the Meet and Greet. We were introduced recently by the Union Station owner." Kragan felt pleasure in knowing no one could see his smile as he moved to the window to look down at the street below. In the distance, he could see Union Station. "What's up?"

"Do you mean Mr. Cruz?" The detective sounded less than engaged.

The rattle of paper being shuffled in the background caused the mayor to bite back his condescension. "Yes. Damien Cruz. Is there a problem?"

"Ms. Spokane was attacked last night at her apartment building."

"Good God! Is she all right?" Kragan took a slow sip of his coffee without taking his eyes from a minivan that had just slammed into a taxi cab.

"Yes. Got a little roughed up, but didn't need any medical attention."

Kragan turned back to his desk to set the cup down then switched the phone to his other ear. "Explain." The mayor felt his body stiffen and his teeth clench, listening to the events of the previous evening. "And you say this character…The Watcher, was it…might have been involved?"

"Looks that way. One dead. Also a lone severed hand. We were able to run the prints however, and the guy has a long history of run-ins with the law. No sign of him yet. Hospitals are on alert. The others are still no shows. With the amount of casings found at the scene I'm sure it's only a matter of time. In the meantime, we have a search warrant for the Spokane apartment."

That news intrigued him. What did the detective think he would find? "And you say Mr. Cruz was with the Spokanes?"

"Apparently had been with the brother all evening playing cards. It checks out. Neighbors thought they saw someone else come to the woman's rescue, but it was dark and they were all pretty shook up. Witnesses aren't good witnesses if you know what I mean, Mr. Mayor. Cruz and the brother managed to get her inside. Didn't want the woman questioned. Insisted you would agree." Jacobs paused for a few seconds, as if he might be insinuating the mayor might be involved. "You being a personal friend."

"Yes. Well, thank you, Detective. I appreciate the heads up. We need to get to the bottom of this. It's affecting the whole city. Let me know if there is anything new you discover."

Before the detective could respond, the mayor hung up and threw his coffee cup. A brown trail of spots now led across the carpet, ending at the wall beneath shards of ceramic. Snatching up the phone he hit the intercom button.

"Get me the chief of police."

Chapter 19

The day felt longer than most. Exhausted and burdened with the memory of being attacked, Catharina promised Father Xavier she'd be careful in going to The Kitchen of Hope. With sore muscles and a headache, she longed to go home, but knew there would be a mess to clean up, since the police served a search warrant. The priest made sure Zane behaved himself during the invasive show of mistrust. An underlying fear of something being found that would implicate her brother or Rocco haunted Catharina throughout the day. With Rocco's intervention the night before, serving the poor would be by the grace bestowed upon her by powers she couldn't begin to understand. The people of the street needed her as much as she needed to perform for them.

Slipping on her gloves as she backed through the front doors of the hotel, one of the curbside valets greeted her and asked about her day. A thumbs up was all she could manage. Sometimes he would tell her how much longer it would be for the bus to arrive or could he get her a cab. Tonight, he nodded toward the curb where a black Mercedes waited. A spiral of exhaust lifted into the cold night air as Damien Cruz exited the driver's side and joined her.

"There's time to go home and change if you like." His overcoat pulled open as his hands slipped into the side pockets. Dark hair fell across his forehead when the breeze caught it, adding a layer of unruliness usually absent from his well-groomed appearance. A five o'clock shadow added a hardness to an already tight jaw line. Opening the passenger door, he waited as if daring her to refuse. "I promised Zane."

She caved with a shrug as she slipped inside the warm car with the heated seats. The smell of leather and the familiar music of Beethoven filled her senses. Damien got behind the wheel and extended his hand to release the parking break when Catharina reached out to lay her hand atop his. The slow turn of his head toward her caused her to squeeze his fingers.

"I'm sorry." The forgiveness in his eyes was almost too much to accept. "You have asked nothing of us. Nothing. I don't understand why you would help us. Only Father Xavier ever has taken an interest in Zane and me. Clearly, I have trust issues."

Catharina started to remove her hand when Damien turned his palm up and waited for her to continue touching him. In the darkness, he looked changed. Although he dressed in an expensive suit and overcoat and drove a luxury car, the night couldn't hide a menacing undertone that warned her to tread lightly.

"Father Xavier has taken an interest in me as well. I will not forget it. We are more alike than you know."

"Was I shot last night or did I imagine that? I know you did not carry me to the apartment. It was The Watcher." When he didn't answer, she pounced. "If we are to have any kind of relationship, Damien, I need answers."

He withdrew to place both hands on the wheel then adjusted the rearview mirror. "A bump on the head can make us believe impossible things."

A sigh drew his eyes back to her. "You stayed with us last night to make sure we were all right? To make sure Zane didn't go looking for those men." She paused to see if he would comment. When he didn't, she continued. "I thought Zane was one of the men with The Watcher."

"Your brother is a good man. You're all he has. I thought it best I stay for a while." He turned to look back at her just as she leaned over and kissed him on the cheek.

"Thank you. I'll be more careful." She couldn't pull herself back. The touch of his breath on her lips and the smell of his essence grew intoxicating. Was it incense? "Can we talk about the Essmalory? Later?"

He nodded, before letting a smile turn up one corner of his mouth.

♫ ♫ ♫

Kragan watched Catharina leave Union Station with Damien. A rush of anger, mingled with jealousy, surfaced as they drove away in the Mercedes. He pushed a button on his phone and waited. When a male voice answered, he gave his instructions.

"Serve that search warrant now at Union Station. Let me know when you arrive." Clicking off, he made one final call to Morgan Knox. "Go now. It won't take him long." Before she could refuse, he hung up.

Leaning back against the seat, the mayor smiled before glancing at his watch.

"Shall we go, Mr. Mayor?" The driver addressed him by looking into the rearview mirror.

With a heavy exhale, Kragan patted the man on the shoulder. "Sure. Just drive around for another twenty minutes or so before you head to that dump of a kitchen. I don't want to be there any longer than I have to. With any luck, I'll get to enjoy the show without having to try any of that garbage served to the pathetic moochers living on the streets."

♫ ♫ ♫

Hearing about the attack on Catharina caused a lot of commotion among the people who had grown to love her at The Kitchen of Hope. Several mothers rushed up to her with hugs. The bombardment of questions as to her well-being helped chase the uncertainty to her subconscious. Father Xavier served meatloaf with a side of mashed potatoes to the line of men passing before him. He sent her a smile and winked at seeing Damien standing at her elbow. Zane stood shoulder to shoulder with him, teasing the little kids as they came through the line. She knew they would get larger portions to chase off hungry bellies. Their sweet smiles at seeing him softened her heart enough to breathe as if all was right in the world.

"Big crowd. Think it's the food?" Damien arched an eyebrow as he helped her remove the leather jacket that looked like it had been designed for a man twice her size. When she cocked her head to look up at him, a smirk toyed with the corner of his mouth, making his eyes narrow. "Cat, if you need to make a little extra cash—"

"We'll manage," she interrupted then bit her bottom lip.

He waited patiently, in spite of raising his chin so he could look down his nose at her.

"I did it again didn't I?" This time she touched his arm, feeling it flex beneath her fingertips. "Yes. I do need to make extra. Zane's car needs new tires and his insurance is due. I told him I'd help with it so he would stay with me a few extra days to recover. You know guest occupancy at the hotel was down in November, too. That didn't make for a lot of customers."

His eyes slid to her hand on his forearm then back to her face. "It wouldn't be charity, Cat. I promise you that."

Reading him grew more complicated as she realized the desire to be accepted by him increased. When she started to withdraw, he reached over and laid his hand on top of hers. The warmth startled her. "Okay. Tell me what you have in mind? Tending bar? Because it looks like to me the bartenders you have don't have enough to do as it is." She offered a smile up at him.

"The Boys and Girls Club have a—" His cell phone buzzed, causing him to withdraw his hand to pull out his phone from a pocket. "Excuse me. I need to take this."

Catharina turned to look around the room, spotting Gideon and his friends sitting near the windows. They watched her until she met their eyes. Like a switch being thrown, they looked down or away, pretending to be unconcerned. Their hunched forms made them look pathetic.

"I'll be right there," Damien said with an element of concern.

Catharina turned back to Damien and watched his jaw tighten and release. "Something wrong?"

When he reached out to pull her closer, Catharina found herself wondering if his mouth would feel like Rocco's. They were shaped the same. Could he imprint his desire on her as Rocco had done?

"I need to get back to Union Station. Somewhat of a problem needs my attention. Will Zane or Father Xavier be able to take you home?" He had already pushed open the door, letting in a gust of frigid air.

"Sure." He turned to go until Catharina grabbed his sleeve. "We're good. Right?"

His eyes caressed her face. "We're good. See you tomorrow and we'll talk about an idea I have." He looked over her head at Gideon and she thought he nodded a greeting. "And us. We need to talk about that." Pushing away, he slipped into the night.

Staring after him until he disappeared, she released the air held tight in her chest, forcing it out in one gust. Moving to relieve Zane at the steam table, she let her eyes scan behind the counter and saw her brother lift a violin case. Thankfully, he'd remembered to bring it. He walked over to Gideon and the others, clutching the instrument like it might be the Holy Grail.

Catharina continued to watch him and the others, in hopes of seeing something that would alleviate the confusion about the night before when Rocco arrived with the others, driving the vile attackers away. They remained stoic, except for Zane who chatted with those around him, only occasionally turning back to Gideon. In those moments, his face grew serious. Leaning in, he would mouth words as if whispering to them. They would nod with some kind of obedience. Zane appeared so forceful in those flashes of saneness. He looked like a Marine commander, his eyes holding determination and resolve.

The last of the food disappeared as she watched Zane and his friends turn their heads toward the door. Gideon looked troubled as did the others. Only Zane remained unaffected at seeing Mayor Kragan enter the Kitchen of Hope.

"Mr. Mayor." Catharina hurried to greet him, in hopes of cutting off the line of sight of her brother's friends. They did not look enthralled to see a politician join them again. "I didn't expect to see you."

From behind his back he pulled out a bouquet of mixed flowers. "A Detective Jacobs gave me a courtesy call. I contacted the police chief after his visit in your shop about the attack." He shook his head before letting his eyes travel around her face, then body. "I wanted to make sure for myself that you're all right." After handing her the flowers, Kragan put a hand on each shoulder. "Tell me they didn't hurt you."

The sudden touch of his hands forced her to flinch. "Just a bump on the head. Still a little shaken up is all."

"I've had the police increase their presence in that area. I understand The Watcher showed up to save the day."

Catharina caught the disbelief in his condescending tone. "I'm not sure who it was, Kragan. I didn't get a good look at anyone. The lights were shot out and things just happened so fast. The next thing I knew—" She looked over at Zane and Gideon who observed her with concern. "—my brother was bending over me in my apartment."

"Yes, so I heard. How do you think The Watcher got inside?"

He cocked his head to the side, provoking a feeling of caution in Catharina.

She shrugged. "I don't know that it was The Watcher. Besides, someone probably didn't follow protocol at locking the back doors. Happens all the time when people bring in supplies like groceries or have deliveries." A forced smile followed as she sniffed at the flowers. "Thank you for these." She hoped the questions would now be concluded. A certain feeling of protection for Rocco and whoever helped him remained a priority in her mind.

Without warning, he embraced her, crushing the flowers between them. His firm kiss on her cheek surprised her. "I'm just happy you're okay. I know you need to get to the entertainment portion of the evening. Let me throw this out to you."

"Okay." A little girl came up to smell the flowers and Catharina ended up letting her hold the bouquet. "What is it?"

"I'm on the board for the Boys and Girls Club. The annual fundraiser and Christmas party will be held at Union Station this year. I suggested you for the entertainment." Her lips parted, but before she could speak, Kragan continued. "It pays a thousand dollars for the night." With a gasp her hands flew to her throat. "I know you're worth more, but we have a budget too. If we used a talent agency I'm not sure what would be available on such short notice." He reached for her hands. "Say you'll do it." He smiled as he squeezed her fingers. "It's really an excuse to hear you in a more grand setting. A setting, I might add that will do your music and dancing justice."

"Yes." She laughed. "Yes. Yes. Yes." Without hesitation, she hugged him.

Kragan watched Zane stand up as a scowl formed on his weathered face. The five men next to the former Marine stood as well then moved to different parts of the room like sentinels. "Your fans grow restless. Can I take you home afterward?"

"I think the Father or Zane plans to do that."

"I promise to drop you off at the door, safe and sound."

Catharina smiled, a relief washing over her about new money coming in soon. "I'll let Zane know. You can fill me in on the Boys and Girls Club event."

Kragan shooed her away. "Go. I'm getting impatient to hear you play."

She smiled up at him. "You don't know how much this means to me."

I think I do, he mused as she almost skipped then twirled around in joy. The spontaneous movement of light heartedness possessed him in a way he found both disturbing and exhilarating.

Watching her run to her brother then wrap her arms around his neck reminded him Zane Spokane might not be so happy for him to drive her home. The brute certainly wouldn't be thrilled at what else he had planned for his little sister.

♫♫♫

"Detective Jacobs. We meet again." Damien leveled a dangerous look at the man.

The detective continued to wear his overcoat as officers began taking Damien's living quarters apart. Watching the detective check the bottom of his shoes then wipe them on a sheep skin rug irritated him.

"Nice place." Jacobs stuck out his bottom lip as he glanced around the room. "Sorry about all this." He offered his hand in friendship, but Damien continued to glare at him until the hand was withdrawn.

Damien looked over the search warrant. "Splendid," he growled.

"Shouldn't take too long."

"I don't suppose you'll be putting everything back where you found it, Detective."

Jacobs grinned. "I'm sure you have staff for that."

"Yes. Of course. What exactly are you looking for?"

"The Ark of the Covenant, Inca treasure, and oh yeah, a murder weapon. Maybe a sword that could cut the hand off a man."

"I see. Well, I can certainly point you in the direction of the Ark of the Covenant and Inca gold. The St. Louis Art Museum has a number of medieval swords in their collection. Perhaps you can go there next since I donated all of my hand choppers to them."

The detective became well aware that Damien's eyebrows were raised in annoyance as he looked down his narrow nose at him. The haughty voice didn't rattle Jacobs. Being a seasoned detective, he was used to poor treatment by suspects being served a warrant. He took out a pen and paper and jotted something down. "Art museum. Got it." The flippant response showed his ability to stay calm.

"This is absurd. You know that, don't you?" Damien stepped around some items carelessly tossed on the floor from his end table. He picked up the phone and placed an order to the night kitchen.

The detective sighed and surveyed the room. "Yes. Not my idea. You're a smart man. If you were involved, and I don't think you are, you'd be smart enough to get someone else to do your dirty work."

"Thank you for the vote of confidence, Detective. I assure you I had nothing to do with what went on last night. Have you found the men that attacked Ms. Spokane?"

"Nope." His grin revealed stains on his teeth. "Probably

won't. You already know that. I figure they're dead or crawled in a hole until they do die. They most likely got the worse of it last night."

A waiter entered the apartment with a cart of sandwiches and several pots of coffee. "It's late. I'm sure you're only doing your job, Detective Jacobs. Please, you and your officers help yourself to some refreshments in between ransacking my living quarters. I'll be downstairs if you need me."

Chapter 20

The sun finally decided to shine in late November. Thanksgiving would be in a few days and the Union Station Hotel had been booked to capacity. That news brought a smile to Catharina's face as she started her routine in the coffee shop. Maybe things were turning around for her and Zane, more customers for the next week and a chance to make some serious money for car repairs. She couldn't help but twirl around to some funky music playing on the speakers in the corridor. Propping open the doors she let the sounds waft in as she waited for the pastry delivery.

"You look happy," Jeremiah chirped as he strolled in looking as if he'd not slept much the night before. "Need a large coffee today."

"What's up? You look like you need a nap." Catharina pulled a large cup of coffee and secured it with a lid and jacket before handing it over the counter to him. "Pastries haven't arrived. I'll bring you one as soon as I can."

"Guess you haven't heard about our little visit from the police last night."

Caught off guard, Catharina could only stare at the assistant general manager.

"Damien got served a search warrant. I came in to calm down the staff." She remained wide eyed and silent. "Guess it had to do with what happened at your place the other night. They wanted to make sure some kind of sword wasn't here." He chuckled before taking a sip of his coffee then sighed as if he'd been given an injection of caffeine. "That whole Watcher thing is stirring up trouble everywhere. If you ask me, the police should sign him up. He's cleaning up the streets of St. Louis faster than they ever could." Another sip of coffee. "He's got the gangs on the run, anyway." He started toward the door after shoving a ten dollar bill in her tip jar. "I'll be in my office, Cat. I'm in need of a bear claw big time. Pretty please."

"You got it."

A cloud of regret tried to cover her as she realized the reason Damien left so suddenly the evening before at the kitchen. This was her fault. His efforts to help her now threw suspicions on him as being a part of a murder in her building. Molly arrived about the same time as the pastries so Catharina decided to pay a visit to Damien with a peace offering.

"Where you going with that? And where is my bear claw?" Jeremiah walked alongside her, grinning with his usual good cheer.

"Thought I'd try and make amends to Damien. I'm sure he's going to wish he'd never gotten involved with Zane and me." She looked down at her attire and wondered if leopard stockings and cowboy boots would be inappropriate on this floor of the building. Catching a glance in the mirror, she noticed her dark hair looked a little more tame than usual and her makeup enhanced her eyes. Licking her mouth made the red lipstick shine.

Jeremiah winked at her in the mirror. "You look great. Don't worry." He laughed. "Not everyone could pull off that Bohemian look like you. The desk girls requested to dress like you as their new uniform." This forced a laugh from her. "Damien, of course—" Jeremiah lowered his voice and started to speak in a British accent. "—said 'absolutely not. Don't be ridiculous.'" He maneuvered her away from Damien's office down another corridor. "I think he's still in the apartment. I'll take you there. But I'm taking one of those bear claws."

A couple of turns led them to a carpeted hall with fine works of art hanging on the walls. The regal feel slowed Catharina's steps, wondering if coming here was a mistake. Jeremiah appeared to sense her trepidation and nudged her with his elbow to keep her walking.

A door opened near the end of the hall and a tall blonde

woman backed out, trying to slip on a high heel. She pushed back her straight hair behind one ear before reaching through the door and patting something. Glancing toward them, she smiled as her eyes narrowed. Reaching in the doorway, Morgan Knox took hold of something and pulled forward. Damien stepped forward with her fingers wrapped around his tie. Without another thought she pushed her body against his while managing to pull his face to her parted mouth.

"What is she still doing here?" Jeremiah whispered as he stopped abruptly with Catharina two steps behind. He turned to look at Catharina's devastated stare and wanted to block a revelation he couldn't explain.

Catharina froze at seeing Damien fail to resist Morgan's kiss. The fact that he didn't respond or close his eyes at her touch overpowered Catharina with the knowledge Morgan Knox spent the night with him. A punch to her gut couldn't have hurt worse. Turning to Jeremiah, she shoved the tray of coffee and pastries at him before turning to run down the hall to escape.

Damien stepped out into the hall at hearing the commotion. Seeing Jeremiah holding the tray and Catharina running away, he shoved Morgan aside so hard she stumbled backward with an unflattering reference to his mother and birth. He stormed past Jeremiah, causing him to plaster himself against the wall to avoid being knocked down.

Stunned at the commotion, Jeremiah wasn't aware that Morgan approached him. She started to reach for one of the pastries when he pulled them to the side from her reach. "Get your own." Turning, he walked away carrying the tray. "Looks like you've been packing a few of these away lately."

The insults hurled at him caused a smirk to form on his lips. He wasn't sure what was going on with Damien and Catharina but he knew enough about Morgan Knox to know she was trouble. Catharina was a nice person. She worked hard and he wanted her to be successful. Unlike Morgan, there wasn't a pretentious bone in Catharina's Bohemian body. Damien Cruz taught him a great deal about running a hotel. It looked like it was Jeremiah's turn to teach him a thing or two about women.

Carrying the tray in one hand, he opened his office door. Those lessons could wait. The smell of pastry and coffee lured him to his desk.

♫ ♬ ♫

How could one person run so fast in cumbersome cowboy boots, Damien wondered as he stood on the balcony overlooking the Grand Hall. Catharina picked up speed as she looked over her shoulder at someone calling her name. With a sudden stop she whirled around to face an approaching man Damien recognized as Kragan LaPlante. His outstretched hands grabbed hers and tugged her closer. Even from where he stood, Damien could see a look of sympathy on his face as he reached up to move Catharina's bangs from over her eyes. The intimate gesture forced his hand to jerk to his shoulder, now hot to the touch. He felt a darkness swallow him as his hands turned to fists. When Kragan took her face between his hands and leaned in to kiss her forehead, Damien knew his body would soon morph into something else if he didn't control his sanity.

Catharina looked as if she smiled before turning away. Now walking replaced the frantic escape he witnessed moments earlier. Kragan stood motionless, watching her like a predator until she disappeared down the corridor to her shop. When he turned to leave Morgan Knox appeared and slipped her arm through his. There didn't appear to be any emotion on his part as she clung to him.

Damien realized he'd been set up. "What are you up to, Kragan?" he mumbled under his breath, deciding to wait on approaching Catharina until she'd settled down from what she thought to be true. His body began to relax as the darkness slipped away from his mind, especially his face. The burning in his shoulder dissipated with a slowness that, once again, forced him to acknowledge living in two worlds presented him with dangerous consequences. Sooner or later, someone would discover his secret. His eyes shifted back to where Kragan and Morgan went down the steps toward the street.

Why had he even made an appearance?

♫ ♫ ♫

Catharina worked so hard Molly ordered her to take a break in the late afternoon. She planned to stay until closing in order to make extra Christmas money. Before she could object, Molly removed Catharina's apron forced her out the door.

"Take a walk or a nap. Whatever. You're wearing me out. This is the slowest time of day. Call your brother or that priest you're always talking about. Just get out of my way. You're driving me crazy." Molly put her hands in the middle of Catharina's back and shoved her all the way to the door. "Go. I'll be fine."

Without work to distract her, Catharina suffered the flashback of the blonde woman kissing Damien. The realization another female came to comfort and support him during a difficult time with the police, sickened her. The depth of her feelings for a man she barely knew drove her to a dark place in her head. Slipping into backrooms of Union Station, off limits to tourists and guests, helped her ignore the pain welling up in her chest. When she found herself standing before a door in the boiler room, Catharina remembered how she escaped through a hatch then down a ladder the night she discovered Rocco hiding in the spaces above the train station.

A basement window revealed the light of day would soon be replaced with the twinkle of streetlights and cars headed home for the evening. Looking back at the door, she pulled three times before it opened. Darkness filled the space as she stepped inside and closed the door. One hand on the ladder, then another, up and up until she reached a platform that felt rickety and unsafe. The comparison to her friendship with Rocco and the platform gave her pause as she considered whether or not to proceed to where he hid by day.

"Rocco?" Catharina couldn't find the right way to go at first, feeling her way along in the deep shadows of emptiness. The pale light of the time between day and night seeped through the windows enough for her to take cautionary steps as she reached the top floor.

The climb left her breathless. Grit caked her hands when she tried to grasp at unsteady railings along steps that now took her to the place where her guardian angel lived. She reflected on the man and wondered if he really was an angel or some psychopath pretending to be a Watcher of the helpless and forgotten?

"Why are you here?"

A raspy voice came from behind her, causing her to stumble back in panic. His head, now uncovered, revealed thick black hair. The wide band beneath his eyes that spread from ear to ear, gave his translucent blue eyes a haunted appearance. The cloak was gone as were the various other sashes and belts he wore to carry his weapons. Except for his shoulders beginning to glow beneath his white shirt that opened to his waist, he looked like a man.

"Answer me." The raspy voice sounded impatient. "Why are you here? It is not safe to be with me."

Catharina let out a strangled cry as tears flooded down her face. She watched Rocco's feet separate in a fighting stance as his hands went out to his side like she'd seen him do before battle with the evil elements of the city.

"Rocco."

His name spilled out as she rushed toward him with outstretched arms. He caught her, holding her tight as she sobbed against his neck. The smell of incense entered her nose as she caressed his neck so tight the press of his lips against her ear offered a degree of comfort. His embrace lifted her feet off the floor.

Between sobs she managed to speak. "I'm such a fool. I put my faith in a man."

The stroke of his hand down her back as he placed her feet on the floor, moved Catharina's grip from his neck to the front of his shirt.

"You are hurting."

Catharina's shoulder began to glow now as he placed his hand upon the spot.

"Who has done this you?"

Catharina shook her head before laying it against his chest. The heat, nearly unbearable, filled her body. "Someone I began to trust."

"You must be careful." He started to take deep breaths, wanting more than he dared. "Is this man Mayor LaPlante?" The growl in his voice caused her to step back and rub her eyes.

"No. He's been wonderful to me. He even offered me a job to perform for the Boys and Girls Club Christmas party." The sudden show of anger in Rocco frightened her. "It's Damien Cruz. One minute he's some kind of hero protecting my brother and me, making me…" She hesitated then looked into Rocco's eyes. "Making me feel gratitude and…"

"Love?" Rocco arched an eyebrow that made Catharina take a step back, feeling the familiarity of his glare.

When she looked into his eyes, Catharina knew something wonderful had happened deep inside her. "It's you I love, Rocco." Her whispered confession softened his stance as he stepped toward her. "But I'm afraid of you too."

He resisted touching her. "This can never be unless I'm freed from this body. Only you have the power to do this."

"Just tell me what to do and I'll do it." She sounded urgent as she tried to touch his face even as he dodged her hand.

"You will have to discover this for yourself."

A look of horror filled her eyes. "You're lying. You don't want me either. Just like Damien." She started back toward the stairs. "What is wrong with me?"

He cut her off at the top of the stairs. "I did not heal your fingers and your gunshot wound because I could. I saved you for my own desire to be free and to walk as any man who loves you. Do not discount Damien Cruz's affection for you. He is a complicated man who tends to the needs of others in his own way."

She felt anger. "What is he to you?" He turned away and moved toward the center of the room. For a few seconds she lost common sense, rushing to cut off his retreat. "He knows you're here, doesn't he?" No answer. Catharina reached out, touching his arm only to have him grab it to twist behind her back before jerking her to his chest.

Rocco's gaze bore into her, fighting the earthly desires known to men, not angels. The look of terror filled her eyes.

"Damien Cruz is a means to an end for me." He shoved her back so hard, she nearly fell. "I tolerate him only because of you and your brother. He knows me for what I really am and can do. If I need to kill him," he said tilting his head sharply, "I will not hesitate. Sooner or later you must decide between us."

"No!" She tried to approach him, but he turned sideways and pointed to the door.

"Leave me, Catharina." The raspy voice softened as he looked down at the floor. "Play your violin for me tonight. Bring me peace before I go into the night to do the job God has set before me."

The weight of the world on his shoulders showed in the way he stood, looking down and to the side. With caution, she approached him until she stood inches from him. The burning in her shoulder triggered his own glow across his shoulders and chest. He raised his head to meet her eyes. The translucent glow in his flipped off like a switch, making them look a normal blue.

"Leave you?" In spite of being afraid, she felt a smile reach her lips. "Never, Rocco." Extending her hand to lay on his cheek, Catharina waited until he laid his hand atop hers. "In the Grand Hall tonight. Listen for me. I will play for you."

Rocco raised his chin in acknowledgment. "Catharina?" Her eyes blinked at hearing his voice change slightly from a raspy tone to something more normal. "Damien Cruz." Her smile faded. "He is the kind of man I wish to be. Listen to his words that I cannot or will not say to you. Listen to Zane. He grows stronger each day. He has been called into service for good." When he stopped speaking, his eyes flipped back to being the haunting glow of power.

The encounter ended with him leading her by the hand back to safety. Taking a deep breath, she turned to thank him, only to find herself alone.

♫ ♫ ♫

After making a stop in the restroom off the Grand Hall to clean up, Catharina took the long way back toward the shop. With downcast eyes and deep in thought, she staggered two steps back when she ran into a man that felt like a brick wall.

"Damien." Keeping the shock out of her voice was impossible. "I'm sorry. I didn't see you." Her eyes fell on the violin case he was carrying.

"This is for you." With both hands he offered it to her. "Your brother thought you might need it tonight."

The eyebrow arched, a movement Catharina now enjoyed watching.

They stood there staring at each other, words failing to bridge the secrets each carried.

Catharina looked down at the violin case then back at Damien. He appeared to roll his shoulders and neck as if they were stiff, before his fingers slipped inside his jacket to rub a spot she couldn't see.

"Is it all right if I play in the Grand Hall tonight? It would be late."

Damien nodded. "Mind if I listen?"

Catharina started to walk around him. "It's your hotel."

Chapter 21

How the hell did you screw this up, Crane?" Kragan stood with his hands on his hips, forcing his suit coat to push back. The shirt looked as if it had just been pressed. The red tie caught the overhead light, making it shine. The president of the board of alderman looked nervous under the mayor's penetrating glare as he towered over him. "I thought you could handle this."

Crane fidgeted in his seat as he patted his thick gray mane. "How was I supposed to know that crazy guy would show up at her place? My boys got beat up bad."

"Where are they now?" Before Crane could answer the mayor held up his hand. "Never mind. I don't want to know. Just tell me if they're still alive?"

When the alderman didn't answer at first, the mayor dropped both hands to his side. "The one that got his hand cut off bled out," Crane said finally. "The others suffered gunshot wounds and—"

"Really? Because my information says they were the only ones with guns. Did they shoot themselves?" The mayor's voice lowered rather than getting louder and angrier.

Crane twisted in his chair. "Guess we'll never know. They won't be any trouble." His eyes grew wider, insinuating a solution to a problem. "Those guys were amateurs. Gang members, pimps, and drug dealers. Unreliable." The mayor huffed before turning his back on the alderman. "The new guys are more like The Watcher," Crane promised. "Bad ass bunch out of New York City. Problem solvers for the Russian mob."

Kragan stood before the window, looking down on the traffic. His thoughts switched to seeing Catharina dance to her music. They had driven around the city, chatting like old friends when he decided to take her home. His plans were to come inside and get better acquainted but her brother waited outside with some other derelicts from the Kitchen. A policeman was standing with them, listening to something that made him smile and nod. As soon as Catharina's toes touched the pavement, Zane was right there leading her to the door. He thanked the mayor but didn't insist on him coming inside.

The notes of *The Devil's Trill* echoed in Kragan's head, as he imagined her spinning around him in her bare feet, teasing him with her pouting mouth and twisting body. The image of a little girl he once knew hiding behind a locked door, crying for him to stay away or her brother would hurt him, also appeared. The brother beat the crap out of him before he rescued little Catharina.

They disappeared into the night after that. A social worker managed to come around, asking his father and mother a lot of questions. Nothing ever came of it. Just two more kids lost in the system. He recognized Catharina the night at the Fox Theater when she'd been on the arm of Damien Cruz. Seeing Zane at the Kitchen of Hope made him take stock of his surroundings and body. The Neanderthal looked like the poster child for "Be all you can be." That gave Kragan enough pause to know he needed to move slowly on the little gutter rat of a sister.

Yet, hearing her play the violin, dancing on tables—as the dead eyes of the homeless, unemployed, and forgotten veterans came alive—struck a chord inside him. Something wonderful and magical clung to her, not only as she played and danced, but as she spoke. As a child, she'd feared and hated him, with just cause. Now with encouragement and deceit, Catharina would come to him when the time was right.

The fear of her discovering who he was remained remote. After his car accident in college and extensive plastic surgery, it gave him an opportunity to create a new life. A life without his abusive and two-faced father, always demanding more of him, presented itself the day he left the hospital, never to speak to his father again. The man didn't know his own son the few times they'd come into contact through politics and business.

Now the old man was dead—killed, according to the coroner. He thought what poetic justice it would be if the killer were Zane Spokane. Revenge was a powerful motive. He envisioned Zane being arrested and the little sister turning to the man who tried to make her life miserable as a child.

A smile spread across his face as he turned back to look at the alderman. "Remember that guy who died in the house and later was ruled a homicide?"

"The Watcher was spotted there too. What about it?"

"I know who he is." His smile widened. "You're going to have to make sure something is done about it."

♫ ♫ ♫

Catharina sent Molly home earlier in the evening when the coffee crowd dwindled. At nine the doors were locked as she prepared for the next day. Even though the customers were increasing for the holidays, she remained concerned about the mounting bills. Picking up her violin case, she flipped off the lights and headed toward the Grand Hall.

The lighting remained dim with candle lights on the tables scattered throughout the hall. The bar extended the length of the hall with three bartenders and hostesses taking care of the customers who were also hotel guests wearing badges of a conference being held in another part of Union Station. Her eyes were drawn upward to the barrel-shaped ceiling as the lights turned from blue to red then to yellow. The ornate details of the Grand Hall never lost their power to amaze her at the craftsmanship of people a century ago.

"Working late again." Damien approached her with caution it seemed. He carried a computer tablet in one hand. "I was hoping we could talk about last night and what you think you saw this morning."

Catharina stared at him and blinked. Without his suit coat, she was aware of his board chest. The missing power tie gave him a casual look that she found very appealing. A five o'clock shadow added to the already mysterious darkness under his eyes. Something about the way he stood, the way he lowered his head then looked up through thick lashes, made her think of Rocco. She looked up in the balconies that surrounded the Grand Hall in search of him, to no avail.

When she looked back to Damien, his eyes flashed from translucent to blue, or so she thought for a split second. "What you do with your time is none of my business, Damien." Her voice sounded tired even to her. The fight just wasn't there.

"I am in negotiations with Mr. Chevon concerning the Essmalory Building where you live." Catharina focused on his face with a frown. "He approached me. Not the other way around, Cat."

She sat down on the round bench covered in red velvet. Being on her feet all day forced her to remove her shoes and rub her sore feet. "Why would he do that without bringing it before the tenants?"

When Damien didn't answer, she looked up at him.

"Someone else is trying to scare all of you into selling your units. Several have sold just in the last couple of days. He wants a partner to make the Essmalory what it can and should be. I have a reputation for restoration." He looked around the Grand Hall. "Just look at this place."

"Why would you consider such a venture? Sounds like throwing good money after bad to me. And you don't owe me an explanation."

Damien eased down next to her. "Maybe. But your opinion of me means a great deal. I'm not trying to run the tenants off or increase monthly fees. For some reason, Mr. Chevon has been denied loans, time and time again, to make improvements. For a small portion of the businesses he wants to put in I'd give him a low interest loan. That's it."

Catharina felt his shoulder touch her when he joined her. The faint fragrance of incense took her off guard. She examined his profile and realized how his looks affected her. "Thanks. I jumped to conclusions. I apologize." In her gut she knew he spoke the truth. "When I overheard you and Mayor LaPlante talking, it sounded like you were planning on romancing me out of my home." She smiled, embarrassed at the suggestion. Look-ing down at the violin case next to her, a kind of relief washed over her.

"Then there's Morgan Knox."

"Again. None of my business." Catharina remembered the kiss, quickening her heart and jealousy. Knowing that she'd just professed her love to Rocco, the thought of Damien being with another woman still made her a little crazy.

"Morgan and I were together for a short time." Damien turned to look at her downcast head. "It was a long time ago. She is a dark soul I wanted nothing to do with. It was strictly physical. Nothing more."

An exasperated chuckle slipped from her mouth. "Oh, gee. That does make me feel better." She took a chance at looking at him, only to find him a breath away.

His smile teased her into chuckling again.

"That too was a long time ago. I'm not proud of it. It was a very lonely time in my life. I finally decided I'd rather be alone than be with someone like her." He laid his hand on hers. "Last night the police showed up looking for proof I was somehow involved in the incident at the Essmalory. She showed up not long after they arrived, trying to pretend to care. The truth is she works for Kragan. And yes, she tried to pick up where we left off a few years ago. I worked through the night putting every-thing back in order and calming the night staff down with Jere-miah's help. She fell asleep on the couch." Catharina rolled her eyes. "This morning what you saw was a parting gesture on her part. It meant nothing. The woman has a corrupt soul."

Catharina looked away, not wanting to feel the surge of warmth in her chest. She tried to remember Rocco and his words about Damien.

"That night at the Kitchen when you played to stop the gang members from bothering the people with your music, took my breath away."

Catharina jerked her head around and stood. "How did you know about that? You weren't even there? Who told you about that? Zane? Father Xavier?"

His face went cold as did his eyes when they looked at her.

He rose to his feet in slow motion to tower over her. "I was there. You just didn't see me." The emphasis on the last sentence sent a chill up her spine. "Open your eyes, Cat. Don't be fooled by some silver tongue devil like Kragan. I'm not the bad guy here."

"I know all about men like him, Damien. They're psycho deceivers. They pretend to be one thing and tempt you into believing something else. He's been nice to me so far, offering me a job performing with The Boys and Girls Club fundraiser. I suspect that's what you were about to do when you got called away last night." She watched him arch his eyebrow and raise his chin in surprise. "I jumped at the opportunity. I need the money."

Damien realized Catharina probably played Kragan into thinking she was a little more than interested to get the job. "Just be careful around him. He's a vindictive man who thinks he's entitled to whatever he wants. I've seen the way he looks at you. He came here this morning to pick up Morgan." He watched the surprise come across her face. "I'm guessing he sent the cops after me followed by Morgan to get information. I can't prove it nor do I need to. But I'm afraid he will use you against me."

"I'm nobody. That would be impossible."

His eyes searched her face then trailed down her entire body before taking a step closer. "You have become somebody to me, Cat." Her eyelashes fluttered in surprise, but she couldn't tear her eyes away from him. "Play your violin. It's getting late and I have much to show you." He held up his tablet. "You are going to be the toast of St. Louis soon." He nodded to the bartenders and hostesses. "They've been waiting to hear you. When you're finished, I'll be waiting over there." Without warning he leaned over and kissed her shortly on the mouth.

Catharina let him withdraw from her but she continued to stare at his mouth that felt very familiar. Backing away, she removed the violin from its case. In moments, she began to play "Larghetto, MaNon Troppo" from *The Devil's Trill*. The slow sweet melody filled the Grand Hall. The music took everyone by surprise as they muted the televisions behind the bar and customers turned to watch her strolling around the floor, barefooted and swaying as she played. Everyone seemed to hold their breath.

By the time she moved into the allegro part of the piece, she could no longer resist dancing as she played. Time and space evaporated for her as people came from their rooms, the restaurant, and the covered mall outside the hall. People began to line the bar, ordering drinks and finding a spot to listen to *The Devil's Trill* and the dancing Bohemian clan girl that twirled and bent backward as she played. At the conclusion, applause echoed throughout the Grand Hall with the fifty or so people who had gathered.

Breathing hard as she lifted her violin and bow out to her side, she managed to bend in thankfulness. As the hall emptied, one of the bartenders walked over and handed her forty dollars.

"Tips for you." She tried to split it with him but he refused. "Are you kidding me? I made more tips in the last twenty minutes than I have all week. Mr. Cruz said maybe we could work together during the holiday season. A few of us are part of a theater group. This is right up our alley."

Catharina looked over her shoulder at Damien who walked to the middle of the Grand Hall with his computer tablet. He was touching apps then looking up, then back down.

"You're going to love this, Cat." The bartender smiled looking up. "Wait until you see what the boss has next." He patted her on the back and returned to his position behind the bar where a few more customers had materialized.

Catharina gazed at Damien who smiled over at her then pointed up. She heard the sounds of a train engine as lights began to flash on the sides of the walls. Dramatic music began as the figures over the arches turned into angels flying over the ceiling. Ornate flowers began to bloom in riots of colors, forcing her to gasp at the awesome spectacle. She began turning around to see the light show explode into mosaics of history and life through the ages.

At the conclusion, the lights all came back on with a bang, causing her to jump forward as she began to laugh with joy. She waited for him to join her.

"You approve?"

Catharina hugged her arms. "It's fantastic."

"I have eleven more."

She flopped down on one of the velvet seats. "Can I see them?"

Without another word, he began punching apps on his computer. There were shows much like the last one as well as St. Louis sports and history. Her favorite one was the undersea light show. By the time she'd watched all of them, Damien sat next to her, looking up very much as she did.

She bumped his shoulder with hers. "Thank you for making a sucky day something magical." Then she realized she'd forgotten about Rocco. Had he heard her play the violin? When she sobered and looked all around the balconies, Damien took her hand.

"I should take you home." Standing, he pulled her to her feet. "I promised Zane I'd make sure you were returned to him safe and sound. He wasn't very happy about Kragan bringing you home last night." He looked over at the bartender who'd brought Catharina the tips. "Want to be a regular? Good for business during the holidays and good for your bottom line. I'll pay you of course."

"I'll do it." The excitement couldn't be contained in her voice as she clapped her hands together.

"Don't you want to know how much I'm paying?" He laughed as he lifted the violin case for her to secure her instrument.

"Truthfully? I'd do it for tips." She replaced the violin then snapped the case shut.

"You're a terrible negotiator. Our first Polar Express train ride is next week, the Friday after Thanksgiving. Will that be enough time for you to get ready?" She nodded enthusiastically. "Weekends for sure. The nights you don't work at the kitchen I'd like you here. Will Father Xavier go for that?"

"I'm sure he will. My little fan club there will be happy for me. We'll make it work." The overpowering urge to wrap her arms around him in thankfulness caused her to take a step back before she embarrassed herself.

Damien sobered as he tilted his head to the side and leveled a penetrating gaze at her. "I can't take you home myself. I'll have someone drive you. There are some things that need my attention tonight."

She held up the tip money. "No need. I can afford a cab tonight."

"Your brother would never forgive me. And, truthfully, I don't trust the cabs considering what happened the other night. I'll walk you down to the valets. I'm sure a car is waiting for you by now. Jesse is just leaving so he'll be taking you."

"Damien?" She met his eyes with determination. "What do you know about The Watcher?"

♫ ♫ ♫

Father Xavier sat in the tattered wingback chair in his quarters, staring into the fireplace. The gas logs warmed his aging bones but not his troubled soul. The social worker now living in Tampa gave him a courtesy call earlier in the day about Zane and Catharina. She had found them on the night of their escape from an abusive foster care home. Nothing else was available, except for a place that ran rampant with juvenile delinquents one step away from jail time. Knowing him through several community action projects they participated in together and later as a member of his parish, she brought the children to him in the middle of the night.

"I'm a priest. What can I do?" He remembered them hugging each other, standing by his backdoor as if wanting to run back out into the snowy night. "Maybe I can find someone to take them."

"There is no place safe to send them. Even if I found someone, they'd be separated." At her words, the little girl began to cry and bury her face in her brother's jacket. He looked older than thirteen. Comforting his sister with pats on her back, the boy never took his angry eyes from the priest. "Please, Father Xavier. Look at them. They've been through so much. Let them stay the night. The storm is getting worse by the minute. I can't be running all over the city with them in my backseat. I've got a family too. In God's name!"

With a nod, he'd agreed. The storm lasted three days. By that time, they were a family he couldn't do without. He was in love with the children. After two weeks of hiding them from others in the church, he found an elderly couple to help him. Together they hatched a plan for the children to live with them if the priest would help out. The social worker made sure the monthly stipend got sent to the couple. When they passed away, the social worker kept it on the books as active. The priest bought a small house across the street, with money the old couple left for their care. They lived there, across from the church until Zane went to serve with the Marines. Hiring a live in housekeeper made it all look legitimate. Very few people in the church knew of the deception and all tried to be supportive in their own way, taking turns with whatever needed to be done.

Then today the retired social worker called in a panic, saying the state contacted her about misappropriation of funds in the foster care system. His name came up but she claimed not to know anything about him receiving funds after the deaths of a certain couple who were foster parents. She wanted him to know if she got investigated it could get ugly for him.

The overpowering urge to pray engulfed him as he left his quarters to find the sanctuary of the church. He kneeled as he crossed himself before the altar.

"You come with a heavy heart, Father Xavier."

The raspy voice no longer frightened him. "Yes. What I thought were good deeds may now come back to haunt the ones I love. I've tried to help others in my life. Sometimes, I had to bend the rules to do it." He remembered selling the little house to put a down payment on The Kitchen of Hope.

"Who burdens you, good priest?" Rocco took the man's elbow as he tried to stand. "Is it money you need? Or does someone threaten your work at The Kitchen?"

The priest turned to the creature he'd come to know as The Watcher, Rocco, a disturbed angel who took great delight in smiting the evil of this world. His sigh bounced off the sanctuary walls. He retold the story of his deception before looking up at the cross to say, "I'm sorry."

"You have given much," the raspy voice continued as he laid

a cold hand upon the shoulder of the priest. "Someone is trying to replace goodness with evil. I won't let that happen. You pray for those who need help and for the ones I intend to make pay for their sins against all that is good in the world."

"Rocco. About the woman." Father Xavier turned his eyes on the creature who kept his face partially covered with his hood. "What of her?"

"She can free me."

"At what price?"

"Death."

The priest caught his breath in his throat and staggered backward. "No. Please."

Rocco reached out to grab the priest and pull him back to within inches of his body. "She loves me. But not all of me. There is much she does not know."

"She is the child graced to me through circumstances. I won't give her up to save you." Father Xavier spoke in a quivering voice of fear, knowing the creature could slash him to bits if desired. "You do not deserve to be human if you take her life."

"I agree, good priest." He touched the spot on his chest where a heart beat in the rhythm of a clock starting to unwind. He closed his eyes. "I love her. That is why I will not harm Catharina, unless—" He stopped speaking to look over his shoulder at shadows emerging out of the darkness as men. "—unless she loves all of me. And only then if someone takes my place for eternity. I cannot take the one good thing that sees me for more than what I have become over centuries of retribution and loneliness. You have nothing to fear."

"But you will not harm her?" The priest looked at the strangers walking down the aisle, dressed in the same manner as Rocco.

"To love someone is sacrifice. I learned that from you, Father Xavier. Once I believed our Lord was the only one capable of such love. She must be willing to give something in return for my mortality."

"What will that be?" The priest hoped that Rocco would abide by his word for her protection.

"Time. That is the price."

The priest watched the others stop with bowed heads. "I don't understand."

"You will. Now, we come for your prayers and blessings. We have much to do this night."

Chapter 22

The smell of smoke tickled Catharina's nose at first. The weight of fatigue made her roll to her side, burying her face in a second pillow on the bed. Not until she started coughing did she open her eyes and sit up. A fleeting thought of leaving the tea kettle on a hot burner surfaced then realized she'd forgone her usual cup of chamomile. Swinging her bare feet to the floor, she moved to flip on the lights, only to see a haze hanging in her apartment.

Running to the door, she placed her palms on the wood to find it warm to the touch. The sound of screams in the hall forced her to run back and slip on a coat then grab her violin case. There weren't many things she valued, but her violin was the one thing she wouldn't leave behind. Someone banged on her door, yelling to get out. She heard the demand several more times as the voice faded down the hall.

Distant sirens impaled her fears of dying and leaving Zane alone. At least he decided not to return to the apartment. He'd left a note that he would be gone for a few days and not to worry.

A last minute decision to slip on her jeans under her nightgown and coat, then her boots gave her a sense of being prepared for what lie on the other side of the door. The sirens sounded closer as she grabbed the doorknob, now hot to the touch.

Flinging open the door, a wall of fire snapped at her. She jerked one arm up to cover her face before falling backward to the floor. Slamming the door shut with her foot, she heard the sound of crackling timbers and falling debris, driving home the seriousness of her situation. Catharina gagged on the thick smoke now pushing under her door. The lights flickered into darkness as she managed to get to her feet and move to the windows. Red strobe lights of emergency vehicles flashed below as she tried to pry open one of the windows with no success. She stumbled to the nightstand next to the bed and grabbed a flashlight to use to bat out the glass. But before she could swing it, a coughing fit racked her body. Tripping over her violin case, she fell to the floor. As she did her head met with the windowsill. Another kind of darkness welled up inside her.

"Save me, Rocco," she whispered as blood trickled into her eye.

♫ ♫ ♫

The bulky man, with his ski mask rolled up to reveal a pudgy face, looked around at the others then down at both ends of the street. "I don't like it. What if the cops come 'round, Dred?"

Another man grinned as he rubbed his hands together. In spite of wearing gloves, his fingers felt cold. He nodded toward the others exiting from an old black van with non-descript detailing. Mostly dressed in dark clothing, they too left no identifying details of who they might be. "The cops won't come around, so shut your yap. They're going to be busy a few blocks away with a fire." Dred took a baseball bat one of the others handed him. "Let's take this place apart and be gone."

"What the hell is a Kitchen of Hope, anyway?" A black man walked up carrying an automatic rifle with a faded image of a skull on the stock. He chuckled. "They better hope we don't find anybody hiding inside."

Dred snarled as he stepped toward the front door then looked back at the black man. "Antone, you go round the back. Take Ice Man with you." He looked at the bulky man who moved to Antone's side. "Anybody comes through that back door from upstairs, shoot 'em. Don't need any witnesses."

They disappeared into the alley.

"Somebody live upstairs?" another man asked as he pulled

his ski mask down over his bearded face.

Dred nodded as his eyes traveled upward. "Couple of families and a few vets. Not more than ten, twelve people. Won't cause us problems. They start down the stairs to see what's goin' on, just wave your problem solver at them. Follow 'em back up if need be to scare the ones with kids." He motioned for everyone to get ready to enter.

With the swing of a bat, and a few kicks, the door gave way. They rushed in to destroy the Kitchen of Hope.

♫ ♫ ♫

The Watcher moved through the darkness like a wisp of fog hovering over water. After the blessing given by the priest, the Nephilim brothers disappeared into the night to rest and reflect on their sins. Under his protection, the men would remain safe against the eyes of the world. They rose up only when called upon by him to do so. His orders led them against the evils of the world when he needed to be in more than one place. They were humble and meek until he breathed the venom of power into them for such occasions. It was then they remembered who they were and how they came to be. Unleashed they could do much damage. They were not pure angels like him. Their bodies and soul could be influenced by the human blood fused with their angelic parentage. Left on their own, the Nephilim could destroy the world. He took a moment to pray for them and for the one destined to replace him when the time came.

The sound of fear invaded his solitude and he knew the Kitchen of Hope faced trouble. His silent footsteps rushed along the alleys and streets. Remaining hidden by his power, he waved his hand, and lamp posts faded to black as he passed. Reaching the kitchen, he cocked his head to hear the cries of little children from upstairs that served as a shelter. He climbed up on the outside of the building and entered one of the windows he knew did not have a lock. Slipping inside he made his way down a hall where he saw a tall man arguing with one of the residents. The resident tried to block the door, only to be shoved aside before the intruder barged inside. A woman screamed drawing Rocco closer.

Tapping the intruder on the back of his leather jacket, Rocco stood ready as the man jumped around, startled at not being alone. He leveled his nine millimeter and pulled the trigger, but not before Rocco slapped his hand down. The bullet exploded through the floor several times. Grasping the man's wrist, Rocco squeezed the gun from the intruder's hand.

Rocco became aware the invader possessed no fear of him as the man began fighting with doubled fists. One blow landed upside Rocco's head, knocking him back against the wall. With a sudden cry of defiance, he pulled his daggers from his waistband, holding them level with his own chest. From the corner of his eye, he could see the woman rush the children into the bathroom and slam the door. The father crawled toward the door as if to block another invasion.

The thug hunched, clearly ready to do battle. "All right, freak. Let's do this."

Rocco realized that this man, unlike the street gangs, knew how to fight, probably even relished the opportunity. "Do you believe in hell?" His raspy voice laid flat against the sound of weeping children.

A smile appeared in the mouth opening of the ski mask. He pulled out his own switchblade and took a swing at Rocco, missing. "No, freak."

Rocco brought his daggers up to crisscross his chest. "Then you must prepare yourself to meet the One in authority."

The man chuckled. "What authority? I'm not afraid of you."

"You should be. For when I complete this task, He has the authority to throw you into the pits of hell after death. This is the One to fear. Prepare to meet the Beast of Hell for your evil deeds tonight. For I am the Soldier of the Divine."

A gritty chuckle spilled from the attacker. "And I'm here to kick your sorry ass into the hall, freak." With a roar of contempt, the attacker lunged at Rocco only to feel the sharp steel of death penetrate both his lungs.

The attacker's eyes bulged as his face fell forward to touch the icy skin of The Watcher. They did not close as his soul left his body and it was shoved out onto the hall floor.

The bathroom door creaked open as the father shoved his way inside then slammed it shut again. Rocco jerked his head around, sensing more eyes watching him from several of the other apartments.

One man nodded his approval as his eyes fell on the dead corpse sprawled on the floor. Dressed in sweatpants and a faded Hard Rock tee shirt, Rocco realized the man was more weathered than old.

Glaring at him, Rocco took a step over the body. Just as the man tried to slam the door shut, Rocco put his hip into it, forcing it to fly back. Rocco eyed him and saw the symbol of an Army Ranger tattooed on his bicep. "You need not fear me. How many more of them are here?"

The vet shook his head. "They're taking the place apart downstairs." Lifting a prepaid cell phone, he frowned. "Called nine-one-one. You better get going." The southern accent no longer sounded like a man afraid. The door across the hall opened and the new friend waved them away. "Sounds like too many for you to handle, Watcher."

Rocco felt his eyes glaze to opaque as they often did during battle. "You know me?"

"We all do. Now, if you're goin' down there, I reckon I'm taggin' along." The vet straightened his body and limped forward, revealing he wore a prosthetic leg.

"Thank you." Rocco turned his head toward noise coming from downstairs. He would have to sneak out the front then surprise them. His eyes traveled to the dead man then back to the wounded warrior.

"All I saw was a dark shadow come up and give the guy an ass whoopin' he deserved after scaring some kids. Then he just disappeared. Like. A. Ghost."

The father of the children emerged out of the apartment and called to them. "That's the way I saw it, too."

Rocco saluted them with a fist over his heart. "Stay here. You must remain safe, and innocent of what I am about to do."

♫♬♫

The sound of pounding against metal, wood, and glass melted with the grunts of laughter as several of Dred's men continued to smash the Kitchen of Hope to pieces. After unplugging the two freezers, the plugs were severed so not to be rescued if anyone discovered the malicious activity. The refrigerator, just purchased from The Habitat Store was like new, but now it looked like the victim of bumper cars gone wrong. Condiment packets splattered on the floor and walls as the men proceeded to rip the place apart.

"Let's beat it," Dred panted, loving the way destruction made him feel omnipotent. He didn't usually get to let off steam like this. He yelled again, calling through the backdoor to the two he'd sent to cut off any escape of the people upstairs. There was always the possibility he would need to feed his pyro fetish. "Anyone feel like torching this place?" Taking out his lighter, he flicked it open and grinned.

A raspy voice responded. "At least that way you'll get to know what you're new address is going to feel like, Dred."

Spinning around, Dred saw the cloaked angel standing on a table with his legs apart and his hands out from his side. Even from where Dred stood he could see the opaque eyes glare at him. The shuffle of the others coming to his side, bestowed confidence. "Who are you and how do you know my name?"

"I am of no consequence. Your name is burned upon the tablets of eternity. It is up to you when you will begin that journey."

Stepping forward, Dred snickered then nodded at his helpers who began fanning out to trap the stranger. "Are you that Watcher character? I'm not scared of you." Pointing at the others, he began moving closer to the target. "What are you, like some kind of psycho or something? Maybe a ninja?" He looked over at his friends and laughed. "There are six of us and one of you."

"Five. There are five of you." The pale eyes never left Dred as the knowledge he'd lost a man wiped the smirk from his face. Sirens turned everyone's head except for Rocco's. "Choose how you want to die."

"Back at ya, Watcher." Dred pulled a revolver from his belt.

He pointed the barrel at Rocco, a split second of surprise crossing his face as The Watcher jumped from the table in front of him, piercing his heart with a sword that, moments before, remained invisible. Dred expelled the gurgle of death as two of the others ran forward with loud yells of intimidation. Dropping the sword, Rocco pulled the daggers from within his cloak. Without turning around, he jammed them backward as the men charged him, forcing them into lungs that quickly filled with blood. Jerking around, Rocco leap-frogged onto several chairs, cutting off the retreat of the others as they tripped over themselves, landing on the floor. Scampering up, they pulled out their guns and began firing at Rocco, who flinched at each penetration. But he did not fall.

When their guns emptied, a look of horror was embedded on their faces as Rocco began to speak. "From Psalm 101:8 'Morning by morning I will destroy all the wicked in the land, cutting off all the evildoers from the city of the Lord.'" Rocco extended his arm toward his fallen sword and it flew to his hand. "Zip ties. On the counter." His eyes shifted to where several spread across the counter. "Bind yourself to the steam table. And remember. Tell the truth of this night or I will find you." When they appeared frozen, Rocco took only one step forward to thaw their resistance. As the sirens neared, the two remaining men made quick about securing themselves, even as a police car screeched to a halt out front.

Two police officers burst into the kitchen, guns drawn. Their shock at the amount of destruction and blood on the floor forced them to hunker toward possible danger.

"What the hell?" one uniformed officer spit.

"The Watcher! It was The Watcher," both zip-tied men yelled as they nodded toward the back entrance.

The officers pursued but by the time they entered the alley there was only the dark silence of the night.

Chapter 23

When he entered the alley, Rocco climbed the outside of the nearest building. The-five story structure provided plenty of hand holds for him to propel himself upward until he reached the roof. Just as he leaned over to gaze down into the darkness, the police ran into the alley, guns drawn in nervous anticipation. No doubt the remaining two men now secured to a steam table, only had to mention his name for a sense of excitement to ensue. He walked along the roofline, stalking them like a wild hunter of the night. The spill of blood sometimes did this to him, especially if he came between evil and an innocent victim. As the two officers ran back, so did he, then knelt down on one knee to watch them reenter the Kitchen.

The red strobe of light from the police car flashed in the street at the edge of the alley. The crackle of police radios boomed in his ears until he placed his hands on each side of his head. Dropping the palms of his hands to his bended knee, Rocco closed his eyes before tilting his head up toward the heavens. "Forgive me, Father. I pray that you have mercy on the souls I sent to fire."

'Save me, Rocco.' The whispered cry for help forced Rocco to jump to his feet then jerk his head to look behind him.

♫♫♫

"My sister! My sister is still in there." A frantic Zane ran back and forth in front of the Essmalory Building. Leaving her a note not to worry if he didn't surface for a few days was meant to give him some time to reflect and plan out his life. Presented with an offer of wholeness and strength, it came with a sacrifice Zane wasn't sure he could make.

Tears gushed from his eyes as others stumbled from the building. Twice, he tried to charge forward, only to be restrained by burly firemen, before being handed over to the police. They forced him behind some kind of safety line, but it didn't keep him from pacing or calling for Catharina.

"Cat. Cat. Cat." Slamming his fist against his chest, shaking his head, and bending over in pain, he felt a world of hopelessness raining down on him. If only he'd returned to her apartment like he promised. If only the Taliban would stop firebombing them. If only reinforcements would arrive or the Blackhawks. This could turn out okay. If only. "Cat. Cat. Cat."

"Zane?" A man in a dark overcoat touched the wounded warrior's shoulder. "Zane. It's me. Mayor LaPlante. Where's Catharina?"

The ex-Marine started shifting his weight from one leg to another, then bent over as if he might vomit. "Donno. Donno. Donno. Inside. Inside. Inside." Tears continued to pour from his eyes as he shook his head. "Gotta get her. Gotta get her. Gotta get her. The Taliban did this."

Mayor LaPlante frowned as he turned to a black police officer that drove his limo. "See what you can find out." The man nodded and walked off. "Zane, pull yourself together."

"Pull together. Pull together. Pull together. We got this. We got this. We got this."

The mayor rolled his eyes in exasperation then exhaled. Looking toward the Essmalory, he realized the firefighters appeared to be getting control of the fire. His officer returned and whispered in his ear. "Are you sure?" The man nodded. Kragan, with narrowed eyes, stole a glance at the giant next to him, feeling little satisfaction at the possibility Catharina might be dead. For years he longed to do this man harm. Now it appeared Zane was already so damaged that telling him the truth about the fire would only send him spiraling into a psychotic episode. "Zane,

I'm going to talk to the fire chief. Wait right here. Okay?"

Shaking his head like a little boy, Zane swayed on his feet. "Okay. Okay. Okay."

The mayor and his officer walked away just as Zane stopped swaying. His body became rigid. Every inch of his body began to change as his mind cleared. The hunched back straightened. Unknown power and confidence filled the muscles that rippled along his chest and arms. Looking up from the pavement, he stared at the fire still breaking through some of the windows. Cocking his head, he began to listen. With a slow deliberate walk, he disappeared into the crowd gathering in the street. He turned the corner to enter the alley on the side of the Essmalory left unprotected by firefighters or police.

Waiting with feet apart and head bowed stood The Watcher. With his hands clasped below his waist, the angel appeared calm.

Zane's footsteps sounded like a shuffle in Rocco's ears, knowing no one else could hear the uncertainty above the chaos. A slow unfolding of hands led the angel to lift only his eyes to examine his protégé. His raspy voice forced Zane to halt. "Therefore take up the whole armor of God that you may be able to withstand in the evil day, and having done all, to stand firm."

"Ephesians 6:13." Zane lifted his chin in confidence then shifted his eyes up toward his sister's apartment. "You doubt me."

Walking up to Zane, Rocco, the Lord's protector, placed his hand on his shoulder. "No. Only you can do that." He now looked up as well. "Time grows short. She doesn't have much time. Together we can save her. Are you up for the task? There can be no turning back."

Pulling his shoulders back forced Zane to stand straighter, taller than ever before. "I'm ready."

"Then it begins." Rocco laid his hands upon Zane's head, filling him with some unearthly power. It lasted only a moment before both men rushed to the side of the Essmalory and scaled the bricks and mortar as if gravity meant nothing to them.

Once on the ledge outside Catharina's window, Zane kicked

in the panes, shattering glass inward. Rocco did the same before using his arms to swing inside. The smoke seeped under the door causing a thick haze. Both men spotted her at the same time, lying on her stomach. Just for an instant Rocco felt Zane's confidence ebb away then gush forward like a shot of adrenaline.

Zane rolled her over to cradle her as Rocco kneeled down beside her. The realization Catharina wasn't breathing demanded he remove her body from Zane's arms. He gingerly carried her to the window where bursts of winter's air wafted inside. Bending his head forward he lowered his mouth to hers, knowing what he was about to do might be too little too late. After blowing life into her parted lips several times, Catharina's chest rose. A sputtered cough erupted from deep within her as Zane exited onto the windowsill.

Handing her off was impossible. Zane's training and faith remained risky. Rocco wouldn't take chances with the possibility of freedom from an eternity of being immortal, now that it was within reach. Only a little longer. Even carrying her in one arm, Rocco beat Zane to ground level.

A cough now stabbed at Catharina's consciousness as her brother stepped in front of Rocco. With fluttering eyelids, she looked up into the glazed eyes of a creature she feared to love. His arms held her securely even as he lifted her to bury his face in her hair. The touch of her brother's arms slid beneath her body as Rocco handed her off.

"Take her forward. She needs medical attention."

"No." Zane shook his head, feeling the sickness creep back into his mind. "You do it. I trust you."

"Do as I say. Then take her to Union Station. You can stay there. I must go." Catharina's eyes, now closed, forced him to reach for her face. The back side of his hand ran along her cheek then across her mouth before he looked at Zane. "You did well tonight."

Zane nodded without any show of emotion before turning and walking toward the street. The excited sounds of first responders as Zane, appearing on the street carrying his sister, drew instant attention. A final look upward revealed flames now licking its way out Catharina's apartment windows. Her soul had been seconds from crossing over, leaving him without any hopes of living the life of a human. Now Rocco realized that without Catharina, he no longer desired to be human. Would she feel the same about him when she discovered the price and sacrifice of being together?

Easing out onto the street, he scanned the crowd until his eyes fell on Mayor Kragan LaPlante standing with Zane at an ambulance. Kagan stroked Catharina's hair and bent down to kiss her soot-streaked face. Rocco could feel a tremble inside Zane and wondered about the growing agitation in him when he suddenly shoved the mayor away. A police officer restrained the wounded warrior until the mayor straightened his coat and nodded that he was okay. Something had jerked Zane back into his confused state again. What was it about the mayor that made him lose himself so quickly? Had the breath of power given to him earlier revealed something about the mayor that diminished Zane's ability to control his emotions?

Evaluation of the matter would have to wait. The need to return to Union Station before Zane and Catharina arrived, forced Rocco to flee into the cold darkness of the night. By now, Father Xavier would have been informed of the break-in. The police might still be questioning the people upstairs over the Kitchen of Hope. The remaining two men he left alive most likely would refuse to talk further without a lawyer. Men like that enjoyed telling everyone they knew their rights. No matter. There remained work to be done to save so much. The Essmalory, The Kitchen of Hope, and the homeless of the city demanded he watch over them. Now Catharina and Zane had been added to that list.

Rocco found the entrance that would sequester him from curious eyes. The knowledge that Zane would soon be bringing Catharina to him, forced him to bolt upon rafters and swing onto steel girders that propelled him upward to the recesses of his hidden world.

Once there he looked out the small oval window to the street below. He felt them. Taking a deep breath, Rocco fell to his knees and began his transformation.

♫ ♬ ♪

"We're taking her to the hospital, Zane, to make sure your sister is okay." The paramedic who now knew the troubled warrior leaned in to come face to face, emphasizing the importance of his decision. "She'll probably be treated and released but we've got to check her out."

"Can I go with her?" Zane's voice sounded strong causing the paramedic to look at him with bewilderment.

"No. You'll have to get a ride." The paramedic looked at the mayor, who frowned, indicating the idea of Zane going in the ambulance would never happen. "Let me see what I can do, buddy." He patted Zane on the side of the arm and yelled out to the crowd. "Anybody here able to take this man to the hospital for his sister?"

Several onlookers who watched Zane carry his sister out of the darkness stepped forward, with one man leading the others. "My car is over there. Happy to give you a ride. It's the least I can do." The old man appeared a little hunched in the shoulders and he carried a cane. "Would that be okay, Zane?"

Zane jerked his head around to stare at the man who said his name. When their eyes met, the old man offered a thin smile and a nod of his head covered in a hoodie. "Yes. Thank you," Zane agreed.

The paramedic wondered about the man appearing out of the crowd who knew Zane. Clearly, the warrior was surprised at hearing his name. The paramedic observed the two staring at each other, as if measuring one another for trustworthiness. Two others stood nearby, eyeing the surroundings with unease. Maybe he should mention it to the police or firemen. As Catharina was lifted into the back of the ambulance, the paramedic walked over to one of the officers. He voiced his concern, causing the policeman to turn around.

"I don't see anything. Where are they?"

The paramedic squinted to where Zane still stood straight and tall, staring at something he seemed to be listening to. Was it another one of his demons from Afghanistan? And where did his ride go? Could Zane have changed his mind?

"Keep an eye on him, will ya? He's gone through some tough times of late. That guy who offered a ride had some sketchy friends with him. I don't have time to look after him. They might know something about the fire."

The policeman agreed as his eyes fixated on watching the wounded warrior. The paramedic rushed to get behind the wheel of the ambulance. The lights started to flash, then it pulled away from the curb.

"Ready?" The policeman walked up alongside Zane and looked over his shoulder as the fire was being extinguished.

Zane's eyebrows lifted as he realized the police officer looked familiar. Was it from the night he was shot? "I know you?"

The officer took Zane's elbow to move him toward a car pulling up to the curb. "Yes. Rocco thought I could serve best with the police. I owe him. I don't understand any of this and I don't want to. Go." He palmed a business card into Zane's hand then opened the car door. "Keep your friends low for a while. Call me if you or Rocco need anything." His eyes shifted to the chaos on the street. "I hope your sister is okay. Lucky you came along."

Zane slipped into the front seat. Shutting the door, the officer noticed two other men in the backseat, hoodies pulled low over their faces. One man was so tall his head nearly touched the ceiling of the car.

"Go." The officer slapped the side of the door as it pulled away from the curb.

Mayor LaPlante strolled up to the officer with his hands shoved into his overcoat. His driver wasn't far behind. "Is Mr. Spokane following his sister to the hospital?"

The officer tried to pull himself to attention to avoid the appearance of being caught off guard. "Yes, sir."

"Who took him? Do you know?"

"No, sir. Someone from the crowd volunteered when the paramedic asked for help. Maybe it was an angel."

A huff of disgust escaped the mayor's lips. "This city is going to hell in a handbag and you think angels are walking among us. Don't tell me you're buying into that whole Watcher thing. He's a thug, murderer, and terrorist. You guys need to get your act together and catch this guy. I would bet next month's salary he was behind this fire. Wants attention drawn to himself. The news hasn't said anything about him now for about a week. I see the news vans over there, just salivating for a story. Keep your angel opinions to yourself if you want to keep your job."

"Yes, sir. Not a word, sir."

The mayor nodded as a shiver followed a gust of wind. He looked at his driver. "Let's go to the hospital. I want to check on the girl." Waving to one of the reporters, who began walking his way, he spoke to the officer in a low voice. "Let the reporter know I'm headed to the hospital to check on the injured and that I plan to get to the bottom of this. This has The Watcher written all over it."

The reporter managed to push his way through the crowd just as the mayor left in his car. "Dang it. I wanted a statement." Squeezing his eyes against the smoke-filled air, the reporter looked up at the now smoldering building. Taking out a small notebook and pencil, he directed his questions to the officer. "Did the mayor say anything about the fire?"

Starting to walk away the officer shrugged. "Said it was a shame."

"That's it?"

The officer paused, as if trying to remember what the mayor said. "I think he said he was headed home. Long day."

Chapter 24

Father Xavier started toward the Kitchen of Hope when he heard on the radio that the Essmalory was on fire. A call to one of his parishioners who worked for the St. Louis Police Department informed him about Zane and Catharina. Said a camera crew caught him walking out of the alley carrying her in his arms. They should be at the hospital by now. Father Xavier found Zane sitting in the emergency room on the edge of his seat, head bowed with his hands clasped in despair.

"Son?" Father Xavier sat down next to the man he loved. He placed an arm around his shoulders and tugged so that the warrior leaned into him with relief. "How's Cat?"

Shaking his head, Zane leaned back in his chair, forcing the tears back with the soot caked sleeve of his camo-jacket. "Waiting to hear. That paramedic who brought her in said she was in good hands."

The priest pulled closer to Zane. "Let me pray, my son." With a nod of his head, Zane closed his eyes and let the words of hope, faith, and love plead for Catharina's health. "How did you manage to get to her, Zane?"

Zane started to answer when the mayor walked into the emergency room, asking about the others who had been brought in for treatment. The nurse stood and answered politely. Turning he glanced at Zane and the priest. Rather than engage them, he let the nurse take him to visit the other injured.

"I don't like that guy," Zane's snarled, clenching his fists.

"But why? He has treated your sister very well and is

respected throughout the city. He seems to be genuinely concerned for her welfare. Are you being an over protective brother?" The priest smiled and began rubbing Zane's back as he leaned forward in his chair again.

"I don't trust him. Something about him doesn't ring true. It's like I know him, but I don't."

The priest sighed as he withdrew his hand. "Son, sooner or later your sister will fall in love, marry, and have children. Don't you want that for her?"

"Damien Cruz. He's right for my sister."

Father Xavier felt panic grow inside him and his heart squeezed tight. "No, Zane. And we both know why!" His voice became low, edged with a growl. "You know that can never be. I had no idea who Damien was when I introduced them. Please forgive me for ever doing that. Damien is a dangerous man—or whatever he is—and I won't have him be a part of either of your lives."

"It is too late for that, Father." Zane's voice sounded calm and controlled as he turned his eyes on the priest.

"Don't you understand that Cat could die? Think, man!" The priest knew he sounded desperate as his whispers grew louder. "The mayor can offer a secure life for your sister. He's obviously interested in her. I've seen how he looks at her. The man is in love. Damien will never know what love is. His touch means death."

This time, Zane slipped an arm around the priest and smiled. "But what does Cat want? She loves The Watcher, Father Xavier. His touch is deadly only if he remains an angel. If he were to become a man, then she would be safe."

The priest shook his head as his hand reached out and fist bumped the warrior's thigh. "That's impossible. He'll take her life to transform to a human because of that love and trust. She will listen to you, Zane. You must stand between them."

A doctor walked up and extended his hand to Zane then Father Xavier. "You're Miss Spokane's next of kin?"

Both men stood as if expecting bad news. They nodded in a kind of hopelessness when Zane spoke. "I'm her brother. How is she?"

"She has all of us a little confused. The others brought in are going to have to spend the night. Considering how long she was exposed to smoke, Miss Spokane should be in a lot worse shape. It's a miracle is all I can say, that she isn't dead. She'll probably feel pretty tired for a few days and needs to rest for maybe forty-eight hours or so. If you notice an increase in coughing, paleness, respiratory problems don't wait to come back. Things can flare up even after a few days." The doctor eyed Zane, figuring out he probably didn't have the means to take care of her. He looked at the priest. "Does she have family or a place to stay?"

Zane nodded as the priest chimed in. "Yes. We'll make sure she is taken care of." He extended his hand. "Thank you, doctor."

"A nurse is with her now. You can go back in a few minutes. The people at the desk can give you a few papers to sign and some instructions for her care." Walking away, the doctor was stopped by the mayor who appeared to be looking around. The doctor motioned for him to follow with his head.

♫ ♫ ♫

Catharina sat on the edge of the bed as she slipped her feet back into her slippers. She couldn't remember putting them on the night before when she got out of bed to check on the fire. The nurse told her someone waited to see her and would be back in a couple of minutes to help her out to her car. Like she had a car. She left to find a wheelchair when Mayor LaPlante walked in the room.

Catharina realized she probably looked like a chimney sweep after a hard day's work, but it didn't stop him from approaching her and cupping her chin in his hand.

"Thank heavens, you're all right." Both his smile and voice was kind and comforting. "I was terrified you wouldn't make it out." He eased down next to her as she lowered her eyes. "I don't know how your brother found you, but I'm indebted to him." Their shoulders touched, drawing Catharina's eyes to him. "Do you need a place to stay?"

"She does not." Zane entered, pushing a wheelchair with the

priest at his side. "I've got it taken care of, Mr. Mayor."

Catharina felt embarrassed at her brother's rudeness. "Zane, Kragan was only trying to be helpful." The priest came to pull her off the bed with a gentle tug then guided her to sit in the chair. "Thank you, Father Xavier." He rested his hand on her shoulder as she looked back at the mayor.

"Zane, I wanted to give you a lift to the hospital, but by the time I came to ask, you were getting in the car with someone else." The mayor sounded almost disappointed. "At least you made it." He extended his hand to the priest. "Father, the police tell me there was some kind of break in at the Kitchen." Their hands clasped only for a few seconds.

"That's right. I haven't been there yet. I don't know what to expect. Hopefully, the people upstairs are safe." Father Xavier rubbed his eyes as if vanquishing the thought of being too tired to continue. "I need to get over there."

"How can I help?" Kragan stood glancing from Zane who stood stone faced to Catharina who looked up at him with watery eyes and a vulnerability that excited him. "Your home is gone for now, Catharina. Do you have some place else to stay?" He looked back at the priest. "Are there any rooms upstairs at the Kitchen, Father Xavier?"

"No. All taken. But—"

"I have plenty of room in my loft," Kragan looked at the brute glaring at him with a renewed interest. "Both of you could stay there tonight if you like."

Father Xavier looked pleased as he looked hopefully at Zane. "A generous offer."

"We already have a place to stay, Mr. Mayor. Damien Cruz is waiting for us."

"Damien!" The mayor didn't realize his voice turned cold and angry. "How—"

"We talked earlier." Zane turned his sister's chair around and rolled it toward the door. "He knows we're coming."

Visibly shaken, Kragan stiffened his spine to cover his agitation. "He has lots of room there so this could be a very good thing." He began to walk alongside Catharina. "Please allow me to take you there. That way the good Father can go see about the Kitchen." Glancing over at the priest he added, "I'll join you later, Father Xavier. I want a first-hand account from the police of what went on. I hope those people upstairs are okay."

Father Xavier offered a tired smile. "Thank you, Mr. Mayor. This city is lucky to have someone so interested in the poor."

Kragan shrugged. "There are many who care, good father." He looked to Zane. "So please let me take you to Union Station." He couldn't bring himself to say Damien's name. The very thought boiled inside him.

Catharina reached out and took the father's hand. "Please, Zane. Father needs to go and he is so tired. Maybe you should go with him," she added as a second thought.

"I could use the help, Zane. I'm really tired. Could you drive me?" Father Xavier stepped through the automatic doors as Zane wheeled his sister through.

"No." Zane's words were curt.

"Zane!" Catharina chastised him. "Father needs you."

The mayor motioned for his car to pull forward, offering a smile. "It's all right. He's only looking out for you, Cat." His eyes went to Zane. "Father, come with us. Then I'll drive you to the kitchen. My driver will deliver you back to your home when you're finished. Give me your keys." He extended his palm out. "I'll have someone drive your car back to the rectory." He wiggled his fingers. "Come on. You do so much for the city. Let me do this for you. It would be my honor."

The priest dug in his pocket and retrieved the car keys. The sincerity and in-charge attitude won the priest over. "Thanks, Mayor LaPlante. I appreciate it." He turned to Zane with impatience. "Happy? Now let's get Catharina to Union Station. It's getting late."

No further complaints were offered by Zane as he helped his sister into the mayor's car. He made sure the priest sat next to her then himself, forcing the mayor to sit in the front seat. A smirk of contempt crossed the politician's face, knowing the lug of a man thought he'd won. The old priest and Catharina chose to believe in the kindness being offered, but the brother needed to be dealt with before too long or Damien Cruz would interfere in his future plans.

The priest would soon find himself in trouble as well. Handing over the keys opened more doors of possibilities than he could even imagine.

♫ ♫ ♫

Catharina opened her eyes with the slow awareness of a person coming out of a dense fog. The heaviness of her arms and legs against luxurious white sheets drove home the exhaustion inside her. The silky comforter composed in various degrees of black spoke of masculinity. Her eyes traveled around the expansive master bedroom until they fell on the sliver of light seeping through the partially drawn drapes. It even smelled like a man, she decided, as the fragrance of soap wafted from the bathroom against the squeaky sound of a shower being turned off. She wanted to push herself up, but the pillows beneath her head felt like she might be on a cloud. A feeling of warmth caressed her so thoroughly that she burrowed deeper into her spot, loving the sight of a fireplace and a small fire glowing across the room.

Suddenly the memory of the fire came crashing back into her otherwise contented reverie. She remembered tripping then hitting her head. The next awareness was the breath of something wonderful entering her body with the will to live. Hearing the voice of her brother, being carried to the alley below and finally the raspy voice of Rocco, brought her to the conclusion that together they had saved her. The hospital visit, Father Xavier and Mayor LaPlante bringing her to Union Station now forced the fog of protection to lift, exposing her to the real possibility she was in Damien Cruz's bed.

Chapter 25

"Good morning." The deep British accent jerked her head toward the man leaving the bathroom as he straightened his tie. He walked over to a silver coffee set and poured hot liquid into a fragile-looking cup that made the slightest tinkle sound after he stirred some cream into the blackness. Carrying the cup and saucer to the bedside, he set it down on the nightstand and went back to messing with his black tie. "Feeling better?"

The aroma of the coffee forced her to take a deep breath and close her eyes. "For me?" She carefully pushed herself to a sitting position after first taking stock of what she was wearing. Apparently, Damien loaned her one of his shirts, now that she remembered, after taking a long hot shower the night before.

Damien handed the cup to her, dwelling on her mouth as she sipped. "You look refreshed." He sat on the edge of the bed where her hand rested seconds earlier. A smile toyed with the corners of his generous mouth. "Did I wake you? I tried to be quiet." The chime of a regulator clock sounded somewhere in another room. He watched her mentally count the chimes. "And before you start worrying, Molly has been at the coffee shop for hours. She's quite capable. Jeremiah helped her with deliveries this morning."

Replacing the cup on the saucer, a slight tremble rattled the china. "Thank you, Damien. Zane and I are in your debt. Taking us in last night—I'm so sorry he burst in on you like that."

Zane wouldn't let Catharina walk up the steps from the street level the night before or take the elevator. He insisted on

carrying her up, as Father Xavier and the mayor followed duti-
fully. As soon as they entered the Grand Hall, she could tell that
her brother had started to slip back into his wounded head of
nightmares.

"Damien Cruz! Damien Cruz! Damien Cruz! I want to see
him now!" His voice echoed across the hall like a small explosion. Thankful that no one was there to hear except some of the
staff, Catharina realized her brother might be dangerous.

"Put me down, Zane," she insisted as he carried her to one
of the plush chairs and deposited her like she was a sickly child.
At least he wasn't dangerous to her. "Stop yelling. Do you want
the police to hear you from the station three blocks away?" She
remembered looking at the mayor as he followed the priest. The
look of contempt and embarrassment was obvious on his narrow face. Before she could evaluate him further, Damien arrived.

Without any concern for Zane's outburst and pacing, Damien squatted down in front of Catharina. He surveyed her condition in one glance before turning his eyes back to Zane. "I'll
take good care of her, Zane. You needn't worry."

Father Xavier sat down in the chair next to her and leaned in
toward Damien. "I don't think this is a good idea."

Damien tore his eyes away from Catharina, leveling a glare
at the priest as his eyebrow arched. "Yes. I imagine you'd think
that." He stood and turned to the mayor. "Kragan. Always nice
to have you drop by."

"He brought us." Zane swayed a little until Damien reached
out and laid a hand on the side of his arm which instantly
calmed him.

"I see that. Thank you, Kragan. I'm sure the Spokanes are
appreciative as is Father Xavier." The mayor's frown and narrowing eyes brought a smirk to Damien's face. "You can all
stay here tonight."

Catharina's voice sounded like a whisper in such a grand
place. "Thank you. I didn't realize Zane had called you. I'm
afraid he's once again taken advantage of your kindness."

She tried to stand and felt the room start to spin. In one swift
movement, Damien scooped her up in his arms, holding her

tight against his chest.

His face came closer to hers. A fleeting thought that Zane would object evaporated as he moved toward the tube-like glass elevator. Her brother backed his way after them, as if on patrol. "Kragan, I'm sure you can show yourself out," Damien called over his shoulder before smiling back down at Catharina. "Father Xavier?"

"The mayor is taking me to the Kitchen then I'll be back." Father Xavier watched Damien nod without giving him another thought.

Now here she was, in Damien Cruz's bed. The thought occurred to her that, on another occasion, this could insinuate a romantic step toward breaking through that iron-clad mystique of his. Her brother had followed them all the way into the bedroom the night before, looking around the room as if it might hide the monsters living in his head. The pacing resembled someone on guard duty. When Damien brought her some clean clothes and showed her the bathroom, which was nearly as big as her apartment, Zane followed. Shutting the door, her brother announced he'd stand guard until she returned for inspection.

Catharina now looked over the edge of her cup as she brought it to her lips. "Where's my brother?"

"In the next room." Damien's mouth turned up at one corner. "Slept on the floor. Father Xavier used the couch even though I offered both of them a room." He reached out to take the empty cup, sitting it on the nightstand. "I suppose their trust of my goodwill only goes so far."

This made Catharina chuckle as she pulled the covers up to her throat. "I'll be sure to let them know my virtue remains intact." She dared to look into his blue eyes, wishing that her brother and the priest would go away.

"You're blushing." Damien reached out and pushed back strands of black hair from her forehead. "They're right not to trust me."

Catharina tilted her head as her hands went to her cheeks. "Why's that? You've been so good to Zane and me. I really appreciate it, Damien."

Damien eyed her with a look of hunger. "Maybe I'm trying

to win you over. We got off to a rocky start." His hand darted out to rest upon hers as she tried to pull it from her cheek.

"Consider me won over." She smiled, all the while pulling free of his hand. "I probably should get dressed and go to work."

Damien stood. "Not today. I rather like the thought of you lying in my bed." He smiled wolfishly, seeing the embarrassment flood her eyes. "Besides, the doctor said rest for a few days. Your brother can keep you company as long as he likes." He nodded toward several blue striped boxes wrapped with black ribbons. "Your clothes may not be salvageable so I took the liberty of having the boutique in our mall send some things up. Keep any and all that you like. Everything in your apartment is gone, Cat."

The truth of her destitution forced a sob to escape her throat as tears rolled down her cheeks. Damien rushed back to the bed and pulled her into his arms, stroking her head and back. Rocking her tightly against his chest, he waited for her to calm.

"Sweet, Catharina," he whispered in her ear as her arms went around his neck.

"My violin." She pushed back only inches, aware that his lips nearly touched her own. "I don't care about clothes or anything else in the apartment. The violin was the one thing that brought Zane and me happiness all these years. Now," she choked, trying to smile through tears. "How will I calm him?"

Damien took her hands in his. "Let me help."

Catharina shook her head. "Just when I think he is getting better something happens to erode his progress."

"Zane has greatness inside him, Cat. Don't under estimate that." He stood. "I need to get going. I'll have the chef prepare our French toast special for you. I'll make sure there's enough for Zane and Father Xavier." Offering a smile, he reached out and wiped away a few tears. "Tonight we'll talk about where you'll stay until you decide what you want to do. Zane is welcome to join us in the conversation. As a matter-of-fact I think that would be a good idea."

"Thank you, Damien." She tugged at the covers again. "For everything. Zane really trusts you for some reason. I'm glad."

"No running off to the coffee shop," he warned. "I've got

security on high alert for that." He grinned as he moved toward the door. "See you tonight."

Catharina waited a couple of minutes before swinging her legs over the side of the bed. She wanted to make sure Damien didn't return. The thought of him gazing upon her half naked could be awkward. When she heard voices in the next room, she cracked open the door enough to hear. None of it made sense.

"I don't want her here." Father Xavier paced, shaking his head and looking down at the floor.

Damien stood with his hands on his hips, feet spread apart in a familiar stance that didn't seem to fit him. Zane leaned back on the sofa with both his arms stretched out on the back. He appeared to be watching the two men with curiosity more than concern.

"I keep telling you, it is not your decision, Father Xavier." The calm voice of reason coming from Damien appeared to insight the priest.

"Like hell!" he roared.

"Keep your voice down, Father." Zane interjected with a logical air. "I don't want Cat to be disturbed. Damien is right. The decision has already been made."

Father Xavier flopped down on the couch next to Zane, laying his hand on his knee. "Son, you don't have to do this. You kids will make it just fine without him. Please listen to me. I'll retire. We'll move away some place where—"

Zane's arm came down around the priest's shoulders. "No, Father." His voice resembled a caring father more than a wounded warrior. "I'm sick, Father. I know that. Nothing helps, except when I'm fighting for justice to help others. Then I'm whole. Don't try and take this from me. It's my choice."

The priest shivered before turning his watery eyes back to Damien. "I trusted you. Ministered to you. Cared for you." The betrayal he felt revealed itself in his voice as he choked back a sob. Father Xavier turned back to Zane. "And what of Cat? Is this what you want for her?" His eyes darted back to Damien with scorn.

With his other arm, Zane finished wrapping himself around the priest and hugged. "It is. But she will be the one to decide both our fates. Not you. Me. Or—" His eyes moved to Damien. "—anyone else. Believe, Father."

Catharina closed the door, confused at the conversation. What was happening? How could she possibly decide anyone's fate? After all, she wasn't so good with her own fate, much less someone else's. More crazy talk coming from a brother whose demons of war refused to loosen their iron grip of post-traumatic stress disorder. Leaning against the door, she let herself toy with the thought of having Zane committed to a VA mental facility for some help. The periodic swings between being normal and threatening could put others in serious danger. They occurred more often it seemed. Did Rocco have something to do with this increasing fall toward insanity?

A pounding heart, forged of grief for what lay ahead, helped her decide to savor the days ahead for however long they had together.

♫ ♬ ♫

The French toast, covered in bananas, caramelized pecans, and powdered sugar delighted Zane and Father Xavier. Even as Catharina picked at her serving, the priest shared that the recipe won first in a city wide contest. She wasn't surprised.

"This is so good, I'm pretty sure it must be a sin," Father Xavier said, trying to catch a drip of caramel with his linen napkin. He pointed at Catharina's plate. "If you're not going to eat that Zane and I sure will. Right, son?"

Before Catharina could comment, Zane reached across with his fork and snagged a half-eaten piece. He still chewed on his last bite.

"No wonder you're so skinny, Cat." He pointed to the priest then Catharina's plate. "Father, tell her she's too skinny."

Catharina decided hearing Zane chuckle and make light conversation was the best medicine she could possibly have after nearly losing her life in a fire. What would have become of him if she died?

The priest forked one of her slices of toast onto his plate. "No. You're perfect." He funneled the toast into his mouth, winking at her. "This is not good for you, anyway. I'm doing you a favor by eating it."

Leaning back in her chair, she smiled at the two men she loved so deeply. "Thanks, Father Xavier. Maybe you and Zane can go jog off all those calories when we're finished."

Zane nodded and pointed his fork at the priest. "Great idea. You used to jog with me when I was a kid."

"That's because you were a handful and I wanted you to burn off some of that energy."

Laughter spilled from Zane's mouth, making Catharina reach over and pat his arm. "I love you, Zane." Her eyes shifted to the priest. "And especially you, Father."

The priest pushed his plate back. "We know that."

"I thought I heard arguing when Damien left this morning. What was that all about?" Catharina couldn't help but notice the smiles on their faces fade. "Everything okay?"

Zane lifted her hand to his sticky mouth and kissed it. "Right as rain, baby sister. Nothing to worry about." He shifted his eyes to the priest. "Right, Father Xavier?"

The priest shook his head and forced a smile. "Nothing to worry about, Cat. We'd tell you if there was."

She eyed both of them, feeling skeptical. "Promise?"

They crossed their hearts at the same time, making her laugh, before speaking in unison. "Promise."

A light tap at the door then Damien's assistant pushed it open carrying a large vase of long stemmed roses. "These are for you, Ms. Spokane."

Catharina hurried to take the card as the assistant placed them on a rod iron library table. "Oh my goodness."

The image of Damien sitting on the side of the bed, consoling her earlier in the morning flashed into her brain.

"That's not all, Ms. Spokane." He walked back to the door, propping it open with his hip, and was handed another large package. "This also came." He nodded matter-of-factly then excused himself.

Tearing into the beautifully wrapped package, Catharina found another oblong box. Lifting the lid, she sucked in her breath, reached in, and pulled out a violin case. With nervous fingers, she opened the case so gingerly it drew Father Xavier to her side. "Oh." The awe in her voice at seeing the exquisite maple colored violin enticed her to lift it up into her arms as if it were a newborn.

Zane rose to come near and stare over her shoulder. "Who are they from, Cat?"

Catharina looked up with concern, knowing how Zane would react. "They're from the mayor."

Chapter 26

Staring out his window to the street below, Kragan turned only when he heard the office door open. Morgan entered with Detective Jacobs at her elbow. The detective's eyes appeared to instinctively sweep the room, as if looking for clues. Unaffected by the grandiose space and person before him, the detective extended his hand toward the mayor while at the same time letting his gaze look out the window.

"Good afternoon, Detective Jacobs. I appreciate you stopping by." Kragan released the detective's hand, fighting the urge to use the hand sanitizer inside his desk drawer. He surveyed the detective's rumpled appearance and wondered if the man slept in his clothes. "The fire marshal called a bit ago and it looks like the Essmalory Building was a result of arson. What do you have for me?"

Without being told, the detective took a seat. Pulling out his notebook, he caught the glances between Morgan and the mayor. He waited until they lowered themselves into their own chairs before proceeding. "Hate to hear that about the Essmalory. My grandmother used to live there back in the day." Shaking his head, he slipped through several notebook pages. "The Kitchen of Hope was badly damaged as you probably saw last night."

Kragan leaned back in his chair until it squeaked. "Yes. A shame." He regretted letting his condescension slip into his voice, drawing the detective's eyes away from his notes. The detective looked like a simpleton, but his accolades over the years drove home the awareness that treading lightly would be in his own best interest. "And the men killed last night? Was it The Watcher again?"

"Sounds like it."

"This is getting out of hand." The mayor let his irritation show this time. "The news is making a circus out of these attacks. The Watcher, or whatever he is, has everyone calling him some kind of vigilante hero that swoops in to save the poor. This city doesn't need a wack-job-of-a-Robin-Hood running loose. He's a menace." He began to rock his swivel chair back and forth, making it squeak. "I'm getting sick of hearing about him."

"Yes, sir. Well, it appears the people living upstairs didn't see a thing. One of the kids did say some guy helped his dad. But when we questioned the kid further, he clammed up."

Kragan stood up and placed his hands on his hips, forcing his suit coat back. "Drag their butts down to the station. See how they like that."

The detective shoved his notebook back into the inside pocket of his jacket. "They're not going to talk. Not the most trusting lot. Whoever swooped in probably saved their lives. The other residents were just as closed mouth. Didn't see anything except the dead guy fighting a shadow. Then he was gone. Downstairs there was quite a ruckus. The two that survived said The Watcher had super strength." The detective smirked. "I'm sure that description comes from getting their asses kicked. They were a little shook up that the others met with justice—"

"Justice," Kragan barked. "Don't tell me you're becoming a fan too. No wonder the police department hasn't caught him." His voice turned into an icy growl. "If you guys did your job, then we wouldn't need a crazy person going around serving up his own kind of retribution."

A patient sigh slipped from the detective's mouth. "We had a number of people at the Essmalory fire last night. Seems like these guys took advantage of a bad situation. Someone left a message for me this morning saying the two were connected."

Kragan dropped his hands to his side then toyed with pulling down his suit coat sleeves. "Connected? How?"

"Not sure." The detective smiled revealing crooked teeth.

"Don't worry. I'll figure it out, Mr. Mayor." The detective stood. "I always do." Pulling back his shoulders, he dropped his eyes down on Morgan Knox. "You and Damien Cruz still…friends, Ms. Knox?"

She began examining her nails. "Not really. We see each other socially on occasion but that's all. Why?"

"Just wondered if you knew anything about Ms. Spokane and her brother staying with Mr. Cruz is all." He watched her eyes widen for a second before turning his own on the mayor. "Nice of you to take them to Union Station last night, Mr. Mayor."

"Yes. They needed a place to stay and I'm very fond of the Spokanes. They've had some bad luck over the years. Mr. Cruz was gracious enough to offer them a place to spend the night. Ms. Spokane has the coffee shop there, so it makes sense."

The detective grinned. "From what I hear it's a little more than just coffee."

"Don't believe everything you hear, Detective," Kragan snapped as he grasped the back of his chair.

Jacobs moved toward the door. "I never do, Mr. Mayor.

"By the way, what have you found out concerning the fire and murder at Glen Forrester's house?" Kragan walked around to the front of his desk and leaned back, crossing his arms in front of his chest. "And the guy on Laclede's Landing where Mr. Spokane was shot?"

The detective chuckled as he eyed the mayor. "We're still looking into it, Mr. Mayor. Fingerprints were pretty smudged. Only got a partial. Not enough to be sure. Could be self-defense just like Spokane claims. However—" The detective clamped his lips together as if he might be concerned about giving out too much information.

"I'm the mayor, Detective Jacobs. I want to get to the bottom of this. The city is in crisis."

The empathic tone didn't fool the detective as his lips thinned to a smile. "We found a print at the Forrester home on the shed doorknob out back. It belonged to Mr. Spokane. The slices across the man's chest were similar to the deceased at Laclede's Landing and the ones that broke into the Kitchen of

Hope. We're also doing a comparison with the victim at the Essmalory. Looks the same."

"But Mr. Spokane was in the hospital at the time of the fire at the Forrester home. How do you explain that?"

The detective appeared to chew on his answer for a few seconds before answering. "Could have had help, maybe came by the day before to threaten the old man, who knows? Records show that Mr. Spokane may have known the deceased."

"You don't say. How's that?" Kragan found himself feeling light headed with anticipation.

"It's a process. You'll know when we're sure of the evidence. Still checking things out. I wouldn't worry too much about your friend."

Kragan rose up from sitting on the desk. "We're not friends, detective. I am concerned about the safety of his sister. She appears to be unaware of the danger he poses."

The detective's eyes went to Morgan who now glared at the mayor. She obviously wasn't aware that something was going on between the coffee shop girl and her boss. Making a mental note to bring it up the next time he talked to the Spokanes gave him an excuse to leave. "On my way there now to visit with the Spokanes."

Kragan glanced at his Rolex. "They may have gone by now. The brother doesn't stay put very long and Catharina is a workaholic." Just saying her name made a smile toy at the corners of his mouth.

"Nope. Already called. Mr. Cruz says they'll be his guests for a little longer. You know Mr. Cruz. Once he decides on something, it's his way or the highway." Jacobs chuckled more for the sour look on the mayor's face than his little attempt at a joke. "Have a nice day you two." He pulled at the doorknob then let himself out.

♫ ♫ ♫

"Are you seeing that rag-a-muffin from the coffee shop, Kragan?" Morgan's voice rose like the beginning of a kindled fire.

Pouring himself a bourbon, Kragan quickly downed it then

poured another. "What I do in my social life is none of your business unless it affects this office."

She stood before crossing her arms across her cosmetic enhanced chest. "Don't get the idea I'm jealous. You're just a way to soothe an urge." A hard swallow nearly choked her as Kragan leveled a sinister glare over the top of his glass. "If her brother is involved in this Watcher business, toying with the affections of his sister could land you in the media cross-hairs in a very negative way." It took some doing, but Morgan managed to drop her arms and stroll nonchalantly to the mayor's side to pour a drink. "Are you sleeping with her?" The words sounded hollow even to her.

Kragan chuckled as he sat his glass down. "Not yet." He eyed Morgan from top to bottom. "Why don't you lock the door and try to change my mind about that?" Slipping one arm around her waist then letting his hand slide down to her buttocks, he kissed her neck. "She's a toy. You on the other hand—" Kragan removed the glass from her hand. "—make this job bearable. I don't know what I'd do without you, Morgan." He smiled as she pulled away then walked to the door to turn the lock. "No more questions about Cat." He began to remove her layers of professional clothing. "We're a good team. Let's not screw that up."

The familiarity of calling the woman "Cat" wasn't lost on Morgan as she allowed Kragan to consume her self-respect. Loving such a man would always be a one-way street. She'd decided a long time ago that getting what you wanted demanded sacrifice. Kragan always came back to her after one of his affairs, usually with a married woman. There was a certain ring of protection by seducing such women.

But with Catharina Spokane the possibilities were endless. Morgan had noticed from the moment they'd met that something intrigued Kragan. His smile and mannerisms changed. The uninterested glare he dropped on people like a hammer evaporated when Catharina spoke. Even his laugh sounded warm and inviting. The woman needed to be dealt with as soon as possible.

♫ ♫ ♫

"Don't you want the new one, Mr. Cruz? It's not likely to have problems like this one." The owner of the music store held up the violin Damien selected.

Damien eyed the turquoise colored instrument and pictured Catharina holding it as she spun around to some hip hop music she loved to play. It fit her Bohemian style, he thought.

"No. I think this one will do."

"It's old and doesn't have any kind of a guarantee, Mr. Cruz."

"Neither does life. If it doesn't suit the lady, I'll bring her back to choose one she likes better. How's that?" Damien passed over his credit card.

The owner nodded then shrugged as if it was a poor decision.

♫ ♫ ♫

Left alone, Catharina crawled back into bed after leaving Zane and Father Xavier. Both needed to attend to other matters so they made sure she was tucked in first. Her feelings of self-consciousness about sleeping in Damien's bed evaporated as exhaustion engulfed her.

The bed felt like a cloud. A familiar scent clung to the pillow cases, drawing her arms around their firmness so that she moved her face back and forth to breathe their earthiness. The luxurious feel of the sheets brought to mind Belle in the Beauty and the Beast. Did she feel like this?

Dreams began to chase her through the dark recesses of Union Station. Something dark and dangerous followed her. Laughter started to bounce off the steel beams that she'd seen crisscross in the upper areas where Rocco liked to escape. Whoever tracked her didn't try to climb them. She could hear him breathing harder with each step. Then she heard him speak.

"Here kitty, kitty."

Catharina started to run then fell. Someone grabbed her foot and tugged hard enough that her knees began to bleed. She couldn't see her captor but heard him laugh between calling her "kitty."

Bolting upright in bed, panting, with tears running down her cheek, Catharina swung her legs over the side of the bed. She took a deep breath before rubbing her face against the sleeve of Damien's shirt. Pushing herself to her feet, she let her heart slow before moving to open the drapes. The first snow fell outside as she rested her forehead against the cold panes of glass.

Years of buried terror surfaced in her dreams along with everything else going on in her life. That horrible bully that used to torment Zane at their last foster care home now stalked her again. He would stand outside her room at night and toy with her name calling "kitty, kitty, kitty." Sometimes he would make suggestions she didn't understand as a child. Zane understood them, causing him to fly into a rage against the boy.

Finally they ran away into the night. Father Xavier mended their broken spirits and memories, replacing them with faith and love.

The news reports of Glen Forrester's house burning caused that whole episode of her life to float to the surface like a bloated body. She looked around her. Somehow she knew this place would be safe for a few days until she could decide what to do next. Her eyes fell on the boxes Damien left for her. Walking around in his shirt and robe might send him the wrong message.

He probably was used to women doing that, but her love life was a lot less complicated.

Grabbing up several of the boxes, she started toward the bathroom for another shower when her eyes fell on a painting. The artist plate said 1777. Catharina smiled at the irony of it all, considering that Damien was British and this depicted a scene from the War of Independence. Then one of the British soldiers caught her attention.

"Damien!" she gasped.

Chapter 27

Damien read the card left on the violin case. It rested on the library table next to the vase of roses. *May you continue to bring beauty to the world with your music. Love, Kragan.* He stared at the card until the words began to blur. Hearing Catharina humming in the bedroom made him decide to place his own surprise in the coat closet. Kragan's violin was exquisite. Anyone in their right mind would desire such an instrument. The turquoise violin now felt a little ridiculous. His assistant could return it in a few days after Catharina decided what she wanted to do.

"Hi." Catharina stood in the doorway as he shut the closet.

Damien eyed her dressed in the new clothes he purchased for her at the mall boutiques down stairs. They were a combination of black, leopard, and pink stripes. Somehow she made it work. Even the silver earrings and bracelets added a layer of funky chic he'd come to love.

"Hi, yourself. Feeling better?" The taffeta skirt swished when she walked. The black stockings hugged her slim legs all the way down to the top of her pink cowboy boots.

"I feel great." She looked down at her clothes. "These are perfect, Damien. I'm surprised you didn't buy me a three piece suit or something regal like this place." She threw her hands up to encompass the room. "Thank you."

Damien smiled as he stepped closer, noticing the tips of her hair were wet. "This place needs a little more fun. You keep it from being too stuffy. Your au-vanguard style is growing on me. I'm thinking about wearing a polo shirt to work."

Catharina burst out laughing. "Don't go all crazy on me, Damien." She hugged her sides from the laughter. "I'm kinda liking that stuffy look of yours." His smile widened, but his eyes narrowed a little. "Besides, you needn't change on my account." She wanted to voice her insecurities without sounding ungrateful.

Damien moved to stand before her. "Why is that?"

"We both know I don't fit in your uppity, fancy, smancy world. I'm pretty rough around the edges."

The look of steel was seeping back into his eyes. "Just like a diamond. We both know how they turn out."

"Sweet talk. I bet the ladies just eat that up." Catharina forced herself to move away to stand near the flowers. It was getting difficult to breathe.

"Yes. They usually do." Damien's voice took on a bland tone that drew Catharina's eyes to meet his. "But not you."

"Not me." She raised her chin as if playing with his temperament. "If you don't mean it, don't say it." Fiddling with one of the flowers calmed her jittery feelings. "I really don't like all that phony baloney."

"Yet you and the mayor seemed to have hit it off." He walked over to the violin and lifted it out of its case. "This is beautiful. Expensive too, I suspect. Kragan never skimps on his gifts to those he cares about."

"Yes. It is quite lovely." Catharina noted no jealousy or irritation as he inspected the gift. Was she imagining Damien's growing attraction to her?

No matter. Rocco was who she really cared about and that was all that mattered.

"It looks so fragile." She reached out and touched it. "I'm intimidated by such extravagance." A chuckle escaped her lips as she withdrew and sat down on the sofa. "Zane and I never had much and what we did have was precious. I'm so disappointed I lost my violin in the fire, but I've learned to count my blessings. At least Zane and Rocco—" She gulped into silence as Damien returned the violin to the case and turned to level a look at her.

"Rocco?"

Damien's eyebrow did that arch thing that made Catharina want to touch it. "I—Huh."

"Did The Watcher help Zane rescue you? Is that what you're telling me, Cat?"

"I'm a little fuzzy on the details." She dropped her gaze to the floor as a knock tapped at the door, followed by Damien's assistant ushering in Detective Jacobs.

"Hope I'm not interrupting anything?" The detective's eyes drifted from Damien, who looked like his usual sinister self, and Catharina, who looked like the cat who swallowed the canary.

"Not at all." Damien's voice turned icy. "Wasn't expecting you, Mr. Jacobs."

"It's *Detective* Jacobs." He smiled. "And I don't usually make appointments, Mr. Cruz." Moving to a nearby chair, the detective reached inside his coat pocket to remove a small spiral notebook. "May I sit down?"

"I see no need in that, since you won't be staying long." Damien knew his British accent always thickened when he grew irritated. It felt like syrup on his tongue now. He leaned against the library table and crossed his arms. "How can I help you?"

The detective's smile faded as his eyes turned on Catharina sitting on the edge of the sofa, hands folded with the look of a frightened church mouse, fear filling the widened eyes. "Glad to see you're all right, Ms. Spokane. Some were not as lucky as you."

"Oh no. I thought everyone made it out." Catharina put her hands on her cheeks and shook her head. "Who are you talking about?"

Jacobs read over his notes. "A Mrs. O'Hanlon died of smoke inhalation after getting to the hospital. The Tripps on the third floor have some injuries but are expected to make a full recovery. Several others suffered injuries trying to escape and will need further medical attention but they too are expected to recover, although it may take a while." He watched Catharina's eyes become watery. "Yet you made it out when the building was fully engulfed. How did your brother get to you in time?"

Before she could answer, Damien joined her on the couch and took her hand in his. "She doesn't remember, Detective."

He squeezed her hand in support, drawing her eyes to his. Could she recognize a warning of caution in his tone? "Her brother is a strong lad. I'm sure it was a case of an adrenaline rush pushing aside any thought of danger for his own safety."

"I asked Ms. Spokane." The detective leveled his own look of caution toward Damien. "Ms. Spokane?"

She looked down at Damien's hand holding hers and appeared to be surprised, then she leaned into his body enough where he dropped her hand to surround her shoulder with his arm.

"I'm afraid I don't remember much." She touched her forehead where a nasty bruise showed near her hairline. "I tried to gather up a few things to get out then tripped and fell. The next thing I knew Zane was carrying me down the alley." She tore her eyes away from Damien long enough to focus on the detective. "I'm sorry."

The thought of Rocco holding her in his arms then passing her off to Zane would remain a secret. She knew the darkness inside the angel held many mysteries she dared not explore just yet. Without his help, Zane would never have been able to reach her. Something else toyed at the recesses of her mind; the breath of life filling her lungs when her body felt as if the desire to live had evaporated.

"I really don't remember, Detective Jacobs. Why is this important?"

The detective took a deep breath before leveling a serious look at Catharina. "Your brother seems to always show up at the wrong place at the wrong time."

"What are you saying?" Catharina's voice took on a nervous tone.

"Do you think he set that fire?"

Catharina jumped to her feet. "No. Of course not. He's a gentle giant who wouldn't hurt a soul. I know he's a little off of late, but he suffers from PTSD."

Jacobs stared at her then down at Damien whose eyes had narrowed to slits of fire. "There's some question about several incidents, involving unexplained fires or deaths."

"Detective, is this line of questioning necessary? Ms.

Spokane has just lost her home and discovered some of her neighbors were seriously injured. She's been through a great deal. Can't this wait?" Damien stood, too, so he could look down his nose at the detective who had begun to smirk at them both.

"If it could, do you think I'd be here?" The detective tried a flippant tone, as if to show Damien two could play the intimidation game. "Do you know a Glen Forrester, Ms. Spokane?" When Catharina's eyelashes began to flutter nervously, he prepared to hear a lie.

"The name sounds familiar." She tried with everything inside her to remain calm. "Why?"

"Apparently, he was one of your foster care fathers when you were growing up." Watching Catharina pale was all the answer he needed. "You and your brother ran away it seems and were never heard from for some time until someone in Father Xavier's parish took you in. Although they were an older couple and died not too long after you joined them. Yet it appears payments continued for your support."

"It was a long time ago, Detective Jacobs. I don't remember the names of the families who took us in. There were so many. The couple you say died kept us safe for several years. I know nothing about payments."

Damien moved to open the door. "Get to the point, Detective, and then leave. Ms. Spokane needs to rest."

"Your brother's finger prints were found at the Forrester home. We think he's involved somehow in the fire and death of your former foster father."

Catharina gasped as her hands flew to her throat. "He was in the hospital when that fire started."

"I thought you didn't remember the man?" The detective shoved the notebook back into his coat pocket along with his hands and glared at Catharina. "Yet you are pretty sure your brother was in the hospital at the time?"

Catharina swallowed hard as her eyes darted to Damien who stood with his feet slightly apart in a stance that reminded her of Rocco. "Yes." Her voice became rushed and breathy. "Yes. I watched it on the evening news. He was a cruel man we both tried to forget and did until we saw it on the news."

"How do you explain the finger print?" The bottom lip of the detective jutted out in a pout.

"I put it there." Zane pushed into the room past Damien to stand next to his sister who looked as if she'd been thrown a hand grenade. With a nonchalant shrug he flopped down on the sofa. The contrast of soft velvet against tattered camouflaged clothing was not lost on the detective.

"Zane." Catharina felt a wave of panic engulf her as Damien came to stand in front of the detective.

"Why were you there, Mr. Spokane?"

Damien bristled as he pushed his suit coat back with his hands resting on his hips. "You don't have to answer that, Zane."

Zane smiled, almost child-like. "I saw the creep at the shop I take my car. Thought he looked familiar so I talked to him. Told me who he was. Didn't recognize me, of course." Zane chuckled. "Wasn't the same stupid kid he like to knock around."

"Maybe you decided on a little payback." Jacobs cocked his head as he spoke.

"Nope." Zane shook his head. "He needed a ride home so I offered to give him a lift."

"Zane, stop talking." Catharina sounded panicked. The night in the hospital he hadn't mentioned he'd seen the man earlier. "Stop right now."

Zane held up his hand for her to hush and continued to smile. "It's okay, baby sis. I carried some things to the garage for him. I bet that's where you found the fingerprints. His neighbor came by to check me out. I said goodbye and never saw him again."

"Did you tell him who you were?" Jacobs wanted to believe him.

"Nah. I was going to but the neighbor came along." Zane's facial expression changed from innocent to menacing in a flash. "Besides 'vengeance is mind saith the Lord.'" The anger faded from his face but not his eyes. They seemed to glow. "Or that's what Father Xavier always says." He winked at Catharina. "Right, little sister?"

Catharina choked on her words, failing to respond in a way that would clear her brother.

"Will that be all, Detective?" Damien again walked to the door and opened it wider. "Next time make an appointment."

Jacobs smiled and moved to leave. "That's not really how it works." He turned back to look at the Spokanes. "You wouldn't know anything about the fire last night, would you Mr. Spokane?"

Zane crossed his legs as if he were at a board meeting. "I know it wasn't an accident."

"And how would you know that? The fire marshal just informed the mayor an hour ago."

Zane looked at Damien then the detective. "A little birdie told me."

His eyes turned into that faraway gaze that made Catharina realize she was losing him again.

"Yep. Little birdie. Little birdie. Little birdie." A cackling laugh escaped his lips.

The detective frowned and shook his head in sympathy. "I'll check out your story, Mr. Spokane. Thanks for your time." And then he was gone.

Damien shut the door as he heard Zane laugh out loud and slap his hands together. Catharina looked both horrified and confused. Zane stood up to gather his sister in his arms. Patting her hand like a little girl, he then twirled her around.

"He thinks I'm crazy." Landing a kiss on Catharina's cheek, he noticed she'd thought he had lost touch again. "I was just acting, Cat. I'm okay. Really. Can't you tell the sickness is leaving me?"

"I—" She looked for assistance from Damien who had arched an eyebrow in impatience. Would he kick them out into the street? Why would he want anyone like them staying at his hotel if there was a possibility of Zane being arrested? "I think we should go, Zane."

"Go where?" Zane started to laugh then realized she wasn't kidding. "The rectory? Impossible. The Kitchen of Hope rooms are full, so that leaves the streets. That's no place for you. Right, Damien?" Zane's voice had taken on a serious tone, indicating he felt in charge.

"We need to talk about that, Zane." Damien sounded forceful as his eyes shot Zane a warning look. "That guy is out to get you. The police need an arrest."

Zane started to pace, flexing his hands open and closed. "I didn't do anything to that man. I wanted to but I didn't. Someone beat me to it. The guy was a monster. How many kids did he hurt after us?"

Catharina grabbed him by the arm to stop the pacing. "Are you sure?"

Jerking free of her hold, he pushed his face into hers and yelled, "Yes!" Realizing he'd frightened his sister, he put his hands on her shoulders and squeezed. "But whoever it was, I'm thankful." His eyes shifted to Damien. "Forever thankful. And when I find that man's son I will kill him." The quiver in her body forced Zane to pull her into his arms. "Don't cry. Don't…" He felt himself slipping into confusion until Damien touched his back with one finger. "I was part of the group that protected the Essmalory from those jerks who broke in and tried to hurt you. But that's all."

Damien pulled Zane back from Catharina. "Let's have some dinner then talk. Zane, I want you to stay here tonight. A foot of snow is forecasted. The streets are no place for you."

Zane slapped Damien on the back, making Catharina cringe at his familiarity. "Don't mind if I do. The Kitchen is closed for a few days while things are sorted out over there. Told Father Xavier I'd be around to help out. Gideon said he'd bring some of the guys to help too."

"Thanks. That's very kind of you, Damien. But I'm sure there's a shelter—" Catharina tried to interject.

"Nonsense." Damien picked up the phone and made reservations for them downstairs at the Railroad Restaurant. He ordered a private alcove for them. "We'll be able to think straighter after we've eaten. I'll leave a message for Father Xavier to join us. I'm sure he's exhausted after today. He may want to be in on this." His voice transitioned from commanding to concern as his eyes turned to Catharina. "Just one more night, Cat. I want to make sure you're healthy before I let you go."

Catharina nodded and forced a smile as she retreated to the bedroom to get her new purse.

Zane raised his chin then turned to face Damien. "You're not seriously thinking about letting her go."

"No. I'm not."

Chapter 28

atharina stared out the windows of Damien's Union Station apartment to the street below. Traffic moved at a snail's pace on snow-laden pavement. Horns sounded muffled against such purity. Most of the snow fell after midnight and the plows didn't appear to be making much headway on clearing the main arteries. From the trickle of cars, it appeared that most chose to stay home. She placed her hands on the icy cold panes of glass and remembered how she'd loved a snow day as a child after coming to live with Father Xavier.

When she was a small child those days turned into a nightmare. Tormented by the other foster children or bullied by an older child of the host family, she was forced into hiding with her brother most of the time. After the Father Xavier took them, those snow days became a holiday. The priest would wear an apron and bake cookies, show them secret places in the church, tell them funny stories about his travels as a young man. But mostly they would play board games and read books together. He taught Zane about cars, caught him up on his math, and showed him how to box. Catharina loved watching the priest teach Zane how to be a man.

He had saved them. "Christ saved all of us so it is my duty to save those who cannot fend for themselves."

The brief explanation would end with a kiss on the top of Catharina's head. Sometimes she prayed that Father Xavier would never leave them, that the authorities would be blinded as to their whereabouts. She lived in fear their happiness might crumble until a familiar social worker promised to keep their secret.

Now another savior stepped forth to protect them. Damien Cruz. She wasn't sure how long his hospitality might last. Being a burden could jeopardize their relationship, even though she remained confused as to what that relationship was. Then there was Rocco, materializing at the most dangerous of moments. The hold he wheeled over Zane both thrilled and frightened her. Since that first night they'd met, Zane often appeared to be healing from the inside out. He joked again, teased her, worked diligently at the Kitchen of Hope, and didn't slip in and out of reality as often. The brave Marine she'd watched march to war, only to return broken and a shell of a man, now carried himself proudly as if the world had been served to him on a silver platter. His eyes sparkled again with life instead of being haunted by ghosts from a foreign land. The strength in his hands and the tightness of his muscles told Catharina her brother was working out again. Yet she feared what it all meant, since Rocco set the metamorphosis in motion. Would it all be for nothing if he became a vigilante for Rocco's kind of justice?

Catharina let her thoughts drift back to the night before at dinner. The storm emptied Union Station Mall early so only a few hotel guests wandered into eat. She did notice a number of what looked to be business men at the bar watching various sports venues on the big-screen TVs. The sound of quiet throughout the Grand Hall calmed her jitters as Damien and Zane talked about their days in the military. The image of Damien in the painting in his bedroom made her look at him differently.

Even now as she stood before the painting, she couldn't resist touching the figure of his likeness. Her shoulder began to burn where the tattoos reminded her of a cruel past. Yet she allowed her fingers to linger until the fire subsided. Usually it was Rocco who made her pain surface. She hadn't realized the thought of The Watcher might burn as her thoughts crowded in against Damien. Both men, if you could call Rocco a man, created a powerful attraction for her that felt impossible to resist.

"Morning." Damien backed into the bedroom carrying a silver tea service. His British accent brought a smile to toy at the corners of Catharina's mouth. "Did you sleep well?" He set the tray down on a table near the window. His eyes stared out at the canvas of white.

"Yes. I hope you did. I could have slept in one of the hotel guest rooms, Damien. This is just too much. I can never repay your kindness." She smiled over at him, noticing how he stared outside with his hands clasped behind his back like some English lord of a magnificent manor house.

"We discussed this last night." He remained focused on the scene outside. "You own a business here that is good for my hotel. If you can't make any money, then you can't pay me." He turned to look at Catharina, standing like a little lost kitten. "I would do it for any of my vendors, Cat." He wondered if that were true.

"Somehow I can't imagine old Jesse sleeping in your bed." She was thinking of the bellman with amusement as she cocked her head to eye Damien.

"Yes. Well, you're right there." He took a series of slow steps toward her. "I'm rather selective on that point."

"I need to get to work. I got a call that the pastries wouldn't be delivered today so I postponed going down so early." The image of a dark panther moving through the jungle flashed in her mind as Damien approached, his hands still clasped behind his back.

"Catharina." His voice drew her eyes to his mouth.

She turned to look at the painting to avoid exposing how she felt. "Explain to me how it is that you're in this painting. The date is several hundred years old. I Googled the artist and he was a British artist in the late 1700s. An ancestor?"

Damien pretended to examine the painting closer. He grinned as one eyebrow arched in that omnipotent way he had about him. "No." His eyes looked down at Catharina who began to feel as if she were being teased. "I'm pretty sure that's me."

"Well, you look really good for your age, Damien." She tried to sound flippant. "You'll have to let me in on your secret for such a long life."

"Some secrets need to remain that way, Cat." He could feel his eyes frosting up and the desire burning his heavenly designs across his body. For now they remained hidden, but he knew they would surface if he wasn't careful. Fortunately, she walked away to pour herself a cup of tea. The ability to breathe became labored as his body begged to change. He laid a finger across his nose, hoping the black band didn't surface to form a mask across his face. "I'll see you later today, Cat. I'll have a couple of rooms for you and Zane tonight." The longer she stayed in his apartment, the longer her scent tortured him, preventing him from living a normal life. He needed to decide soon what to do about that problem.

♫ ♬ ♫

Catharina listened for the living room door to close before she walked into the room. The grand piano caught her eye as did the floor to ceiling brocade drapes. Everywhere her eyes rested, reminded her that she was out of her element. Before she went downstairs she wanted to look for Zane's backpack he thought he left behind the day before. She vaguely remembered Damien placing something in the closet. A single man used to having everything, probably didn't tolerate clutter like she and Zane.

Opening the door caused a light to automatically turn on. There was a black overcoat, an umbrella which made her smile at the British implications of the two items. It was very Damien. The only other thing was a violin case.

Catharina carried the case to the piano bench and opened it carefully. She stood back as her hands covered her mouth against her awe, staring. The turquoise violin with the nicks and dull finish took her by surprise. Reaching in, she lifted the card. *For the one who heals hearts. Damien.* In that moment something warm and wonderful washed over her. A euphoria of love brought a realization to her very soul, knowing that Damien was a good man who she could surrender to without fear of secrets, social justice, or chance of death.

The violin Kragan sent the day before remained where she had opened it. The emotion she experienced yesterday could not compare to finding Damien's gift. Seeing Kragan's exquisite instrument forced him to hide his. She was sure of it. Now Catharina knew that it was Damien who knew her personality and tastes. It showed in the clothes he bought and now this violin that had seen better days. She never planned to keep the expensive gift Kragan sent. Something didn't feel right. Now she knew why. It just wasn't her.

The overpowering urge to find Damien and throw her arms around his neck swallowed her thoughts until she heard the grandfather clock chime. Carefully, she returned the turquoise violin to the closet. The desire of surprising Damien when she played it for the first time, forced her heavy heart to throw off the shackles of a self-induced pity party. Joy welled up inside her like a new found spring. Grabbing the new violin, Catharina carried it downstairs to the concierge's desk and requested it be returned to the mayor as soon as possible.

Tonight she would surprise Damien.

♫ ♬ ♫

In spite of the bad weather, business remained good at the coffee shop. Molly left early to avoid slippery roads when they started to refreeze at the approach of darkness. Jeremiah dropped in to let her know that any employee having trouble getting home would be allowed to stay at the hotel free of charge. As Molly exited he remained to catch up with Catharina. She drained the coffee machine for him to have the last cup.

"I'm not sure how good it will be," she confessed, handing it to him. Jeremiah smiled then sniffed the brew. She grinned. "Are you sticking around tonight?"

"Live too far out to go home in this weather. I'm beat." He flopped down in a winged back chair. "This Christmas decorating is killing me. Have you been out in the Grand Hall yet?"

Catharina looked out through the glass wall that separated the coffee shop from the Grand Hall. The smoky film covering the surface didn't allow her to get the big picture. "From what I can see it's going to look beautiful. Guess the snow came at a good time. Your army of decorators didn't have to worry about guests getting in the way. When will they be finished?"

"Another hour or so. About the time you get off. They're staying the night. Told them they were going to be treated to a rehearsal of your show for Christmas. The bartenders are pumped. For once, I didn't get any complaints about working overtime. The hostesses say they're wearing their outfits you helped pick out." He laughed as he unbuttoned his suit coat. "They are pretty wild, Cat. Has Damien seen them?"

A moment of insecurity forced her to doubt the creative license she'd taken with the costumes. "No. There's still time to change it if he doesn't like them. None of them were very expensive since we went to Goodwill and Salvation Army."

"Don't change a thing. Besides, you only have another forty-eight hours until the Friday night performance then Saturday for the fundraiser for Boys and Girls Club. I doubt you have time to second guess any of this." He stared down into his coffee for a couple of seconds as if pondering what he would say next. "I understand the mayor sent you a violin."

"I sent it back."

Jeremiah cleared his throat then stuck a finger between the knot of his tie and collar to loosen it. "Be careful around that guy. He comes across all smooth and caring, but he is a snake in the grass."

"He's been really kind to me. And to Zane." Catharina thought she should try and defend him, but the feeling Jeremiah might be right kept her from saying too much.

"Really? Because he has a reputation for trying to move the homeless population out of downtown and out to the county." He stood and smoothed his coat then drained the ceramic cup. "Even though—" He walked behind the counter to put the cup in the sink. "—I'll be the first to admit the homeless keep tourists and businesses from coming downtown, there has got to be a better solution for them." He patted her on the arm as he headed toward the door. "Just saying, I don't think he's being kind to Zane because he's homeless. He's being kind because he wants something else. Watch your step. He's not used to people refusing him. Sending that violin back is a big slap in the face."

"I didn't mean it that way. I'm very appreciative of his thoughtfulness."

"I know." Jeremiah tried to smile. "It'll be okay. You and Zane need to hook your lifeline to Damien. He's not afraid of the mayor like most people."

"You make the mayor sound like a monster." Catharina felt uneasy. "Zane and I have gotten along all these years without either of them. Nothing has changed."

Jeremiah opened the glass doors. "Don't worry about it. Close up early. Get some dinner. On the house. Then get ready to rock this place." He waved as he left.

♫♫♫

Panic gripped Catharina as she slammed the closet door shut in Damien's apartment. The violin was gone. She rummaged through every nook and cranny, in hopes Damien had moved it. Nothing.

Tears threatened to cascade down her freshly applied makeup as Zane entered the apartment, dressed in new clothes, or at least clean ones.

"What's up, little sister? You look bent out of shape." He whistled at her. "I'm liking those new clothes. You look better in them than that resale crap from Goodwill. That Damien has good taste." He turned around to demonstrate his own clothes. "These are Goodwill but the clerk said they were from some rich guy in Webster Groves. Pretty snazzy, huh?"

Catharina eyed him and had to agree he looked handsome. Even his shaggy hair had been cut. Another change for good, she thought. "Yes. You look ruggedly handsome. But I'm in serious trouble," she moaned, running her hands through her jagged hair. "I don't have a violin. Rehearsal is in less than an hour." She started to pace. "What am I supposed to do?"

Zane looked around him. "Where's that fiddle the mayor sent you?"

"Sent it back. I found one in the closet this morning from Damien. He must have hidden it there after finding Kragan's. I put it back and now it's gone. What am I going to do? I wanted to surprise Damien tonight and play it during the rehearsal. Now he's going to be irritated because the rehearsal will have to be canceled. Lots of people are counting on me tonight. I'll let everyone down."

She flopped down on the couch and buried her face in her hands until Zane began to laugh. Raising her eyes to meet his, she hoped he wasn't fading from reality. "Oh, Zane. Please don't slip away from me now."

Zane grabbed her by the hand and pulled her to her feet. "I don't do that anymore or haven't you noticed?" He kissed her on the cheek. "Damien told me to return it to the antique store where he bought it but I took it somewhere else."

Catharina felt breathless. "So you still have it?"

Zane pointed up. "Yes. I took it to the attic."

Catharina thought her heart had stopped beating. "The attic? You mean where—"

"Yes. Where Rocco stays. I'll get it for you. Go on downstairs."

"Why did you take it there after Damien told you to return it?"

"Damien doesn't always know what's best, Cat. He thinks you're falling for Kragan." He looked pensive. "You aren't, are you?"

"Of course not. That's ridiculous. If I were going to fall for anyone, it would be…" *Who? Rocco or Damien?* She didn't know. But seeing her brother smile in utter delight was enough to put off thinking about it further. "Stop looking at me like that. Just get me the violin. I can still surprise him." She stood on tip toes and kissed her brother's cheek then wrapped her arms around him. "I love you."

He took both of her hands and tousled her hair until she protested. "We'll be watching."

"Who?"

But Zane hurried out the door to leave her alone with her last-minute jitters.

Chapter 29

Catharina gawked at the Christmas decorations filling the Grand Hall. The biggest Christmas tree she'd ever seen towered in the middle where a balcony jutted out over the staircase leading to the street below. Stained-glass windows behind it added to the color and holiness of the scene. Garland looped across all the balconies surrounding the hall. Bouquets of poinsettias, white hydrangeas, and gold spikes sat in silver vases on cocktail and coffee tables. Lights, ornaments, and fake snow clung to almost every piece of décor. Eye candy was an understatement. More Christmas trees could be seen on the balconies and every corner of the Grand Hall, each with a different theme. Christmas carols played on some invisible pipe organ over the sound system. There was even a Santa's workshop in one corner of the hall, displaying robotic characters that appeared so life-like Catharina first thought they were actors.

It was nearly nine o'clock.

There was still time for Zane to bring her the violin.

Jeremiah walked up next to her with an iPad in his hands. "Five more minutes and I'll start the light show on the ceiling." He smiled at her starry-eyed look. "Pretty incredible, right? This cost a bundle. The kids are going to love it."

"Probably not as much as their parents." She couldn't help but release a breath she'd been holding tight in her chest. "This is the most beautiful thing I've ever seen." She turned her eyes on the assistant general manager. "Where's Damien?"

Jeremiah turned his attention to the iPad and shrugged. "Somewhere. Not sure. He'll probably show up at the last minute. Don't wait on him." He punched in some commands. "Ready. Ten minutes of light show then you're on, Cat." He smirked as he nodded at the bartenders. "Look at those guys. They can't wait to be in on this. Looks like the decorators are here. The guys over there—" He raised his nose toward them. "—they're from the St. Louis Symphony. And them—" He looked down at the end of the bar. "—not to scare you, but they're from the Post-Dispatch. Damien is putting them all up tonight for coming. Is that good PR or what?"

The overhead light show started with the sound of a train coming. Lights flashed on the side of the Grand Hall as if a locomotive had entered the building. Walls vibrated and the floor trembled beneath her feet as the hall became engulfed with the expectation of a runaway train. Catharina felt frozen in fear as she watched the show. Just seconds before the light show ended the presence of someone behind her caused her to twirl around.

"Zane," she said in relief. "Where's Damien?"

He handed her the turquoise violin, his eyes scanning one of the balconies. "Watching." He leaned in to kiss the top of her head. "Break a leg. You're on." He backed away just as the spotlight hit her.

She heard someone cough, a stool scoot, and a few anxious whispers of concern. Music burst from everywhere as she kicked her shoes into the air. Closing her eyes, she began to feel the background rhythms of the prerecorded melody. All the troubles in the world began to dissipate as the turquoise violin reached her shoulder. As the first song ended, the bartenders and hostesses joined her on the floor with a routine of their own. Something inside of her took hold as she began to dance around them, swaying to her own beat of ecstasy. The realization the onlookers clapped to the beat of the music and sometimes slapped the marble surface of the bar drove her into a delirious performance of perfection.

Stopping for only a couple seconds so she could be lifted onto the bar, she caught a glimpse of someone squatting on the rim of the third floor balcony. Hooded in his dark red cloak, Rocco looked down upon her. With every spin, she looked back to make sure he was still there, watching, believing and maybe in his own way, protecting her from the cruelty of the world. He remained in that position until someone from the newspaper pointed up at The Watcher. Catharina wasn't aware of the discovery until her big finish when she leaped down the bar and swung out her arms and bowed.

Through the applause she heard, "Up there! On the balcony. It's The Watcher."

All eyes looked up to the man now standing precariously on the lip of the railing with his feet apart and his hands out from his side. Cell phones came out and flashes started snapping pictures of the creature that haunted the streets of St. Louis. Then they turned them on Catharina. The morning papers would say, *The Watcher Watches New Angel, Bright Angel Captures Dark Angel's Heart.* She would not be aware of her new celebrity status until several days later.

The flashes began to blind her. She took a step forward and realized too late that she'd stepped off the bar and was falling. Arms reached out and caught her up, then spun her around for more flashes. As she felt her naked toes touch the cold tile of the Grand Hall she looked up into the eyes of Kragan. The headlines to follow would be *Angel's Knight to the Rescue.*

Kragan smiled down at Catharina as he drew her into his arms and kissed her passionately on the mouth. When he released her, he stole a glance up at the balcony where The Watcher had stood moments before. The creature retreated instantly as Kragan pulled Catharina around so she couldn't see the monster escape. He felt a slight resistance in her body as he tightened his embrace.

♫ ♫ ♫

Kragan waved the reporters away as he led Catharina to a quiet area off the Grand Hall that overlooked the Union Station Mall below. Coffee drinkers and businessmen often retreated here to take advantage of the view and relax. The wicker chairs adorned with thick cushions often tempted travelers into taking a nap. With the added Christmas décor, something magical seemed to be everywhere. He ordered the bartender moments before to bring them refreshments.

"You were breathtaking, Cat." Kragan continued to hold her hand as he ushered her to a wicker loveseat. His thumb rubbed the top of her hand as he then reached for her violin. "I'm sorry my gift didn't please you."

"But it did, Kragan. I just didn't think I should accept such an expensive gift. My skills are not worthy of such an instrument." Catharina noted the pain in his narrow eyes. She noticed for the first time they were a mix of gray and yellow. The image of Satan sprang to mind then disappeared. "I really appreciate it. The flowers were beautiful. They really cheered me up," she lied.

"Where did you get this?" He removed his hand from hers and examined the instrument as if he were petting an alligator ready to take his arm off. "It's kind of beat up."

"Zane found it and put it in a safe place. Lucky for me he remembered." She chuckled to make light of the situation. "A little shabby chic, don't you think?"

Kragan gritted his teeth. "Very." He laid it down on the other side from him so that it was out of sight. "You deserve better." His eyes began to caress her face and hair.

"I like this violin." Catharina stood to stare down at him. "Am I an embarrassment to you, Kragan? Because I'm a lot like that violin, a little beat up from life."

Kragan stood suddenly and pulled Catharina into his arms. "You are the most interesting, charismatic creature I've ever known. I can't stop thinking about you. When you play the violin, I nearly lose my mind with wanting you." He crushed his mouth to hers as his hands slid down her back. "I'm falling in love with you, Cat." Running his hand along the side of her head, he leaned in to kiss her forehead. "Come home with me tonight. You need not worry about a place to live. I have plenty of room."

Catharina pushed away and bent to pick up her violin. "I have my brother to think of, Kragan."

"He's a grown man, capable of taking care of himself. Don't let him ruin a chance for you to be happy."

Catharina backed away toward the entrance to the Grand

Hall. "Zane makes me happy. He's always been there for me, good times and bad. I won't desert him, Kragan. Ever." She turned and disappeared.

With fists forming at his side, Kragan growled in a low voice. "Then we'll have to fix that, Catharina Spokane."

♫ ♫ ♫

Jeremiah kept expressing how awesome the rehearsal was and that Catharina would be the next star of St. Louis. Between laughter and retelling some of the comments from the guests, he tried to impersonate some of the dance moves of the bartenders. Once, he tripped and nearly hurled over the walkway that led between the Grand Hall and the new building renovations. If it hadn't been for Zane grabbing him by the collar and jerking him back, Jeremiah would have found himself with a couple of broken legs and maybe even his neck.

Zane followed behind them, looking from side to side as if he were on patrol. Something had spooked him, forcing him to be extra quiet. Catharina tried not to look at him with concern. Even though his fatalistic episodes had diminished, she knew it was a tenuous reprieve. He needed psychological help and Rocco wasn't a therapist.

"Here you go." Jeremiah swiped the card for Zane's room and swung open the door. "Not much of a view but it's cozy." He followed Zane inside, noticing how he examined every nook and cranny.

"Smells new." Zane's words were flat, as if looking over a new set of orders from his commander.

"You're the first guest, Zane. Your sister will be right across the hall." Jeremiah thumped him on the back then snatched his hand back, aware of how hard the man's muscles had become. "Stocked the fridge with some fruit and juice. Damien says to make yourself at home."

Catharina remained in the doorway. "We should have a place in a day or so, Jeremiah. I know this is the busy season for you. You'll need these rooms."

He shrugged. "No problem. If the boss isn't worried, then

neither am I. Come on. I'll show you your room. Yours looks out onto the Union Station Mall. The concierge's lounge is down the hall." Jeremiah handed each of them a pass key. "Breakfast, snacks, anything you want will be there. Comes with the room." Walking across the hall he unlocked her door. "See you in the morning, Cat. Great job, tonight. The Christmas season will rock this year."

"Thanks, Jeremiah." She watched him stroll back across the bridge, humming "Jingle Bell Rock."

Zane pushed passed her to examine her room. When he nodded his okay, she carried her violin in and sat on the end of the king size bed with a sigh. Staring down at the floor, she felt a wave of exhaustion wash over her.

"You did good tonight, baby sister." Zane sounded proud as he appeared to puff out his chest and give her a thumbs up. "What's wrong?"

"Nothing." She smiled up at him. "Thanks for saving the day with the violin." His penetrating stare reminded her of two other men in her life who often looked at her the same way. "I saw Rocco. He could have been captured. The mayor was there and he rarely goes anywhere without his protection detail."

"Rocco can take care of himself." It sounded so matter-of-fact.

"And Damien? Where was he?" Catharina so wanted to surprise him with playing his violin.

Zane laid his hand on her head like Father Xavier used to do after mass. "Watching."

Catharina was confused. "I didn't see him."

"Really? You were looking right at him." Zane turned and walked toward the door. "He's waiting for you downstairs in the ballroom." He motioned for her to find him. "Or maybe you're having second thoughts about the mayor." Catharina stomped past him in anger, but he caught her arm then pulled her back so she had to meet his warning gaze. "I don't like him. He can't be trusted. I don't know why he makes me uneasy but he does. If he ever tries anything—"

Catharina jerked free. "Don't be ridiculous. I'm not interested in him like that." She started through the door but Zane cut her off.

"Well, he's interested in you and doesn't like to be told 'no.' I don't want you to be alone with him again. Understand?"

"I'm a pretty good judge of character, Zane. If I thought he wanted to harm me, I'd stay away from him. Besides, I have no intention of being alone with him."

"That's good, because Rocco wouldn't like it." Zane watched her open her mouth to speak then think better of it. "And neither would Damien," he added as an afterthought.

"What has Damien got to do with Rocco? How are they connected?" Catharina wanted to lift the veil of confusion she felt about the two men. "I'm afraid one or maybe both are affecting you in a negative way. I don't want to lose you. One thing is for sure, I do love you, Zane."

Zane nodded toward the hall. "You'll find out soon enough, Cat. You aren't going to lose me. You might say, you'll have me forever." He smiled at Catharina's frown. "Now go. Damien is waiting."

♫ ♫ ♫

She tugged at one of the double doors leading to the downstairs ballroom. The darkness pierced itself with a small light that flickered behind a Mahogany bar at the opposite end of the expansive room. The door seemed to whoosh shut behind her as she moved inside. The thick carpet softened any sounds that might bounce around a noisy dinner or conference. As she moved forward, her feet touched tile where partiers could dance. Tables and chairs stacked against the walls looked like rock trolls waiting for orders to collapse in on themselves.

"Catharina." The voice carried a thick British accent from the darkness where light couldn't touch. "I'm here."

She paused to let her eyes adjust to a thin outline of a man standing off to the side. With a feeling of caution, she took each step with slow deliberation. She felt conflicted as to her loyalty to Rocco, and now Damien. Both men wrenched at her heart so that indecision of what she desired burned against her soul. One was of Heaven and maybe the other of Hell. It was difficult to understand which was which at times.

"Why are you hiding?" she whispered as she stopped far enough away to see his complete outline.

"I didn't want to frighten you." The British accent grew flat as he took a step forward.

"Frighten me?" This didn't make any sense. "The violin." She swallowed hard then moved closer. "I loved it. Why did you hide it? Was it because of Kragan's gift?"

"I thought perhaps I misread your tastes. His gift was as beautiful as you play. You deserve such a fine instrument."

"Pretty trinkets aren't what I deserve." She felt the tattoos begin to burn her shoulder. Her hand instinctively went to cover it. Was Rocco near? She looked around in alarm.

The shadow moved toward the light. "You deserve a life full of love, Cat. Someone to cherish your God-given gifts. You want a family."

"Yes. How did you know that?" she asked.

"God is a good listener." The British accent faded as a deeper voice emerged.

"Are you comparing yourself to God?" She knew she sounded accusing and disgusted. A jab of pain hit her shoulder so hard she bent over with a groan.

"Breathe, Catharina. Focus on what you know and the pain will subside."

She straightened. "Rocco?" The confusion made her shake her head. "I thought—"

"What?" he asked, his voice patient and low. "That I was The Watcher?"

"I don't know." She took small steps, afraid of the unknown. "Come into the light so I can see you."

Out of the darkness and into the light stepped a man Catharina didn't expect.

Chapter 30

Staring out of his penthouse windows near Forest Park, Kragan held a Purple Heart medal in his hand. He rolled it between his fingers, noting its hardness. The tattered ribbon, with a thin layer of grime, hung on precariously, as if it too had experienced battle. His finger ran across the broken clasp where the pin once fastened it to a soldier's uniform. Recovered at the Kitchen of Hope the night of the breakin, the police discovered it lying on the floor under a steam table. They tossed the medal into a clear bag, then sealed it inside, along with a few other items of no consequence. The decision was made later that it was merely clutter which came along with serving the poor. They left it unattended on a counter to deal with later, and the bag was soon forgotten. More important evidence discovered in the destruction of property and dead bodies demanded immediate examination.

If Kragan had not taken Father Xavier back to the Kitchen that night, he would never have spotted the medal being dropped into the bag. Slipping it into his inside pocket with a nonchalant manner, he drew no undue attention. Just as he'd hope, the Purple Heart belonged to Zane Spokane. Placing it in an evidence box with other information from his father's house fire would be a no brainer. Finding the person responsible for the death of the old man who claimed to be his father was of little importance to Kragan. That bridge burned a long time ago. Revenge against Zane for childhood retributions and taking his precious sister from Zane stroked a more urgent chord.

"What are you thinking about, Kragan?" came a sleepy

voice from his bed.

Kragan turned to see Morgan propped up on one elbow, the sheet barely covering her body. "The future." He turned away, not wanting to be reminded how he could barely stomach the woman. The physical pleasure she once gave him now waned. Consumed with the thought of Catharina dancing for him as she played her magical violin kept him off balance. He imagined her stroking him like her instrument as she professed her love. The press of her lips against his earlier in the evening, brought him to the conclusion that he would have her. Completely.

"What is your status with Damien?" He took a deep breath and moved toward the bed. Looking down at the tangled blonde hair, he noticed a smear of mascara at the corner of one eye.

"Status? You sound like love making is some kind of corporate decision." Morgan huffed as she slipped out of the covers onto the floor on the opposite side of the bed, not bothering to hide her nakedness. "Are you jealous?"

Kragan let a burst of laughter escape from deep inside his chest. "Hardly, Morgan. Let's be honest. Whatever is between us is merely urges on a primal level. Most days I can't stand to be in the same room with you."

Grabbing an autographed St. Louis baseball off the nightstand, she hurled it at his head, only to have him catch it in midair. He threw it back so fast she couldn't dodge it, taking the blow on her shoulder. Crying out, Morgan stumbled back as Kragan hurried around the bed and slapped her so hard she fell back onto the covers.

"Don't ever do that again, you stupid whore. I'm going to teach you a lesson you'll never forget for that," he said as he threw off his robe to the floor. "Then I'm going to tell you what you're going to do for me." As Morgan tried to scoot away, he grabbed her by the ankles and jerked so hard tears flowed down her pasty white face.

He began to stroke her legs. "Purr for me like a cat."

"What?" Morgan's voice trembled as she recognized the evil in Kragan's quiet voice.

"Purr." He drew out the sound like it was cold honey. His demand continued as he got on the bed with one knee. "Here kitty, kitty." His smile forced Morgan to shiver, making him chuckle. She tried to purr. "That's better."

♫ ♫ ♫

Catharina stood staring at the man before her, dressed in a cloak she'd come to recognize as Rocco's. Sometimes, it appeared to be black trimmed in silver and red. Other times, it looked crimson, the color of dried blood with streaks of black and gold. She wondered what it really looked like in the light of day, realizing she'd never seen him in daylight.

The man before her was not Rocco.

Frozen in bewilderment, Catharina mentally tried to evaluate the possibilities of why Damien wore Rocco's clothes. Was this some kind of sick joke?

"Damien?" she whispered, causing him to cock his head as if trying to catch her words. It was a familiar gesture of Rocco's not Damien's. "Why are you dressed like that?"

"This is not of my choosing. None of it is." Damien stepped toward her, driving her deeper into the darkness. "Look at me. What do you see, Catharina?"

Catharina eyed him, loving the straightness of his nose, the dark hair that fell down over his forehead, and the mouth that seemed too wide for his oval face with the high cheekbones. He looked more like a Roman god than a British entrepreneur. Even though she couldn't see them in the dim light, she knew his eyes to be the same blue as a spring sky.

A stinging started again in her inked shoulder, but she cringed to avoid touching the designs. "A kind man I've misjudged. You showed Zane and me kindness at the most impossible of times. I've done nothing to deserve that, and yet you offer everything without asking anything in return."

"I wish that were true. Both of you have given me hope the world can be a better place. I've done things over the centuries that would frighten even your battle-hardened brother."

"Centuries? What are you talking about?" Catharina's first thought was that everyone she cared about had some kind of mental disorder. "You mean years."

Damien motioned for her to step closer. "Your shoulder." He watched her look down at her shoulder then shift her eyes to him. "It burns when Rocco is near because of—"

"Wait! How did you know that? Did he tell you?" She dropped her hands to her side and made fists. "Of course, he did. The two of you are in Zane's head. You're up to something. What is it?"

"Look at me."

The quiet demand caused her to take one step closer. Damien began to unbutton his white dress shirt as his eyes bore into Catharina's.

The pain started to seep into his veins as he pulled back his shirt with both hands, making sure the cloak didn't hide his chest.

Catharina wondered if she should run for safety, back to Zane who would protect her. Something held her in place, like stepping in wet cement. The bare chest appeared tan in the dim light but his strength remained evident as her eyes caressed every inch of his skin. Even when he pushed the hood from his head, Catharina found herself admiring the man before her. Then she saw it.

"Damien?" she whispered in horror as she took one step forward. "What's happening?" A shiver ran up her spine.

"It's time for you to know the truth."

Catharina shook her head as she moved within two feet of him. The smell of incense wafted up to her nose as she inhaled deeply. His chest began to rise and fall with labored breathing. To resist touching him became futile. Lines began to form across his torso then up over his shoulders. She reached inside his shirt to pull it open even farther as the lines began to fill in with ink. She was so captivated by the artwork spreading across his skin that she forced herself to ignore her own pain surging through her shoulder and arm. When the designs were complete, she ran both her hands up and down around his chest, feeling the heat radiating from his body.

"I don't understand…" she began as her eyes lifted to see that a black band about three inches wide had formed across Damien's face, from ear to ear. His fierce blue eyes now looked like a ghostly gray, piercing the depths of her soul. She snatched her hands away and stumbled backward.

"Don't be afraid, Catharina." The longing in his now-raspy voice could not be disguised. "It has become too difficult for me to hide the truth. In this state, it is dangerous for us both. God could strike me dead for falling from his grace to seek my own pleasure. I dare not touch you with the longing that is impossible to deny. I am two beings, one of Heaven and the other of Earth. Only you can set me free." He moved forward, only to see her retreat in fear.

"How?" Her voice trembled, but she couldn't help feeling terrified and enchanted at the same time. "I'm nothing."

"You are everything to me. Your love can set me free from being this." He looked down at his body. "I'm tired of man and their evil ways. I was promised that, someday, I would be rewarded. I've waited eons for you to appear."

"Me?" was her breathy reply as she stopped her backward retreat. "Why me?"

"God only knows. But when I saw you for the first time, I understood the gift I'd been given. But it can just as easily be taken away." He stretched out his hand to her. "Wait with me as I return to human."

Catharina covered her mouth to keep from screaming then turned on her heels and ran as fast as she could, through the ballroom doors. Entering the Union Station Mall promenade where large dinners were often held, she turned and took the steps two at a time that led up to the bridge between the Grand Hall and the hotel rooms.

Spinning around in confusion, she chose to escape through the Grand Hall and down toward her coffee shop, knowing it, too, would be bathed in darkness.

♫♬♫

Damien and Zane looked throughout Union Station for Catharina, even the upper recesses of the building where Rocco often escaped to morph into a human or vice versa. They combed the halls and doorways of the shops. The doorman said she hadn't come by him, and the security camera at the far end of the mall showed no one leaving.

"She must have left somehow, Zane." Damien saw the concern etched on the warrior's face. "It was too much for her. I should have had you there. I'm sorry."

Zane nodded acceptance of the situation. "If I remember right, this whole reveal thing was my idea. You didn't tell her everything."

"No. That would have been too much." Damien looked at his watch. Three a.m. "I'll go get my coat. Get whatever you need and meet me upstairs at my apartment. I'll call Father Xavier to let him know she might be headed that way."

Zane nodded and headed to his room.

Damien ran up the stairs, aware that Christmas carols still played throughout Union Station. He thought he recognized "Carol of the Bells," one of his favorites as he opened the door of his apartment. The room had been lit with candle light and a fire burned in the fireplace. Laying on the sofa, sound asleep, was Catharina. He moved to her side and squatted down next to her as his hand reached for a silk throw. She looked like the version of an angel humans fantasized to be true. Just as he started to cover her body, she startled awake.

Damien withdrew his hands, concerned he'd frighten her into running again. "Zane and I have been looking for you." He smiled and couldn't resist touching a piece of hair that had fallen into her eyes.

She stared at him, eyeing him from head to toe as he stood and backed away. She swung her bare feet to the floor and stood before him, seeing the man he really was for the first time. "Are you human now?"

"Yes. I am human."

"Good." Catharina rushed into his arms and pulled his mouth down to hers. All of the years of caution evaporated as her passion swelled inside her. "I love you, Damien Cruz or Rocco or whoever you are. I love you so much it hurts deep inside me. I don't understand any of this and I don't care." Damien's arms tightened around her before lifting her up in his arms. "Just tell me I'm not making the biggest mistake of my life."

Zane pushed into the room and chuckled. "No mistake, little sis." He turned then shut the door behind him as he returned to the hall.

"I guess I have your brother's blessing, Cat." Damien smiled down at her as he moved toward the bedroom. "Do you love both sides of me? I must know."

She ran her fingers through his dark hair. "Both sides. I loved Rocco first but couldn't escape my longing for you. Knowing you are both the same person only makes me—"

Damien didn't let her finish as he laid her on the bed and captured her mouth with his own.

Chapter 31

The first day of the train ride modeled after *The Polar Express*, a children's book by Chris Van Allsburg, started the following Saturday. Every hour on the hour, excited children tugging the hands of parents now captivated by the Christmas décor, entered Union Station from all directions. It almost appeared to be reminiscent of a bygone era when trains carried passengers to destinations across the country. The mall shops on the lower level opened early each day with expectations of a high volume of holiday purchases helping them break even for the slump in sales earlier in the week during the snow storm.

With the *St. Louis Post Dispatch* featuring articles and pictures about the performance and the appearance of The Watcher, a buzz about the grand old lady of a train station caught the interest of local television stations that passed it along to their parent networks. The photograph of Mayor LaPlante catching Catharina in his arms had women across the city and county swooning. Curiosity drove people to the hotel, booking the rooms that remained, and helped sell tickets for the Boys and Girls Club Christmas Fund Raiser and Gala for that Saturday night. It would be a sold-out crowd.

Catharina slipped down to her coffee shop in the early morning just like always. Zane moved into her room, claiming the hotel needed his. He was slipping away again into the streets to live, much to her concern. Their search for an apartment needed to be put off until after the holiday. Damien insisted she and her brother stay close. December and January weather in St. Louis could be brutal. She caved to his suggestion only because Zane would be prowling the streets every night if she moved. At least, here, he felt comfortable and safe. Each day he took a hot shower, wore clean clothes, and ate three meals. Having him assist her in the coffee shop helped her to keep an eye on him.

"So you and Damien are…" Zane let his sentence trail off as someone walked up to the counter and ordered a coffee. Molly was working too since so many customers found their way to the shop. He glanced over to where she wiped down tables as he handed the customer their cappuccino. He elbowed his sister. "So?"

Catharina pushed back at his elbow. "Stop it." She felt a heat flush her face. "I'm trying—we're trying to figure things out."

"What's to figure out? You love each other. Simple." He busied himself washing a few things in the sink.

"You can't be serious." Her harsh whisper forced him to turn his head to her. "Half the time he isn't human. He's never going to age. I've aged ten years since we've met!" she snapped.

"Do you love him?" Zane sounded so matter-of-fact. "Both sides of him?"

For a second, she pictured Rocco standing on the Grand Hall balcony ledge, robed in some medieval garb that frightened those he targeted. The ink across his chest, blazing at the most inopportune times, gave her feeling of connection. Then the image of Damien standing nonchalant, with an irritated arched eyebrow, followed by him staring at her like an omnipotent god. She remembered the first time he'd smiled at her and how his mouth touching hers drove impossible longings to the surface.

"Do. You. Love. Both. Of. Him?" Zane asked again.

"God help me, but I do." Catharina shook her head in dismay as she met her brother's eyes. "But any kind of a physical relationship is dangerous. I'm sure he's told you that." The night he swept her off her feet and carried her to his bed ended abruptly when he transformed into the angel. Their love making would have to be postponed until he figured things out.

"He can be released, you know." Nodding to a new customer, Zane took the order and busied himself pouring the coffee into a cup then passing it over the counter. "Come again," he called as the woman tried to round up her kids watching the electric train in the glassed-in room.

Catharina stared at her brother. "So what does that mean exactly? Rocco, I mean Damien, I mean—" She threw up her hands in frustration. "Why is that you know this and I have no idea what he's talking about? Are you saying God will just let his holy angel fly the coop? No pun intended." She backed up against a counter and folded her arms across her chest. "Father Xavier is never going to believe this."

Zane cringed. "Yeah. About that. You probably should hold off on saying anything. He and Damien are a little on the outs right now." Catharina stood erect, stiffness coming into her posture. Zane held up his hand. "Nothing to worry about."

"The other day I overheard them arguing. What was that about?"

"You, mostly. He doesn't want Damien or Rocco to have anything to do with you."

Between serving customers and side stepping Molly, Zane told Catharina how the priest had been ministering to Rocco for several years. It wasn't until Catharina opened her shop that Father Xavier became aware that Rocco and Damien were the same person.

"He deeply regretted suggesting the two of you get together. By that time, it was too late. Rocco had already fallen in love with you. Until you were able to distinguish your love between both man and angel, Damien couldn't reveal himself. It was too dangerous."

"Is he still in danger, Zane?" Catharina laid a hand on her brother's arm.

"Yes. If, at any time, he begins to change with you, it is important that you show physical restraint. He was punished severely once when he lost control. Do you remember that?" Zane watched a blush creep up his sister's neck.

"Maybe. What will happen to him? Will he die?"

"Worse. He will become like the Nephilim. Like Gideon and the others."

"Gideon is a Nephilim? I thought that was a Bible boogieman story." Catharina edged closer to her brother to whisper so the customers wouldn't hear their conversation. "They were the offspring of angels and human women. Is that right?"

"Yes. But they are believed to have died during the great flood of Noah's time."

"So how can Gideon be a Nephilim? And you saying his friends are also Nephilim?"

"Rocco has never told me. Remember in the Bible, when Moses sent spies into Canaan and they returned saying it was the land of giants." Catharina tried to remember and couldn't but nodded as if she did. "Those giants were thought to be Nephilim. Gideon was there as were the others. They helped the Hebrew people survive and obtain victory those early years. Because of their devotion, God granted them life without memory of whom or what they are. Rocco protects them and calls them to action when times demand it. The name Gideon itself means destroyer. Without Rocco taking care of them, they could unleash havoc on mankind."

Her hands went to each side of her face. "Zane, how do you know all this? You never paid much attention to the Bible stories Father Xavier told us or what the sisters said in school. You got into trouble for cracking jokes." Catharina smiled up at her brother. "Now here you are a virtual biblical historian. What's up with that?"

Taking a deep breath, he looked down at her and pulled her into his arms. "I love you, sister. Thanks to you and to Rocco, I'm almost healed." With a final hug before pushing her at arm's length, Zane looked into his sister's eyes. "I want to stay well, Catharina. Do you understand that?"

"Yes. Of course. I want that, too." She couldn't help letting her concern show. "If what you're saying is true, what kind of life will I have with Damien? Now that you're strong, we can make a new life together. If I stay, I can only hurt the man I love. I'll explain it to him."

Zane tousled her black hair, making her squeal in protest. "Not yet. Let's wait until after Christmas. I'm looking forward to it for the first time in years. Please."

Punching him in the stomach with a soft fist, Catharina laughed. "Okay. But we bring Father Xavier in on this, too."

Turning his back to Catharina so she couldn't see his deception, Zane agreed. "Whatever you want, little sis."

♫ ♫ ♫

The sound of tinkling china and crystal echoed in the lower level. Catharina looked out her window onto the area filling up with guests dressed in their finest. She'd never seen so many furs and sequin dresses. Laughter drifted up to her as she turned her head to look across at the bridge where she would begin her performance. The bartenders and hostesses, who were now a part of the routine, worked in their costumes, which looked like mismatched clothes from a left over storage bin at a homeless shelter. Their hair looked like they'd just rolled out of bed.

Catharina smiled, knowing they loved the avant-garde look. The spiked hair of the guys and the new frosty hair of the girls gave them the Bohemian look Catharina sported most of the time. They would add a layer of glitter just before the performance. She turned away to look back into the room. Zane sat on the bed and Damien stood over him chatting about something that made both of them laugh. Her heart swelled at seeing them together.

"Are you laughing at my clothes?" Catharina sashayed with great extravagance toward the men. Her skirt was a bundle of glitter on black, the stockings red zebra striped, with white ribbons hanging from her waist. The bodice of her well-fitting top was a combination of red and black with an explosion of sequins. The black lace sleeves started at the elbow and stopped at her wrists.

Damien eyed her with appreciation. "You look stunning."

Zane shrugged. "I donno. Looks kinda frumpy to me." He smiled as Catharina tugged at his ear. "Okay. You look pretty good. I think you'd look better in one of those fancy dresses like those rich ladies are wearing downstairs. Maybe that Morgan chick could give you some pointers. She's pretty hot."

"Ha! You can't make a silk purse out of a sow's ear, Zane. I'd look ridiculous in one of those." She didn't really like that her brother had taken notice of Morgan Knox.

Damien wrapped an arm around her waist then tugged her to his side. "I wouldn't change a thing." The burning in his chest caused Catharina to bend double as she grabbed her shoulder. He released her as Zane pulled her to sit on the bed. "I'm so sorry, Cat. It's getting more difficult to control my true nature."

Catharina nodded and smiled up at Damien. The burning had stopped as soon as he released her. "Guess I'll just have to hold my affection in check for a while."

Zane faked a frown and waved a fist at her. "Hey! A brother doesn't want to hear stuff like that coming from his sister." He shifted his eyes to Damien. "You okay?"

Damien nodded. His walkie talkie crackled to life. It was Jeremiah. "Damien, the mayor is looking for you. He seems pissed."

The thick British accent returned. "Of course, he does. Be right there." He turned back to Zane who was pulling Catharina to her feet. He bent to kiss her then stopped. "Break a leg."

Catharina followed him to the door. "I love you forever, Damien." The whispered words in his ear as she stood on her bare tip toes caused him to pause and bring his face within inches of hers.

His eyes traveled around her face as he smiled. "Forever is a long time. I know that better than anyone." He pulled the door open and disappeared into the hall.

"You guys are kind of sickening, you know that?"

Zane started making kissing sounds on the back of his hand, causing Catharina to burst into laughter.

♫ ♫ ♫

"Problem, Mr. Mayor?" Damien's words escaped like a flat line on a heart monitor.

"Where have you hidden Catharina? She hasn't been returning my calls. It would be just like you to take advantage of her during a difficult time. She's homeless. I suppose you have continued to put her up in your apartment. That would be convenient."

The mayor stood next to Damien, sipping his champagne, while he nodded to a few guests who offered a smile and a thumbs-up. His body looked slimmer in a tux, but it also made him look hard. The contempt on his face intensified as he narrowed his eyes to slits.

"She moved out the next day into a room over there." Damien tilted his head toward the annex that overlooked the event below. The mayor shifted his eyes up and spotted Catharina looking out the window at them. "She and Zane can't get a place until after Christmas. There will be insurance and paperwork to tend to in the meantime."

Kragan waved to Catharina. She returned the gesture eagerly and he thought she may have smiled.

"And that would indeed have been very convenient, Kragan, if I were an incorrigible lech such as yourself," Damien continued, responding to the earlier comment. He took advantage of being a few inches taller than the mayor, looked down his straight nose at him, then smirked. "Fortunately for Cat, she has a very protective brother who thinks God Almighty isn't good enough for his sister." He gave a signal to his staff to start clearing the tables. "So you should probably thank me for keeping Zane occupied so he doesn't break your scrawny little neck for pulling his sister onto the Grand Hall balcony the other night." His eyes turned back to watch the hundreds of people finish their desserts. "For some reason, he doesn't like you."

"And I guess you've endeared yourself."

"Soldiers tend to do that. I understand what he's been through. Besides being a victim of war he led a pretty rough life as a kid."

Kragan set down his fluted glass then lifted another glass of champagne from the passing waiter's tray. "I know more than you think, Cruz. My old man liked to pound on me and the other kids in our house. When I left for college—" He gulped down the rest of the champagne. "Sob stories. Hate them." He fingered the glass in his hand. "I guess it was you who convinced Cat to return the violin I sent over." Just the thought of such a refusal irritated him.

"No. I thought she should keep it."

"Where did that pathetic turquoise thing come from?"

Damien arched an eyebrow before giving the mayor a smirk.

"I gave it to her." He thumped the mayor on the back good naturedly and walked away toward a bartender, motioning for his attention.

Morgan strolled up wearing a black gown with a plunging neckline trimmed in rhinestones. "What was all that about?"

Her blonde hair was piled up on the top of her head with a band of more rhinestones keeping it in place. Morgan caught a glimpse of Zane Spokane standing in a window staring at them. If it weren't for his pathetic situation, she might consider him handsome. She sipped her drink as the mayor glared at her.

"Nothing. Just be sure you distract him later so I have a chance to get Catharina alone."

"You think, because she's destitute, she'll be willing to sell you her share in the Essmalory Building?" He cut his eyes to her so quickly she felt as if a knife sliced through her juggler. "The fire marshal says that, although there is extensive damage, it can be restored."

"Yes. Well, the old coot who has it certainly can't do that, even with insurance money. He'll take the money and run, and then sell what's left. That would be a nice little nest egg for his waning years."

Morgan hesitated then shifted her weight to one hip. "Maybe."

"Maybe? What's that supposed to mean?"

"Heard today someone stepped forward to buy the building at a bargain."

Kragan chuckled. "Nonsense. Why would someone do that?"

"The deal stipulates the Essmalory will be restored, not torn down, and that the previous owner can live there as long as he wishes." Morgan swallowed hard, knowing that Kragan might have an internal meltdown before hundreds of people. That would be a nightmare to explain. She noticed an increase in Kragan's breathing and his nostrils flaring as a vein began to pulsate on his neck.

"How did you get this information?" He smiled at the chief of police who paid the $300 dollars for this event he couldn't afford. The chief kept eyeing him as if he wanted to say something.

"I went to the city inspector today and he was there. After he left, I questioned the inspector. You know as well as I do the inspector can't keep a secret. Says it's going to return to the glory days of the 1920s."

"What about the other tenants? Aren't they ready to move on?"

"Some are. I don't know. Maybe all of them. Probably even Catharina Spokane. They want the money. Most of them can't afford to wait around a couple of years while it's being put back together. With all of them gone, it will be a gold mine. No more cheap housing."

"Who is trying to buy it?"

Morgan took a deep breath as the lights began to dim. "Damien Cruz."

Chapter 32

The master of ceremonies announced Catharina as the lights went dark. An explosion of light fell on her as she stood on the bridge above the event in a theatrical pose. She looked like a small doll standing there all alone. As she lifted the turquoise violin to her chin, applause began to filter through the crowd. The hype over the last few days about the entertainment mesmerized them as she was joined by her dancers.

No one knew how nervous Catharina was as she walked out onto her stage. Within minutes, like always, she'd lost herself in the music. Dancing between the beams of light, taking each step down to the main floor with the help of her team, Catharina played her violin harder than she ever had. Somehow, the thought of all those children who used the Boys and Girls Club drove her to perfection. Maybe if the performance was good enough the funds raised tonight would go a long way toward continuing programs so desperately needed for the next generation. Nothing like that had been available for her.

The chill of the aged tiles on the floor refreshed her bare feet as she began to twist her way between the tables, all the while dancing and playing. People got to their feet, clapped along with her music, cheered, and sometimes stomped their feet at the rhythm. At the end of a thirty-minute performance, Catharina was carried half way up the stairs by two bartenders who looked like body builders, and she concluded her song as red, green, and silver confetti rained down on the guests with a bang. Once more, the lights flooded the event hall to whistles and thunderous applause.

The mayor walked up the steps, carrying a microphone. "Isn't she amazing!" He smiled over at Catharina and noticed how winded she'd become. "And the rest of these guys! Wow! You rock." He extended his hand toward the young men and women who were part of the performance. "All of them asked to be a part of this. Be sure you tip them before you leave." More applause filled the hall. Kragan couldn't help but reach for Catharina and pull her to his side by placing his arm around her waist. "Thank you," he said into her ear then kissed her tenderly on the cheek. He then turned to the audience again and gave a short speech about the importance of funding such a worthwhile organization for young people. Imploring them not to hold back their giving, he concluded the evening's festivities.

Catharina whispered into his ear.

"Almost forgot." He clicked on the microphone again as it vibrated for a couple of seconds. "The light show in the Grand Hall will be in twenty minutes and Catharina will play another song for us. The bar will be open while you wait. Merry Christmas everyone!" He waved good naturedly, like a politician running for office.

The crowd began to disperse as Catharina started up the steps with Kragan on her heels. Several people stopped her at the top as she stepped onto the bridge and offered her praise for the performance. It was something new to her. Having the people at the Kitchen of Hope love her was far different than these people who were used to attending Powell Hall and the Fox Theater for big name performers. A shyness swept over her, which prevented her from doing more than nodding.

"I think you're a hit, Cat." Kragan managed to take her arm. "How is it possible you keep getting better? Or maybe I'm a lost soul when it comes to you." He smiled as he led her into the Grand Hall. "Let's find a quiet place to sit for a minute. You need to catch your breath."

There was a long promenade that led to other conference rooms where they could sit. A woman sat at the grand piano, playing Christmas carols, as a few couples began to stroll past them.

"I'm relieved it's over. I was so nervous." She exhaled a breathy laugh as she laid her violin down next to her. A waitress walked up and asked if she could get them anything. "Just some water, Meg. I'm dying of thirst."

"Mr. Mayor?" Meg beamed at the most powerful man in St. Louis. "Anything?"

"Water for me, too." His eyes went back to Catharina who was flushed with excitement. Waiting for the waitress to leave, Kragan finally asked. "Why have you not returned my calls? Have I upset you or done something to displease you?" Sounding hurt rather than perturbed was an act he'd mastered a long time ago.

"No. Certainly not. With working and rehearsals—Thanks again for letting me do this. The money will really come in handy." She reached out and squeezed his hand then withdrew it. "Damien has hired me, too," she said with enthusiasm.

"Really?" Kragan tried to sound pleased with not much success.

"Mostly on weekends but at night, too, when the bar crowd comes in. I was only going to do it a couple of nights so I could still play at the Kitchen of Hope, but—" Her voice caught in her throat.

Kragan slipped his hand over hers. "I'm just glad none of the residents were hurt. I'm sure there must be some organizations that can help Father Xavier get it up and running again."

The mayor knew most businesses in the area would like nothing better than for the place to meet with a match and a gas can. Metal shopping carts pushed along by rag-tag old ladies and smelly men sitting against alley walls did not endear the homeless to most. Even though the police kept most of the panhandlers away, a few still appeared during major sporting events. It was a constant struggle.

"I hope so, Kragan. Many of those people are just down on their luck. They need a little help and then they'll mainstream back into society. Father Xavier's kitchen was a safe place for families and others."

"You're a good person, Cat." Kragan meant it. Never had he felt empathy for anyone. The thought bewildered him.

Nonetheless, he recognized the sincerity in Catharina. She really believed those wretched people could be saved. "I've never met anyone like you." When he lowered his voice, her eyes looked up at his. "You make me want to make the city a better place to live."

Catharina beamed. "Really? I appreciate you saying that, Kragan. If anyone can do it, you can." She squeezed his hand as a sign of encouragement for his goal. When he leaned over to kiss her on the mouth, the realization that the gesture meant something far different to him made her feel a little panicked. "I—" She stood up while smoothing her outfit. "I better go get ready. If I sit too long, my muscles will tense up."

Reaching for the violin, Kragan grabbed it up then examined it like a piece of spoiled meat. Feeling cautious, she reached for it. "Guess I'll need that," she said with a nervous chuckle and a timid nod toward the instrument.

As he handed the instrument to her, he forced a smile. "When you're ready for an upgrade, let me know."

"I will."

Catharina didn't know why she scooted away from the mayor so fast. Something in his eyes reminded her of a time in her life when fear was the emotion of the day. Even his voice brought back memories for some reason. She knew he followed at a snail's pace. Turning briefly to wave goodbye, she discovered an angry scowl watching her. His slow movement forward reminded her of a boy who used to taunt her to tears. A warning whispered from her subconscious that she had to run.

♫ ♫ ♫

Zane and Damien watched Catharina exit the promenade with Kragan not far behind. They looked at each other with concern then slowed their pace to follow at a safe distance.

"I hate that guy." Zane pulled back his shoulders. "Reminds me of a punk kid that used to pick on Cat. He was older than me but I was bigger." He smirked. "Probably showed up at his old man's funeral a few weeks ago. Wish I could've been there to put the fear of God in him."

Damien cocked his head over at his friend. "Funeral?"

"Yeah. That creep whose house burned."

"The one Detective Jacobs was asking about?"

"Same." Zane stopped and put his hand on Damien's arm. "I know you did it."

Damien arched an eyebrow, trying to keep his face impassive as he often did. "Zane."

Zane held up his hand. "Rocco's job is to protect the innocent and make those who harm children pay. I get it." He sucked in a big breath. "Where the hell were you when we were kids, Damien?"

Damien glared into the big man's eyes without flinching. "The job is bigger than I can handle at times. There are more of us, but I'm in charge. The Nephilim can only help so much without being discovered. Most of the time, they don't even know who they are." He watched Kragan disappear into the Grand Hall. "The old man didn't seem to know where the son was. I assumed they were estranged. When I looked into it, the boy disappeared during college after an auto accident. There was no indication they ever had contact again." A feeling of failure swept over him. "I would have gone back if I'd known. The city is sick." He stared toward where Kragan had stood moments earlier. "With men like Kragan in power, nothing good will come of it. That must change. Are you up to the task?"

Zane released Damien's arm. "What do I need to do?"

"Receive Father Xavier's blessing. Then we'll proceed. Cat—"

"Has nothing to say about this. I'm broken without the change. What's so bad about living forever?"

"Loneliness."

"But Cat will be happy. You've earned this. Besides—" Zane shrugged. "—I'll still be able to see her."

"Will that be enough?"

"I can make a difference. If God wills it, then I stand ready." Zane thumped Damien on the back. Another man would have staggered forward, but Damien stood firm, rigid against the younger man's growing strength. "You'll see," Zane continued. "Now let's go watch Cat. That creep probably thinks he's taking her home tonight."

♫ ♫ ♫

The music from the light show began as the two men walked into the packed Grand Hall. Damien knew this one was the underwater show which Zane favored over the others. The former Marine gawked at the barrel shaped ceiling like a little kid with a lopsided grin on his face. Damien shifted his gaze to Kragan, who took a seat at the bar.

With a drink set before him, the mayor turned his eyes to meet Damien's. Lifting the drink in a kind of salute, the mayor swirled his drink as he squinted. He could feel his teeth begin to grind as Damien approached then sat down next to him.

"Isn't it past your bedtime, Mr. Mayor?" Damien waved a bartender away before he could ask him anything.

Kragan smiled as he took another sip of his vodka and tonic. "Don't like sleeping alone." His eyes landed on Catharina who was stretching her legs in the middle of the Grand Hall.

Damien remained silent for a few minutes then leaned in to the mayor. "She's not for you, Kragan. Stay away or else."

The mayor set his drink down and chuckled. "Or else what? You'll throw me out? Call the cops? Oh, I know. You'll have that ogre of a brother beat the crap out of me. It wouldn't be the first time he—" he mumbled as the lights came on for Catharina to begin her routine.

Damien resisted asking further questions as Catharina began to play the violin. His heart skipped a beat as she twirled deliriously. Once she looked his way and smiled. He noticed Kragan nod to her. It occurred to him that Kragan imagined she was playing for him. Damien knew better. His earthly body began to change and surge with holy blood. The designs on his chest started to burn as he stood and took his leave of the Grand Hall. He turned one last time to see Zane clapping to the music as his sister approached him, love in her eyes. The two of them filled him with longing as he escaped to the rafters of Union Station.

By the time he reached his sanctuary Damien had morphed into Rocco. Relief washed over his soul as the true nature of his body returned to its Heavenly state.

How would he tell Catharina he planned to kill her brother? Would he be able to do it? Would she hate him for eternity?

Kneeling to one knee he cried out.

"Father, I beg you! There must be another way!"

Chapter 33

et's get out of here." Kragan took Catharina's hand and smiled. Damien's threat left him more determined than ever to win her. "How about we go for dessert?"

Catharina panted but managed to smile back at her one-man fan club. "I'm exhausted, Kragan."

Disappointment leapt into his eyes. He'd made it possible for her to earn a sizable paycheck tonight.

She wanted him to know how much it meant to her. "Why don't I play your favorite piece of music? Then we'll call it a night." Pleasure brightened his face. "Okay?" she asked.

He nodded. The bar became packed with guests taking one more night cap. Kragan led Catharina to the promenade where he sat down on one of velvet covered sofas. "Thank you, Cat. Please. Begin."

This time she played the slower section of *The Devil's Trill* called "Larghetto, Ma Non Troppo." Closing her eyes, Catharina let the music take her. Instead of dancing, she swayed only slightly with her feet spread apart for balance. The piece wasn't very long so she played it twice before opening her eyes to look down at Kragan.

Shocked to see tears in his eyes, she forgot her trepidation of him and smiled. "You're pleased?"

Kragan rose to his feet and started to pull her into his arms when Zane walked up, slipping an arm around his sister's shoulders.

"You look wore out, sis." He looked amused at the disgruntled expression on the mayor's face. "Thanks for hiring her tonight."

"One of the best decisions I've made in a while." Kragan looked back at Catharina and tried to act pleasant. "I'll call you tomorrow, Cat. Thanks for helping raise so much money for the kids."

He noticed Zane loop his arm through hers in a movement to steer her away or maybe it was a show of possession. Kragan stepped closer to Cat and gave a quick kiss on the cheek, then let his hand slide down her shoulder and arm. As he turned his eyes back to Zane the good-natured giant looked like he might implode.

Catharina felt her face flush as she let Zane lead her away. "You know you were rude, right? I'm grateful for this job tonight. We have enough money to put on an apartment now. When the insurance money comes in, we'll decide what to do next. Kragan helped with that. Can't you be nice?" She jerked her arm free of his hold, only to feel his hand go to her back. "Stop being so overprotective. I can take care of myself. I've been taking care of you for a couple of years, you know?" She realized, too late, how condescending her tone had become when Zane's hand dropped from her back.

He moved a few steps ahead of her without a word. By the time she caught up, he stood at her room door, inserting the key card into the lock. He handed her the key after swinging the door open. "Good night, sis."

As he started to turn away, Catharina grabbed his arm. "Zane, I'm sorry. I was out of line. Please don't be mad. I didn't mean to hurt your feelings. Don't go into the night. I worry when you do that. It's cold."

"I'll be fine." His voice sounded a little raspy so he cleared it and repeated the words.

Catharina stared at him in stunned silence before she tried to speak. "Your voice."

Zane rubbed his throat. "What about it?"

"You sounded like Rocco." Her own voice became a frightened whisper. "Please. Stay with me, Zane." She pulled at his arm without much success.

"I can't. You'll be safe here as long as you don't leave the room."

Tears sprang to her eyes. "I'm sorry. Forgive me. I didn't mean what I said."

He pushed her inside then followed before shutting the door. "There's nothing to forgive. I know how bad I was. I'm better now. Can't you see that?"

"Yes. Yes, of course. I just don't understand why. Has Rocco done something to you? I will gladly take the old Zane if it means I might lose you. I'm begging you to stay. I'm afraid something is going to happen to you."

He wrapped his arms around his sister. "You would have me delusional and sick? Now I have clarity, a purpose. My strength is incredible. There are promises I must keep."

"What kind of promises?" She felt panic attack her calm. "Did Rocco make you promise to do something against the law? Is he feeding you dribble about me and the mayor?"

"No. None of that. You wouldn't understand."

"Make me understand, Zane. Please. I feel like I'm losing you again to something I can't see or begin to fathom. I don't know which is worse—having you relive the war in Afghanistan or partner with an avenging angel and a bunch of Nephilim."

Zane held her at arm's length. "I'm just going to talk to Rocco or Damien or whoever he is at the moment, about a few things. Then I'll be back." He wiped her cheeks free of the trail of tears. "Life is going to be better. You'll see." She nodded. "And as for that scumbag Kragan, I will try and be nicer. That doesn't mean I want him hanging around my sister. There's something about the guy I don't like. He can't be trusted."

Her mischievous smile appeared. "Okay. You know, I'm in love with Damien. Doesn't that count for something?"

"No. It doesn't. I'll be back soon. Don't come looking for me."

Catharina crossed her heart then gave Zane a bear hug. "I'll wait up."

"No. Go to bed. You've had a big day. Sleep in tomorrow. Molly and I will open the shop. Not much action on a Sunday morning until around ten, anyway." He opened the door and

blew her a kiss. "Damien won't be coming by tonight. He strug-
gles with keeping his human form lately." The familiar smirk
spread across his mouth. "Thanks to you."

♫♫♫

Morgan avoided Kragan at the Boys and Girls Club Gala as
much as possible. The lure of his attention kept her coming back
for more abuse. Sometimes their encounters felt magical, almost like their lovemaking had a deep connection. Other times,
it was just rough sex that meant she would get the worst of it,
like the other night. To continue pretending she meant something to him was a waste of time. He made his feelings abun-
dantly clear that the only one who interested him was Catharina
Spokane.

How could that be? A gutter rat with a junior college education who had the fashion sense of a panhandler at the mall. A
coffee-shop girl who felt more comfortable around the homeless than the influential elite of St. Louis couldn't possibly have
much to offer a man like Kragan. Yet he seemed consumed with
her very existence, to the point of being half mad.

Morgan stretched like a lazy feline as the silk sheets rubbed
softly against her naked body. "You certainly know how to live,
Damien Cruz." Her words were but a whisper as she rolled to
her back in his large four poster bed. "Where are you?"

Asking the question out loud sounded lost in such a vast
room. Several years ago she'd spent a number of times wrapped
in his arms, enjoying the pleasures of the flesh.

Never knowing why he'd stopped calling hurt her pride.
Then Kragan came along. At first he was more to her liking,
high society, in the spotlight, and being on the arm of the mayor
for many events gave her some clout in St. Louis politics. Damien was soon forgotten.

Morgan fluffed the pillows and lay back down, spreading
her arms out wide to try and touch the edge of the bed. Damien
never hurt her. His strength overwhelmed her at times, but he
never tried to harm her. If only she had not fallen victim to Kragan's charms. Now look at her, a whore for the mayor, who did

his bidding in order to keep his affections and her job.

The front door opened. Anticipation surged through her, knowing Damien had returned. As he entered the bedroom, Morgan noticed he'd already removed his shirt. The exposed chest drew her admiring eyes. He removed his belt and unbuttoned his pants before catching sight of her in the bed.

"What are you doing here?" His tone was anything but friendly. He moved to the side of the bed, his anger rising.

"You used to like for me to surprise you like this," she cooed as her lips puckered in a pout. "I've been waiting here all night. Where have you been?"

"How did you get in here, Morgan?"

"I still have a key. You gave it to me. Remember?" She raised up, letting the gold sheet start to slip. Placing her hand on his chest revealed her intentions. Morgan cocked her head and wiggled up on her knees. "Come on. I know you're glad to see me." Extending her hand out, she managed to ruffle his black hair before he grabbed her by the arm.

"Stop it," he growled. "What do you want?"

"Isn't that obvious, Damien?" she purred, edging closer so the sheet fell around her waist. She looked down then smiled up at Damien. "Oops. What are you going to do about this?"

Before he could answer, he heard someone at the bedroom door.

"Damien?" The shocked voice of Catharina slammed into his heart as he jerked around, still holding onto Morgan. Her eyes widened as she took in the whole scene. As her hands flew to her mouth, Catharina staggered to escape from the bedroom then broke into a run until she reached the front door. She heard Damien call after her.

Damien pushed Morgan back so hard she nearly fell off the other side of the bed. "Hey!" She snarled her displeasure at the man who once found her body enjoyable. "You can't be serious," she fumed. "That rag doll is nothing," she screamed, feeling the open wounds from being rejected by two men who she once thought loved her.

"Nothing? There is more humanity and goodness in her little finger than in your entire body, Morgan. Now get the hell out of my bed. I'm alerting security that if you come within one hundred yards of this hotel to have you arrested for trespassing." He started to leave then added: "And I'd better find that key on my nightstand when I get back."

By the time Damien ran into the hall, he could see Catharina running down the staircase toward the lobby. Since he was half dressed, he couldn't stop her, knowing that the instant he touched her Rocco could very well take over his human form.

His heavy footsteps hinted at danger as he entered the apartment. He heard water running in the bathroom. Damien waited, pacing very much like Rocco did in the attic of Union Station when he became perplexed or angry. What was taking her so long?

Slamming his fist into the mahogany door Damien shouted. "Morgan, hurry up." Silence. "Morgan. I'm coming in!" His anger peeked as he kicked open the door.

Lying in a tub full of bloody water, Morgan turned her head slowly toward Damien and smiled. Her naked body was partially visible as the water continued to run.

"Dear God in Heaven!" Damien turned off the water then removed the drain plug. He ran to call for help. In seconds, he returned, pulling her up out of the water. "Morgan, what have you done?" He could feel the life slipping out of her. This was his fault. With the gentleness of a new mother, he laid her on the bathroom floor then stood.

He held out his hands from his side and closed his eyes as Morgan watched him. The ink on his body appeared then the hollowness of his glazed gray eyes. Veins began to pop forward as Rocco took over his human self. It took only seconds to become a holy one. Kneeling down beside her, Rocco took both of her wrists in his hands before breathing the gift of life upon her wounds. He felt a tremble in her body, and she raised her eyes to watch as realization flooded her face that Damien Cruz was really someone else. His mouth moved in prayer, speaking in a language that only God and angels could understand.

"You will survive." His raspy voice made her shudder. "Speak not of this." He stood slowly and looked to Heaven. "Father." In his plea, Damien's body changed back as the sound of paramedics rushed into his apartment. "In here!"

The agitated paramedics, firemen, and police forced Damien aside with the omnipotence that came from saving lives every day. They eyed the Union Station manager with suspicion as he moved out of the way. Police waited in the living room with him to take advantage of what they hoped would be a chaotic thought process, perhaps even tripping him up into some kind of a confession of what occurred. With hushed voices, they asked the kind of questions you'd expect.

What did he think happened? Had they fought? Was there any indication she might be distraught earlier? Had they been drinking the night before and was she often an overnight guest?

He knew it was only a matter of time before Detective Jacobs would arrive. But his main concern was Catharina. Where did she go? He could only imagine the pain and betrayal that she must be feeling.

A gurney rolled past where he waited in the living room with Morgan barely conscious. He reached out and took her hand. "I'm sorry, Morgan." Her only response was a look of confusion mixed with fear. A nervous tremble in her fingers forced him to withdraw.

"I'll check on you later."

Morgan whispered so low that Damien lowered his ear to her lips. "Kragan sent me." Then she became unconscious.

The paramedics looked disturbed and more than a little accusing. "You're going to need to talk to the police, Mr. Cruz."

"Yes. Of course."

"How about now?" Detective Jacobs squeezed past the paramedics as he eyed Morgan. "She doesn't look too good. I was in the neighborhood when the call went out."

"Lucky for us," Damien said as his eyebrow arched and the haughty British tone returned to his voice.

"Yeah, Well, you know what they say, 'God works in mysterious ways.'"

Chapter 34

Jeremiah managed to keep hotel guests from seeing the mayhem unfolding by directing the paramedics to take a different exit, explaining that there would be an elevator and a quicker way to the street level. After all, their emergency vehicles were parked along that side of the hotel anyway. Because it was a Sunday, and the snow still caked sidewalks, traffic was almost non-existent. Guests always slept in on a Sunday, especially if parties kept them at the bar later than usual. No one seemed to be stirring in the Grand Hall so fallout would be minimal.

The only concern now involved seeing Catharina run down the staircase then across the bridge to her room. There wasn't enough time to go after her. By the time the excitement dissipated, Jeremiah needed to put out other fires caused by needy employees or grumbling guests.

"Excuse me." It was Detective Jacobs. He handed Jeremiah a business card as he leaned against the check-in desk. "Your boss thought maybe you'd know where I could find Ms. Spokane," the detective continued. "I'd like to ask her a couple of questions." He forced a smile as he nodded to the ladies behind the desk. They quickly diverted their eyes. "Any of you see Ms. Spokane? I tried to call the coffee shop."

He pulled out a little notebook and flipped through a couple of pages. A couple of coins slipped out, hit the floor, bounced, and started to spin. He went after them as if it amounted to a large sum. Dropping the money into his pants' pocket, the detective chuckled and held up his notebook as if remembering his original objective. "As I was saying. Let me see." He looked down at his notes. "Here it is. Molly. She said Ms. Spokane hadn't come in yet. I understand she's still staying at the hotel so I thought maybe someone saw her this morning?"

Jeremiah offered one of his smiles that could disarm a Black Mamba lying in wait for its next victim. He went behind the counter to the warming oven, pulled out several chocolate chip cookies, and brought them to the detective. "Here you go. One of the things we're known for here at Union Station. Best cookies in town."

The detective took them and inhaled. "Umm. Still warm. Thank you. Now—"

"Haven't seen her," Jeremiah interjected as he turned with wide eyes to his employees, warning them not to contradict him. "Any of you?" They shook their heads then tried to appear busy. He began to herd the detective out into the Grand Hall. "Anything else, Detective Jacobs?"

The detective took a bite of one of his cookies. A softened chocolate chip stuck to the corner of his mouth. The goo gave him a cartoon appearance. "Still staying with Cruz?"

Jeremiah put on his best interested look. "Oh no. They've taken a room in the new annex across the bridge." He pointed out toward the mall. "Since Catharina has the coffee shop, it works out for her to be here. They plan on getting a place after the holidays. She's working here at night too."

"Doing what?"

"Entertains with her violin at night. Big draw. Weekends too. The Polar Express event is huge. The diversion should keep them happy while they have to wait. Do you have kids, Detective?" Jeremiah walked alongside the detective, edging him toward the stairs that led to the street.

"Nope. No kids. Three wives though." The detective pushed the last bite of cookie into his mouth. "Single at the moment."

Jeremiah smiled. "That's hard to understand." He forced his voice to show surprise.

"Thank you, sir. " The detective extended his hand. Jeremiah grabbed it and pumped with his usual enthusiasm. "When you see the Spokanes let them know I'd like to talk to them," the detective said. "Don't mind coming back."

They walked through the double doors as the doorman pulled them open and stood at attention. Jeremiah patted the detective's back. "Will do."

He saluted the man then returned inside with a huge sigh before taking the stairs two at a time. Instead of returning to his office or the front desk, he headed to the coffee shop.

♫ ♬ ♫

Father Xavier finished the last Mass for the day and returned to his quarters. Seeing Catharina curled up in a chair in front of the gas log fireplace, gave him pause. He remembered how she'd loved reading books in that chair or sitting on a stool in front of him as he retold stories of his youth in the Appalachian Mountains. Now here she was again. It had been too long since they shared a meal in his home. The Kitchen of Hope and the coffee shop became their meeting places with an occasional visit to her apartment at the Essmalory. He whispered a prayer of thanks that the child he helped raise was safe, even if it meant Rocco was involved.

"To what do I owe the pleasure?" Father smiled as he noticed Catharina had turned the lights on the tiny Christmas tree in front of the window. She'd always loved the real trees better than the artificial ones. They'd gotten smaller over the years as the children grew up, but he always made sure he had one for her. She looked at him with blood-shot eyes. "What is wrong, my child?" he asked.

"Oh, Father," she cried as her legs uncurled from beneath her to run into his waiting arms. "Hold me."

Father Xavier rubbed her back before stroking her hair. He never understood why she dyed the tips blonde or the reason she cut it so jagged. He wondered often if it was some self-induced punishment or just a fashion statement.

"Tell me what brings you here to visit an old man." He pushed her away to arm's length then grabbed a tissue from the box sitting on the coffee table. "Here. Blow." He held the tissue to her nose. She took it, smiled, and then did as she was told.

"Now, I will make you some hot chocolate like I used to do when you were a little girl. I think I even have a piece of peppermint to drop to the bottom."

She only nodded her approval. Neither spoke for a long time. The ticking of the grandfather clock in the corner of the living room at times sounded like a base drum. One of the things the Spokane children loved about his home was the quiet.

"So tell me why you are crying." Father Xavier reached out and laid his hand on hers. "Has Zane gone back to the streets?" She shook her head. "Are you worried about money, because I have savings. It's yours if you need it." Again she shook her head. "If you're worried about me and The Kitchen of Hope, we'll be fine."

"No. It's none of that. I mean maybe it's all of that too. I'm feeling overwhelmed, confused, and hurt."

"Tell me, Cat."

"Damien." She watched as a hardness came into the priest's eyes. "I know who he really is, Father."

"Then you know it is forbidden for you to have feelings for him," he scolded. "I can see it in your eyes and in his." He stood and walked to the fireplace to warm his hands that suddenly felt numb. "This is my fault. I told him I'd had a dream of a woman who came for him. I didn't know it was you." His head bowed in sorrow. "I didn't know. I'm sorry."

Catharina put her face in her hands. "Tell me the truth, Father. All of it."

Father Xavier walked to his recliner and sat down with the caution one might use sitting on sharp objects. "He is Rocco, an angel sent to protect the young and abused. He is a healer, one of the good angels. In spite of taking retribution against those that do harm to the less fortunate, he has managed to live centuries without being discovered as he walks among men."

"Why does he want me?"

Father Xavier frowned. "So that he can be fully human. He has served long enough. It was prophesied that a woman could free him some day when his time had come."

"Are you telling me he has never been with a woman?" Catharina found that absurd. He seemed very aware of how to make her swoon.

"As a human, he has had women over the years. He often tired of them quickly. They were only something that fulfilled the human desire within him. As long as he kept the angelic form he could resist earth women, unlike those who eventually became Nephilim. Because he was void of any human attachment or emotion to the women he interacted with as a human, they remained safe from death." Father Xavier watched Catharina come closer, pulling up the stool like she was a little girl.

"What makes me different?"

Father Xavier took a deep breath. "He saved a musician once from Satan himself who fancied the violin. The two battled for domination. Rocco won. Unfortunately, Satan had already given Tartini his greatest composition."

"Tartini? *The Devil's Trill.*" Catharina couldn't believe it. "And God was displeased?"

"God is a loving God. Rocco promised he'd fight on for eternity to keep Satan from harming another soul." The priest took a deep breath. "I will tell you a secret. Did you know that Tartini's wife's name was also Catharina?"

Catharina looked up at the priest, eyes wide with interest. "So why now? Why me? Because of my name?"

"No. If that were the case, he could have found his love long ago. Rocco told me once that our Lord would free him of his promise for his stellar service when he was ready, if someone would take his place."

"You mean become an angel?" Catharina's voice lowered to a whisper.

Father Xavier nodded and leaned forward to lay his hand upon her cheek. "Yes. Both the human and the angelic side of him had to be revealed and accepted by someone he loved." He shook his head. "I didn't know Damien was Rocco until after I introduced you. I never knew the human side of him. Once I had the dream, I now know he followed me everywhere to see where you were. He could feel my heart, explore my brain to understand the dream. By the time I understood these things, it was too late." Father Xavier leaned back in his chair, exhausted. "I've prayed for God to stop him."

Tears rolled down her cheeks again. "Am I going to die, Father? Is Rocco going to kill me to be fully human?"

Father Xavier pushed out of his chair then pulled her up into his arms. "No, my child." He started to tell her the truth but his vocal chords constricted so that he was mute. After a few seconds, he stopped trying. Whether it was God or Rocco preventing him from telling Catharina the truth, he knew that it was pointless to warn her.

"I thought he loved me. I fell so hard, Father." She buried her face in his chest.

The phone startled both of them as their arms untwined. "I should get this, Cat."

"I know, Father. I learned a long time ago I would have to share you."

After a kiss on her forehead, the priest walked to the phone, hoping deep down it would stop before he got there. "Hello." He turned his eyes to the woman washing coffee cups in the sink. "Yes. I'll be there." Catharina wiped her hands on a dish towel and smiled a silent message that she was much better. "Where? How bad?"

Catharina felt a wave of panic wash over her. The look on Father Xavier's face sent a signal of concern. "Father?"

"I'm on my way, Damien." Catharina hugged her arms at hearing the man's name. "No. I haven't seen her." Seeing the surprise in Catharina's eyes almost made him grin. He hung up the phone, crossed himself, kissed his crucifix, and whispered: "Forgive me, Father."

"What is it? Please tell me Zane isn't in trouble or hurt?"

"It's Morgan Knox. Apparently she tried to commit suicide this morning. Damien found her in his bathroom. "I need to go to the hospital. Maybe you can come too and fill me in on a few things."

♫ ♫ ♫

"I'll say one thing, when you ask Morgan to go to bat for you she steals more than home plate." The Chairman of the Board of Alderman had shown up in his casual jogging suit to show concern and sympathy.

Kragan poured himself another cup of coffee then pointed to extra cups in the glass fronted cabinet. The police chief called earlier to let Kragan know the situation and reassured him Morgan would survive.

"Crane, you look ridiculous in jogging pants. When did you ever see the inside of a gym?" The mayor smirked, eyeing the black man before him. "Anyway, thanks for your concern. The hospital said I could drop in later."

The alderman poured himself a cup of coffee and stirred in enough French Vanilla Cremer to make it look like wet sand. "What happened?"

With a shrug, the mayor took a seat at his kitchen island and glanced at the weekend *Post-Dispatch.* "Guess she and Damien didn't see eye to eye on his role in her life. She is a little insecure."

"Insecure? Everyone thinks the two of you are…" He let his voice fade as Kragan looked up from the paper with expectation. "…an item."

"We had sex. Or at least I did. We were far from being an item. Besides, that was over a long time ago. She had been trying to rekindle interest in her old flame, Damien Cruz." His voice sounded so matter-of-fact, Kragan could have been talking about the weather.

Crane joined him at the island and sat his cup down with a clank on the granite counter top. "So what did you mean when you said you asked Morgan to do something for you?"

"I'm interested in Ms. Spokane and, it seems, so is Damien. I asked Morgan to be her charming self so Damien would realize what a prize she was, and I could have more time with Catharina without being interrupted. The poor girl is really tired of her overbearing brother and her stalker boss hovering over her."

"She said that to you?" Crane asked.

Kragan's frown unnerved him as he reached for his coffee.

"Sorry. She doesn't seem like your type, is all," Crane said.

Kragan sipped his coffee, letting the warmth and caffeine surge through his veins. "Maybe she is and maybe she isn't. I'm never going to get a chance to find out with the *Incredible Hulk* running interference. Which brings me to another matter."

Crane twisted in his swivel bar stool. "What now? Are you going to blackmail me again over that misunderstanding between that summer intern and myself again?"

"Most definitely. I hardly call rape a misunderstanding and she was barely legal. You took city funds to pay her off and used your influence to get her a scholarship at Wash U." Kragan chuckled. "Please. You're going to do my bidding or be hung out to dry. Maybe even lose your license to practice law."

With clenched teeth, the alderman growled a response. "Okay. But this is it. Tell me what I have to do this time."

"There's a box of evidence I need you to bring to the attention of the police chief. Seems there is a Purple Heart medal with an interesting name on the back."

Chapter 35

n the end, Father Xavier dropped Catharina back at the hotel. The afternoon shadows grew long across sidewalks free of snow. Several of the valet attendants waved to her or tilted their chins up in a greeting as they hustled to make their guests happy. The Grand Hall staircase made her legs feel like thick logs as she climbed at the speed of a turtle. With eyes looking down at the white tiled floor, she could avoid making eye contact with any employees of Union Station.

Escaping into the corridor that held computers for guests then into her coffee shop, Catharina saw that Molly leaned against the counter, scrolling through her cell phone. The brown and ivory floor tiles glistened from what Catharina guessed was a good scrubbing earlier in the day. Molly wasn't one to just sit around, so seeing her absorbed in her social media meant no immediate tasks waited to be completed.

"Hi, Cat. Everyone has been looking for you. Everything okay?" Molly slipped the cell in her pocket and walked around the counter to stand before her boss, who flopped in a chair.

"Yes. Thank you for staying so long. Where's Zane?"

Molly shrugged. "Not sure. He left around one. We weren't really busy, anyway. I was wondering if I could leave too. Forecast says more snow tonight."

Catharina leaned her head back against the chair with a dismissive wave. "Sure."

A recap of the day's customers, gossip, and supply needs bombarded Catharina until she felt a head ache coming on. The sight of Molly pulling on her coat as she left offered a kind of relief. A groan emitted through clenched teeth as Catharina pushed up out of the chair and went to lock the doors. At this end of the hall, very little light filtered in from the skylights into the business center. With a few clicks, the switches turned out all of the overhead can lighting except for the artificial glow in the mosaic tiled fireplace. She finished cleaning up and setting the shop right for the next morning. As tired as she was, she knew it was better to just get it over with rather than worry about it all night.

Darkness now forced the Christmas lights to appear magical inside the Grand Hall as the barrel ceiling continued to rotate into a kaleidoscope of color every thirty seconds. There would be no violin show tonight. Jesse, the bellman, informed her as she approached him at his station. But next Friday through Sunday she should expect a full schedule. She nodded her appreciation as a voice sounded behind her.

"Cat. Cat." She turned around to see Kragan approach with a determined step. He shoved his hands into his coat pockets as he offered a slow smile. With his peppered gray hair a little windblown and the sting of December wind against his cheeks, Catharina found him rather handsome. "I was hoping I'd catch you. Can I buy you dinner? You look like you could use some company." When she didn't respond, Kragan shrugged like a naughty child. "It's okay if you'd rather not." She smiled with only one corner of her mouth. "Look. I know I've been coming on a little strong. Let's start over as new friends." This time her smile widened and she nodded. "Okay?" The excitement in his voice drew an expectant chuckle.

"Yes. Can we stay here? I don't really feel like leaving Union Station."

Kragan couldn't resist the deep satisfaction he felt spreading throughout his body. Knowing he needed to slow down his heartbeat was just an added shot of adrenaline to his ego. "Sounds good. I've got no place to be anyway."

In the end, Catharina retrieved her coat from her room and met Kragan on the lower level of the mall. Out back of Union Station where the children took *The Polar Express* ride were two restaurants, a Hard Rock Café and Landry's Seafood. When

Catharina admitted she loved seafood, Kragan insisted they try it out since it was one of the best in St. Louis. After Catharina saw the prices on the menu, she suggested they go somewhere else.

"My treat, remember? Besides, this is not any different than any good eatery in St. Louis. I know you aren't used to splurging but please let me do this, Cat."

His genuine smile won her over as did the quiet conversation. The restaurant continued to be busy but their candlelit table in the corner remained private and intimate. Catharina realized she was actually having a good time. Hearing some of the stories about the city and the quirky requests made by businessmen forced a deep laugh several times. Cupping her chin in the palm of her hand, she found looking into Kragan's hazel eyes was a pleasant experience. Had she misjudged him?

"Snow!" Kragan laughed as he opened his mouth for snow to touch his tongue as they walked out into the frosty night. "It should always snow at Christmas."

Catharina ran to a soft pile of the new flakes and formed a ball, hurtling it at the mayor. When she started laughing as it hit him square in the nose, he sputtered. She squealed as he gathered up a much bigger snowball and approached her at a wobbly run on the slick surface.

Kragan caught her but both of their feet hit ice and they fell in against a compacted snow pile from the first snowfall. With his body pressed against Catharina's, he could feel her laugh as well as the firmness of her body. He laughed too, thinking of how ironic it was that the little Bohemian violin player trusted him so completely.

He struggled to his feet, slipped, and fell flat against Cat again, his face resting against hers. Together they continued to laugh as each tried to gain a footing on the slick surface. Arm in arm they managed to get back inside the mall, shaking the flakes of snow to the floor. Catharina continued to laugh as she reached up to dust the snow from Kragan's hair.

He smiled and shook his hair to send a spray of icy pellets into her face. "Probably hard to see which is gray and which is snow."

They started to walk down the long promenade of the mall shops. Somehow their hands touched and clasped. When Kragan stopped at the foot of the bridge stairs that led up and over to Catharina's room, he dropped her hand and shoved his into his pocket to gain some control.

"I really should go. I'll go out here. It's street level and my driver will be parked nearby."

She eyed him with warm regard. Suddenly, she spontaneously stood on tip toes and kissed him on the cheek. "Thank you for a lovely dinner. Next time I'll treat since we're practicing being friends."

Kragan clenched his jaw, wanting more than she would be willing to surrender. "Goodnight, Cat."

It took a lot of will power, but he turned away and never looked back as he left. He liked to think she continued to watch him as he disappeared. Tonight he would just enjoy the memory of her pressed against his chest, the soft lips against his cheek, and the innocent web of deceit she'd fallen victim to.

♫ ♫ ♫

Just as Kragan's car pulled up, he spotted Damien getting out of his Mercedes. He tossed the keys to one of the attendants like it was a ten year old Chevy. The lack of respect for such a fine automobile was reprehensible. Kragan waited for the thorn in his side to notice him. Damien glanced his way then stopped.

"Have you been to the hospital, Damien?" Kragan tried to look concerned in spite of feeling zero empathy for Morgan Knox's plight.

"Yes. The lack of your concern and appearance today speaks volumes." Damien's black hair fell across his forehead as a gust of wind pushed in under the protective awnings. "Have you no mercy?"

Kragan grinned and looked around him to make sure no one was listening. "None." He thought he saw a spark of anger flash in the man's eyes, but Damien, like always, was quick to cover any amount of emotion he might feel. They weren't all that different, Kragan thought. "Besides, I did have a nice evening with

Catharina. She didn't really mention you. You think that is because you slept with Morgan last night?"

"I did no such thing." Damien raised his chin in his omnipotent fashion to look down his nose at the shorter man. "But I'm sure you already know all that. You've turned this honorable police force into a bunch of tattle tales. I'm sure Detective Jacobs couldn't wait to share his findings."

Kragan continued to look around him between moments of conversation. "Everybody wants to feel special, it seems. Even you." Damien began to glare, causing Kragan to shift his weight from one hip to the other. "Maybe that's why you've taken up with the rift raft of the city."

"Meaning?"

"Zane Spokane and his scruffy friends who scrounge on the city streets. Guess we'll have to move those vagrants out of downtown all together now that The Kitchen of Hope is out of commission."

"They'll be up and running in another week or so."

Kragan chuckled deep in his throat. "Happy Holidays, Damien."

Damien narrowed his eyes and calmly walked away, jarring the mayor's self-confidence.

♫♫♫

Zane watched from the parking lot across the street as the two men conversed in front of Union Station. Puffs of cold breath escaped their mouths as they spoke. He wondered what the conversation might be, city business, the weather, or general pleasantries. It would be odd for Damien to exchange pleasantries with anyone, much less the Mayor of St. Louis. Even from where he stood, Zane could feel the animosity between the two. Damien's heartbeat was strong but gathered speed at one point. The thought occurred to Zane that the topic might be his sister. Then he sensed fear, smelled it, and even tasted it in his mouth, causing him to spit out the bitterness. Although the mayor looked calm, he was anything but that. Zane sensed a familiarity of someone he once knew.

"Problem?" It was Gideon. He walked up behind Zane at an easy gait with some of the others following. Gideon looked across the street, saw Damien, and forced his body to slouch more than it already was. "I can feel him but I don't see him." Gideon looked around for Rocco. "Where is he? I shouldn't be here. He won't like it, Zane. We need to go. We'll be punished."

Zane raised his hand in a sign of authority. "Silence. I'm listening." But the new thread of contact he'd only recently started to embrace suddenly cut him free. He sighed as Kragan slipped away into the night, only to see Damien return to the street and look straight at him. Had he broken faith or a command?

The other Nephilim began to walk backward, heads down, stoop-shouldered, and moaning as if they were in pain. Zane locked eyes with Damien, knowing their strength became closer to equal each day as the transformation took hold. He also realized Damien was still in control and would be until the final act of sacrifice. Hundreds of years of doing God's bidding created an invincible creature that Zane realized he could not match at this stage of development.

With a final check on the Nephilim standing in a safe place from view, Zane ran across the street to face Damien. A valet attendant nodded his way then ignored the two men. "How is your friend?" Zane referred to the woman Morgan.

"She'll be fine. Father Xavier spent a while with her this afternoon and evening. The hospital plans to release her in a couple of days." Damien refused to divert his eyes from his protégé. "Catharina?"

"With Kragan earlier. Dinner. He's up to something." Thanks to Damien, Zane already knew that his sister spent the morning with Father Xavier earlier in the day. "Let me take a crack at him."

"No. Your God-given gift is not to be exploited for personal gain or satisfaction."

Zane frowned but looked up to the sky and nodded. "I need to go. We're going to make sure everyone is okay on the streets."

"Father Xavier opened the church recreational center for tonight. They should be able to get that far. Some of the deacons are already there setting up cots. At least it will be warm."

"Find Cat. Tell her what really happened this morning."

Damien finally broke his gaze and looked out into the street then over to where the Nephilim waited for Zane. "I can't in this current state of turmoil. She may force me to lose control. I can't risk it."

"Just don't wait too long, Damien." Zane grinned. "Better get used to human women being hard to get along with and willing to punish you for eternity for something they think you did."

Damien broke his solemn expression to let one corner of his mouth turn up. "I find the thought of making it up to her forever a viable choice."

Placing a hand on Damien's shoulder, Zane chuckled. "I hope I get a chance to become an angel before you find out the truth of your words." He turned then ran across the street to join his friends.

♫ ♫ ♫

The black woman sat in her recliner staring at the television. Neva Wallace always watched this station because the weatherman would mention several times a week how awful the temperatures were in St. Louis, Kansas City, and Chicago. It reminded of her why she moved to Florida. The sun and humidity suited her just fine. Several times a year her children and grandchildren came down to go to Disney World or the beach. She loved life in the small cottage she'd purchased for her retirement.

Now a simple phone call could ruin everything she'd worked for most of her adult life. Helping children in the foster care program didn't pay very well and the emotional drain on her humanity crippled her mentally several times. Then she met Father Xavier, who was willing to take in two runaway children one winter night. Together they hatched a plan so that he could keep them. The money allotted for the children went to him after she created a fake foster family. Neither the church nor her superiors would have approved. She could have been fired or been arrested for misappropriations of state funds.

Someone now knew the truth. They demanded she step forward, implicating Father Xavier. If she did nothing, then charges would be brought against her. The priest was a good man and saved those children. Could she do this terrible thing to save her own skin?

Chapter 36

The coffee shop remained busier than all the previous months combined. With so many families coming in to do The Polar Express experience, Catharina's bottom line was finally in the black. It took Molly and Zane to help her keep up with the many tasks she'd always done herself. Children loved the train set in the middle of the glass room. Parents loved it too because it gave them a chance to drink a cup of coffee while their little ones focused on the beautiful train speeding through an artificial world.

"You know you're going to have to talk to Damien at some point, Cat." Zane waited until Molly went to clear some tables before approaching the subject of his sister's relationship with Damien. The last two evenings Kragan dropped in to take her to dinner somewhere in the mall below. When Zane protested, Catharina told him in no uncertain terms to back off. "I know you're hurt, but can't you just hear him out?"

"I've been here all week. He's not come by once." Catharina smiled as she handed a cup of coffee over the counter to a familiar policeman who dropped by several times a week. "On the house, Officer Cooke. Merry Christmas." He winked at her and disappeared out the door.

"You know, when emotions run high it can be dangerous for him."

Catharina lifted her nose in the air like a spoiled child. "Emotions? The man, or whatever he is, has the emotions of a robot. He is using me to get what he wants and that is   " Another customer came to the counter, stared at the menu longer than needed then ordered a Carmel Latte.

Zane took someone else's order and decided to let the subject drop.

Catharina handed over the latte and thanked the woman for the tip shoved in the large jar on the counter. "Zane, I know you think he is perfect. I don't see it that way."

"And Kragan? What about him? Is something going on I should know about?"

Catharina picked up on the deepening voice change and sinister tone when he said the mayor's name. "No." She sighed and shook her head. "Just friends. I'm done with romance, big brother." She took a towel and snapped it against his leg, causing him to yelp. "You and Father Xavier are my true loves. Kragan is just a distraction from how bad I'm hurting. His kindness helps me forget how angry I am."

Zane turned her around to see Father Xavier walking Morgan Knox into the shop on his arm. Catharina didn't realize how large her eyes grew or that her lips parted in shock. "She's here to see you, Cat."

"I need to leave."

He grabbed her by the apron, jerking her back in his arms. "Nope." He untied the apron and shoved her out from the counter. "Don't be rude. You tell me that all the time. Practice what you preach."

Feeling his hand in the small of her back, Catharina stepped forward and chose to look at the priest. "Father Xavier. I wasn't expecting you. We're a little swamped today."

"Not so much now, though," Zane called loud enough it could be heard in the Grand Hall. "Have a seat."

"Please, Catharina." The pleading was in the Father's eyes. "Just a few words."

The first thing Catharina noticed were the bandages on Morgan's wrists. Why would she do that? Did Rocco force Morgan to harm herself because Catharina had caught the two of them together? That was one of the reasons Catharina avoided Damien. She was afraid of the questions, as well as the answers. Rocco could manipulate anyone and everything to his liking if he attached God's name and work to it. Would he do this?

Catharina sat across from Morgan in a wicker chair before the glowing fire. Father Xavier excused himself to visit with Molly and Zane. They sat in silence a long time before Catharina heard Morgan take in a deep breath. Catharina couldn't resist stealing a glance at her and noticed tears running down her face.

"Morgan, are you all right? Should I call someone?" Catharina lost the attitude she'd planned to use against the woman when she reached over to lay a hand on Morgan's arm. Catharina jumped up and retrieved some napkins. "Here." She pulled her chair closer. "I'm sorry. I was really rude a minute ago."

"No. It's fine. Really." Morgan dabbed at her face. "I need to tell you about the other day when you walked in on Damien and me." Catharina caught the woman's glance toward Zane and wondered why he nodded at her.

"I know the two of you have a history." Catharina turned her eyes back to the fire. "I guess I thought that was in the past."

"It is. I did spend the night in Damien's room." Catharina dropped her head but held back any tears. She was done crying over romance. "But Damien wasn't there. He came in only moments before you." Catharina jerked her head around in bewilderment. "What you saw was an attempt to seduce him. Yes, I was naked and he was half dressed, but…" Morgan told her the whole story of how things unfolded. "You came in at the most inconvenient of times."

Catharina couldn't help from blinking rapidly, as if by doing so, she would clear the cobwebs of confusion.

Morgan reached over and took Catharina's hand. "I realized that Damien loved you. I could see it in his eyes. I was devastated. After what Kragan did to me, I felt like a worthless whore begging for someone to love me."

"Wait. I don't understand. What did Kragan do to you?"

"I loved him." Morgan now looked away, as if bewildered by her own confession. "He is a vile and cruel human being."

"People break up all the time, Morgan. It doesn't mean you're worthless." Catharina's heart ached for this woman. "I know it seems cruel to be rejected but—"

"No," she snapped. "He is really vile. The only reason I went to Damien was because Kragan wanted time alone with you. I was the distraction. He knew how I loved him."

Catharina covered her mouth with her hands. "Kragan did that to you?"

Morgan pulled up one sleeve so Catharina could see the bruises. "If I ever wanted him to love me, then I had to obey. I'm not even going to tell you what he made me do to please him. But I did it so he would want me." She looked down at her wrists. "It wasn't enough. Even this—" She lifted her hands. "—changed nothing. He never even came to see me. When Damien rejected me, I realized how low I'd sunk."

Catharina's heart burst as she looked at the broken woman next to her. She scooted her chair in front of Morgan and pulled her into her arms. "I'm so sorry, Morgan. Forgive me." Catharina felt the woman stroke her hair. "But you lived. I'm glad Damien got to you in time."

Morgan smiled down at her. "Rocco saved me, Cat." Catharina jerked back, eyes full of horror. "I know the truth." Morgan watched the blood drain from the Catharina's face. "I wouldn't have made it if Rocco hadn't appeared. Somehow, Damien knew I was pushed beyond the breaking point. I'm not proud of that." Morgan looked over at the priest and Zane who watched them. "But I'm going to change my life. Father Xavier says God will forgive me. I believe that. Do you?"

"Yes." Catharina hugged Morgan again. "I certainly do, Morgan." She stood and looked down at a rescued soul. "You must never tell his secret."

"Promise." The weak smile showed signs of hope. "You need to know that Kragan was behind that first attack at the Essmalory." A look of disbelief filled Catharina's face. "I can't prove it but I believe he was behind the attack at the Kitchen of Hope and the fire too."

"But why?" Catharina couldn't believe the man she'd just begun to know could do such a thing.

"Greed. Those properties are worth millions in development. His holding company planned to take them over when no one wanted them because of the crime. He purposely held the police back from that area." Morgan could read the skeptical look in Catharina's eyes. "I'm not trying to get even. I'm doing this because Rocco gave me a second chance to make things right. Do I still love Kragan?" She bit her bottom lip. "Yes. But he is poison for me. He likes to hurt women, Cat. Be very careful. He is a psycho-deceiver."

"What does that mean exactly?" Catharina whispered.

"Same thing as wolf in sheep's clothing." Morgan stood too now. "Forgive Damien. Even if you don't want him, show him compassion."

Catharina stared at her for a good ten seconds, ran out of the coffee shop, then came back to call to Zane. "Can you stay?"

Both Father Xavier and Zane smiled as they waved her away.

The priest slipped the apron over his head as he watched Morgan move to the electric train behind the glass wall. "She's got a lot of healing to do. I sure underestimated the mayor. To think he made her lap milk from a bowl and made her purr."

Zane froze as he stared at the priest. "He did what?"

"Made her pretend she was a cat. When he would call her, he'd say, 'here kitty, kitty, kitty.' Disgusting. Twisted. What's wrong with people today?" Father Xavier looked over at Zane and frowned. "What's wrong, son? Are you ill?" He watched the man he'd claimed as his child morph before his eyes. The overall body didn't change but the look in his eyes turned deadly. His eyes frosted like Rocco's. "Zane? What is it?"

"Kragan. I know who he really is."

♪♬♪

Catharina ran into the lobby of Damien's office where his assistant looked at her in his usual distasteful way. "He's not here."

She swallowed hard as she placed a hand over her heart and gasped for breath. "Do you know where he went?"

"Left about twenty minutes ago. Did you check to see if he went to his apartment?"

Before he could make another suggestion, Catharina ran out

of the lobby, leaving the assistant to huff and comment how inappropriate her manners were to be working at Union Station.

Catharina sucked up her courage and tapped lightly at Damien's door. When no one answered, she pushed the door open. Nightfall left the rooms dark, not that Damien needed light to see, but she knew he was gone. She found the opening that led to the rafters and attic above Union Station. Climbing several rickety ladders then a winding staircase that creaked at each step, she realized the small flashlight she grabbed out of a drawer in Damien's nightstand needed newer batteries. The light would fade until she shook it and became bright again for a few minutes.

Surely, the rooms where Rocco lived when the weight of the world crashed in on him couldn't be far. The sounds of something moving above her on the rafters made her skin crawl. Was it a rat or bat? She became disoriented several times with the distraction of being stalked by an animal. Every time she turned the light to the rafters, the noise quieted. Did demons haunt this place to tempt Rocco with the ways of the world? Her flashlight shined on the ladder that led up to where she'd first found Rocco. The feel of soot and mold made her nose itch as she placed the light in her pocket.

Once inside the cavernous room she tried to shine the light around everywhere but the beam paled again. The batteries rattled as she shook them. This time when she lifted the light, Rocco stood no more than two feet from her. She screamed, dropping the light.

Rocco's face had the black band across his nose, ear to ear. His eyes glazed silver. The clothing he wore was that of Damien, not Rocco. With his tailored shirt removed, his tattoos became visible, even in the dim, dabbled moonlight coming through the windows. His lips, firm and wide, appeared to be glued shut in a permanent frown. Only his nostrils flared, letting Catharina know he wasn't a statue. It was as if he failed to breathe. Slowly the silver faded and his eyes transformed to blue.

Rocco began to back away from her.

"Why didn't you tell me what happened?" Silence. He

continued to back away as his body art started to fade and the black band across his nose disappeared. "Did you think I wouldn't believe you?" The moonlight fell across his chest as he backed farther from her, as if her presence was toxic. "I was hurt. I'm still hurt." Catharina's voice cracked but she kept speaking. "Seeing you with her—"

"There is only you, Catharina." The raspy voice of Rocco still clung to the body of Damien, now transformed to human. He began to breathe normally and stretched out his arms to examine them before dropping them to his sides.

"Are you transformed completely to human?" Catharina's voice sounded small even to her.

"Yes. I—" he whispered so low he wondered if she could him.

She ran to him, slamming into his body so hard that his arms came up around her. Their mouths connected over and over, until their ragged breath seemed to fill the air with the cold vapor that inhabited the ghostly space. Damien knew his resistance grew thin. His desire to devour Catharina was so powerful he couldn't stop Rocco from appearing and vanishing over and over. Finally, he pushed her away with a shove.

"Stop," he panted as Rocco took over his body once more.

Catharina tried to catch her breath as she stepped closer and ran her hands across his chest then down his arms. As she looked up into his eyes, they frosted from blue to gray then silver. "I love you, Damien. Forever. Whatever length of time that is, I love you. If we can't be together, I still love you. I want you to know that. If you need to take my life to be free, I'll gladly give my whole being to you, to God. Just say you love me too." A tear formed at the corner of her eye.

Rocco fell to his knees and pulled Catharina into his embrace, pushing his face into her midriff and stomach. He began speaking in some angelic language she couldn't understand.

Catharina stroked his head, holding it firmly against her body, wondering if, at any minute, she would vaporize into some kind of angel powder that would drift on the wind for eternity. She would do it for him.

Finally, Rocco stood and ran his fingers through her hair

then down her neck and shoulders. The tattoos covering her burns began to ache until he spoke softly. He reached into her blouse, laying his hand upon them, then withdrew, touching the area over his heart. The tattoos she'd worn for so long appeared. The burning disappeared.

"I take your pain forever. You will not die for me, Catharina. Without you, I might as well be an angel." Rocco stood back and straightened to his full height. "The only woman to ever own my heart plays a violin and stands before me. I love you beyond reason. This feeling is new to me. Being a human is harder than I imagined, but I can no longer resist the pull of a heart that beats only when you are present."

Catharina rested her head against his chest. What would be the price? There had to be a price?

Chapter 37

Calm down, Neva. Who called you?" Father Xavier understood only bits and pieces of the hysterical woman's tale. Something about paying back all the money or they would be turned over to the state attorney's office, maybe even the IRS.

"He was a St. Louis city alderman, used to be a local attorney. I remember him from years ago when he first started. A real go-getter at first then turned out to be just another ambulance chaser who did quite well for himself."

Father Xavier could hear her blow her nose. "Did he threaten you, Neva, about helping me?"

"Said if I didn't come forth, he'd make sure both of us went to jail. He knows I never followed through on the death of the Mitchersons." She started to cry.

The priest was well aware of what Neva managed to pull off in order for him to keep the children with him and safe from unscrupulous men like Glen Forrester. He reflected back on that night, remembering that December was the coldest on record for St. Louis. Periodic downpours of freezing rain knocked the power off in parts of the city. Fortunately for the children, Neva found them after checking several places the children often talked about hiding. They were huddled in an enclosed park pavilion that offered some protection from the weather.

She brought the children to him that night. It was late and she had no other choice, or so she claimed. He'd wondered many times if God let her find them at that precise time so there would be no other choice but to come to her priest for help.

Seeing the children both frightened melted his heart. The boy, Zane, had given his coat to his little sister, wrapping it tight around her skinny body that shivered even when they arrived at his doorstep.

The lights on the Christmas tree twinkled so that little Catharina couldn't stop staring at it in wonder. He made up his sofa for the girl and a pallet on the floor for the boy, who wouldn't get five feet away from his sister. Even then, he was protective and devoted to her. Several times, he placed himself in between the priest and his sister, as if he needed to make sure of the man's intentions.

The freezing rain paralyzed the city for a few days without much opportunity for Neva to touch base with him. In those days, there were no cell phones and the aging telephone lines collapsed under the weight of the ice, cutting the priest off from the outside world. Even that made Father Xavier wonder if God was trying to solidify his attachment to the runaways.

By the time Neva did arrive, Father Xavier was ready to lie, cheat, steal, or do whatever it took to keep the children safe and with him. Neva smiled, since she had already hatched a plan. She could tell the children were beginning to come out of their shells and followed the priest around wherever he walked, sat, or stood for more than one minute. Later, she told Father Xavier she thought it was a Christmas miracle to see such damaged children smiling and laughing as they were meant to do.

Neva worked for an independent agency that placed children in foster homes. The agency also trained foster parents. Zane and Catharina's paperwork fell into her lap as a result of too much work for the state agency. It hadn't taken her long to see something amiss at the Forrester household, even though all the I's were dotted and the T's crossed. The Spokane children particularly touched her heart, causing her to make an extra effort to visit them often, as well as bring them little gifts and treats.

After they ran away, Neva and Father Xavier enlisted the help of the Mitchersons, an elderly couple in the church who were childless. With Neva's help, Mrs. Mitcherson secured a kinship license for them, so no extra training was required. They moved in to a small house near the church where a younger Father Xavier could attend to them almost every day. Soon they were enrolled in the parish school attached to the church, where the children thrived. Zane could be a handful, pulling pranks and spooking the nuns, but overall he was a good kid. Catharina, stunted by fear and neglect, began to blossom under the love and guidance of Father Xavier, who enlisted the help of several parishioners to fill in the gaps of parenthood where he or the Mitchersons failed. It became an open secret of raising two children who had no one else.

The Mitchersons loved the children and did their best. With the monthly check each month, expenses didn't eat into their social security. There was always someone dropping off a few personal hygiene items or pair of shoes just when it was needed most.

When the Mitchersons died several years later, Father Xavier was at a loss as to what he should do. By this time, Neva had become a licensed social worker assigned to the case. Fearing that the children would be removed, as well as separated because of their age, Neva never officially reported the death. Slipping the paperwork in with dozens of cases of a caseworker that recently died in a car accident gave Neva another opportunity to purposely mishandle the file. Many of those cases got lost or misplaced, because the person assigned was already swamped with their own work load. It was a no brainer.

At that point, Father Xavier continued to cash the checks sent to the Mitchersons, in order to support the children. Since they willed the house to the priest, he moved in. With the continued help of a few nuns and parishioners, nothing really changed. Even the bishop knew nothing of the arrangement. When Father Xavier needed to stay all night with a family who needed last rights for a loved one, one of the nuns gladly spent the night with the kids. It was a perfect arrangement.

Did he know opening a state check and cashing it was breaking the law? By then, the priest really was more concerned that his little family not be broken up. Father Xavier knew full well that the dioceses had a policy of no dependents for priests. A priest's wage falls short of supporting a child, and the general consensus was that by placing a child with a priest might deprive an earthly mother of a child, not to mention the priest might be unable to fulfill their duties as a minister of the church.

"I can't see where you'd be in any kind of trouble, Neva. You were protecting those children. I was the one who cashed those checks."

"I created a false home study so they could stay with you and that old couple. If I hadn't done that, in six months they would've moved them again. Besides, neither of you were certified by the state to take foster children. I broke the law."

"Not in God's eyes, you didn't," Father Xavier assured her in his usual calm voice, although his stomach began to twist.

"Well, you better tell God to get with the program and get us out of this."

"How do you think the man found out, Neva?"

The sound of rustling paper then a click of a pen sounded close to the phone. "I'm looking at notes I took when he called the first time."

Father Xavier experienced a rush of bewilderment. "He's called more than once?"

"Three times. I asked him that same question. Said someone had seen both the girl and boy at The Kitchen of Hope and recognized them from the same foster home he was in. Reached out to Alderman Crane out of curiosity because they'd runaway, never to return."

"That was a long time ago. People look differently."

"Apparently, the little girl looked the same, only grown up. When her brother showed up, it was a positive identification. The interested party is some kind of city official or something."

"Why would you say that?"

"Crane said someone important in city government wanted to know about where they'd been. How did they survive? I guess it is common knowledge in the homeless population how you treat those kids like your own. I don't know. I guess he's just fishing. Maybe the two of them want to blackmail us." She puffed out a large breath, as if she'd been holding it in, followed by a sniffle. "What are we going to do? I don't have that kind of money."

Father Xavier remained quiet for some time before he

ventured a comment. "My life is richer and more fulfilled because of the chance you took, Neva. I will not let you do anything to jeopardize your life style or security. If I have to come forward and admit what I did, I will. You can remain an innocent."

"What are you going to do?"

Father Xavier looked at the crucifix hanging on the wall. "I know someone who can help, God willing."

♫ ♫ ♫

Morgan looked at the number of the caller on her cell phone before ignoring it.

"Aren't you going to take that?" It was Zane who stopped at a light near Forest Park. He'd volunteered to take Morgan to the doctor and then return her to the apartment that overlooked the park where the World's Fair was once held. Glancing at her, he realized how fragile she looked in her plain black coat, trimmed in faux fur. Her skin looked like a porcelain doll with only a hint of color on her high cheekbones.

"No. It isn't important." She wondered what Kragan would think about her description of his attempt to reach out to her. "Just work."

"Don't overdo it, Morgan. You've been through a lot." Zane turned his car into the parking lot and found a place to park. "Looks like this is as close as I can get. I'll walk you to the door."

Morgan laid her hand on Zane's arm as he started to exit. "Thank you for helping me out." She withdrew her hand. "And for your visit in the hospital."

Zane shrugged and smiled a toothy grin like a little boy. "Who wouldn't want to drive a pretty lady around town? And as for the visit...well, I thought you couldn't ignore me there."

"Just like your sister, and Father Xavier I guess, you don't hold anything against me."

Morgan realized, in that moment, how big and strong Zane Spokane was. He seemed to have transformed over the last few months from when she'd spotted him the first time. Images of him changing from homeless man to resilient warrior continued to pop in her head when she thought about the kindness he'd shown over the last couple of days.

"Are you ready to go in?" Zane could smell vanilla on her skin. "Or do you want to talk for a while?"

"Talk. I think." For the first time in several years, she actually experienced embarrassment. "Do you mind?"

Zane shook his head and relaxed against the seat. "No place I gotta be. One of the perks of being homeless, jobless, and a little off in the head."

This caused Morgan to chuckle. "I wish I were like you and your sister, Zane."

"Something tells me you are and just don't know it."

Morgan turned her eyes out the window to observe the gloomy weather. "You don't know me or the things I've done."

Zane reached out and took her gloved hand in his bare one. "I've got ghosts following me around most of the time because of things I did in Afghanistan. Lately, it's not so bad. Just takes time, Morgan."

"Can I fix you some dinner, Zane?" The words came out a trite hesitant. "It's okay if you say no. I want to explain a few things about who I was and—"

"Yes," he snapped with a friendly nod. "I'm starved. Can I help because I love to cook?"

"Zane—" She felt her cheeks grow hot. "—it's just dinner."

He nodded. "That's more than I've had in quite a while, Morgan. I want nothing from you. I know what it's like to be mixed up. Okay?" Watching the relief wash over her touched something deep inside him. Jumping out of the car to hurry around to her door, he helped Morgan out as if she was the Virgin Mary. When her boot touched some ice, she slipped deeper into Zane's arms. He pulled her upright and looked down into her face. Both burst into laughter as they continued to hold onto each other before making their way across to the double doors of her building.

♫ ♫ ♫

Kragan watched Zane and Morgan slip and slide to the apartment building. He slammed his fist against the steering wheel over and over until he could hardly breathe from the rage rising up inside his gut. To see that hulk of a reject wrap his arms around Morgan, as if she was a helpless child, forced Kragan to turn the key in his ignition. Could he run through the fence and hit them both without anyone seeing? How could she turn to that slob of a human being after all he'd done for her? And to think he'd driven all the way over here to thank her for the sacrifice that put her in the hospital. He was still amazed that she'd tried such a stunt. But this. Seeing her let that half-witted vet touch her sent a chill up Kragan's spine. Guess he would have to teach her another lesson soon.

A glance at the digital clock on the dash diverted his attention from Morgan to someone else as he punched in a few numbers on his cell. It rang only a few times.

"Hello." The male voice was definitely British and coming through on Catharina's cell. Kragan waited, hoping Damien would pass the phone to her. "Kragan. I know you're there."

"Let me speak to Cat." His voice had the warmth of a melted popsicle in July.

"She's unavailable." The line went dead.

In a rage, Kragan threw his phone against the passenger side door, picked it up, and slammed it two more times, before pulling out into traffic and stomping down the accelerator.

♫ ♫ ♫

"Was that my phone earlier?" Catharina's ring tone was the beginning of Mozart's Fortieth Symphony. No one she knew had anything similar.

"Yes. It was Kragan." The two walked out onto the balcony that overlooked the Grand Hall. Catharina grabbed Damien's arm to stop him walking. He turned to her then pulled her into his arms. "I'll handle Kragan. You need not talk to him again."

Catharina played with his tie to settle her nerves. "No. I really should tell him about us. He may have done terrible things to Morgan—"

"And to you, Cat. Don't forget he wanted the Essmalory enough to burn it when no one would cave to selling."

"I know. But I keep remembering how kind he was to me." She looked up into Damien's blue eyes and couldn't resist kissing his lips. He pulled back and cringed. "I'm sorry! I shouldn't have done that. Are you okay?" He opened one eye and smiled. "Yes, woman, I am more than fine. You just might be the death of me yet," he joked as he jerked her tight against his chest. "Don't trust him and don't tell him without Zane or myself close by. Understand?"

Catharina let her eyes take in every inch of his chiseled face with the five o'clock shadow. "I love you." Damien released her so fast she stumbled back then couldn't contain a chuckle. "I'm sorry. I'll stop now."

He shook his head then pulled back his shoulders as if adjusting his control. "No wonder the first angels fell out of favor with our God," he moaned as he breezed past her.

♫ ♫ ♫

The Friday night crowd packed into the Grand Hall. Many children, tugging at their parents' hands or pant legs from being tired or hungry, quieted once the light show started at the top of the hour. The big finish drew applause just before the sound of Catharina's violin echoed across the expansive room where once travelers moved across the country.

A spotlight illuminated her standing on the bar with her head down and her arms lifted out to her side. When she started to play, then dance, a wave of applause started at one end then floated across the entire area. At some point her dance team would lift her to the floor so she could continue to weave a magical spell over the children who now beamed with excitement. A few even joined her on the dance floor.

From five until eleven, Friday through Sunday night, Catharina played her turquoise violin twenty minutes each hour. One of the bartenders placed a jar for tips. Each night, she made close to another hundred dollars to add to her savings.

"I tried to call earlier, Cat." It was Kragan. Catharina noticed him entering the Grand Hall at her last performance of the evening. He stood at the end of the bar watching like a sulking tiger that hadn't eaten in a few days. The mask of warmth and friendliness now revealed what Catharina feared might be the real Kragan. "Damien answered your phone."

Catharina scooted up onto a bar stool, accepting a glass of water that one of the hostesses knew by now she'd crave and sipped before stealing a sideways glance at the mayor. "He told me later. I'm sorry about that." What else was she supposed to say?

"Why did he have your phone in the first place?" Kragan motioned for another shot of something, gulped it down when delivered.

Catharina wondered if this was a good time to discuss her relationship with Damien. "We're together a lot here. It's not unusual for us to be together. I must have been changing into my costume for tonight's performance when you called."

Kragan sat his glass down a little too hard, causing Catharina to flinch. "Seems a little cozy."

Catharina could sense the threat level elevating and wanted to escape to a safer subject. "We're all a cozy bunch here at Union Station." She smiled at a passing bartender who caught her comment. "Isn't that right, Sean?" She leaned over to whisper loud enough for the bartender to hear her. "Sean's a law student at Wash U. You may want him to work for City Hall someday."

Sean gave a thumbs-up and moved on. "Cozy is an understatement. Tips are behind the bar, Cat. Don't forget."

"We're one big family here." Catharina thought the spark of anger lessened in Kragan's stiff posture. "I'm notorious for leaving my phone lying around. Don't hardly ever use the thing. The only reason I have it is to stay connected with Zane and Father Xavier. Up until recently, they were the only ones who called me." She wondered if the smile on her face looked fake until Kragan smiled too.

"I sounded like a jealous lover, didn't I?" He shook his head in disgust. "Guess I can't keep pretending I don't have feelings for you, Cat."

"About that, Kragan—"

Kragan moved a breath away and kissed the side of her face as his arm went around her waist. "How about we go back to my place. Take tomorrow off." Just then, he felt an iron grip on his hand that jerked him free of Catharina, spinning him around like a toy.

"Keep your hands off my sister, Kragan." Zane towered over him, looking like an angry bull ready to charge. "Stay away from her permanently, or I'll make it impossible for you to be with any woman."

"Zane! Please!" Catharina looked around, noticing people pausing conversations to look their way.

"Are you threatening me, Spokane?"

"I'm promising you, Kragan, that if you ever get close to my sister again, I'll find a way to not only remove you from office, but from this earth. Understand?" Zane gave the mayor a shove that slammed him against the bar.

Kragan glared at the man who once beat him up as a kid. He could feel his own nostrils flare at the rage building inside him. Knowing that he was no match in strength, the mayor savored the thought of other ways to deal with Zane Spokane. "You have no idea what you've just done." He straightened up and walked away at a brisk pace, making a mental list of all the things he planned to do to Catharina Spokane. His plan just rived up a notch.

♫♫♫

Crane opened the door to his row house and instinctively flipped on the light switch. Lights failed to flood the kitchen with brightness, giving him the thought that he may have forgotten to pay his electric bill again. He kept a flashlight in the junk drawer which he retrieved in quick order then pushed the on switch. When he turned around, someone stood in front of him, hooded and dark. Crane stumbled backward with a gasp as the realization hit him that The Watcher stood before him.

"What—what do you want?" For such a rotund man, his voice sounded squeaky.

The Watcher glared at him for effect then took a slow step

in his direction. A moan of discomfort emitted from the alderman's mouth until the press of the kitchen cabinet jammed into his back.

"I want answers." The raspy voice sounded cruel, edged with sinister intent.

"Answers to what?" Crane tried to edge away from the tall man before him, but only managed to make the beast invade his personal space. "Okay. Okay." He held up his hand, dropping the flashlight as he turned his head away to avoid looking into the frosted eyes of death. His heart pounded and he wasn't sure if he could wait to go to the bathroom.

"You called the social worker in Florida. I want to know why."

Chapter 38

Detective Jacobs listened intently as Alderman Crane ranted about The Watcher invading his home. "I could have been killed!" he shouted, choosing to pace back and forth across his living room instead of sit like the detective.

"What did he want?" The detective took out his notebook, touched the tip of the pencil to his tongue, and scribbled to make sure it worked. It didn't. "Do you have a pen or pencil, Mr. Crane?" He started patting his overcoat pockets then checking the inside for something to write with. "Sorry."

Crane exhaled like a gale force wind kept him from breathing normally. "Here." He tossed the detective a pen from the top of his desk. "What are you going to do about it? This has got to stop. Now that looney tune is targeting city officials."

"Was there anything taken?"

"Not that I could see. I interrupted him."

"No computer thumb drives or files accessed? I'm sure you keep some city business notes here."

Crane hurried to his computer and turned it on, made a quick search, then sighed with relief. "No. Nothing."

"I'd change my passwords just the same." The detective wrote down a few things. "Were you hurt?"

"Startled is all." Crane didn't want to admit he'd wet himself when The Watcher put his ornate dagger to his throat. He'd changed clothes before calling the police. "He didn't stick around long."

"What do you think he wanted, Mr. Crane?" The detective

looked around the house and, although nicely appointed, most of the décor could have been purchased at any IKEA or furniture outlet.

Crane diverted his eyes and began the pacing again. "He never said."

"Was your security system armed?" The detective stood. "I noticed you have a camera on the front and backdoors. Maybe we can get something off of that."

Crane rubbed his face, as if by doing so he'd lose the look of fear and irritation. "It had been disabled. He thought of everything."

"If you don't care, we'll take a look, anyway." Crane nodded and another officer set about checking things out. "Did he say anything to you? Threaten you?"

"No. No. Just said I should take better care of the people in my ward." Crane burped his Mexican dinner, apologized, and continued. "He is dangerous, detective."

Jacobs nodded in agreement, wondering why there wasn't more evidence of a crime. "Are you sure it was The Watcher? Maybe it was just a burglar. The Watcher usually leaves a calling card with a little blood on it. Did he cut you?"

Crane pulled out the turtleneck of his sweater for the detective to see. "What does that look like? I sure as hell didn't cut myself shaving!" he shouted so loud the extra officer hurried back into the room, only to have the detective wave him away.

"So you changed clothes before we got here." The detective appeared to make a note. "You should have that looked at, Mr. Crane. What did The Watcher use to cut you?"

"Some kind of dagger. I don't know. I gave him a shove. He fell and then I punched in the emergency code on my security system. He took off." Crane puffed out his chest as if he'd done something heroic.

Detective eyed him over the rim of his glasses. "I thought the security system was turned off."

Crane frowned before stuttering an answer. "I—I mean I grabbed the phone and hit nine-one-one."

"May I see your phone, Mr. Crane?" The detective walked up to the alderman as he shoved both the pen and the notebook in his pocket.

"No you may not!" Crane blasted, hoping the detective would take a step back. "What's going on here? Are you accusing me of something?"

"No, sir. Just doing my job. Part of the interview process. Don't worry about it. I'll make a note in my report." The detective smiled with as much condescension as he could manage without being too disrespectful.

Alderman Crane had a reputation for being a tantrum-thrower when things didn't go his way. It was bad enough the detective found himself in the bad graces of the mayor, or so the police chief had informed him earlier in the day. Politicians. You couldn't live with them and you couldn't kill them.

"Since you said earlier he wore gloves there probably isn't any fingerprints, but we can double check."

The alderman moved to a cart that held a variety of liquors and poured a double of a bronze liquid. "Don't bother. I gave you a positive ID. If your stupid police department hasn't gotten anything by now, they won't." His growl, meant to be insulting, only managed to cause the detective to motion for his officer.

"I'd be happy to take you to the ER to have that cut looked at. Maybe we can swab it to get some information."

In the end, the alderman thought that might be a good idea after all. He insisted a police officer stay at his home until he returned in case The Watcher reappeared.

♫ ♫ ♫

Catharina sat on the edge of Rocco's unmade bed, sobbing as her brother glared down at her with the patience of a rattle-snake. Sometimes he'd start pacing, swinging his hands over his head, yelling like a crazy man reminiscent of bygone days. He even slipped back into his repetitive behavior of repeating himself over and over.

"Stay away! Stay away! Stay away! Danger. Danger. Danger."

"What are you talking about?" Catharina tried to sound calm as he dragged her through the upper workings of Union Station toward Rocco's sanctuary, where he could exist without fear of being discovered during those moments when being a human was just too hard to maintain. "Let me go!" she snapped as the twisting and jerking movements did nothing to free her.

By the time they'd reached the eighth level of the bell tower floor, Zane had spun himself into a dangerous and irrational lunatic. He'd shoved her on the bed and told all he knew about Kragan LaPlante. The story of how he was living under a new identity to hide from his father, the car accident that disfigured him, leading to drastic plastic surgery, and his rise to power on the backs of many.

Catharina was already quaking at the information but it was the discovery that Kragan was really the bully son of Glen Forrester, their last foster father that sent her over the edge into hysteria. Zane retold all that Morgan had confided in him about the mistreatment, the saucer of milk, the acting out of being a cat, the abuse, and finally how Kragan wanted to take the Essmalory and Kitchen of Hope for his own personal gain and to punish them. "He cares nothing about the people of St. Louis, especially the homeless or you. He wants to get even with us, with me for beating the crap out of him before we ran off that night. And you—" Zane pointed down at her and yelled at the top of his lungs. "—you cozy up to him, making sweet like he's a nice guy."

Catharina choked as she tried to speak. "I didn't know, Zane. I wanted to give him a chance."

"He's a liar and a monster. A monster. A monster!"

"Breathe, my friend," came the comforting voice of Rocco as he slipped a hand on Zane's shoulder. He could feel the raging heartbeat beneath his fingertips as he squeezed slowly. "It's all right. I'm here." The warrior whirled around to confront Rocco, but froze as penetrating silver eyes punctured his madness. "Repeat with me Psalms 23: 'The Lord is my shepherd, I lack nothing. He makes me lie down in green pastures, he leads me beside quiet waters, he refreshes my soul. He guides me along the right paths for his name's sake. Even though I walk through the darkest valley, I will fear no evil, for you are with me, your rod and your staff, they comfort me...'"

In seconds, Zane was speaking the words with his eyes closed, chin held high toward the rafters cloaked in darkness. His breathing decelerated to normal and his heartbeat resumed a strong rhythmic pace, causing Rocco to withdraw his hand. The angel then turned his attention to Catharina whose eyes already looked swollen from fear and grief.

"Is this true, Rocco? Is Kragan the boy who abused us?"

Rocco patted Zane on the back now that he'd gained some control and went to Catharina. "I believe that it's true. Father Xavier came to me with the information Morgan told him, as well as threats against him and the social worker which led you to a safe home."

"Ms. Neva?" Zane shook his head in exasperation. "I can't imagine what would have happened to us had she not taken us to Father Xavier."

Rocco turned his eyes on Catharina, who still cried with her head buried in her hands. "Nor can I." He moved to sit by Catharina and instantly felt the designs on his body catch fire. A silent prayer of strength and control, whispered to God's ear, forced him to wait until his body cooled. "Catharina, look at me."

With a sniff and a swipe at her eyes and nose, she looked over at him, the desire to be held clearly in her body language. Ignoring the pain that shot through his limbs, Rocco pulled her closer so that her head rested against his chest. Her body began to shake with the sobs of tortured memories.

"He can't hurt you now."

"I'm going to kill that demon once and for all." Zane started the blustering once more until he locked eyes with Rocco, who was trying ever so hard to change into a human. His look of reprimand stopped Zane in his tracks.

"I didn't know. How could I not know who he was, Damien? How?" Catharina wrapped her arms around the half angel-human as he fought to change. She could feel the power and the heat leave his body, in spite of her physical touch. She would try to evaluate that at a later time.

"Because you are good," he said as his body kept flashing between the two creatures he'd lived with for hundreds of years.

"That was so far in the past that it was unthinkable anyone might find you."

"What's going to happen to Father Xavier and Ms. Neva? They saved us." She pushed back and saw that the anger had forced back the human and replaced it with Rocco.

He tried to breathe deep and long to control the back and forth, but she knew her proximity prevented him from total control.

Rocco rose from the bed. "God saved you, Catharina," he reminded her. "Father Xavier and Ms. Neva were but instruments to God's design. They fulfilled His will and I intend to protect them as I always have." Rocco looked over at Zane who stood transformed into a calm warrior whom he knew would survive the battles ahead.

"I'm sorry, Cat." Zane took a seat next to her then gathered her small frame into his arms. "That man makes me crazy. I can't stand to see him touch you."

Rocco bristled at the words and waited for Zane to tell him what happened in the Grand Hall.

Rocco placed his hands on the hilt of his weapons. "You are in danger, Zane. Tomorrow you are to go to Father Xavier for The Blessing. Gather Gideon and the others to meet you there. Time is drawing near."

Zane nodded as Catharina wiped the last tear away. "Blessing? What Blessing? Why should Gideon be there?" Rocco faded suddenly into the form of Damien and joined Zane in smiling at Catharina.

"I want you there, Cat. Will you come?" Zane leaned over and kissed the side of her head. Before she could answer he looked back at Damien. "I want Morgan there too."

Damien frowned. "That's not a good idea. Making an alliance with her is dangerous business."

Zane twisted his lips as if considering what his friend said. "I can handle it. Don't worry, Damien. I won't let you down."

"What are the two of you talking about?" Catharina spoke with slowness as if by doing so would give her clarity. She eyed her brother. "You like her, don't you, Zane? I mean really like her?"

Her brother shrugged and grinned like a ten year old with his first crush. "Nice to have someone to talk to that doesn't order me around or demand to know every move I make." He faked being agitated. "And she doesn't think I'm crazy."

Catharina punched him in the arm then snuggled against his shoulder. "I love you so much, Zane. Never leave me."

As the warrior and the angel locked eyes, knowing the events that soon would change both of them, Zane rubbed the side of Catharina's head with his other hand so that she was shielded from seeing them. "I love you too, Cat, and I will forever."

Chapter 39

This is my one day off, Crane. What is it?"

The mayor answered the door still wearing the bottoms of his silk pajamas. With his chest bare and peppered-colored hair not yet combed, the alderman drank in the unusual rumpled appearance, seeing a less menacing Kragan LaPlante.

"The Watcher paid me a visit last night." Crane stormed in, went to the island bar, and started drumming his fingers on the exotic granite. He opened his collar for Kragan to see the scratch left as a calling card.

Kragan took a skeptical look before moving to pour himself a cup of coffee. "Doesn't look too bad. Guess it could've been worse." His smirk incensed the alderman. "Relax. I'm glad you're okay. Did you call the police?"

"Of course I called the police. I'm not an idiot." The alderman went to pour himself a cup of coffee but managed to only get half a cup. Looking for cream and sugar he found nothing. He set the cup back down and proceeded to tell about the questioning and how insulted he felt.

"It's their job, Crane. You haven't exactly been a friend to the police. What did you expect? I don't care about that, anyway. Tell me about The Watcher."

Crane shivered as he walked to the windows overlooking Forest Park. "He knows everything."

Kragan moved, with surprising quickness, up to Crane and spun him around. "What does he know?"

"That it was me who threatened the social worker, that I

knew about the priest taking funds to raise those kids." The alderman's voice began to sound like a whining little boy who couldn't get his way. "I'm telling you, I was never so scared in my life. That thing isn't human. His eyes glowed like some kind of horror movie and he was a lot bigger than reports indicated."

"Well, most people don't survive to give an adequate report, you idiot. What else?"

"He wanted to know who I was working with and why I would bully such a wonderful woman."

"Please tell me you didn't mention my name," Kragan growled through clenched teeth.

Crane shook his head and looked down at the floor. "No. No. I told him it was that nosey detective that's always showing up asking questions. And wouldn't you know he would be the one to come take my statement after the attack."

The mayor cocked his head. "Detective Jacobs?" When Crane nodded enthusiastically, Kragan patted him on the shoulder. "Good man. I never quite know which side that guy is on. But did The Watcher buy it?"

With a shrug followed by a large exhale of air, the alderman felt his eye begin to twitch and drew his hand to rub the lid. "Hard to say. Told that beast that Jacobs was nearing retirement and, with several divorces under his belt, he needed to start building a nest egg. Then he asked about you."

The mayor remained silent for a few seconds as he took another sip of his coffee before leveling a dangerous glare at his alderman. "What about me?"

"Wanted to know if you knew Glen Forrester, the guy found after his house burned." When the mayor's eyes narrowed to slits of warning, the alderman hurried on with his tale. "I told The Watcher you became concerned at the murder, knowing the neighborhood was on edge. So you attended the funeral." The mayor's glare didn't waver. "I told him I thought you knew him from your childhood. That's it!"

"That's an understatement as you well know. Did he buy that?" Kragan asked in a skeptical retort. He turned away and moved to the living area, finding a comfortable chair near the window. "The only two people who know my connection are you and Morgan." His blood boiled at remembering the affectionate way Zane helped her the day before. "I need to pay a little visit to her and make sure we're on the same page. Maybe later today." He crossed his legs as he set the cup down on the glass end table. "In the meantime, I'll have a guard posted downstairs. There's a great deal of security in this building already."

"Humph. Like that would stop him. He disabled my system. If he comes after you, I don't think something like a guard downstairs will matter much. I'm telling you he's dangerous and evil. Better watch yourself. He has it in for the city." Crane left out the part about The Watcher asking if Kragan had anything to do with the Essmalory Building fire. Since Crane only suspected a connection, The Watcher appeared to believe him when he denied any involvement.

"You're not holding anything back, are you, Crane? Remember, I don't like surprises."

Crane shook his head then wiped some beads of perspiration from his forehead with a handkerchief shoved in his pants' pocket. "I told you everything. He doesn't suspect you of one thing. What really worries me is what he said before he left."

"What was that?" Kragan felt a strange curiosity at knowing his name had been on the lips of such a dangerous felon.

"Tell the mayor I'm watching him." Crane shuddered. "Then he cut me, shoved me to the floor, and used me like a doormat before he left. I still get goose bumps thinking about it. I'm terrified to stay in my own home."

Kragan pondered the implications of the information. Crane was too much of a coward to share anything that would inevitably come back to disrupt his cushy lifestyle. That included staying on the mayor's good side. He caught himself staring into thin air when the alderman cleared his throat. Kragan shifted his eyes back to the man to scan his bulbous face and body before speaking.

"I have a feeling I know who has really been watching me all along." Somehow when the mayor chuckled deep in his throat, it didn't sound so light-hearted. He ran his tongue across his lips before addressing the alderman again. "Now about that incriminating evidence on Spokane."

"I put a bug in the police chief's ear to assign someone to look into it. I suggested Jacobs, since he was already snooping around. Not sure if they got anywhere."

Kragan nodded. "I'll make a few calls. I want this taken care of as soon as possible."

♫ ♫ ♫

The afternoon traffic was heavier than Catharina anticipated. Snow showers began earlier in the morning but none of the flakes appeared to be sticking to the street, thanks to the road crews spreading a thin layer of chemicals before daybreak. Frantic Christmas shoppers caused unnecessary delays when they didn't use crosswalks then darted out into traffic. Turning into Morgan's parking lot gave Catharina a chance to breathe. In spite of the creep and crawl traffic situation, she managed to get to Morgan's ten minutes earlier than expected. Since she didn't have Morgan's cell number, she decided to just go in, but by the time she'd reached the lobby, Morgan met her.

"Thank you for swinging by, Catharina." Morgan's timid voice shocked Catharina. The times before her suicide Morgan displayed an uncommon amount of self-assurance. Along with the make-up not being quite so heavy, her clothes, although stylish, seemed a great deal more office casual than sexy secretary. Morgan pulled on her black coat with the faux leopard collar. "I'll tell you I'm a little nervous. It's been a long time since I was in church."

"Call me Cat."

Morgan nodded at the request. "I hope lightning doesn't strike. Maybe we shouldn't sit together."

They exited the building just as Catharina started to laugh then unexpectedly linked her arm with Morgan's. "Trust me, if lightning strikes, it won't be hitting either of us."

Morgan and Catharina both hit a slick spot and squealed as they clung to each other, taking baby steps to Zane's car which he'd loaned to his sister.

"What is this all about, Cat. Zane called really late last night to check on me and ask if I'd come?"

"I'm not sure." Catharina started the car, looked both ways, and pulled out. She stole a glance at Morgan and, once again, realized how pretty she was, although fragile like a China doll. The image of her naked body pressed against Damien nearly made her miss an oncoming truck. "Sorry. Got distracted." She stopped at two stoplights before speaking again. "About my brother, Morgan."

"I understand if you'd rather me not be friends. I really do. I've done some really awful things to you and Damien." She laid a hand on Catharina's arm and felt it flex. "I'll do whatever you suggest. It's just that Zane has been so very kind. He asks nothing of me." She chuckled. "He really likes to talk."

Catharina couldn't help but smile. "Yes. He does. I think he likes you, Morgan. I just don't want him to get hurt. You are so glamorous and fragile. Just the kind of person a man like Zane likes to rescue. He is more damaged than you think. It's been a rough couple of years since he returned from Afghanistan. Something has come over him in recent months that make him seem almost normal again." Catharina knew it had to do with Rocco's guidance and Damien's friendship. The combination was better than any VA doctor.

"He is very special, Cat. I have no intention of hurting him. I would like a friend who doesn't expect anything from me—if you know what I mean."

Catharina glanced over at Morgan and wondered if the blush was from the cold or her declaration. "Maybe we can be friends too."

"I'd like that very much."

♫ ♫ ♫

Kragan experienced a mini panic attack when he watched Catharina and Morgan link arms then walk to the car. "Where are you going?" he mumbled aloud as he waited to follow them. When Catharina parked the car at St. Matthews, the mayor noticed Zane standing on the church steps with his hands shoved into the pockets of his camo jacket, bouncing slightly against the icy wind.

He loped down the steps, sliding a bit, then hurried to walk the women to the church entrance. He kissed both women on the cheek, which deepened Kragan's resentment. He turned the car around and decided to wait for Morgan where he knew she'd eventually return.

♫ ♫ ♫

When the Goliath size doors slammed shut, echoing into the sanctuary, a group of men clad in dark clothing at the front of the alter, turned in the front pew and momentarily looked back at the cause of the disturbance. Zane released the women and walked away, disappearing into a hall off to one side.

Catharina dipped her fingertips into Holy Water then made the sign of the cross.

Morgan stood ill at ease as she watched. "I'm not Catholic."

"It's okay. Come on." Catharina tilted her head toward the front of the church. "Let's sit down." Finding a place near the front, Catharina turned down the pries-dieu, or kneeling bench, and lowered her body in order to pray. Surprisingly, Morgan joined her, locking her fingers together so tightly, it gave Catharina the impression the woman may have been afraid she really would be struck by lightning.

This place gave Catharina peace. Since the first time she'd walked into the sanctuary, she realized that here nothing could harm her. Even now, with a chill in the air and only a few lights burning in the wings of the church, Catharina let the warmth of God's protection engulf her. The altar was covered in dozens of lit candles of various sizes. She couldn't imagine a more beautiful place. No music. No sounds at all. A fleeting thought of hearing that famous church mouse run across the floor caused a smile to form on her lips as she slid back onto the pew.

Stained-glass windows let in enough light to keep the sanctuary from being dreary and ominous.

She hoped Damien would take her to Midnight Mass on Christmas Eve. She and Zane always went together, joining Father Xavier afterward to spend the night then open gifts in the morning.

In that moment of reflection, she appreciated that, for the most part, her life had been good, especially since Father Xavier took them in. The last few years, when Zane lapsed into someone she hardly knew, made her appreciate that at least he had returned from Afghanistan.

Morgan leaned over to Catharina. "What is going on? Do you know?"

Catharina shook her head. "No. Something about a blessing."

Father Xavier walked out wearing white vestments trimmed in gold braid. A sash of gold hung around his neck down to his waist. Two more men followed him, heads bowed, dressed in white hooded robes that were unadorned, tied with a common piece of rope. By the size and gait of their bodies, Catharina knew them to be Zane and—maybe Damien or Rocco. She couldn't be sure who he would be at this moment.

The five men sitting on the front pew stood, pulled their hoods up over their heads, and began to chant some melodious tune that felt centuries old.

Catharina felt Morgan slip her hand in hers, tightening it as she scooted closer. Even though the traditional Mass began, it was not the same. Something filled the air as nothing ever had before. Was it the Holy Spirit that the Father and the Bible always spoke of? Was it the sight of such tall men singing in a voice and language that sounded holy and terrifying at the same time?

When one of the five men turned to face the priest, Catharina saw that it was Gideon and, as the others turned, she recognized them to be the group that always stuck close to him. It dawned on her who they were. Nephilim. Now she could see it. They were strangely beautiful with their near seven foot height, standing erect and confident. Most of the time, they looked so hunched over and withdrawn that Catharina never paid much attention to their height.

"Who are they?" Morgan whispered.

"You wouldn't believe me if I told you." Catharina stood and slipped out into the aisle, prepared to take communion that the Nephilim now took.

Father Xavier met her and administered the sacrament, but uncharacteristically, avoided looking at her. She returned to her seat and sat down.

The last two men turned and faced forward where Catharina could see the outline of their faces. Zane stood a little taller than Rocco who looked dark and foreboding, even covered in white. With bowed head, it was obvious he was pure angel, unable to conceal the black band across his face that once so terrorized Catharina. Now she thought him a beautiful creature and wondered if this blessing meant their time was drawing to an end.

The two men she loved took communion then walked up on the raised altar and lay prostrate on the floor. Gideon and the other Nephilim began to chant in, what Catharina could only imagine was an angelic tongue, as Father Xavier lifted his hands toward the crucifix hanging over them all. He spoke Latin and openly wept, touching Catharina more deeply than she'd ever experienced.

The Nephilim moved to the two on the floor and lifted them to their feet.

"And this is the Blessing from our Almighty Father in Heaven that these two join as one."

Catharina jumped to her feet in horror. "No!" she screamed.

"Let this earthly man take his place among your creations of Holy Service and release your servant Rocco to the world he has given so much to."

Catharina edged out into the aisle. "Zane! No!" She stumbled forward. "You are my brother! I love you! Zane!"

"We will now lay hands upon God's chosen one to receive infinite blessings from our Lord Jesus Christ."

Catharina felt Morgan's arms wrap around her, then she buried her face in her new friend's shoulder, already wet with tears pouring from Morgan's own eyes.

Both women moved side by side, watching the conclusion of the ceremony as all the men pushed back their hoods. They smiled at one another and clasped forearms like Roman soldiers.

Finally, Rocco looked down at Catharina as she stepped

forward to meet him coming down the stairs. He gathered her into his arms as she wept. Zane did the same with Morgan.

Father Xavier put his arms around Rocco and Catharina. "This was not my will, Catharina. God has spoken. I am but an instrument to His Will. It is greater than even my love for you and Zane."

Catharina let Zane pull her into the crook of his arm. "How long do we have?"

"Maybe a few days, maybe a few years."

Rocco's raspy voice jerked Catharina to face him. "This can still be stopped, Catharina." The blackness across his nose and cheeks hid any kind of emotion found on a human. "I will not torture you to choose between us. But only you have the power to free me. If I must continue to serve, then it will be my honor."

Zane pushed Morgan to stand beside his sister. "This is my decision. I am crippled in the head, Cat. Now that this has happened—" He jerked his chin toward Gideon and the others, who stood patiently waiting. "—I feel whole again. Everything is clear and as it should be. I like helping others. I understand now that all the pain and suffering we went through as kids only prepared me for what lie ahead. The war, as bad as it was, gave me a pain that others feel on the streets. If I don't do this, who knows what will happen to me? Do you know how many times I've stood on the McKinley Bridge and thought about jumping?" Catharina caught her breath and covered her mouth with a trembling hand. "I even tried to drink anti-freeze once but Gideon stopped me," he continued. "He found me and helped me find my way. His gaze turned to the angel who looked him squarely in the eyes. "Then Rocco found us. I'm happy again. God has healed me. You have to let me go."

Catharina fell against him, wrapping her arms around him. "Are you doing this for me and Damien?"

Zane stroked the back of her head. "Not this time. I'm doing it for God and for me. I'll either end up in jail or die if I don't, and I think deep down you know that. This is a chance for both of us to be happy."

Morgan watched the two siblings and tried to understand. "Are you leaving, Zane?" Her voice came out small and more than a little bewildered.

Before Zane could answer her, the front door of the church burst open, spilling several police officers with guns drawn into the vestibule. Detective Jacobs pushed to the front and chastised the officers enough that they slipped their weapons back into their holsters.

Father Xavier moved forward as he stole a glance over his shoulder. Only Zane and the two women stood in the aisle. Rocco and the Nephilim had vanished. "What is the meaning of this?" the priest demanded. "You can't come barging into a house of worship."

Detective Jacobs looked past the priest as he handed him a piece of paper. "I have a warrant for Zane Spokane's arrest."

"On what charge?" Morgan spoke up, showing some of her old vim and vigor. "Let me see that?" She took it from the priest. "It says you're being charged with murder." Morgan pushed herself in front of the priest. "There must be some mistake."

Jacobs continued to look at Zane who removed his white robe and carefully handed it to his sister. "You can't arrest him in the church." The priest spoke with a calm resolute that gave Jacobs pause.

"That is a pretty old tradition that really doesn't hold much weight these days. But if you like, I'll wait outside if you'll give me your word Mr. Spokane won't run."

"Thank you, Detective." Zane took the arm of the priest, who seemed to sway on his feet. "I'll be out in a minute. Just let me say goodbye."

Chapter 40

Morgan pushed the door to her apartment open then laid her keys on the unadorned table. She caught a shadowy glimpse of herself in the mirror and stared at her image. The weight of confusion pressed against her heart, knowing her time with Zane might be cut short. Now he was incarcerated, which chipped away at the possibility of a developing friendship. Something about the man touched her so deeply that it frightened her more than the disturbing thought he might become an avenging angel.

"Where's your boyfriend?" came a familiar voice from her small living room.

Kragan startled her. Morgan shivered as she remembered Kragan still had the key to her apartment. She didn't move. "I want you to leave." She swallowed hard to cover the anxiety welling up inside her.

Kragan pushed himself up off the sofa and moved toward her, much like a panther stalking its next meal. "Did you get my flowers?" His smile, meant to unravel her anger, didn't appear to have much influence.

She nodded her head. "Yes."

"I don't see them." He looked around the room as he reached out and took Morgan's hand, pulling her back into the open space.

Sucking up what little courage she had, Morgan met his deceptive gaze of opaque affection. "That's because I threw them in the trash."

His mouth narrowed. "I understand you're probably angry

with me." He tugged her stiff body into his arms and forced his mouth against hers, only to feel the absence of her usual passionate response. "Come on, Morgan. Are you angry because I didn't come to the hospital?" Another kiss on her neck before running his hand down her back to her buttocks forced her to try and shy away, without success. "You know I couldn't be caught up in that. Besides, I never told you to attempt suicide." He smiled before nipping at her bottom lip. "Nice touch, by the way."

Morgan pushed him away and started toward the door. "You should leave. Stay away from me. You'll have my letter of resignation on your desk Monday morning." Before she could lay a hand on the doorknob, Kragan grabbed her by the hair and yanked her back against him.

"You little bitch," he growled in her ear. "After all I've done for you. So are you giving it to that homeless piece of crap now?" He shoved her so hard against the door that she bit her lip. When she turned around, his eyes fell on her bloody lip, making him wipe his sleeve across his mouth as if wanted to taste it.

She tried again to open the door, but felt Kragan's arm go around her neck.

He dragged her into the bedroom before slapping her to the floor. "Did you tell anyone about me being Glen Forrester's son?"

"Leave me alone," she begged as she tried to crawl toward the bed to be able to pull herself up.

Grabbing her arm, Kragan jerked her up only to slap her again. "Did. You. Tell. Anyone?"

This time tears burst forth as she realized she was in serious danger. "Yes."

"Who!" he roared.

"Father Xavier," she sobbed as she tried to free herself from Kragan's iron grip on her arms.

"Anyone else?" When all she did was cry uncontrollably, Kragan shook her violently. "Tell me!"

"The Watcher." This made Kragan step back and stare at her in shock. "I told The Watcher, and Zane," she yelled. She gathered up her courage to spit out one last insult. "You are not good enough for Zane to wipe his boots on, Kragan. Whatever you've done to hurt him, I will make sure you pay!"

"We'll see about that," Kragan managed to say through clenched teeth.

♫ ♫ ♫

Detective Jacobs turned off his ten-year-old car and wondered about the knocking he heard in the engine. With a sigh, he knew he needed to make a decision about those new tires he had on hold, but now this new concern might mean it needed attention first. In his head, he clicked off the cost. Staring out the windshield at Morgan Knox's apartment building, he remembered he could pick a few hours up at the hardware store to make ends meet. He knew the owner and the guy always offered him the work around this time of year, since he wanted to do Christmas things with the family.

As Jacobs pondered when to approach his friend about the best time to start working, he watched Mayor LaPlante exit the apartment building. He was pulling on his gloves, looking mad at the world as he stormed toward his car. The thought popped into Jacobs head about the rumor of Morgan Knox and the mayor having some kind of relationship outside of work. What did he care? She was a looker and both were single. Big deal. If it didn't get in the way of the job, Jacobs didn't really care what they did outside of the office.

Only now, seeing her at the church with the Spokanes brought a new layer of questions, which was why he'd decided to let the officers take charge of getting Zane Spokane to headquarters.

The detective slipped out of the car and tried to lock his door with the key fob, but it didn't work. *Maybe someone will steal it*, he thought then remembered he didn't have any kind of insurance that would come near replacing the vehicle. He took a deep breath and pretended he didn't care one way or another as he moved toward the front door of the building.

♫♬♫

Kragan paced on the living room rug, worried only slightly about what he'd done to Morgan. He was pretty sure she'd learned her lesson this time and wouldn't be testifying concerning any of his past indiscretions. After some persuasive measures, she admitted quite loudly she still loved him.

"Make sure Spokane shares a cell with one of those misfits who survived The Kitchen of Hope fiasco."

The police officer on the other end of the phone was new to the department and impressed that the mayor even knew him. He agreed straight away to do his best.

Kragan smiled. "Thanks. I owe you."

Maybe he wouldn't have to take further action if those tattooed troglodytes discovered Spokane was the one who may have killed their buddies. Kragan's mouth turned up on one side as he went to pour himself a drink.

"Life is good," he mumbled then downed the drink.

♫♬♫

Damien eyed Catharina as she stared out his office window that got a long-distance view of the St. Louis Arch. The weather had cleared several hours earlier just as darkness began to fall. The evening festivities were to begin soon. *The Polar Express* experience was completely booked, and families meandered up and down the mall, hoping their number would be called for the standby tickets. Christmas music floated throughout the space as onlookers from the balcony connected to the Grand Hall stood watching shoppers while sipping on their vanilla lattes or holiday cappuccinos that Catharina's coffee shop offered. Damien would have been exuberant over the success, if it weren't for Zane being in jail and Catharina looking at him as if he'd ruined her life.

"I want to go see him," Catharina declared.

"I just told you Father Xavier said he wouldn't be arraigned until Monday morning. Hopefully, he can get bail."

Her eyes rolled to the ceiling as she ran her hands through her hair. "How much will I need?"

"I'll take care of it, Cat. You needn't worry."

Damien's British accent was so thick Catharina turned her eyes on him as if she'd not understood. She stepped toward him as he stood and gathered her into his arms. She could feel an instant heat start in his solar plexus and creep upward. "Hold me just a little longer if it doesn't hurt too much."

Damien pulled her tight against his chest, cringing at the pain and the desire welling up inside him. "Do you want me to call off the performance tonight?"

"No. The children are expecting me and I don't want to disappoint them. Besides, it's good for business. The hostesses and bartenders are also counting on me."

"They'll understand." Damien inhaled the scent of her hair. "Thank you for being at the church today." She nodded then smiled up at him, feeling the heat begin to radiate into her own body. What felt warm and inviting to her must be causing him great pain. Releasing him, she stepped back.

"I know you're worried about Zane," he said, "but trust me, he has the power to protect himself now. No harm will come to him." He watched disbelief flood Catharina's eyes. "Trust me, Cat."

Her smile proved she loved him once again. "I do."

"What did Morgan say when you told her what was happening?"

"She didn't believe it at first. Then she put two and two together. I think she was disappointed." Catharina leaned against Damien's desk and looked back out the window, where Christmas lights flooded the street below. "She cares for Zane. Maybe not in the same way I feel about you, but it's there. Maybe if they had more time—"

"They don't," Damien was quick to point out, drawing Catharina's gaze back to him. He looked at his watch. "It's time. Ready?"

Catharina picked up her turquoise violin and stared at the surface, as if seeing it for the first time. "Tonight I play for Zane."

♫ ♬ ♫

Detective Jacobs washed the last glass in the sink that, a half hour earlier, was so full of dirty dishes he couldn't see the drain. The only reason he decided to make the effort to wash them was because he'd run out of paper plates and disposable cutlery. His shotgun house on The Hill, an Italian section of St. Louis, was rundown, but at least it was his. He wanted to fix it up, but things like tires and a knocking car engine always circumvented the good intentions. When he retired, he could attend to those things. Maybe even put in a few tomatoes and make his own salsa like his sister did each year.

He dried his hands on a paper towel and noticed the lights were out in the living room. His cat jumped up on the table and arched his back, letting out a mournful sound that made the hairs on the detective's neck stand up.

"What's the matter? You see a mouse? You're worthless." He tried to stroke the feline, only to have him back against the wall and continue staring into the dark adjoining room. Jacobs chuckled. "Come on. It's time for *60 Minutes*. Let's see what's messed up in the world tonight."

He walked into the darkness and tried to turn on the TV with the remote, shook it, tried again with no luck. He then reached for the table lamp next to his recliner. The bulb shot as he rolled the knob between his fingertips. It was then he felt a presence in the room.

Where did I leave my gun?

As if reading his mind, a raspy voice came from the corner of the room, near a window Jacobs could see had been opened. "Looking for this?" The Watcher stepped out of the darkest part of the room to let the kitchen light hit him across the face and chest. He laid the gun on a bookshelf.

Jacobs took a step back, trying to ignore his fear.

"Did you and Alderman Crane threaten a woman named Neva Wallace?" The Watcher asked.

Detective Jacobs tried not to make any threatening moves. "I don't know any Neva Wallace. Why don't we sit down and talk about this, buddy?" Even in the dark Jacobs could see the wide grin revealing white teeth.

"I'm not your buddy, Detective Jacobs." Rocco moved closer and decided that, as much as he found the man a nuisance, it was possible he was telling the truth. "Neva Wallace was a social worker at the Lafayette Children's Agency."

"Get on with it, Watcher. That's right. I know who you are."

"What's the hurry?" Rocco asked as he cocked his head to the side to observe the detective better.

"Well, *60 Minutes* comes on soon and it's the only show I watch all week."

"Set your DVR."

"If I could afford a DVR, I'd have more than one favorite show, now wouldn't I?" Jacobs meant to sound hostile but it didn't appear to anger The Watcher. "So what about this Neva person?"

Rocco looked around the sparse surroundings and thought the detective had good reason to blackmail someone. "She's being blackmailed."

"That usually means she did something wrong." It was a fact. "And someone found out about it."

"Not that simple."

"It never is. Now I'm a little busy. Oh and you're under arrest," Jacobs added self-confidently which brought an immediate chuckle that sounded more like pebbles in a rock tumbler. "So if you'll assume the position, I'd appreciate it."

Rocco eyed him in silence so long it made the detective fidget. "Alderman Crane says you and he planned to blackmail her for check fraud and forging papers so Father Xavier could take care of the Spokane children." Rocco could tell by the stunned expression followed by an angry pucker of his lips, that Jacobs probably didn't know anything about Neva Wallace.

"You cut him the other night," Jacobs said. "That's aggravated assault. Add on breaking and entering and you're in more than a little hot water. I'm not going to even get into what threatening a police officer will do for your jail time."

"I didn't kill Crane. That should count for something."

The Watcher's flippant tone drew a smirk from Jacobs but he quickly recovered. "And I won't hold that against you. Sorry.

Not the way I roll. Now I don't know what you're trying to pull, running around St. Louis being the underdog vigilante, but as far as I'm concerned you're just another anarchist thug with his own agenda."

"Zane Spokane didn't kill Glen Forrester. I did."

Jacobs began chewing on the inside of his bottom lip, wondering what his next move should be. "That's not what the evidence shows."

"The evidence lies. Ask Morgan Knox."

"Yeah. Well, I tried that. Went over to her place yesterday after arresting Spokane. Imagine my surprise when Kragan came slithering out the front door of her building. Guess he was in a lather because she wasn't home."

Rocco tensed and stepped so close to Jacobs he could smell the tuna fish on his breath. "What are you talking about? Catharina Spokane drove her home."

Jacobs grimaced at having such piercing eyes cut into his mental fortitude. "And how would you know that?"

Rocco turned away and became statue still, as if thinking about the information. He moved toward the window. "Did you try again?"

"Went back couple of hours later, called several times. Nothing. Thought maybe she was at the police station, checking on Spokane, but she never showed. Thought I'd try again tomorrow." It dawned on Jacobs now that something wasn't right. He could see it in the way The Watcher stood and the tone of his voice.

"Kragan," The Watcher spat. "He's done something to her."

"Whoa there. Kragan is a pompous ass, but I don't think he'd hurt anyone." The Watcher glared at him. "What'a ya say we head over there and do another check," Jacobs suggested. "She did just get out of the hospital for attempted suicide." He grabbed his coat off a hall tree by the front door. "You comin'?"

He turned to look into the darkness and realized The Watcher was gone.

Chapter 41

As he exited the car, Detective Jacobs stole sideway glances at the dark figure robed in some kind of hooded outfit. He waited in the shadows, as if he knew the detective wanted to be in charge. The cold night forced Jacobs to pull his collar tight around his neck. The thin shirt he wore underneath was meant for a relaxing night in the recliner, watching Leslie Stall on *60 Minutes*, not investigating a problem with a possible murder suspect.

The Watcher edged out of the shadows as the detective placed a gloved hand on the narrow chrome bar across the front of the door. "Locked," he grumbled. "We need to call the super or fire department to let us in."

The Watcher touched the handle and Jacobs could hear it unlock.

He frowned as he yanked on the door. "I'm not even going to ask how you did that."

They walked to the elevator and the doors swooshed open immediately, without so much as a button pushed. Jacobs glared at The Watcher and wondered at the possibilities. The light had been dim in the foyer but here it was bright. Or at least it was, until they stepped over the threshold, causing the doors to shut and the light to fade to only something an alley cat might enjoy. Jacobs kept his eyes on The Watcher, but the man didn't seem to notice. When the doors opened, The Watcher was the first one out, followed by Jacobs who looked over his shoulder at the sudden burst of light in the elevator.

"Let me," Jacobs ordered as he knocked on the door. "Ms.

Knox, it's Detective Jacobs. I just want—"

The sound of a latch being thrown halted Jacobs from speaking.

The door cracked so that only one eye of a battered woman showed. "Yes?" she whispered, as if it were hard to speak.

The Watcher stepped around the detective and placed his hand on the door.

A choke caught in her throat as she pulled open the door. "Rocco."

Morgan's eyes rolled back in her head as she started to collapse to the floor. The Watcher scooped her up as if she was a ragdoll and moved inside to lay her down on the sofa.

Detective Jacobs took out his phone and dialed but nothing connected. He looked down at The Watcher kneeling beside the battered woman he barely recognized. He hit redial. Nothing. The cell phone was fully charged. A feeling of something out of his control connected with him.

"Who did this to you, Ms. Knox?" Jacobs asked, as if he were coaxing a child, then pulled up a leather foot stool to sit.

Her eyelids fluttered as they focused on The Watcher who held her hands. When she tossed her head back and forth in rejection of disclosing the attacker, The Watcher touched her body. Immediately, she relaxed, as if her pain had subsided. The Watcher stole a sideways glance at the detective, as if to see if he noticed, but Jacobs couldn't keep his eyes from widening at seeing the power the man appeared to possess.

"She has multiple injuries." Rocco reached up to touch her bruised and bloodied face, only to feel her cringe then pull away. "Let me continue to take the pain, Morgan," he whispered in his raspy voice.

"No. I want others to see what he did to me." Her breath was ragged. "Detective, use your phone to take pictures of my face." She looked back at Rocco. "I'm not going to the hospital. Catharina is in danger." She tried to lick her lips. "Must help her. Go, Damien." She didn't even realize she'd dropped his name.

"Damien?" Detective Jacobs was confused as he looked at The Watcher—Rocco, she'd called him—hovering over Morgan. Then he saw the resemblance. "Holy Mother of God." His words gushed from his mouth as he stumbled back several steps. "What the hell is going on?"

What was the creature before him? It certainly wasn't human and it wasn't the Damien Cruz Jacobs tried to irritate on a regular basis.

Yet he knew the two were connected somehow.

Rocco slowly rose to his full height and pounced on the detective, grabbing him by the collar. The man squirmed beneath his fingertips, and Rocco could feel his eyes begin to shade from gray to silver orbs of light. "I go for Catharina. Stay with Morgan so that she remains safe. Her injuries are no longer life threatening but she does need to be looked after." He shoved the detective several feet. "Can you do that, Detective Jacobs, or do I need to emphasize each word with a blow to the head?"

Jacobs looked over at Morgan, who could now rise to a sitting position on the couch. His eyes shifted back to The Watcher and he nodded. "Go."

Rocco turned to leave as Jacobs grabbed his arm, causing the angel to over react and slam the detective back up against the wall with an iron grip around his throat.

When he withdrew his hand, Jacobs rubbed his throat. "We're not done here, Watcher. Now that I know where I can find you on any given day, I'll be paying you another visit."

As if to add insult to injury, Rocco put his hand on the detective's face and slammed him into the wall with such force, the wind was knocked out of the him. Jacobs bent over and staggered forward, before looking up to see if another assault was imminent.

"He's gone, Detective Jacobs," Morgan said, trying to stand and help him to a chair.

Jacobs accepted the help, but quickly pulled himself together. "Yesterday I was here. I believe I saw your attacker leave, Ms. Knox, but I need you to tell me who did this to you so there's no misunderstanding."

She touched her bruised face. "Kragan LaPlante."

♫ ♫ ♫

Zane jumped to his feet and roared an insane yell of rage,

raising his fists over his head. At the sudden commotion, the cellmate fell out of his top bunk but landed on his feet behind the tortured man in front of him. Zane had managed to invade Rocco's vision as he'd gazed upon Morgan Knox.

"What the hell is wrong with you?" the cellmate demanded. "Do I need to teach you a little respect for a sleeping man?" It was one of the hired men brought in to attack The Kitchen of Hope.

Zane grabbed the bars to focus on the vision of Morgan being carried by Rocco. She was badly hurt. Another roar of rage drew a reprimand from the security speakers.

A light filled the tiny cell, causing the other occupant to gasp and cower against the back wall where the toilet stood. He nearly fell inside it as he saw five men, nearly seven feet tall, appear on the other side of the bars, dressed in what looked like old fashion monks' robes.

"Who are you guys?" the terrified criminal asked then started calling for help.

One of the giants stepped forward and opened the door of their cell as if it had always been unlocked. Zane now appeared to be calm as he slipped outside with the others. He turned back to look at the man who had taunted him all evening. "You should not tell of this."

The black man ran forward and grasped the bars. "I ain't no Obie-Wan-Kenobi, weirdo. I'm not lying for you."

Gideon reached in and jerked him so fast against the bars a tooth chipped.

When the man looked up into the eyes of the stranger, he started to tremble. "Okay. Okay."

"Enough," Zane said with such authority that Gideon released the man and backed up. "We need to get to Union Station. The time has come."

♫ ♫ ♫

The thunderous applause echoed throughout the Grand Hall as Catharina was lifted onto the bar to dance her last few minutes of "In the Hall of the Mountain King" by Edvard Grieg. She wore a black taffeta skirt that hung down the back of her legs to just above her heels. In the front, the skirt was cut away above the knees. Her green glittery tube top had black fish net draped over it. She wore elf ears with strands of green ribbon twisted through her jagged hair.

To start the show, she gave a short version of the story of *The Piped Piper*. All the bartenders and hostesses put on mouse ears, whiskers, and attached a wiry tale as she spoke. With encouragement, Catharina got the children in the crowd to come dance with her as she played, along with following her as if she were the Pied Piper of Hamlin. Before long, even their parents were dancing. After playing the song through twice, she finished with a bang on the bar, like always.

As the audience quieted down, Catharina played "Silent Night," followed by all of the staff calling out "Merry Christmas."

That was at seven and eight. The nine, ten, and eleven o'clock show would have very few children so Catharina replaced the elf ears and slippers with a red cowboy hat and boots. She played something different each time, dancing slower at those shows, mainly because she was exhausted. The worry over Zane weighed so heavily on her subconscious that Catharina stumbled twice and slipped on the bar at the last show. Fortunately, no one noticed, thanks to the quick thinking of two burly bartenders who grabbed her and swung her to the floor or up in the air.

"The kids love it, Cat. We should keep that in for your weekend performances." One of the college-age hostesses hugged Catharina then waved her evening tips at her. "I get off in thirty minutes. Do you want me to bring you anything?"

"No. Thanks, Kimmy. Have you seen Damien? He said he was going out tonight, but I never saw him come back."

Kimmy shrugged. "Jeremiah just left so I'm guessing Damien is back." She gave Catharina's hand a squeeze and hurried away to a customer waving for service.

Several guests complimented Catharina as she headed to her hotel room. Being gracious under such circumstances grew tedious as she made a stop at the check-in desk to ask about Damien. Once again, no one remembered seeing him from earlier in the evening. She knew he planned to pay Detective Jacobs a visit to find out more information, but dealing with such a man could go terribly wrong. "I'll just go leave him a note in his apartment with my violin. If you see him—"

"We'll tell him, Cat."

Catharina forced yet another smile. With no sign of Damien in his quarters, she decided to retire to her own room. Maybe Damien would join her later to tell her any new information.

"Cat?"

The sound of Kragan's voice coming from behind her, as she started out onto the bridge that connected the old Union Station with the renovated hotel rooms in the new section, unnerved her. Remembering all that Zane told her two nights earlier forced her to pick up the pace.

"Oh. Kragan. I didn't see you." Trying to sound nonchalant wasn't as easy as she hoped. "Were you here for my performance?" She stopped in the middle of the bridge when he came alongside her and smiled with what Catharina took to be a rakish attitude.

"Just the last one. I couldn't make it any earlier." He reached out and placed his hands on her upper arms. "I heard about Zane. I'm sorry. What can I do?"

"Get him out of jail," she quipped then dropped her eyes. "Sorry. That sounded rude. It's not your fault. I'm just so worried."

Kragan looked down and noticed her hands were opening and closing into a fist. "Do you need to talk about it? I'm a good listener."

The hairs on the back of her neck prickled as she tried to step back from his touch. "No. I think I'll turn in. Zane has a hearing in the morning. I want to make sure I'm there in plenty of time."

"I understand." Kragan moved as if he meant to kiss her, but she side stepped him and hurried off without even a good night. The embarrassment and rejection infuriated him, yet drove him crazy with desire at the same time. His cell phone vibrated in his pocket. Slipping it up to his ear, he heard the police chief inform him that Zane Spokane had escaped and was at large. Clicking off, Kragan walked back into the Grand Hall to stop at the bar. Catharina didn't see him as she ran toward the elevator leading to the balconies that overlooked the Grand Hall. Her frantic appearance drew his observant eyes as he watched her run along the balcony dividers.

"Zane Spokane must already be here," he mumbled.

He dialed the police as he reached into the pocket of his coat to let his fingers caress the pistol he'd brought. Instead of waiting for the cops, he followed in the same direction Catharina took to escape. When he reached the hall that led to a number of offices, he discovered a door that hadn't been completely closed.

Upon entering it, he realized it accessed the upper levels of Union Station. The concern could be heard as Catharina called for her brother.

Then the sound of her footsteps circled back toward him. Stepping back outside, Kragan waited like a hungry animal.

Catharina rushed into the hall, smack into Kragan, causing her to gasp and jump back. "What are you doing here?" she panted, terror in her eyes.

Kragan narrowed his eyes at her as he began to invade her personal space. She moved back so fast the wall bounced her into his chest where he encircled her waist.

"I might ask you the same?" Gone was the nice guy façade he could no longer mange. "Is that where your brother intends to hide since he's on the run. Do you know what the penalty for harboring a fugitive is these days?"

Catharina shoved at his chest, which only resulted in him jerking her back and forth several times.

"Let me go," she demanded as she began to twist and turn in rebellion against his grip on her forearms. "Or I'll—"

"What? Call for you half-witted brother just like you used to when we were kids."

Catharina froze at hearing his words. "So it's t—true," she stuttered.

Kragan's eyes filled with hatred as he jerked her after him. "Wonder what the almighty Damien Cruz will think about me taking you in his own bed," he growled through clenched teeth.

When she started to scream, Kragan slapped her hard

enough that she dropped to the floor. Catching a tight grip on her arm, he began to drag her toward Damien's apartment at the end of the hall. The whimpers and protests only managed to excite his already warped desires.

He realized the door was unlocked as he started to open it. When Catharina rose to her knees, Kragan kicked the door open then pulled her inside, locking the door behind them. With this, he released her only to see her scamper up and try to reach the house phone. Kragan beat her to it and jerked it out of the wall, hurling it across the room to crash against the fireplace.

Throwing his coat on the sofa, he began to unbutton his shirt in slow motion as he stared at the woman edging along the wall like a wounded animal. "Good, kitty." He smiled. "Remember how I used to call you that?" He started pulling his shirt out of his pants. "Kitty. Kitty. Kitty."

"You're a twisted and sick man, Kragan." Catharina quaked at watching him narrow his eyes at her then let them slide down her entire body as if she were already naked.

"Nonsense. It's just that I have—" He rolled his eyes up then over at her again. "—a rather specific taste in pleasure." His eyes fell on her violin, nodding toward it as one corner of his mouth lifted. "Pick it up." When she didn't move, he shouted the order again. "I said 'pick it up'!"

Catharina ran to the library table to retrieve the instrument.

"Play *The Devil's Trill*," he ordered.

"Now I understand why you love it so much." Catharina lifted the violin to rest beneath her chin as she brought the bow to the strings.

Chapter 42

ike a swarm of bees, the police arrived, frightening the few people left in the Grand Hall. Out of curiosity, some stayed to watch. Others made an exit, not sure if what they possessed in their rooms needed to be flushed down the toilet before anyone asked too many questions. Union Station was well known for not letting any illegal business take place within its walls and would take appropriate action, as needed, without mercy. One of the reasons the police generally liked Damien Cruz was because he supported them, offered scholarships for the children of slain officers, and tipped them off to some unlawful stuff that almost always led to an arrest, making them look good.

They asked about the mayor at the front desk, but no one had seen him. It was only when a bartender said he thought he'd left that the police grew more than a little concerned. They followed up by inquiring about Zane Spokane. When one of the officers saw a hostess look up at the balconies then quickly look away the lead officer started toward her.

"Halt!"

The word echoed over the Grand Hall. Several screams, followed by the sound of feet scurrying out of the way, created a tension-filled arena of guns being pulled from their holsters.

The officer looked at the six men standing in the middle of the Grand Hall at the top of the stairs that led up from the street. Police gawked at the five, as if the hooded giants may have a future in the NBA. The one standing in front of them all was Zane Spokane. The officer recognized him immediately. It appeared the man wore his street clothes beneath his camo jacket. Even *he* looked formidable with his head held high, surveying the police and the weapons pointed at his chest.

"Mr. Spokane," the officer said with a firm voice. "I need you and your friends to lay face down on the floor with your legs spread apart and your hands out to your sides." He reached for his weapon and realized it wouldn't release from its holster. With a quick glance at the snap which held it in place, he saw that it was open, but the gun wouldn't budge. With a concerned shift of his eyes back to Zane, he saw the war vet was not afraid. "I repeat—"

"Get out of our way, officer. We mean you no harm. I need to find my sister and make sure she is safe and then I will surrender myself to you." Zane lifted his hand which forced the other officers to stiffen and adjust their weapons.

"I can't let you do that. I'm sure she's safe. The mayor is here somewhere so he's probably taking care of her."

The officers were stunned when Zane and the others raised the palm of their hands toward them, causing the safeties on their weapons to lock in place so that they couldn't be fired. As the officers started to check their weapons, Zane and his Nephilim started to walk away.

"Stop!" the lead officer commanded as he took out his nightstick. The other policeman did the same. A chill ran up his spine as Zane turned to stare at him with eyes that appeared to glow for a second. The giants with him pushed back the hoods of their robes to rest on their backs. Each one took out a long dagger.

The officer watched Zane speak from the corner of his mouth and wondered why.

"Stop them. But no permanent harm is to be laid upon their bodies. Understood?" Their bald heads bobbed obediently. "Let's get this over with."

♫ ♫ ♫

"Again. Play it again," Kragan ordered as he sat on the sofa with his shirt open to his naval, smoking a cigarette. "This time dance, kitten." He smirked as he exhaled a stream of smoke from the corner of his mouth. "Then we'll do something else."

When she did not start instantly, he scooted to the edge of the seat cushion. This prompted her to play *The Devil's Trill* one more time. He began to tap his foot and periodically closed his eyes as if enraptured. "Very nice," he whispered as his finger moved like the wand of a symphony conductor.

♫ ♫ ♫

The mayhem below increased, as the police officers fought with everything they had against men who didn't appear to hold an ounce of fear as they moved, trying to lead the police away from the elevator. It temporarily distracted the lead officer when he spotted Damien Cruz run into the Grand Hall dressed in some kind of weird garb that looked like a reject from a video game. He didn't look so different than the men whirling their medieval daggers at his officers.

"Go!" Zane ordered as his eyes looked at the upper balcony. Before he could continue, Damien ran to the stairs that circled the outside of the glass enclosed elevator that resembled a M.C. Escher drawing.

The lead office confronted Zane and managed to slam his nightstick on the back of his neck which should have brought the man to his knees. Instead, Zane turned in slow motion to meet the officer's eyes and smiled like a man drunk on his own power. "That wasn't a good idea, Officer McNeal."

McNeal took a step back with a stunned look. He looked down at his shirt to reassure himself he wore only a badge number. He tried to stop panting and rapid heartbeat. "How do you know me?"

Zane took a threatening step in his direction, causing him to back up more with his baton in front of him. "Your badge number is on file."

McNeal knew that bewilderment flooded his eyes before he could hide the feeling of trepidation. He lunged at Zane, only to find himself with an arm of steel around his neck. "Tell your men to assume the position, Officer McNeal, so they don't continue to get hurt." McNeal struggled only long enough to find the choke hold increased. "That's better. I'm not sure how long I can control my men. I'm kind of new at this."

♫ ♫ ♫

The Devil's Trill ended. Catharina dropped the violin to her side as she watched Kragan stand up and swagger toward her with a satanic smirk on his face. He began to applaud in slow motion as he came to stand inches from her. Reaching down, he removed the violin from her trembling hand then smashed it against the nearest piece of furniture until nothing recognizable remained.

Catharina burst into tears and slid away from such close proximity. "Please. Just let me go."

"I can make all the problems for your brother go away, like that." He snapped his fingers and exposed a wide smile. With a quick snatch of her arm, he pulled her back into his embrace where he placed his hands on her face and then ran them back through her hair. "Would you like that, Cat? Or I can make sure the evidence shows he murdered my father. Wouldn't that be interesting for jurors to find out that he had been your foster father years ago? My testimony could go either way." He kissed her on her neck, making her whimper with fear. "I could tell them what a mean SOB he was or another version of the truth." A light chuckle gurgled in his throat as his hands slipped down her neck then shoulders. She managed to hit him in the jaw with a small fist, driving him a step back. "I like a kitten with claws."

Catharina bolted for the door, only to be caught and slung backward on the couch. She bit him and scratched until he slapped her to the floor. She'd doubled up, afraid he'd start kicking her, when a banging on the door started.

"Cat!" It was Damien.

With a second wind, Catharina pulled herself up onto her knees and lunged for Kragan as he moved to push a piece of furniture in front of the door.

He reached down and shoved her away.

"Damien!" she screamed. She watched Kragan grunt as he

unsuccessfully tried to shove a chest in front of the door.

"I think I want him to come in. Come on," he growled, yanking her to her feet then dragging her toward the bedroom. A last-minute grab of his gun gave him an added molecule of confidence. "Just remember you wanted this when he finds us. If you say otherwise, I'll make sure your brother fries in the chair." He put his mouth to her ear. "Or maybe I'll just shoot him and be done with it. Him and Damien Cruz. I think my day just got better."

♫ ♫ ♫

"Catharina!" Damien yelled once more as he slammed his shoulder into the oak door. His strength was fading. He held his hand out to unlock the door with no success. Again he slammed his body into the door as Detective Jacobs and Morgan ran up.

Jacobs, seeing the problem, pulled his gun. "Move back!" He aimed and pulled the trigger multiple times.

Damien, this time, could bust open the door as he stumbled against a chest pulled away from the wall. "Cat!" he roared.

But he could hear the commotion in his bedroom, even with the door shut. This too was locked as Damien instinctively tried to break through with zero success.

Once again, the detective shot at the door several times, but missed the lock the first two times, causing it to be more difficult to break through. Both men put their backs to it and managed to break through, splintering the door.

Catharina lay across the bed flailing with a wild instinct to survive as Kragan tried to contain her fight. Kragan was absorbed in his attempt to subdue her and didn't realize Damien was there until he felt a grip on the back of his collar. Damien managed to throw him across the room with some kind of unnatural strength.

Kragan landed against the wall with a thud and began to survey the new threat against him. With a wild howl of rage, the mayor ran at Damien, swinging. His fist connected with the man, staggering him back. He blinked in surprise as Damien came back with his own punch to Kragan's gut.

Morgan hobbled over to Catharina, slipping her arm around her to help her stand on the floor when Zane stormed into the room. He first ran to his sister where she fell into his arms, clinging to him like a lifeline.

Damien could feel the angelic strength leaving him. The distraction caused Kragan to get another blow to his chest and face. For the first time, Damien felt physical pain from a human. He staggered back as Kragan ran to grab his pistol off the nightstand.

"If I can't have her, then neither will you!" Kragan roared.

"No!" Morgan jumped in front of Catharina who cowered away from her brother as three shots rang out.

Morgan fell to the floor and looked up at Kragan. "I forgive you."

Zane dropped to his knees, gathered her into his arms, and held her tight.

Damien reached inside his cloak and withdrew his dagger, stained with centuries of blood of those who committed crimes against humanity. "It ends here," he panted.

Kragan still held the gun and shot at Damien, hitting his hand. Blood poured from his arm as the dagger dropped. To Kragan's horror, Zane rose up like a slumbering giant and turned to face him. Kragan watched the man he'd hated his entire life become a monster then step toward him.

With little effort, Zane reached out, knocked the gun from the mayor's hand, then shoved him to the floor. He did not see Kragan grab the dagger as he reached down and jerked him up to his feet. When he did, Kragan plunged the angelic dagger into Zane's chest, piercing his heart.

Damien straightened, throwing his arms out as his voice screamed out, "My God!"

Later, he would remember Catharina cry out and see the detective pull her away to the other side of the room. A lightning bolt traveled from Damien's chest to Zane's, who now stood with his arms out, facing Damien, whose body began to flash between being Rocco then being Damien. With a blinding burst of light that filled the room, everyone cowered, throwing their arms up in front of their eyes.

When the light vanished with a loud bang, Zane stood erect and transformed. He now held the dagger in his hand and kneeled next to Morgan, laying his hand upon her wounds. Catharina ran to her brother, but he vanished before her eyes.

"Zane! Please don't leave me."

Kragan scrambled for the gun on the floor. As he turned around, he leveled it at Damien and a shot rang out. Kragan staggered back, dropping the gun. He turned to stare at Detective Jacobs and opened his mouth to speak, when the detective shot him two more times, ending his life.

"She's alive!" Catharina stroked Morgan's hair and let her tears fall on the woman's face as she tried to smile.

Damien stared at the detective who slipped his gun back into his holster. He met Damien's eyes and frowned.

"Does anyone care to fill me in on what just happened before I call it in?"

Epilogue

Four Years Later:

The three-year-old bounced, skipped, and twisted as the two adults held her hand. One of the adults was a priest who smiled down at the little girl's antics that reminded him of her mother long ago. The other adult let a laugh escape her throat as she lifted the child's arm at the same time as the priest, causing the child to giggle. When they lowered her back down, she gasped.

"Daddy!" her voice was so loud it echoed across the Grand Hall of Union Station. She pulled free and ran to a tall man with dark hair. He turned to smile as his arms opened for her.

Damien Cruz gathered the little girl into his arms and stood up to spin around, much to her delight. "And how is Angelique today?"

Catharina loved seeing them together. "For a three-year-old, she's extremely precocious." She cut her eyes over at Father Xavier. "I wonder who encourages that kind of behavior."

He responded by rolling his eyes upward then clasping his hands behind his back as if he had no idea what she was talking about.

With a hearty laugh, Damien first kissed his daughter then his wife. He took an extra second to meet her eyes. "I love you," he whispered.

Catharina wrapped her arms around both Damien and Angelique, laying her head against his shoulder.

"Daddy, can we invite my guardian angel to Christmas

dinner?"

Both parents looked at each other, then at the priest. Father Xavier shrugged and shook his head, as his brow creased in confusion.

Catharina's heart lurched at the thought of Zane. She'd not seen him for four years. "What guardian angel, baby girl?"

"He said he'd come see you soon, Mommy." Angelique's smile was so wide it made all three laugh. "Ask Aunt Morgan. She knows." The little girl pointed up to the balcony that circled the Grand Hall. "See. There he is." She waved as if she were afraid he wouldn't see her.

The three adults looked up at the second floor balcony at the end of the Grand Hall and saw a man standing on the railing, cloaked in a red and black robe. His hood pulled down over his forehead gave him an ominous appearance. He lifted his hand in greeting then jumped back into the dark recesses of the unused space behind the railing.

It was time.

The End

About the Author

Tierney James decided to become a full-time writer after working in education for over thirty years. Besides serving as a Solar System Ambassador for NASA's Jet Propulsion Lab, and attending Space Camp for Educators, Tierney served as a Geo-teacher for National Geographic. Her love of travel and cultures took her on adventures throughout Africa, Asia and Europe. From the Great Wall of China to floating the Okavango Delta of Botswana, Tierney weaves her unique experiences into the adventures she loves to write. Living on an Indian reservation and in a mining town continues to fuel the characters in the Enigma and Wind Dancer series.

The love of teaching continues in her marketing and writing workshops along with the creation of educational materials and children's books. Try some of her other books to bring a little adventure to your life. http://www.tierneyjames.com

Books by Tierney James

Enigma Series
- An Unlikely Hero
- Winds of Deception
- Rooftop Angels

Stand Alone Novels
- The Rescued Heart
- Dance of the Devil's Trill

Wind Dancer Series
- Dark Side of Morning

Education
- African Safari

Children's Books
- There's a Superhero in the Library
- Zombie Meatloaf
- Mission K9 Rescue